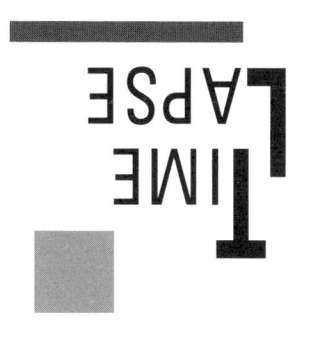

TIME LAPSE

A NOVEL

Alvin Greenberg

TUPELO PRESS DORSET, VERMONT

TIME LAPSE

Copyright ©2003 Alvin Greenberg

ISBN: 0-9710310-6-1   Time Lapse

Library of Congress Catalog Number: 2002112459

Printed in Canada

All rights reserved.
No part of this book may be reproduced without the
permission of the publisher.

First edition, 2003

Tupelo Press
PO Box 539, Dorset, Vermont 05251

802.366.8185 • Fax 802.362.1883

editor@tupelopress.org • www.tupelopress.org

Cover Photograph: "Dark Hat and Shadows" by Jennifer Michael Hecht

Cover and Book Design:
Sheila Selden, Sheila Selden Design Peru, VT

TIME LAPSE

A NOVEL

Alvin Greenberg

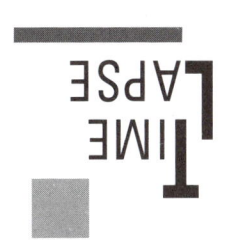

"I've never heard of a crime which I could not imagine committing myself."

Goethe

CHAPTER 1

1. Morning News

All those deaths for which he's been responsible bother him not one bit so much as the single life that pursues him now. Bothers him indeed! Distracts him from thoughts about his upcoming lecture and, as happens ever so rarely, turns him into the monster of the household. His two young daughters, home from grade school and pre-school on a spring vacation which fails to coincide with his own, are in their separate bedrooms, drying their tears and tending each to her own psychic wounds, each no doubt wondering what she did to deserve an ogre-father who would drive her away merely for playing hide-and-seek under the breakfast table, each perhaps rediscovering on her own the myth of the foundling: when would the real father come to rescue them?

The real father sits in the kitchen, brooding, his coffee cold, slowly re-opening the newspaper that he carefully folded shut before allowing himself that rare moment of explosion, the fragments of which he can still feel drifting down around him. And the real mother, the real wife, has meanwhile simply left, trailing a cashmere sweater from one hand and her favorite tapestry purse—purse, he thinks: ha! it's practically a suitcase, and I'm supposed to be the traveller—from the other, easing her little blue convertible out of the garage and into the street without the slightest show of anger but, as usual, leaving the double garage door open. As usual, he is certain, it's the only open garage on the entire block. And where has she gone? To the shopping center? To visit a woman friend? To play golf? To meet her lover? Who cares!

Walter Job does, but it's more than he can concentrate on right now. He loves his wife dearly, but he has just read in this morning's paper that a new federal agent has been assigned the responsibility of solving a large number of murders which have occurred primarily in midwestern states over the past decade and which there is apparently reason to believe are, somehow, linked. Walter knows who committed many of those murders: and more. Walter could easily stretch the geographical limits of this morning's news reports to include both coasts. The south and southwest. A little Canada.

Walter does not need to read the newspaper to know that many of those murders have been committed by the same person. Gratuitously—enough to upset anyone at breakfast—the newspaper tells him that all the same, though it neglects to present the reasoning that has led to such knowledge. It admits, to the contrary, that the distribution of all this death appears random, its motivation, in most cases, unknown. Even as newspaper articles go, it tells very little. Walter tells himself that for all they know, they might as well be trying to tie together a random collection of automobile accidents.

Nonetheless, the newspaper assures him, the new federal officer is certain that a speedy solution is now possible, that the murderer or murderers will soon be brought to justice. For security reasons, the government has refused to reveal the identity of the agent. Walter, approaching the end of the column, is for security reasons of his own not too taken by the newspaper's protective apologies. All the same, he tracks the article down to where, in the humble confines of the last page of the first section, it continues to express confidence. The agent expresses anonymous confidence. His superiors express superior confidence: this is the same agent who has broken up an underworld ring dealing in stolen securities, who has twice retrieved not only the kidnapping victim alive and well but the ransom money besides, who has only in the past year solved a pair of previously unlinked murders which occurred decades apart, one in the east and one in the west, by connecting them to a recent apparent suicide in the middle of the country.

It is, Walter realizes, folding the newspaper neatly down upon all this confidence, the most talent that has yet been brought to bear on his activities.

2. A Biblical Excursion

Walter Job, who constantly busies himself explaining, even unasked, that it is not Job with a long o, like Job in the Bible, but Job with a short o, as in a job of work, goes on all too easily from there to consider himself in biblical terms. He has chosen this way of introducing himself to his classes, and then to almost everyone else, since his second year in graduate school, when he was unexpectedly assigned a course on The Bible as Literature. He stood in front of a large room full of undergraduates, many of them religious study majors who had signed up to take this course from an elderly Professor of Religion who had died during the summer and all of whom doubtless knew far more about the Bible than he did, and devised his personal analogy. Not a single sign of enlightenment shone in their eyes as they dutifully copied his name from the blackboard.

If he wasn't Job from the Bible, he wondered, as he went on to explain that they would begin by examining the Book of Job as a work of fiction, as a classic short story in fact, then who was he? He wasn't Jonah, that much he knew. Though already, by then, he felt himself swallowed up inside the body of a great beast, he was well aware that no one had sent him. Not to do what he was doing. Ishmael, he thought, as he wandered away after class in something of a daze, not the Ishmael in the story but the real Ishmael, might be more like it.

He felt somehow profaned by his participation in this particular class, wondering just what it was he was doing there. Call *me* Ishmael! he cried out silently to himself back in his office when he had finished reading the relevant passage from the Bible. I too have been cut loose from my home and sent to wander fatherless in the desert. This desert. Illegitimate by nature rather than by birth, like Ishmael I have watched the kingdom left behind me pass into the hands of my younger siblings, incompetents all. More power to them.

Yes, and he too, he recalled, like Ishmael had become something of an archer: a marksman, at least. The desert is a learning place.

3. Natural Talent

What he recalled was how within a year after his college deferment ran out he was drafted into the Army, in spite of extremely weak vision and obviously thick glasses. Like millions before him, he stood naked except for his glasses in the drafty examining room of a shabby induction center, which seemed to be nothing more than a sort of lean-to appended to the great stone edifice of the Post Office, while the officer who conducted the eye examination instructed him to remove his glasses and read the chart on the opposite wall. Ever the good kid, quiet and obedient, he did as he was told. He held his glasses in his hand and peered helplessly into the distant blur. The officer, also a blur, waited, drumming his fingers on his desk. Finally, Walter announced that he could see nothing there at all.

The officer, bored, grumbled, "Walk forward until you can read the top letter."

Walter edged carefully forward several steps, barefoot on the cold linoleum. Nothing. Further still. Grey blobs on the wall began to indicate at last the general position of the chart. He moved cautiously onward, a step at a time, still waiting for things to clarify.

"That's far enough," snapped the officer, "get the hell out of here."

Out he went. His visual testimony discredited by an officer who seemed to feel that he had overstepped the bounds of propriety acceptable for even the most determined malingerers, he was shipped off at once to basic training, there to remain until the doctor who examined him for GI glasses uncovered the true extent of his disability and initiated discharge proceedings.

In the meantime, he did what every other draftee does with the weapons thrust into his arms: he struggled to learn how to handle them. In the cold rains of an early spring he lay himself down on the muddy firing line of the rifle range; into the hot and dusty bunkers he dragged himself through the fiery weeks of almost summer. And yet, though he had never before in his life fired anything more than a borrowed BB gun, there turned out to be, for Walter Job, no struggle at all.

Like magic did the sand pit receive his hand grenade, the cardboard cut-out of the enemy disintegrate before his blazing carbine, the most distant target, a mere blur in his sights, open its center rings to his riflery. Weapons of all sorts exposed their intricate workings to his hands and then gracefully gathered themselves back together, oiled and immaculate. He can still picture the chagrin of his commanding officer who, at the graduation ceremonies for Walter's basic training class—when others were about to move on to tanks, to advanced infantry, to Officers Training School, to the paratroops, but Walter alone to civilian life—found himself handing Walter a discharge certificate with one hand and a sharpshooter's medal with the other. Both of which, of course, Walter well deserved. Ah, he should have known.

But who learns so fast? How long does it take for the kid with the natural swing to wake up to the fact that he's the genuine article: that, in fact, to be a major leaguer is what he's wanted all along? Now, of course—realization long since achieved—it's very different. Time has passed, over a decade now, which means, for Walter, that much has been done. The way he finally got around to putting it to himself was simply: I am what I am. What he often wondered, however, in those early years, was why he didn't feel worse about it: didn't tragedy come with awareness? Wasn't that what Sophocles had taught him: that one is pursued not by external forces but by the very nature of who one was, what one did?

But the fact was, he was quite comfortable with what he did, and how many people did he know who could say that? "Find something you can do well," a college career counselor had once told him, "and then find someone who'll pay you for doing it." Now, he not only did it well and was handsomely paid, but he derived from it the satisfaction of a job well done. So where was the tragedy?

4. Fixing Things

Walter's first urge when he entered graduate school in the fall after that sojourn in the desert was to become a scholar of the ancients, of medieval literature in particular. He plunged into the learning of the languages—Latin and Middle English and Old French—and into Chaucer and Langland, Boethius and the Pearl Poet, only to find himself brought up short at the edges of the texts themselves. Here was where his seminars taught him both crisis and solution lay. His killer instinct, honed well and quickly by the United States Army, surged ahead: pin down the emendations, the alternate readings, the variant spellings, the precise contemporaneous usage, and you had it all. Just resolve the textual mess, fix it once and for all: that was the job.

In the University library, pouring over the efforts of nineteenth century scholars armed with insufficient technology for achieving their aim of "the final version," he daydreamed his own solutions. Backwards in time he rushed, carrying a high-powered rifle mounted with a precise telescopic sight. Hidden in a clump of bushes on a hillside behind the monastery, he watched at high magnification, through a distant, narrow window where a solitary monk labored slowly, quill in hand, over a heavy manuscript. Then, just as the copyist paused and looked up, considering in his kindly, tonsured head a minor alteration—something ever so slight: a spelling more elegant, a word less profane, an added mark of punctuation—he squeezed the trigger, sending a quick bullet through the head of the would-be muddler.

At the same time Walter found himself being drawn to an English exchange student who worked as a receptionist at the Student Union, where Walter ate lunches, bought newspapers, watched movies, and chatted with graduate students from other fields. She emerged from behind the Information desk to join these conversations whenever she was free, an active and intelligent participant, whatever the subject, who turned up the corner of her mouth in a quirky little moue whenever one of the graduate students said something particularly foolish. Soon she became free whenever Walter was a part of the group, and eventually Walter began to wait around in the late afternoons till she was done working and ready to take him back to her apartment, to feed and love him. Her breasts were soft and heavy, and the first time she released them from the armor of her bra and he felt them yielding under his fingers, he knew his life was about to change.

Caught in a sudden, passionate triangle, he rushed from seminars in Old English Literature to a library of dusty English texts to the arms of this lovely English girl. He took to staying with her overnight—the only way he could keep the triangle from expanding to an unbearable pentagon, its other two sides composed of the Student Union and his own apartment—and even to writing his papers on a tiny table in her living room. He also took to sharing with her his lust and rage for medieval literature, though it wasn't many months before she turned sharply against the praise his professors lavished upon his intense and meticulous research into problems of textual validation.

"You're bonkers," she announced early one evening when they were still lying in bed together, both of their stomachs growling for a yet-unprepared dinner, his one leg still stretched across her, the fingers of one hand still buried in her soft breast with a grip he thought he just might not ever be able to release.

"You're all crazy," she said, shaking off his leg and hand and sitting up, "you people who think you can get something down permanently and immutably and just the way you imagine it was supposed to be."

"I can do it," he said quietly, looking up at her. She was leaning over him now, her breasts hanging softly down toward him.

"Oh no you can't." He looked up and watched that corner of her mouth make its own amused commentary and knew, with a sudden certainty that required no textual validation, that he loved her.

"You just can't," she continued, "not you or anybody else. There's no such thing as a perfect text, and if there were it wouldn't make any difference. It's what it's about that really counts, that's all." By this time she was leaning far over him, one arm on each side of his body, her breasts whispering against his chest. He could feel his cock beginning to rise toward her again, a testimony to what it was about.

"Marry me," he said, "and I'll take up modern literature."

5. Going Modern

It was during Christmas break, while Penny was in England visiting her widowed father—who, Walter was finally informed, wasn't really English after all, only an American manufacturer's representative who had taken up residence in Liverpool for purely practical reasons—that Walter Job committed his first murder: not, however, before having first paid a visit of his own to his faculty advisor to announce his change from medieval to modern literature.

"It's killing work, this restoration of dubious texts," agreed that red-faced old man, a famous literary historian whom Walter had only managed to see once before.

And Walter, too, quickly agreed, recalling his Thanksgiving fantasy in the library's rare book room: with his carbine he had gunned down an entire troupe of traveling players whom he had found ad-libbing their own version of *Everyman* in the courtyard of an English inn. Meanwhile, the high professional standards he had already established for himself had earned him his advisor's praise and the news that he had been recommended for an endowed fellowship in the fall.

"Keep up the good work, Mr. Job," said the old historian.

Walter's next stop was at a dingy bar that sat alongside the canal underneath the bridge he always crossed on his walk home. No college drinking place this, it had a graveled parking lot usually filled with pick-ups and now and then a couple of rusted, banged-up motorcycles, advertised double shots and boilermakers rather than weak beer by the pitcher, and was staffed by an undershirted bartender who sidled back and forth behind the bar like a linebacker nervously watching the offense set up. This afternoon hardly anyone else was in the darkened tavern. A very literary place all the same, much in the manner of, say, Hemingway or Mailer, thought Walter, adapting to his new vocation in modern literature. Or Nelson Algren, he considered, watching the working men who soon began to drift in by twos and threes.

Walter had ordered a bourbon on the rocks, and as he sipped it through the melting ice he shifted about on his bar stool, trying to catch bits of conversation on either side of him. But there was nothing of interest, and the flurry of after-work drinking was soon over, the bar almost empty again within an hour. Walter ordered a second drink and carried it over to a booth, next to the only other occupied booth in the place, and listened to the voices rising over its wooden back. Primarily it was one voice, and Walter, who had glanced into the neighboring booth as he sat down, recognized it as belonging to a man who had been here on each of his own few previous visits, a steady drinkers of shots with beer chasers. It was a voice that spoke with disgust and anger, its violence punctuated now and then, to no apparent avail, by the low, placating voice of his companion. It was a voice that spoke quite passionately of a woman, and how it would do anything to get rid of her.

"I could kill that bitch!" it said, quite clearly, just as Walter was picking himself up to leave.

"Now Jimmy," said its companion voice, "you know you won't do anything of the sort."

"She's a fuckin' liar," said the Jimmy voice. "Never spoke a true word in her fuckin' life. Hates the kids. Stranglin' their little souls, that's what. Hates me. Better off dead. All of us. What's the use?"

Outside, his feet crunching in damp gravel, Walter found it was dark already. He held out his hand to feel night air so moist it seemed it ought to be raining. Gravely footsteps directed his attention to a woman pacing the path alongside the dark canal that led under the bridge, glancing occasionally toward the tavern as she walked. Walter, pulling on the plastic raincoat he was carrying under his arm, approached to ask if he could be of help. She hesitated, nervously pushing her hands at her stringy gray hair, pulling her gray coat fiercely around her: did he know Jimmy, who always hung out there? Had she seen him tonight?

"Heavy-set man with a little moustache?" Walter asked.

That was him.

"Just went off a little while ago," Walter informed her, pointing down the path under the bridge.

"Fucker," she said and turned and walked away. She set off at a pace that surprised Walter, her wide body lunging angrily forward from one thick leg to the other: a woman with a mission. And hell-bent on its accomplishment, thought Walter, striding along not half a dozen paces behind her, his own footsteps muffled by the harsh crunching of her own on the gravel path.

If, years later, Walter were to think about this moment, it would be with some chagrin: not for what he has done—and done and done and done—but for the amateur way he went about it on this first occasion. For his vision of that gray old head in front of him—frustrated, sad, confused, angry: what would he know?—as yet one more in the long history of thoughtless gray creatures about to inflict their whims on a future that would have to struggle forever after to straighten out their messes. For how—the first, last, and only such slip in his decade-long professional career—he succumbed to both a knowledge of and empathy for the one on whose behalf he was about to act. For the act without forethought, for the unsolicited act, for the act in which—never again!—he was . . . involved. If Walter were to think about this moment years later, a possible but unlikely scenario, perhaps what he would see in that first, amateurish approach to his new career was the world spreading its grubby, ink-stained hands before him, daring him to stop it before it went ahead doing what it did best and most often.

By the time she reached the darkness under the bridge, well beyond the mist-dulled glow of the tavern's neon signs, Walter was beside her again. With a rock he had picked up from the side of the path, he struck a single, neat, and perfect blow along the side of her head, sending her at once into unconsciousness and the dark canal.

6. CRIME AND PUNISHMENT

That night he dreamed of *Crime and Punishment.* Penny was home waiting for him when he got there, returned from England so swift and early that she arrived ahead of the phone call from her British travel agent announcing her revised return schedule, which interrupted them an hour later in the midst of their lovemaking. The phone rang and Walter reached out from the bed to answer it, listened without saying a word, then dropped it back into its cradle and burrowed his own way back into Penny's arms.

"It was you," he mumbled, his face buried between her breasts, "it says you're coming, with love."

"Oh right," she said, quietly, distantly, "oh lovely English message."

When they had gone out and eaten their fill of the White Castles she suddenly craved, and when she had explained her abrupt return on the basis of her father's flying off to spend the New Year's weekend in Greece with his mistress, leaving her alone and cold in England, and when they had hurried back to her apartment to make love again and had done so with such great gusto that Penny, already exhausted from travel, had afterwards dropped off to sleep at once, and when Walter had risen to fill his briefcase with the books and notes he would need for the work he planned to do at the library the next morning, and had at last returned to bed beside her, then he too fell immediately into a deep sleep, in which he dreamed that he had to go into the basement of the house, not this apartment building where they were now living or any house he particularly remembered, but a house that was clearly his, in order to prepare for something, he didn't know what, and he stood at the top of the basement steps, holding the telephone in his hands, about to carry it down with him since its long cord was plugged into a jack down there somewhere, and frustrated because the only light switch for this dark basement which lay before him was down there in the blackness at the bottom of the steps, when suddenly he realized that there was something peculiar about the way the phone cord was attached, as if it were snagged on something down there in the darkness, but not really snagged, it was almost as if someone, or something, had hold of the other end of the cord from down there, that was certainly what it was, but before he could release his grip on the phone, whoever, or whatever, had hold of the other end suddenly jerked at it very hard and he was yanked violently forward, spilling head over heels down through the darkness towards the arms of whatever waited for him at the bottom of the steps, crying out in fright as he fell. And he woke up, aware that he really had cried out in his sleep, and that Penny was sitting up beside him, her hand caressing his hunched shoulders, asking if he'd had a bad dream.

"Yes," he confirmed, so totally exhausted that he wondered if he could speak clearly enough for her to understand, "a bad dream. I'll tell you in the morning."

Then he fell back asleep and dreamed of *Crime and Punishment*. He realized, as if he were a spectator at or a critical commentator on his own dream, that he was not dreaming about *Crime and Punishment,* but that he was dreaming *Crime and Punishment*. His mother was present, and although there was something vaguely wrong with her—her head seemed to be slightly awry—she looked on his activities there with smiling approval. He was quite pleased with himself, though he did nothing. The dream was a perfectly formal dream, rectangular, three-dimensional, in the shape of a book, and though the book was not only closed but also wrapped up in brown paper, unlabeled, with no title visible, and sealed tightly along all the seams of the wrapping with masking tape, he knew without a doubt that it was *Crime and Punishment*. It was not, he also knew, Dostoyevsky's *Crime and Punishment:* it had no characters, no scenes, no content whatsoever; it was perfectly shaped, wrapped, sealed, like a rectangular box, tilted slightly backwards and over to one side, unsupported in open space; his mother was no longer there.

He woke up feeling particularly pleased with the formal perfection of this dream.

7. An Unattended Lecture

Alone the next morning in a quiet study carrel in the library, Walter silently addressed the unassembled multitudes. What he thought at them was this:

What would it take for you to kill someone? Not much, I'll bet. Maybe you already have. Violence is the currency of our age, and the motto on all the coins reads "Spend, Baby, Spend!" And as you know—if you read the papers, watch television, live in a city, drive a car—we have spent in the proverbial fashion: as if money were going out of style. You may—if you don't drive a car, if you've avoided the military, if you don't live in the inner city—still be hoarding your own untouched lode of violence, but who's to say how long it will take you, when the right moment comes, to mine it, mint it, and cash it in? The only question is: what's the right moment? An anarchist mob at your door? The Klan at your neighbor's? A quarrel with your spouse? An attack on one of your kids? A driver who doesn't respect your rights on the highway? A neighbor's pet fouling your garden? The fool who turns the other cheek? What would it take? Passion? Honor? Duty? Money? Or simple necessity? What would it take?

After a long morning rehearsing these words till he had got them down right, Walter concluded that in spite of his continuing work with The Bible as Literature, this sort of diatribe, more or less in the manner of the prophets, was not at all his style.

8. A Well-Attended Lecture

Man kills, that's a fact, Walter, pausing in midcrossing to lean against the rail of the bridge, announced to the gulls. His army career having confirmed his eye for the facts and his early graduate work having trained him in corroborating the data, he knew he had a genuine text here. This too he told the gulls, who flew over his head and under the bridge, skimming the dark waters of the canal, dipping their beaks into it after fish or garbage, real or imagined. Walter never saw them come up with anything.

Their loud cries were distracting, as was the rumble of an occasional car crossing the bridge behind his back, but now that he had his text, he knew that the point was, to consider what it was about. Man kills, that's a fact. To the gull perched only a few yards away on the iron railing, Walter also added that he does it quite naturally. Why, he explained, it's no more a perversion to kill than it is an inhuman act to die. Both are, in the appropriate circumstances, the natural thing to do, whereas it's staying alive or refraining from violence, that's often the real act of perversion, requiring, such an unnatural and uncomfortable act of will, such stress, such determination.

The gull departed from its perch, but soon another took its place. This was like lecturing on relativity theory to a second grade class gathered on the beach in the middle of the summer, but who could better understand what he was trying to express than these busy, perpetually hungry omnivores, forever intent upon survival. You're precisely right, Walter assured them: the meaning of killing is synonymous with the meaning of living.

And yet, he complained, these simple, natural acts, these things we do readily, with incredible ease, on the least pretext, and with whatever means come to hand—and here pages of statistics flipped, unexpressed, through his mind, detailing war dead, slaughter on the highways, urban murders—yes, these acts which are among the most natural and common things we do, are turned into perversions merely because we say so. The gulls wheeled and screeched above his head now; he was, as always, continually amazed that such ugly sounds could emerge from the midst of such graceful flight. If there's a real killer on the loose here, he concluded, its name is language. The basic text is as hard and clear as anyone could want, but how is it that we go about spinning our meanings out of it? With words of course, turning, among other things, the natural into the perverse. And yet meaning, I have been told, is everything. What can be done? Perhaps nothing, if only because, language being what it is, namely something everyone mucks around in, we're all implicated.

Three gulls settled side by side on the rail; to them he addressed his final remark before he turned to go: Perhaps it's only the basic text, the genuine act, precisely executed and fixed in reality forever, that's truly capable of expressing any meaning at all: a purely formal meaning, at that.

Not a squawk of protest did they utter on his departure.

9. A Too-Well-Attended Lecture

Later in the afternoon Walter crossed the bridge once again, in company with Penny this time as the two of them returned to campus to attend a lecture by a famous visiting writer. More gulls than ever flocked about the bridge now, all of them in continuous flight over the sluggish waters that moved through the canal on the outgoing tide. Through the swirling white cloud of gulls Walter, who at lunch had read in the morning paper about the discovery and identification of his victim and had learned that she had a name, too, May Jorgenson, was surprised to see Jimmy, visible from above as a portly figure with sandy hair, entering the tavern below the bridge at his regular time.

The lecture hall was filled to standing room capacity when they arrived, for the speaker was a famous novelist who was already being labeled an American Joyce or Proust and his new book, *Time Lapse,* was a subject of much heated discussion among Walter's fellow graduate students, who had been wrangling for months not only over its meaning but even over the facts of its opaque and contradictory narrative. This was the first lecture he had ever agreed to give on any campus, and his announced topic was "The World of *Time Lapse.*"

Walter, catching a brief glimpse of the famous visitor over the heads of the crowd as he was brought onstage for his introduction, was reminded less of Joyce or Proust than of an old photo of Chekhov he had once seen, looking very small, bearded, dark, foreign, and suspicious. Then he and Penny abandoned the struggle to see the distant stage and settled down on the concrete floor, against a rear wall, to listen. Walter, tired—they had been in bed, about to nap after making love, when suddenly Penny remembered it was the day of the big lecture—closed his eyes. The disembodied voice of the writer, deep and rhythmic, drifted out to him over the heads of the gathered multitude.

This is what Walter heard: "Although there are some people who make light of the quest for explanation—who see it, indeed, as the tragic flaw of our age—there are others, far more numerous I believe, who cry out for explanation at every turn of events. And why not, if that's what they need. Not that I consider explanation *per se* a virtue. Myself, I can do without it, quite as well as I can do without public appearances, and if you can too, well and good, pass on. There will be more to come.

"Others, however, many many others, can no more tolerate events without explanation than the albino can suffer the direct rays of the sun. Nor is the quality of explanation of any more interest to them than the source of shade to the albino. Trees, clouds, umbrellas, roofs, what matter: shade itself is the goal. Nor are there many who are incapable of coming up, in a pinch, with their own handy explanations, no matter how farfetched, should one fail to have been provided, of even the most fantastic sequence of events. Human ingenuity, bless it, knows no bounds.

"But, depending on what's being explained, there comes a time to step in. There is a level of the personal that needs to be spoken to. Why should I sit helplessly by and put up with myself being explained by others out of desperation—and into the realms of improbability—when I myself can be so much more to the point. Like anyone else, I don't want to be the object of someone's fantasy. Like anyone else, I want to be understood. Therefore, in order to forestall such nonsense as might arise—ha! has arisen!—from the efforts of the needy, to their satisfaction perhaps but to the detriment of my own comfort and self-esteem, I offer the following by way of explanation."

At this moment, in this crowded, smoke-filled room resonant with the deep voice of the famous author of *Time Lapse* beginning the only public lecture of his lifetime, Walter fell, his back against the cinder block wall and his head tipped over on Penny's shoulder, into a deep sleep.

10. First Person

A decade later, an associate professor in the midst of editing a critical edition of *Time Lapse,* for which he is also preparing an extensive introduction, Walter remembers waking up amid the scurry of departing feet in the aisle, surprised most of all to have slept through the thunderous applause.

"No applause," Penny told him in her usual direct way in the quickly emptied lecture hall. "In fact, no author."

He had, she continued, been in the midst of explaining why he had chosen to write his novel in the first person when someone rose in the center of the auditorium to shout out that the book was not written in the first person at all, at which point he had simply stopped, gathered up his notes—Penny had risen on tiptoes not to miss what was happening, Walter had slumped back undisturbed against the wall—and walked off the stage, shaking his head. He had never made another public appearance, granted an interview, published a further word. What Professor Job, scholar and editor, wouldn't give for a few minutes in his presence.

Even the gulls were absent when Walter and Penny crossed the canal bridge on the way home. Walter, still groggy with sleep, stopped to lean against the rail of the bridge, considering the absence of gulls so early in the evening. When the canal was low on garbage or fish, did they ask for explanations? No, being gulls, they just went and did whatever it was they had to do. Down below, Walter saw the neon signs of the tavern flicker on, the door open, and then, after a pause, portly Jimmy waddle forth. He crossed to the edge of the canal, looked into its dark water, then seemed to gather himself together, shaking his head, and walked off down the path, under the bridge, out of sight.

One morning a decade later, Walter Job, who has never been able to get the author of *Time Lapse* to respond to a single one of the inquiries with which he hoped to elicit information—particularly about that speech both missed and undelivered—for use in his critical introduction, who has never even had confirmation that the publisher was forwarding his letters to the man whose address they persistently refused to reveal, still remembers quite clearly his first personal encounter with Jimmy on the day following the aborted lecture. He already had seated himself in the back booth, late in the afternoon, and he already had Jimmy's usual shot and beer chaser sitting across the table from him when Jimmy entered and the bartender, as Walter had requested, nodded him silently toward the booth where he waited. Jimmy downed his shot still standing up, and only when he had picked up the glass of beer and begun to sip at it, eyeing Walter over the rim, did he at last begin to edge his bulk into the booth.

"Do for you, young fella?" asked Jimmy, raising his hand to pat down his thinning sandy hair. Walter raised his own hand to the bartender, who quickly brought Jimmy another shot and chaser, Walter a fresh bourbon on the rocks.

Walter sipped his drink: "Sorry about your wife."

"I'm a reg'lar, no reason not to come," said Jimmy defensively. He drank the shot down, rolled the beer glass back and forth between his hands.

"I know," said Walter, "I'm here off and on myself."

Jimmy nodded, acknowledging Walter's own regularity, while Walter, sipping his drink, proceeded, very slowly, to mention how it was said that death was sometimes a blessing, even for those left behind,

"As," he continued, "is no doubt the case with you, remembering what I heard you saying to your friend the other day."

Jimmy set down his beer glass, still half full, and stared at Walter, hard.

"Buddy," he said at last, "if you think for one minute that I . . . ."

"Not at all," said Walter. "I did it for you."

And then, taking a sip of his drink and his first step along the road to professionalism, he added: "And now I want you to do something. I want you to pay me for the service I did you." And he named a figure that he had decided would both show that he was serious and still be within Jimmy's means.

After a lengthy silence interspersed by beer sipping and frequent patting at his hair, Jimmy finally made the little speech Walter had been waiting for.

"Listen," he said, "this is crazy, people say things like that all the time. What're you tellin' me? I wouldn't know if I was paying you for getting rid of May or for blackmailing me or . . . ."

A decade later, not even knowing why he's thinking about beginnings—and such easy beginnings, too! how did it all happen? —these many afters later, when others, as he is about to discover, have their sights set confidently upon his ending, Walter easily remembers what it was he said to Jimmy at that moment before they began to make arrangements for the payment: "You are paying me for what you want."

Then, in the midst of this recollection, on a bright early spring morning with sun pouring its low rays through the kitchen window and lighting up the gleaming white appliances like icons of the well-ordered life, with his wife on her way to the breakfast table with a platter of eggs and his daughters playing hide-and-seek around his feet underneath the big round table, he picks up the morning paper.

CHAPTER II

11. Time and Money

Walter Job stands beside the breakfast table, newspaper folded neatly on the chair he has just abandoned, his mind already tucking him safely away beneath the sheets in his Kansas City hotel room. It is a long way from this, a different time zone, and yet how amazingly fast he can be there—assuming, of course, Penny's swift return to look after the girls, to drive him to the airport. Sometimes he is equally a long way away from this himself: rooming in his own Kansas City, as it were, also a different time zone, no, a different time scheme, which he can reach almost instantaneously, with the speed of a telephone call. A simple gesture, the action of one finger, and there he is. But here, this morning, he sees sudden slippage, a tear in the thin membrane that divides his two worlds, times. He has done nothing in particular, not at this moment anyway, to bring it on, and yet he is faced, suddenly, with news of the collapse of the discrete: intrusion of another time into that in which he is busy dwelling, advent of the future . . . or is it the past? Wrong words for parallel times. For someone else's time, intruding into his own.

Time to be going, anyway: ticket in his pocket, suitcase packed, briefcase filled with copies of the talk he will be delivering. It's only a weekend conference, very professional, very professorial, seminars with some of the best new people in his field, meals with a few old ones, some who claim to remember him from graduate school. Walter remembers no one. He remembers, however, to check his wallet for money: I am the man who always pays his own way. Counting, he looks around. There's money everywhere he turns, a straight vista just now through the dining room and into the living room: money in antiques, furniture, draperies, art work, carpeting, china. Walter has had a heavy hand in all this spending, and give or take a few cash outlays for special items, say the small Persian rug and the framed sixteenth century maps, it's all come from his academic salary.

And has taken a lot of time, during which he's earned a lot of other money: unspent, mostly. Oh, the rug, the maps, the growing collection of first editions of the major modernist poets—Yeats, Eliot, Stevens—nothing at all in terms of the real cash his right forefinger, that used to dial, now pushes buttons, can summon forth. He humors himself that it ought to be insured by Lloyd's, the way they used to insure Betty Grable's legs. And if it spends most of its time just turning pages or helping to hold the pen that makes insignificant marks on student papers? Well, didn't Grable's legs also, most of the time, just walk?

His luck, though, the way things have generally gone, and he'd collect on the insurance, when the years have already added up to more cash than he can cope with. Modern first editions have their limits. He spends as much again on the current press: not just the local morning paper, its ominous news innocently folded away on the kitchen chair, but the Sunday *New York Times*, to which he devotes his Tuesday evenings; *Newsweek, Harper's,* and *The New Yorker*, all inhabitants of the overflowing bathroom magazine rack; the literary magazines, established and new-born, where he hopes in perennial disappointment to find the latest advances in fiction; even the occasional copy of *Crime Fighter* or *True Detective,* the semi-annual issue whose cover blazons "Ten Greatest Unsolved Murders of the Century"—which, unenlightened, he soon deposits in his office waste basket. Just like he does with the receipts he's handed by those dedicated volunteers who come soliciting at his front door—GreenPeace, the Kidney Foundation, the American Cancer Society, the Humane Society—and who depart amazed, their fists, pockets, envelopes full of fifties.

He spends more, in fact, on a single dinner for himself and Penny at their favorite gourmet restaurant of the moment than on Pound or Williams, and would do so more often if it weren't for the problem of having to counter, each time, Penny's last minute alarm at squandering so much on just one meal.

"It's only food," she says, once a month, as she tilts her head forward, pulls her long hair aside, so he can zip up the back of her dress.

And once a month, glancing at his watch, he replies, "Let's get going. Our reservation is for seven."

12. Making Points

In the same way that he lists points to be made in a lecture—though not, in this case, on a note card, but only in his mind—Walter, wandering around the living room, his suitcase and briefcase stacked by the front door, goes over the various points in his favor.

He is, after all, a respected professor of modern literature. Not that professors of modern literature are invariably above suspicion, but he has published widely in his field—on Conrad and Faulkner, on Joyce and Camus and Kafka and Beckett, on their themes and styles and influences—and is frequently invited to appear as a visiting lecturer at various colleges and universities. For some of these lectures he is paid; others he does gratis. He drives or flies or goes by train; stays with academic acquaintances or in campus housing or at anonymous motels; returns home at once after the lecture or stays on a day or two to see a ball game, attend the theater, visit museums or tour the local literary or historical sites. Except for recording travel expenses and such honoraria as he receives for tax purposes, he keeps no better records than any other academic. Who's to notice that there was no lecture in Ann Arbor last October? Or how he spent the weekend in January following the post-modernist seminar at the University of Minnesota? Or where he stayed over, last year, to break the long drive to Norman, Oklahoma?

He broods, for some minutes, before proceeding to his next point, over all the time he has spent in traveling. How far he has gone. Or come.

And who is to connect him with any of these murders? He knew none of the victims, they were merely names and addresses, passed to him over the telephone, committed to memory, never written down, briefly seen and then only for a single purpose. Neither did he know who wanted these murders done. To them, whoever they were—friends or enemies, lovers or spouses, partners or competitors, parents or children, the list of possibilities was endless—he didn't even speak on the phone. He was merely the last— or next-to-last if one included the victim—in a long chain of contacts, and even there he was neither name nor phone number but had, for a long time now, insisted on making the calls himself, to the next contact up the line, and that on an irregular basis, to find out if there was a job for him. His payments he always asked to be left in different places, at times even different towns; they were always in cash, and the cash was hidden away in the safe deposit boxes of a good many banks around the country. On a couple of occasions, pressured by time, he had not even picked up his payments; he has no idea what ever became of them.

Why, he pauses to wonder, is murder so inextricably bound up with money? It's a complication, a pleasant one at times, and one he's aware he signed up for from the very first, in—or so he recalls thinking—some sort of quest for respect, some acknowledgment that here, too, he was a professional, but not one from which he has ever felt there was anything to fear. Cash has no connections. And all his own are academic and respectable.

He is, after all—a final point in his favor—an intellectual, right? And intellectuals: aren't they denizens of the mind, given to thought, not action, inhabitants of a world outside of time, where ideas are born and suffer, die and are resurrected, where there are indeed vendettas, pitched battles and hand-to-hand combat of a sort, but where no blood is shed, no guts spilled, where no graves are dug and no mourners grieve? Who out there—what officer of the law, what dreamer, what novelist even—would imagine that such a person would do such things? What more is there to say? His mind emptied, Walter stares at the packed bookcase on the opposite wall, lit up brilliantly by the morning sun which pours through the window behind him. He is unable to make out a single title.

13. Reservations

Walter's reservation is on a ten thirty flight. Now that the disaster of breakfast is past—eggs eaten, coffee drunk, wife and daughters in flight in different directions, newspaper folded and laid aside—it is eight thirty. Walter likes early starts, likes to be places early—classes, concerts, plays, ball games, appointments—and especially to be at the airport at least an hour before plane time. It is a forty five minute drive from the house to the airport, so leaving any time within the next fifteen minutes will assure him of his requisite time. And he could leave now, taking the station wagon which, peering out the window over the kitchen sink as he wanders in there to empty his coffee cup, he can see sitting in the open garage. He can drive himself in the station wagon and leave it in the airport parking lot, though that is something he never does. But if he takes the station wagon himself, it will mean leaving the girls in the house, and they are too young to be left alone. If he's to drive himself and leave the girls alone, he has to go next door at once and see if Mrs. Nichols is at home and willing to look after the girls until his wife returns. But if he goes next door, he will have to tell Mrs. Nichols that he does not know when his wife will be home, and he won't be able to explain why he doesn't know this. Mrs. Nichols is a sometimes helpful neighbor, not a friend.

So he does not go next door, but when he has rinsed his cup, he refills it from the coffee pot, adds his half teaspoon of sugar and splash of milk, and sits back down at the breakfast table, sits on the folded newspaper he has laid on his chair. He should have taken a later plane: after all, registration for the conference doesn't open till afternoon. The only activity of the day is a business meeting, and one way or another he will be there for the evening's socializing; the real conference takes place tomorrow and Sunday. No, he should have taken an earlier plane, been up and out before anything happened, had breakfast at the airport coffee shop so Penny could have hurried home before the girls awoke. If he had been up and out before anything had happened, nothing would have happened. At seven o'clock he would have been reading his newspaper in the airport coffee shop, and there would have been no possibility of reacting, no one to let out his reaction on.

He is, meanwhile, conscious of what he is sitting on: enough so that he rises before finishing his coffee, picks up the paper from his chair, carries it out into the hallway and stuffs it into his briefcase. He will carry it away with him whenever, however, he goes to the airport, and when Penny returns later on and whines that the paper has disappeared and she has not even had a chance to look at it, he will not be there either to demonstrate his lack of sympathy.

From the hallway he can hear the voices of the two girls coming from behind the closed door of one of their bedrooms. He cannot tell which. It must be Janey's; she is the one who always makes the overtures, offers the invitations, for her younger sister to play, while Judy sits and waits, does not ask herself lest she be refused, but leaps up eagerly when her older sister calls her to come, play. And playing they are, Walter can hear, giggling wildly away, the incident of the breakfast table forgotten already, but their door closed, perhaps to forestall intrusions on their world of play. What Walter would like to do is to open their door and look in on them at play. Would that spoil their fun? Would it spoil his to forget his conference, cancel his reservations, and stay home this weekend? This is no excuse, this is a real conference. But face it, he thinks, if I do not deliver my paper, the world will not come to an end; in fact, I can save it for another time. Wandering down the hall toward their bedroom, briefcase under his arm, he considers rapping lightly at their door to see what reaction he gets. Silence, probably, at least till he could explain what he was up to. Then what?

Then the front door opens behind him, Penny calling out, "Come on, girls, we have to drive Daddy to the airport," and the girls come tumbling, squealing, out of Janey's bedroom, swirling around him, plucking his briefcase out from under his arm and racing each other to the station wagon.

Forty five minutes later, apologies made, goodbyes said, kisses kissed, and return arrangements repeated two and three times until even Judy has his homecoming flight number memorized, what Walter says, looking dumbly into his briefcase as he backs out of the car, is, "Oh, I seem to have carried the newspaper away with me."

And, laying it on the front seat next to Penny and closing the door, what he thinks is: I do not know what I am doing.

14. A Voice in the Wilderness

I just do what I do, thinks Walter: I am what I am.

For some reason, there is no getting away from this biblical tone. He is aware of the danger of pretentiousness, but if something fits, what can you do? Illegitimate by nature, he has said of himself to himself: not by birth, that's for sure. Well, he realizes, he's probably no true Ishmael then, but the fact is he was off on his own even as a child, a denizen of dreams, including the ones called books, long before his younger siblings began to arrive and take up the burden of fulfilling his parents' expectations. Little wonder, then, that the small kingdom of his father's soft drink bottling business should have passed, on the old man's death, into their hands, the only surprise being their continuing inability to run a perfectly well-established company successfully. Walter, for his part, has all these years stayed well away from family discussions of the business.

Seated now in the bar of the Kansas City airport drinking his usual bourbon on the rocks as he waits for his flight home after delivering his paper on "The Fallen World of *Time Lapse*"— no, there's no getting away from it—Walter is engaged in conversation by a traveling salesman on his way to Minneapolis.

Sunday flights are so damned depressing, this gray-suited stranger tells Walter, but if you have to start calling on industrial accounts at eight o'clock Monday morning, what can you do? Walter nods his assent, his sympathy, though he doesn't have to teach his first class till ten thirty. Part of him is busy considering that there must be a million lost sons of the United States Army with sharpshooter medals, or worse, tucked away in a drawer somewhere, behind the rolled socks and folded handkerchiefs, for most of whom the experience of killing, perhaps the most common human experience of their age, has been denied. Like him, they were too young to fight in World War Two, they were drafted only after the Korean hostilities had drawn to a close, their military careers were over before the beginning of American fighting in Vietnam or didn't begin until after the American flight from Southeast Asia. Before and behind them—yes, even in front of them, on television, nightly—death has raged and raged, while they did peaceful tours of duty in Germany and Guam and Alaska and then returned quietly to school, to work, to raising a family. Not that they were violent men, not that he ever thought of himself—or that those who knew him would ever think of him—as a violent man. No, he never found himself in those situations, in the streets, in bars or ball parks or dark alleys, where man does violence—where he often seeks, if he can, that terminal violence—to his fellow man. No, even as a child he was rarely involved in scuffles with other children, and then only against his will and to little effect. Like so many others in this, his murderous age, he is not a violent man. And yet.

"Listen," says the manufacturer's rep, swivelling on his stool in the bar of the Kansas City airport on Sunday evening after having just explained, extolled, his own career in industrial adhesives, "what do you do?" And Walter looks up at this man over his raised glass, out of the dim pages of his self-acknowledged pretentiousness: peers out at him through the brambles of his burning bush.

"I am a professional killer," he says. And wonders, briefly, what this fellow drinking companion now looking at him, amused rather than shocked, sees: a face more long than round, clean shaven, pale; hazel eyes behind a pair of thick but elegant designer glasses; short brown hair, neatly trimmed, thinning; an open-collared white shirt—no tie for travel, thanks—under a blue wool blazer. Does what he sees look like someone who would do the sort of things he just claimed to do? Does it?

What Walter Job has done, he has done in airports, hotels, insurance offices, barbershops, classrooms, laboratories, clothing departments, boardrooms, bedrooms, once even in a baseball stadium, in the midst of fifty some thousand people, during the seventh inning of a crucial stretch drive game between Cincinnati and Los Angeles (3-2, Reds, in eleven innings). All this he remembers, but the details bore him. Logistics, technique, are things of the moment. Important as they are, to become hostage to them, to use them and re-use them until they become wholly identifiable with oneself, is, he knows, certain death. Variety is not the spice of life: it is life. Whereas repetition is pattern, pattern is knowledge, knowledge is identification, identification is recognition, pursuit, capture, the end, goodbye. Walter knows this and, having read the paper, knows that there is someone else who also knows it and is in pursuit of the end. Walter chooses not to be engaged with the end. Each time he steps out to a new task he likes to feel he is only beginning. Always beginning. Beginning again and again. Each beginning a new little fragment of time. Small starts. Forever fresh.

But the books he reads astound him with their mass and repetition of detail. If the details of his own activities bore him, as in retrospect they always do, those in the mystery novels he breezes through on planes and in hotel rooms amaze him with the detail of their details: not just the caliber of the small lead slug pried out of the wainscotting, but its tell-tale markings; not just the sly introduction of the exotic poison into the vermouth, but the precise way it finally comes to rest in some particular organ. To say nothing of the complex pattern of the ringing of the bells, the changing of the guard, the barking of the dog, the cutting of a precious stone . . . . On and on the details accumulate, precise and useless as the books in which he discovers them.

He is particularly impressed by the detailed clarity of violence in American crime fiction. There is nothing he knows quite like it, either in his own experience or in any other fiction. Nothing quite like these precise descriptions of the way a blow cleaves the air, the grimace on the face of hate in action, the crunch of the body assailed, the pure physics of violence, turmoil of flesh and furniture, the way blood pumps from the punctured heart, brains spill from the shattered skull. If you like detail, nothing surpasses this, and it is available over and over again. Walter Job—precise, efficient, effective himself—admires in his own way the number of times a private eye can be waylaid, mugged, punched out, shot, pistolwhipped, and blackjacked in just a single evening. Look at the time all this takes to happen, the expansion of detail allowed: it could go on like this forever— often seems to, in fact, in books like this—and still not get anywhere. Infinity, too, is death. It goes on and on and gets nowhere. Walter is very much a devoted reader of such fictions, but he believes nothing.

15. Mysteries

Why do I read such stuff? he wonders. He has left hotel rooms strewn with the likes of Christie and MacDonald and Simenon. In fact, he has frequently found hotel rooms stocked with Tey and Queen and Hammett and Carr and left these same paperbacks, himself, in still other hotel rooms: left Dorothy Sayres in bus stations and Dick Francis on airplanes and Conan Doyle in restaurant men's rooms. Perpetually dissatisfied: it all begins with such promise and then resolves into such tedium. Almost all. He has yet to read one that he wants to reread, and yet he does reread them all the time, never realizing until he is in the midst of the denouement that this is a Chesterton story or a Gardner novel that he has already read once before—if not twice.

Seated at his wide oak desk in his upstairs study adjoining the bedroom he and Penny share, a pile of student papers stacked neatly to one side and the manuscript of a study on recent fiction—pretentiously titled *Gnosis and Chronos,* it has aroused his worst prejudices before he has even looked at its Table of Contents—on the other side, waiting to be evaluated for a university press, he looks around at the tightly packed bookcases on all four walls, not a mystery novel to be found there. Or anywhere else in the house, so far as he knows, though perhaps Nancy Drew will be making her appearance in the not-too-distant future.

Television police and mystery shows hold no interest for him, and he never watches them, though Penny does, sometimes, in disgust, and his daughters, more regularly, in confusion, never quite able to keep up with their dubious motivation and needless intricacies of plot. He likes to think that murder mysteries, which Penny turns her nose up at, hold no interest for him either, but wherever he goes he reads them. And only when he goes does he read them: only in connection with hotels and waiting rooms and transportation of various sorts.

He used to worry about reading so much and forgetting so much—practically everything—so fast, whereas most other things he reads, even newspapers, certainly the fiction and literary criticism his career has been constructed on, he can remember in meticulous detail. What does it mean, he used to worry, what does it mean? Now he only wonders, with not much more than idle curiosity, how did it happen? An intelligent, well-educated, astute, articulate, thoughtful, reasonably sophisticated and mature man of my age, and this is not only what I read but what slides off of me as if my mind were made of Teflon. How did it happen?

16. A Promising Career

Things happened very fast: more like a medieval romance, Walter often thinks, which fairly ripples with action, than a modern novel, in which it generally seems that nothing happens. Jimmy paid up, in four easy monthly installments: a tribute, Walter believed, both to the careful estimate he had made of the value of his services and to the American way of handling one's debts. He was in the process of becoming a professional in those days: developing, therefore, professional standards. You did good work and you valued it highly. In a world running more and more to the slipshod and chaotic, to random patterns and statistical averages and a casual way of leaving a mess behind, a quality job, precise and accurate, neat and complete, would always be admired, always command its price. If the professionals didn't maintain these standards, and those seeking to become professionals strive to emulate them, what was left?

Such high-minded efforts brought Walter not only the valuable fellowship his advisor had mentioned, not only the opportunity to teach the course in The Bible as Literature left open by the death of the Professor of Religion during the following summer, not only the growing respect of Penny, his professors, and his fellow graduate students, who saw him progressing rapidly toward his doctorate with a promising academic career ahead, but also, before the end of the summer and the beginning of the fall term, two additional contracts in his new field of endeavor.

The first of these, which came about because he continued to run into Jimmy occasionally, stopping by the bar on a late afternoon while Penny was still at her job in the Student Union and having the unavoidable drink with him at times through the winter and on into the spring, was a telephone lineman whose name was also Walter. One day Jimmy had raised his heavy head from staring into his shot glass and mentioned that subject which had never been re-opened after their first discussion of it.

"You do that very often?" Jimmy blurted out one afternoon, quite out of nowhere. When Walter failed to reply, Jimmy nodded knowingly and said, "Can't talk about it. Course."

Jimmy then launched into what promised to be a long, sordid tale of adultery, but Walter pushed him ahead to the point of it, that telephone lineman whose background was of no more importance to Walter than the publishing history of some recent paperback crime novel, and whose very name he would gladly have skipped over if the question of identity weren't so important. What Walter demanded this time was a gun and a slightly higher payment, half now, the other half later.

Later came quickly. Walter dropped his bike—Penny's bike, actually—in the weeds by the side of the country road where the telephone company truck was parked and waited till the lineman descended from the pole through the drizzly June afternoon.

"You Walter?" he said when the man was standing at last between the pole and his truck, and when he saw him nod took the gun out of his jacket pocket and shot him twice, quickly, through the center of his chest, got back on his bike, and pedaled away down the wet, empty road, pausing only once on the way home, to toss the gun, wiped clean, far out into a swamp that bordered the road. Completion of the payment also came quickly, through Jimmy a few days later at the bar. Walter said nothing, bought them both drinks, several rounds over which they sat silently into the late afternoon. Only when he rose to leave did he, considering the dangers of reputation, at last lean over to speak to Jimmy.

"Listen, Jimmy," he said, "just one favor. I don't want any more talk about all this between us. Never. Understand?"

Jimmy nodded, lifting his beer chaser in acknowledgment.

Someone must have talked to someone else, however, for it was only a few days later, fortunately at a time when Penny was out, that the phone rang and Walter, a towel around his waist and his hair still dripping from the shower, struggling with one hand to get his glasses adjusted on his face, heard a voice, which he immediately decided could only have been learned from the movies, say to him, "You, friend, are a real pro."

Practiced from having received similar academic praise over the past year, Walter accepted the compliment graciously. He was puzzled at the trouble someone must have gone to in order to track him down at Penny's apartment; but his pride in a job well done and the firm sense he had already gained of his skills, led him to wonder, in the midst of saying his Thank you's, where this might lead: a fellowship in homicide?

    It led, in fact, to a quick and easy piece of work, considerably more profitable than either he had done to date. He simply showed up late in the evening at a suburban dental office to keep an emergency appointment that had already been made for him in a false name, waited till the accommodating young dentist whose face he never really saw turned his back to load his equipment tray, and plunged a long blade into him with a single, swift stroke. The knife, cautiously cleaned in the dentist's own sink, was soon back in Penny's cutlery drawer; the money was passed to him the next day in a grocery bag in a supermarket parking lot in a neighborhood where he never shopped by a man in a station wagon with three happy tots playing in the rear seat. Back to Penny's apartment Walter carried the first watermelon of the summer.

17. Tuning In

Walter looked on none of this as grants-in-aid or even as an outside job that might help support him through graduate school, like so many of his fellow students who worked as cab drivers, bartenders, and night watchmen through the cold and drizzly academic year or devoted their summers to accumulating funds on construction jobs or in canning factories. He had already been named the recipient of the best graduate fellowship the University had to offer in his field, enough to get by on comfortably, given his minimal needs. Such dire warnings his mother had cast at him when he passed through home on his way from the Army to graduate school: never would he be able to earn a decent living, support a family, enjoy the finer things of life. And yet this work seemed so right to him, so ideally suited to all his interests, as natural as . . . well, as this other activity. He would gladly have paid for the privilege.

Limited as his experience was so far, the fact was, he liked what he did. Unlike what he had come to understand, from listening to the gripes and whines of his parents' friends in earlier days and to men in bars and barbershops now, was the general experience—that people hated their jobs and made no bones about it—his own work gave him both pleasure and satisfaction, not only from the way it revealed his natural skills but, as well, from something in its very nature. Or, he considered, from the nature of his relationship to it. Reading his way voraciously through the summer, both in delight and in the attempt to broaden his knowledge in his newly chosen field of modern literature, he came at last to the passage in one of his favorite contemporary novels which announced: "The point is, to get everybody in tune."

And who could be more in tune, he argued to himself: with himself, his skills, his feelings, his desires, his activities, his standards?

Sitting up in bed beside Penny after a well-attuned hour of lovemaking, he watched the late night news on television, a vision of death and destruction all around: clips of careening semis jackknifed across a rain-slick highway, giant mudslides flicking houses off the sides of the coastal range, reports on burgeoning weaponry stockpiles, political bombings, death by bee sting, tainted meat, medical mishaps. In tune with this? he wondered, or does it really matter with what?

He watched, with only commercials to divert his attention, an interview with the widow of the latest gunshot victim, listened to the screech of furious threats at an unintelligible political meeting, saw films of an anonymous air strike in a country whose location he couldn't have found on a map, followed the camera as it zoomed in on the canvas covered shape on a stretcher two fireman carried from a still smoldering building. Oh he was tuned in all right, waiting for the baseball scores or the report on tomorrow's weather or the late movie that followed the news or simply the next commercial break as a reminder to turn off the set, and meanwhile simply taking it all in, comfortably propped up in bed on a pair of soft foam pillows, Job indeed, patiently in tune with—or, at this stage of his life, still carefully attuning himself to—the world around him.

Well, there it is, he kept thinking, the tornado sweeping through the playground, the berserk sniper, the botulism in the potato salad at the family reunion, the overturned canoe, tractor, light plane, baby carriage . . . and here I am.

Penny, mumbling, face in pillow, sheet slipping down off her smooth bare back: "Is it over yet?"

18. Helpful Honeymoon

Married in late August at City Hall, Walter and Penny spent the week before Labor Day honeymooning at a resort perched on a cliff above a high falls in the Cascades. They splurged on money which Walter explained his mother had sent as both a wedding gift and an offering from funds she had managed to hold back from the dwindling resources of her deceased husband's declining business. Walter knew she had accumulated a safe margin of private investments: savings had always received a high priority in his family. So much so that Walter, even though he had not saved one bit of himself for that family but had spent all on the outside—or his own inside—world, had not failed to hide half of his recent cash earnings in his newly-acquired safe deposit box.

Life in the mountains was, for Walter and Penny, not substantially different from life in the city: they made love in the mornings and evenings, they made excursions along forest trails as clearly marked as city streets, they made much to-do about their bountiful meals, they made conversational acquaintances among other couples beside the pool. Things were much the same even when it rained and they lay in bed most of the day, reading when not, as Penny liked to say, fooling around.

It was on the first sunny afternoon after two days of rain that Penny talked beside the pool with a slim, dark-haired woman in her thirties while Walter swam length after length through the cold water. When he emerged shivering and exhausted after half an hour, to find Penny alone in her deck chair, reading, he dried his face, put on his thick, goldrimmed glasses, wrapped a beach towel about his shoulders and, taking a chair in the sun beside her, asked who her friend was, what their talk had been about.

"The usual," said Penny, looking up from her book. "Trouble with a man. She wants your advice. I mean, she doesn't know what to do, and neither do I, and I suggested that you were sensible and full of ideas. But don't get any. Just be a help."

Walter was. After dinner he sat with her on a bench in front of the hotel, where Penny could see them from the porch if she cared to watch, which he doubted, and, surprised by her tears and how much older she seemed than he had thought at the pool, listened to her anger at a man he recalled having seen with her at lunchtimes. Trim, expensively suited, grey streaks in his dark hair, he pursued her by day from the city, returned to the city at night, burdened her afternoons with guilt and accusations.

"If he doesn't leave me alone I think I'll die," she cried softly. "The things he says! The things he says he'll do!"

Walter stopped her with a finger across her lips, assured her that he could make sure she had nothing to worry about any longer, then watched the growing calm in her eyes turn suddenly to something startled and frightened when he said that there would, of course, be a price for his services.

"What I mean is this," said Walter, feeling her shrink away from him on the bench. And as he named his price, listened to her one, almost whispered, outburst of astonishment—"You do this? People do this?"—and extracted from her the promise that not a word on the subject would be spoken to his wife, to anyone, ever, he watched her dark eyes begin to grow soft once more.

After their late breakfast the following morning, Walter excused himself, telling Penny he wanted some time to be alone to think out their new friend's problem, to take a walk by himself. "Why don't you go swimming with . . . .," he started to say, but then he was aware he didn't remember her name. No, he had never even learned it.

He left the dining room absent-mindedly carrying his napkin in his hand, returned before lunch to find the two women sitting quietly beside the pool, both reading. The woman entered the dining room alone at lunch, joined Walter and Penny at their table; dark-eyed and sadly smiling, her appetite was quite a surprise to Walter. She joined them again for lunch the next day. It was her final meal at the resort, and when Penny left for a few minutes to go to the ladies' room, she reached under the table and discretely laid a white envelope on Walter's lap. Later in the afternoon, dressed for the city, she stopped at poolside to say goodbye to them.

"It's been a pleasure meeting you both," she said, extending her gloved hand to Walter.

And then, to Penny: "Your husband has been so helpful."

Penny, squinting up into the sun beginning its descent above the woman's head, smiled.

18. Rapport

Walter moved steadily through graduate school by knife and gun, essay and carefully prepared lecture, never as prolific as in that second year, in which his vocation had been revealed to him, but always dependable, accurate, skillful, his work marked by enthusiasm and precision, ever avoiding the messy contours and random structuring of the bomb or the discussion section. He declined to speak to his freshman class on the banalities of Salinger, to sit through tediously delivered and mindlessly extravagant seminar papers on Freudian criticism, to murder the chair of the English Department at a branch of the University of California where he was interested in applying for a job. He had a chapter of his unfinished dissertation accepted for publication by Modernisme, but took his exams indifferently and passed them with barely acceptable marks. In spare hours he studied anatomy and pharmacology texts in the library and jogged alone around the indoor track at the University fieldhouse, sweating out Dadaism and the shenanigans of the American expatriates, Soviet realism and the so-called Southern Renaissance.

His rapport with his fellow graduate students was satisfactory but minimal. "Ignore rapport," the Director of Freshman English told them monthly as they assembled in the Committee Room for the required pedagogy sessions. "We are not interested in rapport; we are interested in results."

Rapport for Dr. Whitbread, Walter soon realized, meant looking a student in the eye until he woke up to exactly whom you were addressing. And if the student were an attractive female, rapport assumed the proportions of sin, for Dr. Whitbread was a ferocious classroom visitor, before whose pre-announced appearances even third year Teaching Assistants were known to spend entire nights sweating out the perfect class preparation.

Results, on the other hand, were clearly visible, evidenced simply by the apprentice teacher's success in excising, through the lethal device of the failing grade, a sufficient number of students from the freshman class. "Results" did not mean success; "results" meant failure. Walter, more concerned with learning his job than with questioning its values, was successful at failure; getting results, he also got Dr. Whitbread's respect.

To Whitbread's dismay, however, Walter was a failure at rapport: each time he visited one of Walter's classes he seemed to feel obliged to reprimand Walter, in the subsequent consultation, not only for achieving too much rapport, but for apparently striving after it. Walter, listening to these admonitions in silence, knew, however, that rapport was only a technique; like a lesson in paragraphing, it helped you to get results. In fact it was the *sine qua non* of technique: it allowed you to be there, and by being there to get results. Rapport was presence; the knife could do nothing on its own. Walter had rapport.

On the few occasions when he argued this thesis, with less violent analogy, among his fellow graduate students, he ended by questioning the rapport he thought he had attained with them. As he and Penny had moved away, on their own, from the discussions which used to take place in the Student Union, so the discussions themselves had moved: to a crowded, noisy beer parlor blocks away off on the far side of campus from their apartment and hence, unlike the bar beneath the bridge, well out of his way on the walk home, so much so that only on a rare Friday afternoon did Walter stop there to pursue rapport among a collection of graduate students who were, he saw, bright, articulate, slothful, petty, creative, pernicious, ambitious: a veritable society.

Did he, Walter wondered, want rapport with a society or was that too much presence to be of any use. "Rapport!" they all chorused above rapidly emptied pitchers of dark beer: of course they understood rapport. If you could achieve rapport, it meant you were liked. Except for Walter, who like Dr. Whitbread wanted results, everyone wanted to be liked. It was either the cheap beer or this response that left a bad taste in his mouth. Walter didn't know if he really wanted to be liked by a whole society, much less most of the individuals with whom he came into contact, though they made it difficult for him to leave, dragging in yet another round of full, dark pitchers.

Walter excused himself to step to the pay phone that hung in full view at the end of the bar, called Penny, either got no answer or, because of the noise, could not hear her answer, returned to the table to say he was sorry, he had to be going. Full of rapport and beer, he began the long walk home in the rain.

20. And More

There is something in Walter that appeals to everyone. Not only did the traveling salesman in the bar of the Kansas City airport not flee in terror, to safety or the police, at Walter's revelation, but the woman at the mountain resort was positively relieved to find that he was what he was, and not what she first thought he was. Even his victims turn toward him, like his students, with trust and expectation. The platinum-blonde call girl who has been holding out on her employer bares her chest to his blade without even asking for payment first: unbuttons her blouse to the hands rising toward her breasts without even seeing the glitter of the blade. Their rapport is instantaneous. The embezzling vice-president of the import-export firm sits in his expensive Hilton suite toasting Walter and the deal they will never close with his drugged scotch and water. The shoe clerk, alone in the store on a rainy Tuesday morning, leads Walter back into the stockroom to make his own selection, saying, even as Walter, a step behind him, uncoils the thin wire in his hands, "You're about the nicest customer I've ever had."

Even his contact likes him. Stopping at the drugstore after that last Friday session with his fellow grad students to buy a bottle of aspirin and use the pay phone to dial home again, then recalling, just as he was about to drop his coin in the slot, that this was an afternoon when Penny was working late at the Student Union, he decided to cross campus and meet her so they could walk home together, maybe stop for tacos or rellenos at the Mexican restaurant on the other side of the bridge. But he let the quarter drop anyway and dialed instead the current number.

The number changed every couple of months, though there was always someone, usually a woman, at the old number to give him the new one. When she answered this time, Walter identified himself, remained silent after she said, "Hey, man, where you been? I was about to come lookin' for your sweet ass myself," and hung up when, after a pause, she recited the new number. Walter fished out another quarter, dialed, and this time got the deep, accentless voice of his contact, a voice that could have belonged to a radio announcer anywhere in the country and could, with equal ease, imitate any region's accents: that now went flat, friendly, midwestern at Walter's identification: "Nice ta hear from ya."

And with no contract to offer at the moment, still kept Walter on the phone almost ten minutes with compliments on his work, complaints about how unfortunate it was that they couldn't get together socially.

"Ah, buddy," he said, dropping the midwestern for something vaguely eastern, "such a time we could have."

Walter, struggling to hold, for the first time, something resembling a real conversation with his contact, mentioned the difficulty of lacking of a real name to address. "Anything'll do," he explained, "it doesn't have to be the real thing."

"Call me Buddy," the man said, "buddy."

"Thanks, Walter said, still struggling with it, "Buddy."

When Walter at last wiggled free from the phone booth, briefcase under his arm, he bumped into the old woman who lived upstairs from Penny's—now their—apartment, waiting with a quarter in her own hand, and apologized to her, explaining that he'd been trying to get hold of his wife.

"You two sure make a cute couple," she said, her eyes bright, amused, "but that ain't who you was talking to. She just walked by outside a minute ago."

Walter rushed out of the drugstore, settled into his easiest jog, ignoring gulls and rain, caught up with Penny just across the bridge, taking her by the elbow and guiding her into the doorway of Su Casa: "Lady, I sure do like the food here."

"Mister," she said to him, inside, slipping out of her hooded raincoat, shaking her dark hair free, "I sure do like you."

21. Wrinkle-Proof

The chairmen of several midwestern universities liked Walter enough to make appointments to interview him at the Modern Language Association meetings in New York that December: liked his credentials at first, then liked him well enough in their personal meetings, though he had only just passed his exams and had yet to complete his dissertation, to bid for his services. While Penny visited museums, stores, Greenwich Village, in the winter rain, Walter sat knee to knee in stuffy hotel rooms with men who held his packet of credentials on their laps.

Walter daydreamed of Penny returning to their own room later in the afternoon soaking wet and chilled from her excursions, of soaping each other in the hot shower they loved to take together. He was deeply impressed by New York water pressure. Meanwhile the chairmen always paused when they had thumbed their way through to Walter's letters of recommendation, to point out how highly it appeared he was thought of. By some very respected scholars. And sooner or later the chairman was joined by a couple of younger colleagues, who informed Walter how much he would like living in Cleveland or Detroit or Indianapolis. Walter looked at them blankly. Omaha? Columbus? St. Louis? Where was he? The towels in these older hotels always seemed worn, rough: where he rubbed too hard, toweling Penny dry, red blotches appeared on her skin: all places to go over, after, with his mouth, tongue.

From the after-Christmas sale counter in Saks' men's department, after his last interview was finished early in the afternoon, Walter selected a cashmere scarf he liked as much for its color—plum: all the scarves on the counter were plum—as its softness. He removed the price tag and wrapped the scarf around his neck when he paid for it instead of letting the clerk put it in a bag. Outside, in the rain, cold but very fine now, almost like home, he walked, hatless, to the Tishman Building, pausing in the lobby to wipe his face with an end of the scarf, clean his glasses with his handkerchief, before he entered the elevator.

"Corrigan to see Mr. Schaeffer," he told the secretary in the thickly-carpeted waiting room. He never questioned, was only rarely informed about, either the name he was given to use by those who made appointments for him or the name he asked for. The grey-haired man who belonged to the latter met Walter in the hallway, led him into his paneled office, sat down in the leather swivel chair behind his desk as Walter closed the door behind them, approached.

"I was asked to give you this," said Walter. Slipping the scarf from his neck, he leaned across the desk, laid it gently around Schaeffer's own even as the man began to rise from his chair, lifting his arms to fend it off. Walter pulled down on the scarf, dumping Schaeffer back into the chair, spinning it halfway around: twisted, drawing tightly into Schaeffer's throat the knot he had tied into the center of the scarf as he walked out of Saks; then watched, not the man but his own watch, the circuit of its sweep second hand, till he was satisfied to let Schaeffer's limp body slump even further down into the chair, to untwist, unknot, the scarf, slip it back around his own neck, depart with a slight smile at the secretary: a man who had enjoyed his visit, gotten the results he came for, liked his work, of course.

"What I like about cashmere," he said, explaining his extravagance to Penny back in their hotel room: "doesn't wrinkle."

He demonstrated by squeezing the scarf into a ball, letting it hang open again. She had returned before him, bathed already, lay in bed with her hair still wet, reading movie listings in the *Times*. Walter let the plum-colored scarf drop to the floor as he leaned over her paper to kiss the skin she'd rubbed red between her breasts.

22. Paper Chase

Did Walter read the newspapers back then?

Yes, even then: in New York, in his office, at the barber shop, standing in the check-out lines, all over the little house they rented when the only job offer that materialized brought him to a university of dubious distinction in a place of none at all; in the kitchen and the bathroom and the bedroom and the tiny living room, which were all the rooms there were in that house. In the early fall, when the weather was still mild, on the front steps, too, but mostly, back then, in the bedroom, in the bed.

"This," he replied back then to Penny's curiosity about his obsessive newspaper reading—did he never skip a single page?—"this is probably where modern literature is truly to be found."

"And what have you found?" she inquired, kicking, bare-legged, at the sports section, till it slid to the floor. As often as not, their bed was full of newspapers, the comic pages shredded beneath their thrashing bodies on Sunday morning, the sheets smudged with newsprint.

"Little enough," he hedged: "I read for style, not content."

And it was true, in a way, since the content he sought—or looked out for—he rarely found there. Hardly ever did his victims make their way into print. And certainly not in this new place, where he had none. But still he read the papers and wondered: what became of them? Did no one know? Or care? Were they all so insignificant? But here, he read, was the report of a decomposed body dragged from a drainage canal, and there the unidentified body of a young woman found in the weeds beside the golf course, and over there the unknown old man dead of exposure in the railroad yards. Well then, too significant? But here was the report on the dead union leader, corrupt to the end, the murdered captain of industry, the pioneer of modern military tactics mysteriously dead in the shower in his country home. None of it Walter's doing. But he wondered: wasn't anyone paying attention?

If he read the newspapers for style, as he claimed, the style he found was absence: gaps everywhere, the word unwritten, the event unreported. It did indeed seem no one cared. Well, for that matter, the thing itself undone for some months. But he read on all the same: reading nothing though there was always something: turmoil domestic and international, turmoil beneath the seas and in the skies above. Enough that he did not, really, miss not finding anything else. And though it did occur to him that such a lack of that anything else that he wouldn't have liked to encounter anyway was perhaps—what was the word? controlled?—he continued to find its absence not only acceptable but right.

If he read the newspapers because that was where he thought modern literature was to be found, he would have been sadly disappointed. Fortunately, he never really thought that. But even back then he read the newspapers: more often than not in bed, where, though he read that nothing much was happening, still, Penny was there beside him, and one thing often led to another.

23. A Miracle

The first year in that new academic position passed quickly and quietly as Walter prepared for and met his new classes, kept required but usually lonely office hours, and completed his dissertation. With some violence to context, but always careful to cover his tracks, he slickly extracted from it several articles which were immediately accepted for publication by the leading journals of modern literature, and then he set about exploring the job market once again, for a position at a real institution of higher learning, in a real city.

That contact—Buddy, which he kept having trouble thinking of him as—whose last phone calls, just prior to this move, had been coming to him, rather than his to, OK, Buddy, seemed slow in catching up with him now, though he was sure both that his skills had been sufficiently demonstrated and that his employers were sufficiently skillful that they would not remain separated for long. Meanwhile, he set about explaining to the scholarly community the meaning of "modern" and to his students the meaning of "literature"; gradually retreated, with Penny, and in the face of a bleak and early winter, from exploring this flat prairie town which seemed limited to dull contemporary wood or stone church buildings, to exploring, inside their own rented bungalow, what seemed to be the more unlimited hills and valleys, rivulets and rain forests, of their own fine contemporary bodies; and listened, as the season darkened, to faculty members muttering dire threats against department chairs, to regents raging at state legislators, to students imagining the destruction of their roommates, their parents, themselves, to janitorial anger directed at gum-chewing, cigarette-smoking students, to violent secretarial curses whispered at the backs of inconsiderate professors, and to angry maintenance men hammering fence posts into the frozen ground to keep trespassing students, faculty, administrators, everyone, off the dying grass and on the narrow, cracked, concrete paths that criss-crossed the campus.

"It's a miracle the people in this town haven't all killed each other off by now," claimed Penny one dark December afternoon, just returned from her part-time job behind the perfume counter of the town's one, small department store.

While Walter kneaded spices and breadcrumbs into the weekly meatloaf, she reported to him on ill-tempered Santa Clauses, surly salespeople, kicking children and slapping parents, stockboys who rammed loaded carts through aisles packed with customers, and surly department managers. Walter shaped the meatloaf in its oblong pan, shoved it into the oven, washed his hands at the kitchen sink as Penny narrated the day's quota of violence. He smiled as she reached the end of her long catalogue, tossed the dish towel he'd used to dry his hands onto the counter, reached for the top button of her blouse. Just then the telephone rang.

It was not only the first contact in six months, but the first such call he had ever received in Penny's presence. Therefore did Walter, with great care, refrain from giving himself entirely over to the telephone. Still, it was Penny herself who stood there and finished the unbuttoning, reached behind her back to unsnap her bra, guided Walter's limp hand under her soft breast. With his right hand Walter, standing almost at attention in the middle of the kitchen, clutched the telephone, saying only little things: "Yes" and "Right." Under his left hand Penny's nipples hardened as she moved it back and forth across her breasts: left, right, left, right, left . . . . Her head drooped against his shoulder: she would have been looking at the floor if her eyes had been open. Walter looked out the window, staring away between left hand and right as he committed to memory the facts that were being passed to him over the telephone. Dirty snow was what he saw.

CHAPTER III

24. Facing It

Dirty snow, messy snow, patches the ground six miles below Walter now. According to the calendar, spring has arrived, but the sunshine up here only serves to illuminate winter's remnants of dirty snow down there. In disgust, Walter, in his window seat, pulls the curtain shut. Dirty snow, old snow, snow of a distant city, mostly forgotten, and a first job, long since left behind, is not what he wants to think about. But snow, dirty white, past his view of Penny's soft shape, is what he still keeps seeing: until he closes the curtain.

All the way home from Kansas City Walter has been thinking continuously about his wife, but try as hard as he can, he has been unable to call up into his mind a picture of her face. He was sitting in a bar at O'Hare, sipping a cold beer while he waited for his connecting flight and still thinking about Penny, as he had been doing for the past hour or so, when he first became aware of this inability. And he was buckling himself into the Northwest 727 for the last leg of his flight home when he realized that he had, in fact, not ever been able to call up into his mind a picture of his wife's face when he was away from her.

The rest of the flight home he has spent trying to "see" her in a variety of places and actions: at work in the kitchen, reading in her favorite chair, asleep in bed, making love, sitting across from him in the Chinese restaurant, buttoning Judy's coat as she heads out to play in the snow, waving goodbye as she dropped him off at the airport. At each of these visions he has been moderately successful—to the extent that when he envisioned making love to her he was glad he had a copy of *The Chicago Tribune* to lay across his lap—but what he was successful at was getting a sense of her presence into these portraits: in general, a sense of color and light, shape and gesture; in particular, the fine texture of her hair or the way she dangled a shoe from her left foot. What he was not successful at was seeing her face.

Her face is the first thing he sees when he gets off the plane, however, and he has no trouble recognizing her: wide mouth with thin, pale lips and straight nose, high cheekbones and clear brown eyes, hair the color of the darkly-stained woods he has often admired in fine furniture. People coming off the plane pile up behind him as he stops in the middle of the exit ramp and stares at her, at all these details he knows perfectly well—the tiny scar where the mole on her chin was removed, the delicate lines around her mouth, the feathery curve of her eyebrow—until a briefcase nudging him in the back propels him forward into the waiting room and her arms.

"Walter," she laughs, when she leans back from kissing him, "why were you staring at me like that? You looked like you were trying to figure out who I was."

"I knew perfectly well who you were," is what serious Walter says in reply, "I was just enjoying the sight of you." And that's true: he enjoys being able, suddenly, to see her again. Face to face, his image of her is extremely clear. But what he thinks, as they head toward home with Penny behind the wheel of her little blue Spyder, is: Perhaps I do not know who she is.

On the freeway he closes his eyes to picture her as she is, driving the car, or as he recalls her from one day last summer, in the garden, smiling up at him, squinting in the sunlight as she straightened up from pinching back the white impatiens. Then he opens his eyes again to check his vision: a perfect match, right down to the squint.

"Could you get me my sunglasses out of my purse?" she asks. He does, then closes his eyes to see her face again, this time framed against a white pillow, looking straight up at him. No doubt about it, it's her, right down to the tiny holes in her earlobes. He thinks about how some people respond to hearing their names called by saying "That's me" while others say "That's my name": I am Walter; my name is Walter; or, as he remembers the literal translations from Spanish or French, I am called Walter. Which is to say, perhaps, I am not really Walter, that's just what they call me, a name I have, or have been given. And Penny is a name my wife has, which I can carry away with me and use whenever I want, duplicate as often as I want in speech or print or thought. And others can be called by it as well, who in no way resemble her. Whereas her face is her. To which, or whom, I seem to have complete access when I am in her presence and practically none when I am not. The fact that when I am away and thinking of her I cannot see her is therefore a reminder that it is not really her I am thinking of but only some concept, some faceless concept, I have of her, maybe not much different from the concept I have of myself. Anyway, he concludes, her face is her, she it: not just it, of course.

Having rationalized the disturbing discovery he has made on the flight home and begun, now, to think of her breasts and thighs, which are also her, he opens his eyes to see that they are coasting down the freeway exit ramp toward a stop light.

"You seem tired," she says, glancing over at him, her face bright in the late afternoon sun. "You can nap before dinner, the girls are out. Maybe," smiling, "I'll nap with you." At the red light he reaches over and gently touches her right breast, from beneath.

"Don't."

25. Other Times

Walter does, eventually: in the afternoon, before the girls return home, and again in the night: does in the big city now, not the little prairie town, does in a new house big enough for all and with no dirty snow on the lawn now, does in a bedroom devoid of newspapers, which never make their way to the second floor here, does behind drawn shades and a closed door after his daughters have gone to bed, does when the time is right and he and Penny have stood facing each other on opposite sides of their wide bed, shedding their clothes onto the beige carpeting before entering, together, the printed bamboo forest of their sheets. And does with a gusto matched by Penny's, thinking, even as he kneels above her, about to enter her, Oh how I need to do this: Oh how I need to do what I do.

Who would doubt it, especially at a time like this?

But there are other times, too.

Other times, thinks Walter, other things.

There are always, he sees, other times: probably all times are other times, bringing with them other things.

When Walter thinks back, he can remember lots of other times much like this one but bringing with them other things. Lying in bed, now, with Penny, he can remember lying in bed with Penny: other times: with a dry hard penis instead of the limp wet one that flops down between them now; or with both of them back to back on opposite sides of the bed, altogether dry and hard and silent. Yes, he can remember times like that, though they've been rare. And he can remember other times: lying in a bed without Penny, lying in a different bed with Penny, lying in a different bed, years past, with someone other than Penny: other times and other things. And such is the reality of other times that his penis begins to harden with the memory.

So he can remember, know, even in the dark, that there are other times: that he who prides himself on always being on time is also always in time, and that these times he's on and in are always, somehow, other times. But what he cannot quite conceive of now, in this particular midnight time—among sleepers and dreamers beside and around him all lost, for a time, to time—is how this business of getting from one time to another time works.

Somewhere out there—or should he say out then? out now?—there is, he now knows, another someone paddling along in the stream of his own time, seeking, expecting, expressing a confidence in his ability, to merge it with Walter's. How is this done, wonders a weary Walter, his mind wandering into images of confluence, of swift waters bucking and breaking in the sudden turbulence of their coming together.

Just how and when—at what time?—does one time manage to become or join with some other time? When he leaves the house he imagines taking his own time with him, so some other time must be left behind, inhabiting the house. How little he knows of what that other time of Penny's is like, when he's not around. How little he understands how their two separate times manage to come together, as they have tonight. We are time travelers all, he thinks, and we haven't the slightest idea how we do it. Other times, other times: what lies between them and just how do we, he wonders, winding his sleepy sleepless mind up while his penis winds back down again, just how do we get through that, across the in between, from one time into another time? And into the other things that other times bring?

It is, finally, rather easily that he does it: this time. Even in the dark he manages this miraculously ordinary movement from one time to another. He closes his eyes, turning softly toward Penny, wet penis and all. Turning softly in against her sleeping body, he closes his eyes. He closes his eyes.

When he wakes, it is another time.

26. Cold Soup

So other times shouldn't worry Walter; but they do: there are always other times, into which one simply awakens or—last night's turbulent vision—is abruptly awakened. It happens and it isn't all that difficult. But other things: such other things! Walter can hardly believe them, at times, though he may know, even now, that their very improbability speaks for their possibility. But still: at the next table in the chic little department store restaurant where he and Penny have met for lunch, in this other time to which he has wakened, simply because they decided it would be nice to meet for lunch before Penny has to go off shopping for birthday presents for Janey, where she has left the table for a few minutes after they've placed their orders and just as their cups of soup were being set down before them, two men are discussing, so loudly and clearly that Walter keeps looking around the room to see if anyone else is paying any attention to them, the merits of certain types of weapons.

One of them swears, gruffly, by his old Smith and Wesson .38: "I wouldn't have anything else."

The other, the little fellow in the out-of-style blue suit Walter caught a glimpse of when he looked hurriedly around the restaurant, insists on a nine millimeter, any nine millimeter.

"You really want a job done," he argues, "you do it with a nine millimeter. Nothing else."

Walter looks quickly around once again, manages to see that the Smith and Wesson man is jowly, unshaven, even wears his hat at the table, the brim pulled well down over his eyes. No one else seems to be paying them any attention, but Walter, eyeing the cup of gazpacho he hasn't touched yet, cannot believe he is actually hearing this conversation, conducted at this volume, by these characters, in this crowded place.

"I never use nothin' but a nine millimeter no more. Never will."

"Neatest little tool in the world, that's what your Smith and Wesson is. A classic"

Because no one else seems startled by this debate, Walter has trouble believing he's actually hearing it either: probably some sort of aural hallucination. If it were really taking place, wouldn't everyone within hearing range be looking over at them suspiciously—or taking cover under their tables? On the other hand, if it were really taking place, wouldn't everyone within hearing be doing exactly what they're doing right now, keeping their eyes on their food and their friends? Doing their best to ignore what they, too, can't believe they're hearing? Who would want to risk, with these two, the eye-to-eye contact that says, I know what you're talking about?

"Surprise. Compact, see. Quick. That's the way you do it."

"You got size, you do the job right the first time."

Walter doesn't know whether to prop his elbows on the table or keep his hands in his lap. What bothers him most about this conversation is its unprofessional quality. Oh it sounds very professional, in its accuracy of detail, its knowledgeability. They are not stupid men, and when Walter hears them discussing range and velocity, impact force and reload time, he knows that they know what they are talking about: he has given considerable attention to the same things himself. But at the same time he finds them as unprofessionally narrow-minded in their knowledgeability as certain other so-called professionals he has encountered: a football coach he has read about so committed to his running game that he dropped his best quarterback from the first team for passing on third and ten; or his own colleague Sandra Brennenburg, true believer in—vocal disciple of—Walter Pater as the culmination of the entire tradition of English literature, he whose genius burns with a hard, gem-like flame within the chambers of the British Museum, wherein she spends her every summer.

Himself Walter prefers to think of, more broadly, as a kind of modern Renaissance man: able in one situation to use a knife, in another a high-powered rifle, at the right time a handgun, or, for that matter, a rock, if it's appropriate. A professional is not one who picks out a single tool and uses it over and over again, however well—how long would a pitcher last, who had only his curve ball to rely on?—but one who knows the available tools and how and when to use them. Walter, who certainly considers himself a professional, knows a lot of them and knows the circumstances in which each is best used, but also knows he does not know them all. A professional is always learning, he thinks.

27. Cold Thought

When Penny returns to the table, she finds that her soup is also cold, though a hot soup was what she ordered.

"You were certainly gone long enough."

"I don't really care much for chicken gumbo anyway."

Walter considers reporting to Penny on the conversation he has just overheard. At the same time he wonders if it's a good idea to get involved in that subject with her in any way at all. At least he will make sure that she gets a look at those two before they leave: they are enough of a sight to evoke the tourist in him. So he begins to make covert gestures in their direction, behind him, covering his pointing finger with his own body, lest they see, but also aware that this will cause Penny to think he is pointing at himself, unless accompanied by some sort of eye-rolling, over-the-shoulder nod of the head, which he is about to toss in her direction when he sees that she is already looking over his shoulder.

"You don't usually see that sort in here."

"Becoming quite the snob, aren't we," Walter teases. But the truth has its snobbish side: glancing about, they see the tables occupied, mostly, by middle-aged women, and older: just what anyone would have expected to see in the tea room of the city's most fashionable department store, but here are these two who have not even learned to chew with their mouths shut.

"Distance, too. Impact. You got to know you can take a guy out across the room."

"What you got to know is, you can get close enough without making a guy suspicious, see?"

Walter does not see: he does not see what the point of this discussion is, when both of these characters have made up their minds for a lifetime; he does not see why they are carrying it on in a crowded public place with their voices raised above normal to compensate for the noise level in the restaurant; he does not see why none of the other patrons, busy as they are with their food and their own conversations, seems at all aware of this bizarre conversation. And most of all he does not see why it has to be taking place at the table next to his, right behind his back, leaving him sitting so stiffly and uncomfortably, folding and re-folding his napkin in his lap, as if the whole routine has been staged to test the reactions of those who overhear it: to call attention to him.

Finally he sees that his soup bowl is still sitting on the table in front of him, as it has been for some time. When he takes, finally, the first spoonful into his mouth he is shocked to find it ice cold. Then he remembers that it was, in fact, the gazpacho that he ordered.

"But I really do like this place," says Penny, as if fending off some silent criticism in the way Walter has looked over the room and its occupants.

The waitress, elderly herself, delivers Penny's chef's salad and Walter's plate of cold cuts and breads, smiling as she sets the dishes delicately, fussily, on the table. When she departs, Penny leans forward toward Walter and whispers, "But those two behind you, I wish we could hear what they're saying. They look like they're plotting a murder."

The first thought that bursts into Walter's mind—before he can hoist to his lips a smile suggesting the absurdity of such a notion or voice the possibility that Penny has been seeing too many old gangster movies on late-night television—is: I could kill you for saying that.

The second thought is: I could kill them, too; it's hoods like that who give the profession a bad name.

The third: I'm a professional, but I do not belong to a profession. I have nothing to do with the rest of these assholes.

The fourth is hardly a thought, merely a surge of hostility directed at everyone seated in the tea room, daintily stuffing bits of food into their mouths: This whole place is irrational.

Next: No, I am irrational, what's going on here is probably quite normal.

And: Nothing is normal, it's all irrational.

What emerges aloud from this sequence of thoughts, as the individual elements begin to echo and collapse into one another, is simply: "They have to eat, too."

"I suppose you'd think it was perfectly fine if they were sitting here eating club sandwiches and planning to kill someone?"

"Depends."

Penny dumps the cup of vinaigrette dressing over her salad: "And if you were king, you'd probably have quite a number of people done away with yourself?" It is only half a question.

Walter shrugs his shoulders.

"A cold thought," adds Penny, plunging her fork into her salad.

Walter shrugs again.

"And that," says Penny, looking up with a bundle of lettuce, cheese, and tomato poised on her fork: "you'll probably become famous someday for that shrug."

Walter demonstrates it for her once more.

"Mmmm," she growls, thrusting the forkful of salad into her mouth. Then, mouth full, she adds: "Sometimes I could kill you for that."

28. Cold Consolation

Walter would never say such a thing. In fact, it is terribly important to him that he not say such things: I could kill you for that; Drop dead; Disappear; They ought to fit you with a pair of concrete shoes; Throttle yourself. These are lethal words, and words are powerful, fearful things: to Walter, there is nothing like them. He has always feared the language of violence—You want a punch in the mouth? I'll get you for that!—even more than violence itself: as if it has some lasting, unshakable hold on him while the real violence—the physical violence, that is, which for Walter is no more real than its verbal counterpart—is, at least, quickly done and over with.

Walter has no idea where this dread of violent language—I'd like to smash your face; What you need is a good beating; How'd you like a kick in the balls?—comes from. He certainly never heard it in the house where he grew up. Walter and his siblings practiced name-calling rather than threats, and never did he hear his parents raise their voices, speak in terms of violence, to each other or to their children. His parents did not argue. That was an unspoken rule of the household.

The closest he can remember ever having heard them come to an argument occurred one summer evening after dinner while he was taking his turn helping his mother wash dishes. Through the window over the sink they could see his father pacing back and forth on the front lawn, as he often did in the evenings, picking up debris—chewing gum wrappers, fallen twigs—while he smoked his after dinner cigar. At some point—Walter recalls wielding the dish towel around the inside of the heavy, black, cast-iron skillet that his mother always used for frying liver—his father paused in front of them to speak to his mother through the open screened window.

"I'm going over to Harold's to play cards."
"No you're not, not tonight."
"Yes I am."

That, Walter is quite certain, was the whole extent of the conversation: no one swore, no one yelled, no one threatened violence or retaliation. Not a word was spoken in anger. Like the mature adults Walter took them to be, his parents had confronted a difference of opinion, an unresolved difference even, coolly and with no show of hostility. Then his father's face disappeared from the open window and he and his mother returned to their task of finishing the pots and pans and not another word was spoken on the subject: no bitter harangue of disappointment, no burst of resentment from behind closed doors, no passionate How could you's and Don't you dare's and You'll be sorry's: not the least little verbal expression of passion, anger, violence.

And yet.

And yet, thinks the older Walter, was not even the younger Walter aware, though he could not have said it then—it was all he could do to hang onto that gigantic black skillet without dropping it on his toes—of the forces, the possibilities, that surged along beneath those quiet words: the forces that louder and more concrete words—the words that Walter and his brothers and sisters never heard in that family, the words Walter still dreads hearing—might have released, had they ever been spoken; the forces that were kept in control, perhaps only barely, by the equally strong counterforce of silence? What did the very silence signify: that even when there wasn't violence, there was . . . violence? Did the young Walter pray, in his bed at night, for the violent words never to be spoken lest the violent things that the silence sat hard upon leap up and follow swiftly after them? Not that the older Walter can remember, who in fact never remembers praying at all. And yet.

Never did his mother rage, in tears, his father pound fist into palm to accentuate his shouts: cold consolation, that.

29. He Who Slaps

"I have never laid a hand on any of my kids," was what Walter's father announced whenever the subject of child rearing came up, as if that alone served as adequate parental policy. As far as Walter can remember, his father's claim was true, though he also recalls some sessions of arm-gripping, shoulder-clutching, and ear-pulling to which a quick swat might well have been preferred. His youngest brother has claimed, to the contrary, to have often experienced the violent laying on of hands, but the distant incidents he has named, always the same ones, are ones that Walter recalls, from the point of view of terrified onlooker, as sessions of rather low-keyed verbal abuse, vague warnings, and temporary ostracism: to which, again, a quick swat quickly over and done with might have been preferred.

Walter has laid a punitive hand on both his daughters' bottoms from time to time: and despised himself for it after each such time. He wishes he could make the same statement his father always made so proudly—as if he alone, in the midst of a contrary cultural tradition, refrained from abusing his children—but without the sense of suppressed violence that always underlay his father's boast. Walter does not think of himself as a violent man, which makes it all the more difficult to comprehend the sting in the palm of his right hand.

This very afternoon he has, in Penny's absence—it is one of her volunteer days at Planned Parenthood—just sent a weeping Janey off to her room. What he has slapped her for at this moment—a failure to stop jabbing her forefinger into her frustrated little sister's midsection—is nothing more than the identical thing he was not moved to slap her for yesterday. My, how violence has poked its childish finger around in here since Walter's return from Kansas City. No, since Walter's departure for Kansas City: since the morning he opened the newspaper with the girls playing under the kitchen table and read that . . . . And what is happening there now, he wonders; behind that public silence, what strange beast slouches his way? Does it not indeed deserve to be slapped down? But how and where and when?

Rare as such slaps have been in his attempts to enforce

some measure of control over his children's behavior—and he is sure, as he counts back over them, remembering each one of them all too vividly for comfort, that there have not been more than one or two in any year—and common as this sort of behavior is among his children, among children in general, so far as he can tell, he can't help concluding that the slap has considerably more to do with him than with the child he slaps.

And he does not like what it has to do with him. Here, in this living room, with its gauzy blue curtains and tile-faced fireplace and prints by artists both local and famous on the walls, here on this Saturday afternoon like so many other Saturday afternoons, with a vindicated Judy playing quietly by herself on the oriental rug and the overly-dramatic wails of banished Janey still drifting down the hall from her bedroom, here on a warm spring afternoon in the place where he lives, Walter does not like to think of himself as a violent man.

And yet for the prissy way in which Judy, smug now in her rightness, pushes a pair of Tonka trucks in a line down the serpentine pattern of the oriental rug, Walter could slap her.

"Go out and play."

30. The Scene

Coffee mug in hand Walter stands in the crucially situated kitchen doorway, from which he can see the dining room and most of the living room, the front hall, the bottom of the staircase to the second floor, a bit of the porch at the far end, and looks around the house: at the carpets and furniture, at the books and artwork. He has read enough mystery fiction to know that you do not spend any time developing a scene in detail early in a story if it is not going to be of considerable relevance by the end. But what possible relevance can there be to this red and black oriental rug laid on top of the carpeting in front of the fireplace, to the blue tiles of the fireplace itself, the plants on the mantle, the blue and white rectangles of the abstract that hangs above them, the white wall against which it hangs, the blue drapes that cover the windows on either side . . . ? These are not items in a scene in a mystery story, no matter how rapidly the corpses pile up and the agents of the law draw near: these are the furnishings of his own life.

Never did he think he would have grown so attached to them. Not that there is anything here he could not bear to part with. The nameless abstract—"the box thing" is how they have always referred to it—is by no means his favorite piece of art in the house, and there are other things he would be just as happy to see above the fireplace. The ferns on the mantle are dusty, pale from lack of light, by no means his favorite house plant: he should associate them with lush and watery places, but the desert is what they generally remind him of. Even the oak, refectory-style dining room table that he devoted so much time to selecting has its drawbacks: it is rather too narrow for serving a large- sized dinner party, and the ends tend to droop when pulled out. Glancing over the bookcase in the living room, he knows that even its prizes he could stand to do without: the four volume set of Eliot's   for example, for which he paid something over forty pounds to a London book dealer whose catalogues he regularly receives: a "fine set," as the catalogue described it, and great poetry as well, but if it were lost, stolen, burned up or sold, stuck together with chewing gum by the children or sloshed with coffee by himself, he would not feel bereft.

It is not these individual bits of household furnishings, then, to which he feels so attached: not these walnut end tables and delicate floor lamps, tasteful and expensive as they are, not the Louise Nevelson silk screen print over the couch or his grandmother's pair of gold candlesticks on the dining room table, but the whole which they construct around him, literally around him where he stands sipping at his coffee.

Upstairs, room by room, he could find still other such wholes, and around all of them, and him, the house itself, out of its white siding and green trim and shutters constructing still a greater whole, and around the house the yard, with its Kentucky bluegrass and drooping spirea, the three oak trees and the one apple, doing poorly so far this spring, Penny's small rose garden and the children's little vegetable patch: a whole encompassing all these others. Though beyond that, Walter knows, drawing his mind back from the white fence, in need of a fresh coat of paint, that separates his yard from the house behind it, back into the kitchen doorway so crucially situated, where he now stands draining the last of the coffee from his mug, back into the center of this whole that the years have so carefully constructed around him: beyond that, other forces intrude, beyond his control, and things begin to fall apart, the edges fray and all sense of an ordered whole soon disintegrates.

It is here, in here, in the dead center of his own world, that the scene is set.

31. The V-Shaped Story

The scene, thinks Walter, not a scene. A scene is something he can recollect, somewhere he's been, something he's seen, the locale of something he's done. A scene is in the past, maybe even in the future: other times, other scenes. A scene happens here, happens there: happens all around him.

But the scene: the scene is where he is, the scene is where he lives.

The scene is right here: and he stands, as always, right in the middle of it, rinsing out his coffee cup—actually Penny's cup, one she received at a dinner to honor Planned Parenthood volunteers and bearing the organization's logo—and setting it carefully in the sink.

He sees, standing here, that as the scene develops for him it always narrows down into one final, precisely defined, focal point, like this: that if he were ever to step aside from his chosen profession of unlocking the secrets of the modern novel for the literary community and his own students and decide instead to construct a novel himself, it would move in just such a direction, everything squeezing together toward some only possible, small, and all-too-imaginable, if as yet too distant to be seen, point in the future towards which all things gather.

When he thinks, as he does at times, like almost any literary scholar, about writing a novel, he recalls a story he once heard—he knows none of the details, but never mind: if it ever comes down to the actual writing, which isn't likely, he'll invent them to suit his own needs anyway—about piracy on the inland waterways of the United States back in the nineteen twenties. He can't actually remember the story, if there was a story. All he can remember is the fact, if it is a fact: piracy on the inland waterways of the United States in, say, the nineteen twenties. Make it the twenties, he thinks, standing here in the midst of a scene of, naturally, his own making anyway. What he wants is mostly a formal design, which he thinks of as V-shaped. Such a V-shaped work, he believes, will reflect the essence of his own experience regardless of its content: the preference for a movement away from masses and crowds, down through small groups, gatherings of colleagues and family, eventually arriving at the level of one-to-one relationships, individual encounters, which is where he feels most comfortable: in bed with one woman (the appeal of group sex quite mystifies him), across the desk from a single student (how, he frequently wonders when the clock summons him to the classroom, can you talk to the diversity of a such a group?), face-to-face with his solitary victim (and then, finally, not even the one-to-one anymore: just himself). That's what it always comes down to for Walter, probably always will so long as he can have his way, though he's willing to admit that someone else, for reasons incomprehensible to him, might choose to construct a work which could also be called V-shaped but moves in precisely the opposite direction.

Not for him: in his novel, piracy would begin in the Atlantic Ocean, out there on the high seas, involving a sizeable crew, merchant fleets, pursuit by the navies of several countries, and then grow more and more narrow as it proceeded, taking his protagonist to progressively smaller ships, manned by fewer and fewer crew members, attacking less and less significant targets, as he retreated—or was driven—into smaller and smaller bodies of water: the Caribbean, the Gulf of Mexico, gradually up the Mississippi from its broad and tangled delta toward its northern sources, finally perhaps up into the narrowing Minnesota River. What acts of piracy, he wonders, can be committed in the upper reaches of the Minnesota River, where it is only barely navigable? Attacks on fishermen? And in what sort of craft: a flat-bottomed pontoon boat? a rowboat? At what point would his pirate escape the jurisdiction of the Coast Guard, limited as it is to watching over the nation's coastlines and navigable waterways? Who would be responsible for bringing him to justice then?

If Walter were ever to write this novel, the scene with which he would conclude it would present a distant image, a cinematic long shot, perhaps from the point of view of his pursuer, of the pirate of the inland waterways paddling alone, in a canoe most likely, up a small stream, through the fields and pastures of the northern plains.

32. The V-Shaped World

If Walter wants a world that narrows down, as toward the bottom of a V, rather than one which opens out, as toward the top of a V, it is perhaps because he is a firm believer in cleaning up his own mess: and aware that the narrower the scope, the smaller the mess. Therefore he dusts his own desk and bookcases, wipes out the bathroom sink after shaving, grades his own term papers rather than leaving them for his student assistant, washes his own clothes (and others') when he's around, loads and unloads the dishwasher, avoids spilled blood and shattered furniture, carries out the garbage. It occurs to him that much of this activity involves cleaning up after others as well as after himself, but nonetheless he does not expect—does not even like—others to clean up after him.

It will occur to him in a couple of months—how Walter loves the University's summer stipends that allow its scholars to flit about on research trips from that library to this, the Widener for him this summer—as he sits outside a rooming house in Boston in a rented car, observing the comings and goings of a young man named Steve whom he will kill later in the day, that an awful lot of what he does involves cleaning up after others: making marks on student papers to correct the ungrammatical messes left behind by inept high school teachers; crawling around the den floor on hands and knees after his daughters have gone to bed, picking up toy cars and scattered doll furniture, hair ribbons, and wooden building blocks; wandering around the front yard, shovel in hand, to scoop up the messes left behind by the multitude of wandering dogs in the neighborhood; patiently serving out a two-year term on the local zoning commission, trying to keep the wrong kinds of businesses from slopping messily over into the right kinds of residential neighborhoods; calling up American Express, toll free, to point out the latest mistake they've made on his billing and calling up the University registrar to clear up the half dozen wrong names on his computerized class list and calling up his mother, too, to find out why she's remembered Janey's birthday early this year after she forgot Judy's altogether.

This is a lot of mess, he will conclude, for one person to

be cleaning up after, mostly by himself. But there is always a lot of mess to be cleaned up: which is why he does not feel he can sit around waiting for others to do it.

So he will get up and out of the car and cross the street to the rooming house which he has just seen Steve enter for the last time. Steve will be no more than twenty-five, with dark, curly hair, broad shoulders, and a carefree smile on his face during all his comings and goings that Walter has observed that day. But in someone else's world Steve constitutes a mess: which Walter, nudging open the front door with his foot and climbing the stairs to Steve's second floor room, will be paid to clean up.

33. Questions

When Walter opens the unlocked door at the top of the stairs after a pleasant voice has called out "Come in" at his first knock, he will find Steve's room a great mess, not unlike the rooms of teenage sons of friends whom he and Penny have visited. There will be clothes everywhere—Walter is always amazed by the quantity of clothing teenagers own—clothes on the bed, on the floor, on chairs, in open closets, spilling off dresser tops: several pairs of pants, which could all pass for the same pair in progressive stages of decay, and a remarkable array of shirts. Walter has been in men's clothing stores that had less variety than this, and he will think with some dismay of his own walk-in closet at home, where hang some dozen or so shirts, all plain solid colors, that could all be the same shirt: unlike this wild collage of stripes and prints, plaids and silk-screened pictures, madras and polka dots and patterns of awesome variety.

In the midst of which, on the edge of the bed, a spot of pale and simple order in the center of this hectic flood of color, will sit a naked and totally hairless Steve, thick black hairpiece curled up and resting like a kitten on his left thigh.

"It just gets so damned hot and itchy sometimes," he'll say, lifting it, shaking it, dropping it to the floor at his feet.

Walter will half expect to see it leap up and scamper away. Steve, placid, on the edge of the cluttered bed, he'll see as a remarkable model of order, neatness: not a hair on his entire body. Starting from the floor, where the hairpiece lies, Walter will note: no hair on his legs, in his crotch, on his chest, under his arms, on his face or head. At this beacon of clear skin shining over billowing waves of fabric and color, Walter will outstare the bounds of politeness before remembering to close the door behind him. Steve, miraculously fishing up a matching pair of socks from the froth of clothes on the bed, as if the clarity of his own flesh were enough to light up the depths of the mess around him, will motion Walter to a chair beside the door, inquire, as Walter sits, unbuttoning his jacket, what he, Steve, could do for him, for . . . ?

"I'm sorry," he'll say, "I'm afraid I don't know your name."

"It doesn't matter," Walter will respond, "you wouldn't

remember it for long, anyway."

"Aha," Steve will laugh, "just try me. I'm very good at the unpronounceables. I do foreign names others wouldn't dare to mumble. I speak seven languages fluently and others . . . ." But suddenly he'll fall silent, in the midst of pulling his second sock on, as if he has no words, in any language, for the thing he sees in Walter's hand.

If Walter hesitates, it will be out of admiration, not doubt or fear. He could silence all of Steve's tongues with a single shot before he half began a scream, and will do so in just a moment, probably with no further communication, no contact, between them. And that won't be what gives him pause either. Almost always, when there has been time and privacy, he has allowed others to have their say—like the doorman in Kafka's parable of the man before the law—lest they feel they have left something unsaid that might have made all the difference. He has let women proposition him with their bodies and men with money and both with hatred, gratitude, revenge, love, whatever emotions they could summon up in their last moments. He has not enjoyed—has, most often, not even really heard—what they were saying, but has merely opened these moments for them, for their final needs, and then, at last, taken the final moment, quickly, for himself.

But this time it will not be his victim's voice that fills, for Walter, this last and unrequested, pause, but his body, his appearance. Nor will it be desire that makes Walter hesitate, unasked, but, still, sheer astonishment at the absolute nakedness before him, flesh clear and bright and totally hairless, the purest and most uncluttered vision of an adult human Walter has ever seen, from the top of his head down to . . . well, Walter will see, down to, now, only the tops of his blue socks.

"Why are you going to do this thing to me?" Steve will blurt out, his own vision doubtless as clear as Walter's on the future of their encounter: "¿porque? pour quoi? perche? warum? pochemi?"

All those words, from that class of words that could only add to the existing mess, will tickle like countless tiny hairs at the back of Walter's throat, and for relief, for order, he will pull the trigger and the gun will speak almost silently and the young man will slip backward on the bed, more silent still.

CHAPTER IV

34. Answers

I do it for the money, thinks Walter, and yet time is passing—has passed, another whole year gone by—and he has spent nothing to speak of out of all that cash he has salted away in various safe deposit boxes, in numerous cities, under a variety of names. And if the past year, a quiet one for the most part, by his own choice, out of his own concerns, and to the sometime bafflement of his contact—"What, you don't like doing business with your Uncle Buddy no more?"—has added little to his coffers, neither has it contributed to last spring's anxiety. On that front—or no, he thinks, it's my back I should be watching—he's seen, heard, read, not a sign. Disappointment in his losing teams and dismay at world events aside, the newspapers have become a great comfort to him. He is, he imagines, perhaps the only subscriber who reads the papers to see what's not in them. But maybe, he also considers, what's not there is exactly what I should be worrying about. The sense of the violence that hides behind silence is never all that far from him: the world in its well-known, cunning disguise of quietude—which he learned about early on and is now, as he well knows, his very own methodology.

Into one of his lecture notebooks, the one for his seminar on Postmodernist Literature which he offers every second or third year, depending on demand—the demands of students for that seminar and the demands of his colleagues for their own seminars—he has coded his record of the cities, the banks, the deposit box numbers, and the names he has used. A few coded notes on one page, a few on another, on and on, interpolated through author's biographies, titles, analyses of technique, summaries of articles, even some random ideas, insights, analogies, of his own: it all adds up to quite a lot.

Walter's colleagues tease him for his old-fashioned ways in lecturing from a ring-bound notebook. They are lively and enlightened scholars and teachers, most of them. Most of what they know is in their heads, constantly exercised and readily available, and much of the rest is inscribed in the margins of their texts, from which they can quickly astound a class with three alternate readings of a line from Hamlet or a dozen critical resources for a study of Marvell's "To His Coy Mistress." They lecture little but are adept at inspiring ferocious classroom discussions. Their students disappear for weeks at a time into the library, for semesters into the social sciences, for years to England and France, for decades, even, into graduate schools and teaching careers, but always return to challenge them with new ideas, more thorough research, and more amazing conclusions, with articles and books and professorships of their own.

Professor Job does many of these things too, and equally well for the most part, though he has not been around long enough yet to have his former students come back outranking him. And he does not really lecture any more than most of his colleagues. But he continues to carry these notebooks to class more like one of his own old professors, classical scholars of another generation, than like the professorial image his colleagues dream of for themselves.

Therefore, particularly when the weather is pleasant in the spring and they gather on Professor Hapsburg's screened-in porch overlooking the south end of campus for a pleasant wine hour after a long Thursday afternoon of meeting their seminars and Walter shows up on foot, the station wagon still in the nearby parking lot, lugging home, sometimes, two or three of his black notebooks, they take time between passing the wine and cheese and narrating anecdotes about their favorite students to tease him rather relentlessly about his antiquated habit.

"It's only for security, you know," confesses Walter one pleasant Thursday afternoon this particular spring, after an unusually heavy barrage of teasing.

Walter doesn't mind the teasing. It is, after all, the only eccentricity they have ever found to tease him about—with the exception of his habit of traveling to every conference, symposium or workshop in his field—and he has come to recognize, by attentive listening over the years, that the quantity of teasing he receives on these Thursday afternoons occurs in inverse ratio to the satisfactions of his colleagues concerning their own teaching. It is an amusing release of tension for them, and it is, in fact, the truth for himself when he confesses that "It's only for security."

"Like swearing on the Bible," says young Dora Sibley.

Walter, amazed, watches a bead of sweat drop from the tip of her nose into her glass of iced tea. Dora, a year out of graduate school, no teacher of seminars yet, runs five miles every afternoon, shows up for wine hours in a sweaty sweat suit, forswears alcohol, devours cheese. Walter, lifting sherry to his lips, is in the midst of a dim vision of Dora's lean, sweaty body in the shower when Cameron Fosberg, Chair of the Department, intrudes.

"May I?" he says, lifting the top notebook from Walter's pile of three set on the couch beside him and beginning to flip through the pages.

Walter is amazed once more: nothing like this has ever happened, and before he can react it has already gone beyond the point where he can stop it without appearing defensive and boorish. Walter hears Roger Gruneberg, elder statesman of the department, stifle an unstifleable chuckle; sees their host, Howie Hapsburg, head for the kitchen, as is his wont whenever things get ticklish; and is suddenly amazed for the third time: after all these years it finally occurs to him that nearly half the people in his department, seven of eighteen to be precise, have names ending in -burg or -berg. What does it mean? he wonders.

"What does it mean?" echoes Fosberg, the eminent Victorian, pointing to a series of letter-number combinations in the margins of random pages.

"That," says Walter, looking Fosberg in the eye, "is the secret of modern literature."

35. More Answers

Yes, thinks Walter, I do it for the money, and there is enough socked away to send both Janey and Judy to private school, to summer camp, to riding academy and ballet classes and prep school, to the orthodontist and the dermatologist, to college and graduate school and postdoctoral training and, as they used to do in my mother's day—as long as we are being antiquarian in our habits—on the Grand Tour. Young as the girls are now, higher education and foreign travel are apt to cost quite a bundle by the time they're ready for such things, and by then, who knows, the Grand Tour may include the moon and Mars, but no matter: there is money enough for all that and more.

Yet time is passing and Walter has spent none of it to speak of, none that he could not have accounted for out of his salary and a few cash bonuses from his inherited stock in the failing family enterprise. Meanwhile, each passing year only sees more money added to what's already there: more cash, more bearer bonds, more rare stamps and coins and jewels paid for by cash and with no haggling over price. These things, these small storable valuables, Walter has purchased from only the most reputable of dealers, hither and yon about the country—an emerald in Dallas, a one penny black in Baltimore—and he has never gone back to the same source twice.

He would like to buy original oils and sculpture for their home, pay off the mortgage—which is even now less a financial burden than a monthly duty—and travel. Nothing extravagant: no Caribbean cruises or African Safaris or weekends on the Riviera, no quick jaunts to Chicago or New York for dinner and a show. But he would like to see the cathedrals of Europe, about which he knows absolutely nothing, or the fountains of Rome, the Mayan ruins of Central America, the slopes of the Alps, the Serengheti or the Great Barrier Reef, the bridges over the Seine or the countryside of England, about which he has heard so much.

But he isn't going anywhere, according to Penny, who knows to the precise penny the state of their family fortunes, until they've saved enough for the new car that will be needed to replace the aging station wagon, until the girls' college savings account begins to show some signs of growth, until the next sabbatical year comes along to provide a continuing income, until the balky furnace and the wheezing refrigerator and the cracked walk and the gold crown for her lower left molar and . . . .

"And," Penny has said, sitting at the kitchen table, balancing the checkbook, as Walter, just back from a seminar on "The Bourgeois Modernist" at the University of Virginia, broaches the subject of travel once again, "until the girls are grown up enough so that we can enjoy the trip."

And Walter has stood beside her, swirling a bourbon on ice in one hand, jingling the coins in his pocket with the other. Aside from a few expensive dinners at conferences, where he has occasionally helped the bill to mount by treating an old acquaintance from graduate school or someone he has just heard deliver one of those rare interesting papers he so seldom encounters in his scholarly travels, he has been notably unsuccessful at finding ways to indulge himself with his riches. For women who would be happy to provide him with costly nights he has no use: it is an area where he feels rich enough without cash. For clothing there is a definite limit: nothing escapes Penny's observant attention to his wardrobe, over which she feels she presides with great success. For personal jewelry he has no desire.

The best he has been able to do has been to bring back, from many of his trips, expensive bracelets and pins and earrings for Penny and the girls, an occasional over-priced sweater, hand-knitted and imported, for Penny, and just once, also for her, a watch whose price tag astounded even him: always explaining how he found these things at an auction or met a salesman on the flight to Tucson who sold them to him at cost.

Even the quarters in his pocket have jingled uselessly while he watched Penny's precise hand set down the even row of numbers in the right hand column of the checkbook. I do it for the money, thinks Walter, but the money does nothing for me.

36. More Questions

I do not do it for the money, thinks Walter, taking the long way home after the wine hour, through the meandering boulevards of the city's park system: if I were to lose this notebook with all its codes and combinations today, it wouldn't bother me in the least. But even as he thinks this, he lays his right hand protectively across the stack of notebooks on the station wagon's wide seat beside him. The hand that instantly lights on his own belongs to sweatsuited Dora Sibley, lounging back against the door on her side of the front seat and staring across at him.

"Walter," she says.

He glances at her briefly, then slips his hand out from under hers to maneuver the complex curve at the end of the boulevard, which with its big loop and sudden straightening, followed by a stop sign, has to Walter always resembled a giant question mark. At the stop sign, he turns left onto the avenue and then glances back at her again, both hands still on the wheel.

"I hope this is OK," she continues. "Dropping in on people on short notice always worries me, and I don't feel like I really know your wife. I only met her once. And I'm not exactly dressed for the occasion."

Walter recalls that meeting himself, at the departmental Christmas party this past December, a menagerie of faculty members and spouses, students and friends. On the way home Penny made only one response to Walter's asking what she thought of his new colleague: "Oh, I thought she was one of your students."

"It's OK," says Walter reassuringly. "I called her, and there's enough rump roast to feed the entire department. She'll be happy to have a chance to get to know you."

That last is not precisely true. What Penny has actually said when Walter called her from the Hapsburgs as the wine hour was breaking up was, "What made you decide to do that?"

Walter's only answer was that it just seemed like a nice thing to do. But he did call ahead. Walter always calls: when he is late, when he is away, when there is even a small change in plans. He knows too much about the nature of surprise to want to use it on those he loves. Thinking this he turns, predictably, right, off the avenue and onto the next segment of serpentine boulevard, where it winds around one end of a small lake, to which he is happy to see the mallards have returned again on their northward migration. The grass and trees and shrubs around the lake glow softly green, muted by the yellower tones of spring, and the evening sky is bright and clear. Walter is always, predictably, excited by this annual phenomenon, by that regular bit of seasonal magic which produces increasingly later sunsets, by the ducks and the grass and the crocuses and the buds on the spirea and the high lake level and the evening sky: by all these ordinary activities of the cyclical routine. All that is surprise enough, he thinks, just before he senses that he is, quite unpredictably, developing an erection. And that Dora has been talking to him again.

"What?"

"It's just that you've seemed so thoughtful," she repeats, "that I wondered if you weren't maybe having misgivings about your invitation. Also, I wish I could have taken a shower and changed out of this grungy sweat suit."

"Not a bit," replies Walter, instantly resuming his vision of Dora's lean, sweaty body in the shower at exactly the point at which Fosberg had intruded three quarters of an hour ago, her head arched back, her breasts pulled up. But, as the last minutes of their drive proceed in silence, he is unable to advance his vision beyond this point: perhaps because he doesn't know that he would want it to advance beyond this point, perhaps because it has just become permanently fixed at that point.

"Fosberg," he mumbles, disappointedly, as he swings the station wagon at last into the driveway.

"That's funny," says Dora, "I've been thinking about him, too. He strikes me as a man who's not very comfortable with what he does. That worries me. I like what I'm doing, I want to keep on liking it, I don't want something like that to happen to me."

Walter sits, silent, turning off the ignition, picking up his notebooks, commanding his erection to subside.

Dora stares across at him. "Do you like your work?" she asks, abruptly.

"I do not," he says softly, "do it for the money."

CHAPTER V

37. Doing It

What Walter does or does not do for the money, he does a few weeks later like this:

At dusk, after a long afternoon's waiting, he leaves his car in the empty parking lot, crosses behind the darkening pavilion, and steps out onto the narrow dock, at the end of which an old man is neatly tying up the line of rental canoes and rowboats. Walter has spent the day in his car: driving to this destination, sitting in the parking lot, circling the lake, driving about in search of an ice cream cone. To his surprise, because it has been an abnormally hot late spring day, he has discovered that there are very few places open around this city where you can buy an ice cream cone, but at least he has spent the search in the comfort of the new Pontiac he rented in Milwaukee early this morning, not knowing how grateful he'd be for the air conditioning in this unexpected heat wave. And having spent most of the day in his car, driving and sitting, he will soon get back in it to spend considerably more time, driving it through the night back to the Milwaukee airport to catch the first morning flight home.

Meanwhile, strolling out on the dock, he is surprised at how hot it still is, even with the sun no longer up, and wishes he could have left his jacket in the car: by the time he gets back to it, he'll be soaked through with sweat. Somewhere out on the Interstate, he figures, he can stop to put on a fresh shirt.

At the end of the dock, the old man straightens up, holding the lines of the last two rowboats in his hands, clearly surprised at Walter's appearance. He gathers the ropes in one hand and uses the other to point at the sign alongside the dock that Walter has already read for himself: NO BOATING AFTER SUNSET.

"No boats after sunset," he says as Walter draws near, but the way he drops his voice at the end of that redundancy says he knows Walter hasn't come to rent a boat: as Walter's suit and tie and well-shined shoes, across which the old man's eyes flicker, also attest. So he just stands there motionless while Walter approaches, roundfaced and a little wide-eyed, the multitude of wrinkles that Walter knows are there fading in the dusk, and the sweat and dirt that stain his white uniform fading with them.

"Maybe I been expecting you," he says, in a gruff old man's voice as Walter stops in front of him.

Just then the boulevard lights go on along the lakeside drive, and both of them turn to look at the jewel-like effect they create. Across the far end of the lake a police car, only poorly visible in the twilight, cruises slowly along the park drive. The old man raises his free hand to wave at it, and the officer on the passenger's side of the car leans out, as it glides away, to wave back. The old man turns around again to face Walter, still clutching the two boat lines in his hand.

"Why don't you go ahead and tie those up?" Walter suggests.

"Ain't no hurry," answers the old man, his voice a little gruffer yet: as if, thinks Walter, he is working his way into this role of gruff old man, finally getting to use some lines he's had prepared for a long time now.

Walter, for his part, is busy resisting the first lines that come to his mind. "Suit yourself," is what he's moved to say, but he doesn't see that yielding to this temptation to laconic dialogue will get either of them anywhere. Movie-style verbal fencing doesn't appeal to Walter, who, in this heat, in this open place, just wants to do his job, do it well, and be on his way. Therefore he takes a small step closer, studying the old man's thin white hair, yellowed slightly by the glow of the street lights, the fat mole under his left ear, the necklace of polished stones: turquoise they're supposed to be, but Walter can no longer be certain in this light.

"Oh I am who you think I am," says the old man, taking a step backward himself.

But he can't go far: it's only a few more feet to the end of the dock, and the dock is so narrow that without Walter cooperating by moving sideways, there's no room to get by him, either. Off and on during the late afternoon, Walter watched crowds of teenage couples and parents with young children maneuvering gingerly along this narrow space to and from the boats: half expecting to see someone get bumped off into the water. But it didn't happen. Now the old man backs up another step toward the end of the dock, tossing Walter the boat lines.

"Here," he growls, "you're in such an all-fired hurry, you

take these."

But Walter just lets them drop onto the warped boards of the dock, and the boats, lying motionless on the still water of the lake, drift neither closer nor away.

The old man, looking down at his feet, takes one more step back, leaving not enough room to sit down in between himself and the end of the dock. Then he looks up at Walter: "I suppose you got to do this?"

38. As He Has To

More or less all his professional life Walter has hoped, without even knowing he hoped it, that no one would ask him that particular question.

Only once before does Walter remember ever having had to deal with anything of the kind, and that was during his first year as a graduate teaching assistant when he was administering a standardized test to a freshman composition class. One of the students, a dark, squat, football player with a menacing way of slouching in his desk and almost no academic ability, had looked up as Walter distributed the test booklets and asked, in his usual surly voice, "Do we have to take this?"

"Yes," Walter had snapped, "you have to take this."

And that was all there was to it, though Walter knew, of course, that actually there was a great deal more to it: Why do I have to do this? Out of what motives and toward what ends? To meet whose needs? To satisfy what obscure necessity? Why? Why are you doing this to me? Why do you have to do this to me?

The old man's eyes, which glow amazingly wide and white and clear in the twilight, raise all those same questions again, in the wake of the simple one that penetrates to the heart of the action itself: Do you have to do this? And he looks as if he would be happy to step back a pace or two, if there were room, to open up some space for Walter's answer to this question. But there is no room: he already stands barely a full step from the end of the dock, and Walter stands, arms hanging loosely at his sides, unthreateningly, directly in front of him. If Walter is not moving at this moment, it is not because Walter does not know what he is going to do: what, as he seems to have to put it in the current context, he has to do. If Walter is not moving at the moment, it is because he finds himself in a quiet, darkening place, because the evening is finally starting to cool down, because he has no reason to be in any hurry, because he is almost alone, almost: all in all perhaps the most ideal moment that has ever come upon him for considering, just as he is about to do something, what he does and does not have to do.

One thing he knows is that he does not have to think about

this now. He also knows the pointlessness of considering it afterwards. Afterwards he would only rationalize: I did what I had to do; I did what I do. He also knows that he does not have to think about it at all. He can just go on doing what he does, thinking in the practical terms that suit the action about what he does and how he does it, as the occasion arises, but not directing himself toward the question the old man has raised: I do not have to think about that. If I think about that, it's because I choose to think about it. If I think about it right here and now, in front of this old man, it's because I choose to think about it right here and now in front of this old man.

Walter chooses to think about it right here and now in front of the old man. Maybe only to silence a little voice nagging at him from an obscure corner of his mind that, yes, he has to think about this, Walter chooses to think, right now, about what he does and does not have to do. But he does not choose to do this thinking with the old man. Walter has always known better than to engage in more conversation than is absolutely necessary with his victims, certain that no matter how rational or humane it started out it would likely end in a morass of pleading, wheedling, begging, whining, crying: humiliating, finally, to both of them. He's probably right about that: if he has to do this job—no, if he's going to do this job—isn't there much to be said for providing both parties with the dignity of doing it right?

That, thinks Walter, I really do have to do: professionally, personally, humanely. But that's still only a matter of how he has to do what he does or doesn't have to do, and not the old man's basic question, with which Walter is finding himself more and more alone, out here near the end of the dock. He is thinking about this question hard and fast in the face of the old man. Around both of them, night is falling harder and faster yet.

39. As He Chooses

Listen, Walter thinks into the darkness, the reasons I have to do this are: it is my profession, I am being paid to do it, I have agreed to do it, one has to fulfill one's obligations, I have already gone too far to back off. These are all real reasons, both true and good. There are other possible reasons as well: such as, if I don't do this someone else will. But Walter doesn't believe in that as a valid reason for doing something, thinks it is only an excuse for doing anything. Or: I have to do this because I can do it better than anyone else. That strikes pretty close to home, actually, but Walter is still aware that there are, in any profession, a lot of very talented professionals around. He is secure in his abilities, not conceited about them: and this, after all, isn't a very difficult job.

The old man is still standing motionless in front of him with his eyes open wide and white. The two rowboats push their bows against the side of the dock as if to demand attention to their condition. The boulevard lights sparkle around them in the humid night air like a lopsided, enormous crown. All this doesn't take much time because it happens at the speed of thought.

The main reason of all these, thinks Walter, that I have to do this, is: because I said I would. If I do not do the things I say I am going to do, what hope is there for the future? By saying I am going to do a certain thing I project myself into the future. By doing the thing I said I was going to do I meet and match up with that self I have projected into the future. If I do not do the thing I said I was going to do, then I fail to make that connection, fail to arrive at that meeting in the future, and in such a future I am unattached and lost and at the mercy of future time itself. Some other time arrives and who is there? Not me. Some other me, maybe, whom I do not know, may not even recognize. Moreover, if I do not do the thing I said I was going to do, then others will not know who I am when we get there, or will not want to be involved with the who I have become by not doing what I said I would do. They will not make room for that me in that future. If I do not do what I said I was going to do, the future looks like a place where there will be no place for me: a place where I will not know who I am or what I do.

Therefore I have to do this, he concludes with a nod of his

head that startles the old man and causes him to edge back even more into the small space remaining at the end of the dock.

On the other hand, Walter realizes, I do not have to do what I said I was going to do just because I said it. Like everyone else, I have a certain right to change my mind, to reassess a given situation, to act on whim, even to lie. I was lying when I said I was going to do this, says Walter to a self that knows perfectly well he was not lying. It's possible to try anything on for size, and even if it fits, he still doesn't have to wear it. "I have to do this" makes a nice verbal fit, but he can still choose not to do it: not to live in that particular outfit.

At the extreme, as Walter knows perfectly well, he doesn't have to do anything: get up and get dressed, eat, talk, work . . . . If others are unhappy with my not doing what they think I have to do, or even what I told them I was going to do, that's their problem. There's nothing I have to do or do not have to do. I do not even have to acknowledge that I am or am not doing what I said I was going to do, or that doing it or not doing it becomes the source of certain subsequent effects, or that those effects concern me or anyone else, though they do. There's nothing I have to do: I don't have to stand here in the dark or kill this old man or return the Pontiac to the rental agency or board my plane in Milwaukee or go home again, ever. Nothing. There's absolutely nothing I have to do. Ever.

This time he shakes his head in a quick motion from side to side, and the old man, with no more space behind him to move back into, spreads his legs a little, for stability.

Nothing, concludes Walter with another slight jerk of his head, except one thing: I have to choose. I have to choose whether to leave or do the thing I said I was going to do before I leave, whether to stand here till I drop or jump in the lake or fall to my knees. Whatever it is I'm going to do, and for whatever reasons I'm going to do it or not do it, I have to choose. And the choices I make are the choices I have to live with, the choices other people have to live with too, though that is not my problem. To do or not to do is a choice. What to do is a choice. To choose or not to choose is a choice. One thing after another, big things, little things, nothings, the alternatives are to choose . . . or choose. It's all choices, wherever we turn, whatever we do. To live is to choose. Therefore I have to choose. No one will do it for me.

Walter glances around: towards the pavilion, the parking lot, the path that circles the lake. He's right, there's no one there. The choice, as always, is his alone.

Walter chooses with a nod of his head again that edges the old man back to where his heels are right up against the end of the dock and he himself chooses not to drop backwards into the lake but to lean forward, cooperatively, into Walter's choice. Walter chooses to take a small flask of chloroform from the inside pocket of his jacket, to unscrew it quickly and pour it over his handkerchief and lift the handkerchief quickly between the old man's upraised arms and press it firmly against his mouth and nose. And he chooses to catch the old man under the arms as his knees give way, to catch him and lower him gently, head first, off the side of the dock into the water between the two unattached rowboats, which bob up and down in the small ripples caused by the body's entry and then begin to drift slowly away from the old man floating face down beside the dock, into the darkness of the lake.

40. He Chooses

Now there is one old man who does not have to make any more choices. Thanks to Walter's activities over the past decade, there are quite a number of people—men and women, young and old—who no longer have to make choices. Walter has not been so effective in this area—the reduction of choice—as some others any resident of his century could name, but for an individual acting alone and in secret, he has not done so badly, either.

He doesn't think of his work in this cumulative fashion. He is strictly an *ad hoc* laborer in the killing fields, tending to one case at a time, maybe three a year, only one or two some years, four just once, each a discrete incident, unrelated to any of the others except through its agency, Walter, and, to be sure, its final effect: relief from the burden of choice.

And he knows that he is only one of a multitude of agencies engaged in producing that final effect which everyone is going to arrive at, sooner or later, anyway. The chances are that an aneurism or a speeding automobile, the uncontrolled violence of the earth's great masses or the body's tiny cells, will get there first: if the Hitlers and Stalins, the hijackers and terrorists, don't. More people get there tumbling headlong down the staircases of their beloved homes each single month in his country alone than will be offered the opportunity *in toto* by Walter even if he extends his career beyond the end of the century.

Walter is not thinking of extending his career to the end of the century, nor is he thinking of not extending it that far: no more than the bear in the woods thinks, after blueberry season is over, about whether he will feast on blueberries each July for years to come. Come the middle of next summer and a good crop, he'll gladly choose to gobble blueberries, if they're there: and ditto the following summer, and ditto . . . . The suspension of choice, deliberate or not, confirms the ongoing process of choosing, whereas the elimination of the possibility of making choices is, in effect, the elimination of everything.

Whereby, Walter reasons, not to choose is not to be. To choose not to choose is to choose not to be. Every time a choice is made, and is henceforth no longer open for choosing, a little being is lost: because of which Walter, cruising east through the night on the Interstate on cruise control, having chosen to stay within a reasonable range of the speed limit, feels a little dead just now. He attributes his feeling to tiredness, but tomorrow, with not a lot of sleep behind him and quite a number of new choices before him, he will be feeling a lot livelier: a sure tribute to the power of choosing, without which Walter, like everyone else, would be nothing. And time will pass, as he well knows: at some point, in some way, depriving him of his ability to choose: making him, as he has made others, nothing.

Nothing is worse than nothing, Walter chooses to think: therefore I choose to do what I do, even if, like the bear in the blueberry patch, I would do it anyway, as long as I could.

41. A Choice Time

Walter cruises dully east on the dark Interstate, which carries him straight toward his destination with hardly a choice to be made: leaving him feeling somewhat less than himself and a great deal bored. Time is simply passing, in which he barely participates. No wonder he can't remember how he gets from one time to another. Choices, which he has been choosing not to make, are his means of entering time. But now he chooses to pull out and pass the big, white, refrigerated truck ahead of him and seconds later to flash his turn indicators and pull back in, well in front of the truck. Time has passed and now he has done something with it. Choices take time. They take time by the balls and twist it this way and that: squeeze time and make it move the way you want—though in general the direction will always be much the same. Not to make choices, he fears, is to let time take you by the balls and squeeze you and let you flow away: into nothingness. Not to be able to choose is to have time flow on its own over and past you and be gone, for now, or, perhaps, forever. To choose not to choose or to be chosen, deliberately or at random, by someone or some natural force, to become one of those for whom choice will no longer be possible, is to fall out of time, a lapse from which no recovery may be possible. Time will continue to flow by, but it will not flow by you. If it is still within your power to choose to choose, rather than to choose not to choose, you may enter, once again, its flow: disoriented, not exactly having a firm grip on it, unsure of just where, or when, you are, but knowing at least that you are in it again, that in the choice to choose you have thrust yourself back into the flow of time again, and there you are. But if this choice is no longer in your power, if it has been taken from you quickly by two tons of screeching metal or a ruptured heart valve or slowly by the silent multiplication of cancer cells or the half-expected hiss of gas through the shower nozzles, then there is nothing you can do about it ever again. The only real power, he concludes, is the power to choose, which is the power to enter time, to live: only death remains to the powerless.

Does it seem to Walter, secure in the right hand lane at a steady and only slightly above legal speed in the middle of the night with no traffic in sight before or behind him now, that, making this distinction, choosing for himself and bringing to an end the possibility of choice for others, he is exercising power not only over life but over death as well? Concentration camps and mass starvation and apocalyptic upheavals of the earth aside, who, even in the one-to-one relationships through which Walter operates, has a right to such power as that? Anyone?

Surely, if anyone, the one who loves his family, trims his lawn, lives up to his responsibilities, obeys the speed limits, and exercises his power with professional neatness and restraint.

If anyone, then, surely Walter.

Or: If anyone, then anyone.

42. READ!

The "Fun Facts" column in the Sunday comic pages which he reads to his daughters two days later informs Walter that most of the people who have ever lived on Earth during the entire course of its existence are alive on it today. Not half so amusing, adds Walter out of his own repertoire of fun facts, as the fact that we have already murdered in this century, thanks to the combined efficiency of modern warfare and the automobile, more people than ever even lived on Earth prior to this century. And it isn't over yet. If his daughters sit on either side of him on the blue couch, silent and puzzled in their matching red corduroy robes, it is because he has not made this contribution to their Sunday morning education aloud: there are some things they do not need to know, not yet anyway, and after all, we still have a few years left in which to mend our ways. If we do not blow ourselves up in the meantime. If we have not already committed some irreversible act of destruction. If we don't actually prefer to keep things going the same way as in the past.

"Read, Daddy."

Well, Sunday morning is for moralizing, is it not, even for the likes of Walter, those who do not go to the Sunday places where others can do their moralizing for them.

"C'mon, Daddy, read."

And the comic pages, thanks to the advances of modern print technology, provide a kind of simplified morality themselves: a four-color version appropriate to a Sunday morning. In them the disobedient are chastised, the pompous take their pratfalls, the schemes of schemers backfire, smart alecks open their mouths once too often, the reckless pay hilariously—and often painfully—for their recklessness, and those who do not listen learn to their dismay—and our amusement and edification—that they should have.

Together: "Daddy!"

So Walter listens and reads. But while he reads in a slow, soft, Sunday morning voice, he thinks, between the four-color comic lines, in a voice more appropriate to a Tuesday or Friday. We have listened, he thinks, to the seductive wail of violence. We have listened and answered, from somewhere deep within and with the knowledge that it was calling to each of us, individually. We may have answered in whispers, at first, a little hesitant about just who was calling, a little unsure about our rights to answer, but we answered all the same. And when it became obvious to us that we would have to speak louder to be heard in the midst of the din of violence all about, then we raised our voices, too. We listened—no one can accuse us of not having listened—we listened and answered and then, finally, we joined in. And it has not been amusing.

And we have done everything right, besides. We have kept our mouths shut and our schemes simple. We have obeyed orders and, mostly, avoided letting our accomplishments go to our heads. And most of all we have avoided recklessness: there was nothing rash about the way we entered into violence, and why should there have been, with all the material around to observe before, at last, we acted ourselves: well-read by then, well-educated in the subject, well-equipped, well- . . . .

"Go on, Daddy."

Well, it has not been amusing. No doubt it has been rewarding, in some way. Perhaps it has provided satisfactions from time to time. Certainly it has become efficient, practical. It has even led to a kind of knowledge: this we know we can do. And a sense of finality, for sure. But it has not proven very amusing. Comic strips aside, this is a surface on which the four-color process does not seem to have printed its morality well at all: the effects are terribly blurred and difficult to read, and one is no longer certain one wants to continue.

"Now this one, Daddy."

At the bottom of the page, where his daughters are pointing, an unidentifiable furry animal stuffs an unidentifiable feathered creature into a meat grinder. In the next panel only the feet are visible—three-toed and purple—from the top of the grinder. Feathers drift everywhere.

43. Nothing To It

What Walter discovered early in his career was how easy it is to kill: how frail the human body is, and how little attention people pay to what's going on around them. Around some people, of course, stand others employed solely for the purpose of making certain that no killing goes on in their presence, unless—as Caesar found, or Indira Gandhi—they do it themselves. Walter has been aware as long as anyone who lived through the Kennedy era that even that extreme precaution hasn't always been successful. And if you can kill a head of state, an act that history has certified as business as usual, what ordinary citizen is safe?

Walter's been far too interested in his own safety, having long since learned about the frailty of the human form, to be interested in making attempts on the lives of heads of states or anyone so nearly approaching their exalted status as to warrant the protection of bodyguards. Though he knows as well as everyone else—just from keeping up with the news—that you can kill such people—ask Gandhi, ask King, ask Malcolm X or any Kennedy—he also knows that your own chances for survival are not at all good: the bodyguards will be too late, but they'll be there.

So he does not kill at the level of high politics or extreme wealth, where considerable precaution rules, though he doesn't doubt that he could if he wanted, knowing the risk. And he doesn't kill in Dubrovnik or São Paulo or Munich or Cairo, knowing that the documentation of international travel poses, eventually, too great a risk of identification, though that hasn't prevented him from an occasional foray to Vancouver or Toronto. But that still leaves plenty of human beings whose frailty and inattention make them ready targets for his activities.

What Walter means by frailty is not lack of strength—for he's brought his talents to bear on the young and strong as well as the aging and halt, on athletes and muscular laborers who've outweighed him by a hundred pounds and more—but simply the ease with which the biological machinery of the human body can be shut down: vital organs punctured, blood vessels severed, skulls crushed, breath stifled: all these things that have been done to so many people with such great frequency over so many centuries that Walter can only conclude that there's nothing to it.

What he means by inattention is simply that, in spite of the frequency of violent death—than which, Walter often thinks, nothing except birth itself is more common—no one ever seems to think it can happen to him. Which means that it can, in fact, happen with amazing ease: that what no one is expecting Walter can easily deliver: that he can walk nearly into the arms of his victims, weapon in hand, before a last final step carries him, too late, over the threshold of their awareness: that in privacy or in the midst of a crowd he can act and be gone before anyone notices what's happening: that, in short, there's nothing to it. Simple and effective, as operating policies go: there's nothing to it.

44. True Belief

Walter also finds himself protected by the general belief in human incompetence. On a television cop show, he watches a professional killer, a stiletto in one pocket and a pistol equipped with a silencer in the other, attempt to strangle a woman to death with his bare hands in broad daylight in an open field. Of course she fights him off and her friends arrive in time and the killer is successfully hunted down: with such incompetence at work, what other result could there be? Only by such a vision of the incompetence of death, thinks Walter, is humanity shielded from reality: unless what we actually have here is not a vision but the real incompetence of the scriptwriter. Unable to find another way out of the corner into which he has written himself, he has chosen a solution that takes for granted his audience's belief, no doubt the equal of his own, in incompetence.

What Walter's aware of is the human need that creates such a belief. The man who can't find the blown fuse in the basement or balance the checkbook, the woman who can't get the lug nuts off her flat tire or keep her cakes from falling, need to believe, for their own survival, in the equivalent incompetence of others. Ditto their young apprentices: the kid who can't make his long division come out the same twice, who can't keep her ice skates tied tight enough. Above all they prefer to see their incompetence mirrored in those richer, more glamorous, more powerful—though, of course, not nicer—than themselves. Given the vision of perfection with which television ordinarily taunts them—perfect cars and meals and bodies and laundry—such reminders of incompetence—the singer's drug habit, the actor's suicide, the politician's failed marriage—are necessary food for the sustenance of their own self-images. And if it is the major incompetencies of evil they are shown, then they can rest assured that the minor incompetencies of good, which is to say themselves, place them in no grave danger.

It occurs to Walter that his society's passion for sports, more than anything else, reflects this negative attitude toward human competence. While presenting on the surface a vision of human achievement—wholly consistent, Walter observes, with that romantic dream of human perfectibility that served as the very foundation of his country—in fact sports draws its life from human failure: from the tribute so consistently paid to courage in the face of defeat; from the perennial acknowledgment that records are made to be broken; from the failures even among the great of muscle, bone, eyesight, judgment, temperament, equipment. What an athlete accomplishes on one occasion, it may not be possible to repeat on the next: or, perhaps, ever after. A single mis-step, hesitation, flinch of an eye or lapse of concentration, and all is lost, to which months, years, of preparation have led. The skier wipes out, the runner drops the baton, the slugger takes strike three. And at the critical moment the model of human achievement is revealed as incompetent as the rest of us.

A curious paradox, thinks Walter: by holding up an ideal of what we ought to be able to do, sports demonstrate instead what we cannot do. And nothing, reasons Walter, a sometime fan, accomplishes this better than the national sport itself, through its passion for statistics which only confirm that you cannot maintain a perfect batting average, fielding percentage, or e.r.a. Good grief, superiority at the plate still allows the hitter to be incompetent two thirds of the time! Walter's all too aware of how long he'd last if he performed at such a level.

His father, who during the brief period in Walter's youth when he worked part-time in the family business made him go over everything he did three times—who had a plaque on his desk that read "Check and Double Check"—was the most fervent subscriber he has ever known to this belief in human incompetence, which he was always careful to extend to himself as well, making a great show of his activities as he sat at the adding machine running his figures through again and again, checking them against the tape, then calling his secretary to go over them one last time. Leaving the factory at the end of the day was an interminable process: lights were turned off, turned back on to check that everything had been put away, turned off again, the burglar alarm set, doors closed, locked, tried, reopened to check again, which meant calling the alarm company to report the re-entry, then resetting, turning out the lights, locking up, and exiting once again.

An exhausting task, perhaps an endless one Walter used to

think, to seek security through a belief in fallibility.

He wonders if the police subscribe to this theory, though naturally he doesn't feel like asking. There always have been, he knows, plenty of unsolved murders—most of which he has had nothing to do with. And though the police are as likely as anyone else to rely upon human incompetence—which is to say, the incompetence of others—to make their jobs easier, given the multitude of unsolved crimes as evidence, isn't it likely that deep down they believe in human competence? It's a curious issue on which to find himself siding with the police: a question of deep belief that draws them together here, though in fact he's long been accustomed to siding with them on such practical matters as the treatment of speeding and public drunkenness and child abuse.

Besides, Walter wonders, where are all the other professional killers? If they're as incompetent as society likes to believe everyone is, then the usual hour limit set by the television program format ought to be sufficient to flush any of them out. But it doesn't happen like that: ergo, competency. So long as we are competent, Walter concludes, right back where he began this line of thought, we are protected by that belief in human incompetence which doesn't open its eyes to the fact that we can be doing what we're doing and getting away with it.

But having arrived at this point, he now wonders who it is that comprises this competent, and therefore inaccessible, "we." Where, he repeats, are all the other professional killers? Are they, like him, people with two kids, two cars, a house in the suburbs, and a legitimate job which they perform reasonably well? Where do they buy their groceries? How do they treat their children? What do they do for entertainment? Who do they vote for?

Have they reached such a level of perfection that it is, forever, impossible to know them?

Or, thinks Walter, backpedaling a little worriedly, is such a knowledge of perfection—well, competence: that brings the threat close enough to home, him—only available to the agents of the law? Walter is well aware of how contrary this runs to the usual vision of a police force fully versed in human depravity, but he can't help thinking that perhaps to know the worst is also to know the best: or at least the possibility of the best. If one extreme can be achieved, so, perhaps, can the other: whereas to know the ordinary is only, well, to know the ordinary. And nothing seems to be more ordinary, in the view, and the lives, of Walter's fellow citizens, than incompetence.

In a smug, superior way, Walter takes this as evidence that his fellow citizens do not know him. Just as well, he supposes: he does not believe that knowledge yields understanding, that understanding produces virtue, that virtue dictates forgiveness. For competence alone, he's sure, they would never forgive him.

But what am I thinking? he thinks: I don't want to be forgiven, most especially for that. I do not want to be understood. I don't even think there's anything to understand. I don't want to be known: I don't want to be known.

He doesn't seem to be in much danger there: certainly not from himself.

45. Therefore He Is

Walter would like to discuss this theory of incompetence with someone, but since it doesn't engage him except for its counterbalancing theory of competence, and since he cannot with any personal safety discuss the evidence for that, he finds he has no choice but to remain silent on the subject and to watch, with some dismay, the daily celebration of incompetence that takes place all about him. A tennis star is fined a considerable sum for proving incompetent at controlling his temper on the court; a politician entrusted with the secrets of state proves incompetent at keeping his mistress a secret; a five star general demonstrates his incompetence as a political thinker at three consecutive press conferences, each of the last two called to redeem the mistakes of the preceding one. The press and the public join in the celebration of each of these events: this is the evidence on which they live.

And in between each of these major events, Walter hears how people continue to circulate, in support of their needs, stories of doctors prescribing the wrong drugs, mechanics misdiagnosing engine problems, team owners trading away their best players. Without these tales of woe, Walter begins to wonder, how would people manage? Even his own colleagues boast about their incompetence: at getting student papers graded and returned, at doing the advising and committee work the University has assigned them, at paying their bills, mowing their lawns, caring for their health, raising their children.

Look, they seem to be saying when they stop Walter in the halls outside his office or classroom with these tales of incompetence—with stories of lawns gone to seed, badly played squash games, lost books, and broken marriages—Look, they seem to be saying, I'm human, I really am, and all this, all this incompetence, proves it: what about you?

Walter remains silent.

If he could talk to anyone, he would like to talk to his victims. He would like to assure them that they are not the victims of incompetence. To stop and say such things to them, however, would itself be an act of incompetence, so there too Walter remains silent: and hopes that his actions clearly demonstrate what he cannot say: namely that he, for one, does not share this general belief in human incompetence.

Oh, there are plenty of incompetents about, to be sure: dedicated incompetents, as he's already noted, show-offs of incompetence, magna cum laudes of incompetence. But, he would like to say—if there were someone to whom he could say it—no matter how many people continue to demonstrate the reality of incompetence, an area in which we will probably never lack evidence, still it only takes one, one competent person, to demonstrate the possibility of competence.

And Walter, Walter likes to think, is one. He is competent, therefore he is.

Too competent to deny the possibilities of competence, the voice with which he speaks to himself on this subject cannot help suggesting to him that the unnamed agent who now pursues him is possibly another. Even the fact that he has so far—over a year now since that news item triggered a moment of his own incompetence—seen no sign of this mysterious pursuer Walter takes as likely proof of competence. Incompetence, after all, he reasons, takes many forms, is visible everywhere, leaving the incompetents loudly busy themselves, chattering about, comparing and contrasting and explicating, the content of their particular incompetencies. But competence has, always, only one form: one perfect form, which speaks for itself, leaving its rare practitioners silent: what more is there to say? A scary thing, competence, Walter thinks, realizing at the same moment that his victims must think much the same.

Leaving Walter wondering just what form this silent, invisible, and possibly all-too-competent pursuit of himself might be taking. And where. And when.

CHAPTER VI

46. Form and Content

Because of this abiding concern with form, Walter has not for many years been much interested in the content of his acts.

How I do it, how well I do it: these are his concerns.

These are the survivors, he tells his contemporary fiction class as the semester draws to an end, looking at the remnants of modern civilization who straggle across the pages of the novels they are reading: see how they survive. Like a long line of wartime refugees, each isolated from the other, they slump along in single file from one vision of the holocaust to the next: from them we shall learn. We shall learn how to be. Or how not to be. What does it matter, so long as we learn how.

Walter himself has learned how with a vengeance, thanks to good teachers like the army, which said: we'll tell you what and where and when and who, never ask why; all you have to learn is how. Always a quick study, Walter learned how. His mother had always liked that quality in him. "Walter, you're a quick study," she'd said whenever he picked up anything new: how to make his bed, peel apples, do long division. How to. Walter was always a quick study, though he never heard that expression from anyone except his mother, another of his teachers.

The other was himself. Walter would never have called himself, as his father, founder of his own soft drink bottling business, called himself, a "self-made man." He would have considered that a bit arrogant. But he does take most of the credit, whenever he thinks about the matter, for turning himself into the person he is, who is not the kind of person who would call himself a "self-made man"—even if that's what he thinks he is. Self-determining, independent: there are plenty of other phrases capable of paying tribute to the fact that Walter himself, among others, has played a leading role in teaching Walter how to be.

Mostly, he has learned by doing: how to do each little thing that conspires with all the other little things one learns to do to make up a life. Little does Walter, yet another year later and with more doing done, know this. Standing on a chair in the master bedroom late one afternoon late in the spring term putting up book shelves, Walter naively thinks that he's putting up book shelves.

What he's actually doing is exercising practical skills he learned how to do a long time ago: how to find a stud, use a screwdriver, measure and level. He'd be just as pleased hanging a picture or a mirror; content makes no difference to him; it's Penny who wants the book shelves put up here.

Stepping down from his chair, moving it along to the spot already marked where he'll install the next support strip, hefting a Phillips screwdriver in his hand, Walter smiles, recalling his colleague Niles Warberg bouncing excitedly into his office before class this morning, having just bought a new gaspowered chain saw. By the time they parted in the hall outside their classrooms ten minutes later, it sounded to Walter as if Niles had already leveled everything on his own bit of property—only a small city lot where Walter and Penny have attended many a departmental barbecue—and was seeking new territory to conquer. Having learned how, with only a few scrapes and bruises to show for it, and some aching muscles, a broken window, and a yard full of tree limbs, what he wanted most of all now was just to do.

The eighteenth century scholar, thinks Walter, who would once have been happy with a handsaw but has now mastered the tools of the twentieth century and won't let go: lord help us all. Walter helped himself by patiently explaining—and explaining again at lunch and yet again in the parking lot as they were both leaving in mid-afternoon—that he has nothing in his yard that needs cutting down. As intense as Warberg is, as determined and enthusiastic in everything he does as he is in his teaching, Walter is left feeling, especially when he thinks about the condition of his apple tree, which Penny says is showing brown signs of cedar-apple rust, that he has somehow betrayed him, frustrated new skills and energies. No, not Niles, Walter has to remind himself: nothing will stop Niles once he has learned how.

So Walter climbs back up onto his chair accompanied by an image of Niles relentlessly sawing his way out to the suburbs, tree after tree falling aside from his path as he forges ahead, his dark eyes focused in the distance on Walter's own oak and apple. Walter chuckles softly, turning the screwdriver steadily in his hand, feeling the brass screw crunch through the plaster beneath its pressure and bite securely into the hard wood of the stud beneath. There: that's how to do it.

47. KNOWLEDGE

What Walter would like to tell Niles, but won't, is: just because you know how to doesn't mean you have to. An argument that can be applied to many things, from Dora's long distance running to nuclear stockpiling, Walter has not neglected to apply it to himself as well. A random selection of such applications over the years might go like this: Just because you know how to type, you don't have to. Just because you know how to drive, you don't have to. Just because you know how to cry, you don't have to. Just because you know how to raise African violets, grow a healthy lawn, test liquids for sugar content, listen with care, eat asparagus, use the semi-colon, hit to the opposite field, balance a checking account, remove a fish hook, prepare a compost heap . . . you don't have to.

And lots of times he doesn't. He's just as happy to take a taxi or let Penny drive, turn his manuscripts over to the department secretary, and forget he ever worked in a soda pop factory. Only a small depression in a corner of the back yard reminds him of the compost pit he started some years back, the lawn gets its fertilizer when someone thinks to buy it, and when it comes to playing softball he always gives in to the urge to swing away, no matter what the situation calls for and he knows how to do. He doesn't have to balance his checkbook or his sentences—Penny could do the one and nobody would ever notice the other—but he does. A fish hook in someone's scalp, however, is another matter; if he doesn't remove it, there's usually no one else around who can. An Australian doctor once taught him how. Cry he doesn't; listen he usually does.

But just because he knows how to, and does, doesn't mean he has to. What he does, he does both because he both knows how and chooses to. Neither alone is sufficient: for Walter, anyway, who learned long ago the logic of the necessary but not sufficient. That's what how to is: necessary but not sufficient. Not for everybody, Walter realizes: there are plenty who blunder ahead into action without ever considering the necessity of knowing how. For them choice alone suffices—and maybe not even conscious choice at that: what presents itself, they do. Or don't. For the rest of humanity, who knows what determines their actions?

For Walter, thinks Walter, first comes the knowledge how, then the choice to, or not to.

For the Walter who knows how to fuck and kill, acknowledges the Walter who fucks and kills, when—so long as the opportunity was presented—did he ever choose not to do either?

Oh well, thinks Walter, fishing around for examples. Among the handful of women he's had sex with, surely there's been a time or two when he chose to say no? But the only occasion he can bring to mind is the time when Penny was so hot for him the day he came back from the hospital after his hernia operation, and he feels that hardly counts as a genuine opportunity. But it's still just a matter of choice, isn't it, even if one always does choose the same? Maybe one night this week he'll choose not to, just to prove a point. Doesn't sound like much fun, though. Doesn't sound much like Walter, either.

As to the other, thinks Walter, it's much the same. A few times he has turned down jobs, when, as with the hernia, the timing just wasn't right. Not really a choice there. Once, he recalls, just once, because he didn't want to—certainly not a phrase he's ever used with Penny. It's not as if an opportunity is presented every day, of course. But each occasion presents the same freedom of choice, nor is that choice circumscribed by the choice made each previous time, in which case it would not be choice but merely dull repetition. But no: each occasion is a new occasion; each choice a new choice. And it's the form of the choice that counts, anyway—the fact that it's there, a shape to be dealt with, its presence confirming his own—not its content. It's just as I thought, he thinks: to choose is to be, even if one always chooses the same thing.

But some time, he considers, I will make not just a new choice but a different choice, though that isn't an easy thing for a professional, who is naturally oriented toward using his professional skills, towards choosing, whenever he can, to do what he knows how to do. Particularly when he does it well.

How he does it, how well he does it: these are the forms of Walter's concerns.

But what, he wonders, shapes this connection here between sex and death?

48. And Action

If he ever figures that out, he'll know an awful lot more than he does now about the problem of form and content. Meanwhile, he won't tell Niles what he does know because that in itself would be bad form: telling other people how to shape their lives generally is, especially when they haven't asked. That's the how to, concedes Walter, for which there are either no training guides or all too many: as many as there are other people on whom to model oneself, though that just pushes the problem back one more stage: how to choose among the multitude of models. On-the-job training is really all there is, and it isn't too great: too easy to pick a faulty model, read the wrong manual or read the manual wrong, learn too late, end up with the wrong form constructed around the content known as the self.

That's not right, thinks Walter: "the content known as the self." Why not "the form known as the self"?

For all his emphasis on form, Walter has made, this afternoon, quite a mess; there is plaster dust all over the top of Penny's dresser, above which he has been hanging the book shelves, and plaster dust around her perfume bottles and jewelry boxes and inside the drawer of scarves, which he only now notices has been left slightly open, and presumably over the carpet behind the dresser, which will now have to be moved for vacuuming. Though the shelving supports have all been screwed tightly into the wall, Walter still stands on the chair with the screwdriver in his hand: not exactly the appropriate tool for cleaning up his mess, but then, the tools that make the messes rarely are.

What about me? Walter wonders, stepping down from the chair. If I am the instrument for making the mess, can't I also be the instrument for cleaning it up? He stuffs the screwdriver into the back pocket of his jeans and rummages around in one of his own dresser drawers until he comes up with a brown sock with holes in both heel and toe, with which he then begins to dust the top of Penny's dresser. There isn't much of a mess, actually, just some scattered, fine, white bits of plaster, but one by one Walter picks up each object from the top of the dresser—each of the small vials of perfume, each little jewelry case, several loose earrings, Penny's house and car keys, a package of thank-you notes—and dusts it off and dusts the walnut surface of the dresser beneath and then puts the object back as close as he can remember to where he found it. Last, he takes out the scarf drawer and sets it on the floor, removes the dozen or so scarves one at a time, shakes and refolds them and, when he has dusted out the inside of the drawer as well, places them neatly back into the drawer and slides the drawer back into the dresser.

Now all that remains is to hang the shelf brackets, which are in a hardware store paper bag on the bed, from the support strips, bring the wooden shelves in from the hall outside the bedroom and lay them across the brackets, put the chair back at the desk in his adjoining study and throw the paper bag in the waste basket and drop the sock down the laundry chute, no, throw that away too, and put the screwdriver away in the tool box in the basement: and everything will look just right. Walter's ideal, for any kind of job, is for things to look, when he's done, as if they had always been that way: form so perfect, so well finished, that it appears inevitable. No: appears not even to have been done. He doesn't want his guests to enter the house after he has rehung the art work and comment on what a beautiful job he's done; he wants them not even to recognize that the art work has been rehung, so well-ordered is each piece individually and the collection as a whole. He wants his students to leave his courses at the end of each semester full of new ideas about how literature has shaped their perceptions yet feeling as if they had those ideas themselves all along. He would like each body he leaves behind to appear, likewise, in its posture of death, so inevitable that there will be no surprise or outrage, that those who discover it will have little more to say than, with ease rather than shock, "Yes, I knew it would end like this."

It doesn't end quite like Walter expects, however. When he has completed his job and returns to the bedroom with Penny, each of them carrying an armload of books, to show her his handiwork and put it to use at once, she is quick to notice bits of white plaster on the carpet around the dresser.

"Oh," she says. "Put the books on the floor here and I'll go get the vacuum cleaner. You pull the dresser out from the wall.

Better take everything off the top first."

By the time she returns with the vacuum cleaner and another dust rag—"For the shelves," she says, acknowledging the effort he's already made—Walter is sitting on the edge of the bed surveying the room: books stacked against one wall, dresser askew in the middle of the room, bottles of perfume on top of his own dresser, jewelry and assorted other objects lying on the bed. More of a mess than he'd realized.

49. Order and Disorder

The content to which he's tried to give some form lies scattered all around him. Soon these things will be returned to their own places and, for a moment, form will prevail. But then the bed, now so neatly made except for the wrinkles around where Walter is sitting, will be opened for sleeping, bedspread and blanket and sheet pulled back; his own pockets will be emptied, wallet and keys and coins and comb and handkerchief dumped on his dresser top like the perfume bottles randomly placed there now; and clothes will be shed, Penny's shoes and socks and underwear dumped on the floor on her side of the bed for the night as usual. And content, if that is what it is, will poke its clumsy head up through the thin film of form and shake its shaggy curls, tangled with twigs and leaves, and, probably, laugh.

And Walter, sitting on the edge of the bed, hands clasped in his lap, will continue to think: What can I do about this?

Is it so terrible for a man like this to want to put his world in order? He lets himself fall backward, tired, on the bed, bumping his head against the edge of an antique silver jewelry box, English, and listening only to the ferocious roar of the vacuum cleaner, disruptive force of order. Walter?

Uh, no: not terrible. That's the wrong term, he thinks, from a whole wrong category of terms: makes a moral issue out of order. Or disorder. This is not a matter of morality but a matter of life and death. Mine, among others. How to survive in the midst of chaos: molecules and cells, organs and limbs, mind and body struggling to hang together in a ferociously stormy world that is constantly eroding their frail connections. High tides of chaos surging in, washing away at them. Nothing worse since the Dark Ages, though doubtless all ages are more or less equally dark. Only difference is: some ages acknowledge it by withdrawing from the darkness into warmly lit little enclaves of civilization, others by reaching out into it with the bright lights of civilization: which only serve, of course, to illuminate how much darkness there is out there. Out there nothing changes. It isn't terrible; it simply is. The only question is: what are we to do?

That's enough, Walter. Head back across the bed, glasses

pushed up on his forehead and legs hanging down to the floor, he drifts into the soft, pleasant chaos of sleep. The only answer he knows to his question, anyway—which is the same answer he's always known—is to try to create, as best he can, whatever order he can in the small area right around himself that he can reach with his own hands, screwdriver, voice, gun . . . .

But then, of course, there's the chaos unreachable, unseen, both inside and out: those sneaky cells that could even now be doing their chaotic, duplicitous duplicating inside this organ, that bone; the equally mysterious presence or absence of that federal agent likewise threatening, even now, as silently as those cells, to erupt chaotically into his life too late for him to ever bring order to it again.

Right around him now the vacuum cleaner roars with more complexity than, awake, he was quite prepared to deal with: chaotic sound grinding away in the service of neatness and order. None of it disturbs his sudden sleep, though Penny, having once begun, continues now to vacuum the entire bedroom, and downstairs the pot of spaghetti she put on for the children's dinner suddenly begins to boil over, unwatched, and on the television, also unwatched, the six o'clock news erupts precisely on time, featuring the weatherman as hero of the hour with the rest of the staff bustling excitedly about him amid reports from around the nation of heavy rains, rapid snow melt in the mountains, and record flood threats, and in Janey's room, unwatched by anyone except themselves, the two girls play, on an old chess set of Walter's, a strange, silent game of pawns (Janey) against royalty (Judy) that allows them to move pieces however they please.

The silence that fills the room when Penny switches off the screech of the vacuum cleaner wakes Walter abruptly from his unaccustomed nap.

"Unh," he says, shielding his eyes from the bright overhead light beneath which he has had five minutes of deep, dark sleep: "that's terrible."

Then, sitting up and pulling his glasses down on his face, he looks at Penny, neatly winding the vacuum cleaner cord around the brackets on the handle: What're you doing?"

"Waiting for you," she answers. "It's time to get up out of this mess and get ready to go."

50. A Formal Sort of Party

This, thinks Walter, must be the mandatory department party scene: and I hate it. In the center of the living room, one hand holding a wine glass and the other taking refuge in his jacket pocket, he exchanges pleasantries with Camilla Fosberg, his hostess. She's looking over his shoulder as she talks and her voice has dropped to a mumble, so Walter, supposing she's said something that calls for an answer, asks her to repeat herself.

"I said here we are again in our usual scene, the annual end-of-semester spring party."

That's exactly what Walter thought she said. It makes him feel all the more like he has been wandering through the local department store, looking for a pair of socks, and somehow ended up in the mandatory party department, where he finds the same party that was going on the last time he accidentally stumbled in here. The talking manikins are holding their half-filled wine glasses in gracefully curved hands and reciting the same lines. They look out over the shoulders of the people they're talking to, their eyes on other groups, other people. When Walter follows Camilla's gaze, he sees that it's taken up residence in a far corner in the midst of the American literature gang, all standing: Constance Keen and her husband, whose name Walter's inconstant mind can never recall; Roger Gruneberg, the O'Caseys, John and Joan, or Shem and Shaun as Silverstein, the Joyce scholar, calls them—and where is Silverstein? Walter wonders: probably leching around Penny as usual—plus an out-of-place Dean, rumored to have once been an historian of the colonial period.

Gruneberg's eyes have taken leave of American literature, however, and Walter follows them through the archway into the dining room, over the crudites and sour cream dips, over the cheese and crackers, over the bundt cake and brownies, over the red and white jug wines at the far end and into the midst of a group consisting of Penny, the Warbergs, and, as he suspected, Sheldon Silverstein, who nervously gulps down his glass of red wine, refills it from the jug, and begins to drink again.

Penny, not tall enough to look over Silverstein's shoulder, is looking, instead, around him, into, Walter presumes, the kitchen, where, out of sight, another group has probably assembled, Fosberg himself no doubt among them, leaning up against the refrigerator in his favorite pose, tall enough to be looking out over everyone's head through the other kitchen door, which opens onto the entrance hall, to keep an eye out for late arrivals, a number of whom Walter can hear coming in through the front door just now, behind him, chattering away, some of them very likely letting their eyes drift, even as they talk to each other, across to the center of the living room where he stands with a wine glass in his hand exchanging pleasantries with his hostess.

Walter excuses himself, muttering something about refilling his wine glass. Only then does he note that his glass is still full and that Camilla has already departed. He looks around and finds her greeting the newcomers, a pair of political scientists and their spouses. Maybe it isn't exactly the same party, he muses: every year there are a couple of new people, and besides, I used to be able to drink this wine. Now it's quite intolerable.

He wanders into the dining room in order to abandon his glass on the sideboard, wondering what it is he's doing here: these are people he works with and likes, people he ordinarily goes out of his way to be with, and yet they too seem to be wondering what they're doing here: their eyes all roving off in search of something else.

He picks up a sliver of carrot as he moves by the table, stabs it into the dip, pops it into his mouth. At the far end of the table, Penny catches his eye and rolls both of hers up with patient impatience at Silverstein, standing behind her now gulping at a wine glass clutched in both hands. Walter glides past, touching her gently on the arm, then out through the French doors at the end of the room and onto the sunporch, bright and humid. The glare of the evening sun through the far wall of windows makes his eyes blink and tear. In the moist green atmosphere of Camilla's amazing plant collection—they're everywhere, on the floor, on tables, stands, shelves—he feels as if he's entered another world altogether. On the white wicker couch down at the end of the sunporch to his right, he sees, through blurred eyes, his colleague Dora Sibley, ensconced in a bower of giant ferns.

"God," she says, her eyes boring up at him as she lowers the book she's been reading to her lap, "I hate parties like this."

51. A Parting Sort of Form

Walter wonders what other mandatory scenes life will impose on him. Driving home from the Fosbergs, the sun still held above the horizon by the annual miracle of daylight savings time, Walter waits for the sound of the horn that will send the walls of self-determination tumbling down and leave him exposed to the mandatory discovery scene, the mandatory chase scene, the mandatory courtroom scene, the mandatory . . . . A horn honks, demanding that Walter move on through the intersection on the green light. Penny, who's been leaning back resting, eyes closed, sits up straight, looks out at the green light, then looks over at Walter, who quickly accelerates, anticipating an absent-minded-driver scene and forgetting that never once, in all these years, has Penny criticized his driving.

This time she admits to wondering what made him wait there at the light so long: just as, she also admits, she sometimes wonders what makes him go.

"We all do what we have to."

"Don't lecture, Walter," she says gently, sliding over to lean her head on his shoulder: "I was just wondering. Sometimes I wonder if I really do know you."

Walter sits up a little straighter behind the wheel, as if his posture could disguise his evasive response: "If you don't, I don't know who does."

"I mean, you didn't look very happy at the party, and here you're sitting at a traffic light when we could be getting home."

Walter glances over at her: "How do you mean, I didn't look happy?"

"Every time I saw you, you were standing and talking with one person and looking around for someone else."

"I did that?" he cries out. Again they are waiting at a traffic light, but this time Walter's ready for it when it changes to green, steps down hard on the accelerator and moves quickly ahead.

"Yes, you did that."

"But," he wails, "that's what everyone else was doing!"

Now she sits up again, still close beside him, turning to face him: "Are you so different from everyone else?"

"Aren't I?"

"More alike than not," she says, almost in a whisper.

When Walter hesitates, slowing down for the turn into their street, she continues: "Oh you may be nicer than a lot of people, Walter, and you may be smarter than some and gentler than most, less talkative than others, a better lover, teacher . . . . "

"Hmmm."

" . . . and a dozen other little things, most of which I generally think I don't even know, that make you you. Or me me. But when they get all added up, I still don't think they come out making us particularly different from everyone else. And I don't just mean everyone else at that party. I mean even if everyone else includes people we don't think are like us at all, terrible people even, rapists and murderers and child molesters and dictators and schizophrenics and . . . and I still think we're more alike than not. Them and us. You and me, Walter. You. Especially if we look at the way we really are and what we really do and not just at the ways we think of ourselves being and doing."

Walter pulls up into the driveway, clicks the garage door opener, waits for the sluggish mechanism to trundle slowly up, and meanwhile just sits there, both hands on the wheel, looking over at Penny. She doesn't usually make speeches like this, so it must be something important—something, Walter's aware, that has to do with him. The level rays of the sun, perched just above the horizon, light up the inside of the car so that half her face glows warmly while the other half hides in shadow. And Walter, knowing that his own face, turned toward her, must appear the same, thinks: good grief, do I really know myself so little as that? Don't I know that I'm just like everyone else, more or less? Am I just like everyone else?

He decides, as he pulls into the garage, turns off the ignition, opens his door, and backs out, away from Penny, that as soon as he gets in the house, while Penny takes care of the baby-sitter, he'll lock himself in the bathroom and stand in front of the medicine cabinet and attempt to look closely at just how much he is, and isn't, like everyone else. What he finds his life imposing on him at the moment is the mandatory mirror scene.

52. The Mandatory Mirror Scene

Standing in the bathroom still wearing the blue blazer and khakis he wore to the wine party, standing in the bathroom with the light on and the door locked, standing in the bathroom in front of his own image in the toothpaste-splattered mirror, standing in the bathroom waiting for some shock of self-recognition to flare up in this mirror behind that locked door in these same ordinary clothes, standing around waiting, as it were, for confirmation that he is or isn't just like everyone else, Walter decides he doesn't want to be in any more of these mandatory scenes. He simply will not put himself in them. He hopes that no one else insists on his presence in them either. If anyone tries to put him in one, he will do his damnedest to get out of it as soon as possible.

There's a knock at the door: "Daddy, can I get in there?"

"Right away, sweetheart." He lifts off his glasses, splashes water on his face, grabs a dirty hand towel off the rack to dry off with, sticks his glasses under the faucet and dries them with his handkerchief, puts them back on, runs his pocket comb through his hair, and finally opens the door to his older daughter.

"Why didn't you use your own bathroom upstairs?" She's on her way to bed in yellow cotton pajamas with blue butterflies.

"I was in a hurry, sweetheart."

"Me too."

53. A Dizzying View

If Walter Job has given up mirrors for examining more than the condition of his hair, he still has, secreted away on the dusty top shelf of his bedroom closet and unexamined for half a dozen years, a rather more telling vision of himself: a photograph: actually two photographs artistically coalesced into one, an image that he can't bear to look at.

It was taken by the one person Walter knew in the art department, a painter beginning to make a name for herself in photography with some new techniques she'd devised. She hailed Walter one bright fall day as he was passing the art building on his way to his office, hustled him into her studio in spite of his protests that he had a class coming up in ten minutes, sat him down on a stool, and while she fussed with the lights complained herself about the difficulty of finding portrait subjects. When she was ready she had him sit straight, head turned just slightly to one side but eyes on the camera lens. Walter looked at her over the tripod-mounted camera and wondered what he was doing there. She looked like a gypsy, with a scarf tied around her head, a flowing blouse that hung down over her wide belly, and a skirt that trailed on the floor: all in different prints. But then the shutter clicked, she tinkered with the camera, and he turned his head to the other side, as ordered, until the shutter clicked again. He was late to class.

A week later the campus mail brought him a large envelope containing a portrait of himself that looked like this: below, neck and shoulders wrapped in one of the turtlenecks he often wore at that time, tan in fact, grey in photo; above, his hair, darker than it really was, and a broad forehead he knew was more expansive than it really was. He kept focusing on the forehead: a forehead, he thought, that rivaled Shakespeare's. He was stalling. He was stalling because he didn't want to release his eyes and let them slide on down over the center of the photograph, across which they had already skimmed as he pulled it from its manila envelope. He didn't want to let them move on down because he wasn't sure he could cope with what he was going to see there.

What he saw there when he could no longer avoid looking was this: three eyes, two noses, a wide mouth, and a broad chin:

all his: him. What he saw was that in between a singular scalp and a singular neck, two of him—or maybe one and a half—looked out at him. Too many Walter Jobs stared at him, their odd chin and mouth, their two noses and three eyes—resulting from a perfect overlap of the left eye of one face with the right eye of the other—mocking the fact that they were encased in one body.

Looking at it made him very, very dizzy.

He quickly stuffed the photograph back in its envelope, laid it on his desk, and forgot to take it home with him that afternoon. When he remembered a couple of days later, and gave it to Penny to take out of its envelope while he turned his back and stared out the living room window at his two daughters playing on the front lawn, she cried out in amazement. She wanted it framed, but Walter, objecting that it would have to be hung where he would never see it, took it from her, after she had slipped it back into the envelope, and put it away, up on that top shelf of his bedroom closet, next to the cardboard box in which he stored canceled checks and copies of income tax returns.

To be sure, he did indeed take it down and look at it again over the winter and spring and summer that followed: once a week at first, then once a month, finally one last time just before the fall semester began. He kept thinking that if he could only get a little used to it, then he could get it framed for Penny for Christmas. He remembered a handsome eight by ten of his father, encased in a silver frame, that used to sit on his mother's dresser. But each time he took the photograph down off the shelf and hesitantly edged it out of its envelope, instead of being able to live with it a little more comfortably, he found that it only made him feel dizzier than the time before.

The final time, home alone, sitting on the edge of the bed. the photograph laid out on his lap, he actually felt nauseous.

Not a chance, he thought, clenching his eyes and waiting for his sense of balance to return: I cannot live with this thing.

Neither could he throw it away. Eyes still closed, he turned it upside down and slid it back into the envelope. Then he stood up, slowly, opened his eyes, and—still a little wobbly—crossed the room and stuck it away again high up on the top shelf of his closet. It's still there.

54. Stasis

Much there is, Walter has learned, that people do not pay attention to: and not just what's hidden away in dark closets. People simply do not pay attention to what goes on in front of their very eyes. The world is a moving entity which glides past them at a relentless pace on the moving belt of time, but people are so preoccupied with hanging on to their precious little nows that they do not see what goes by, no matter how bizarre, unless—or until—it reaches over and cracks them on the head. The manufacturer's rep in the airport in Kansas City to whom Walter introduced himself as a professional killer is Walter's primary example of this phenomenon: their conversation proceeded exactly as if no such phrase had been interjected into it: complaints about cuts in airline schedules, viewings of wallet-sized photos of wives and children, discussion of weather past and passing and yet to come. Time's merry-go-round, Walter began to realize then, spins at such a rate that unless most people shut their eyes most of the time to what was passing before them, they would become dizzy and fall to the ground, fearful of ever getting up again.

But Walter's own opinion is that it does not really move fast at all except by comparison to the stasis which most people seem to desire: a fixed and unchanging world, not necessarily a pleasant one but one where they know where they are and are sure that nothing new and therefore threatening can enter: a safe world. Walter knows, just as he knows that somewhere inside of them each of these people also knows, or they would not be doing what they do, that there is no such thing as a safe world, not so long as the moving sidewalk of time trudges by, bringing with it the anything possibles, as it always does. But he is not frightened by this. He knows that it goes by slowly enough for you to see what is coming at you, so long as you do not blink or sneeze or look aside. He knows that from time to time everyone blinks and sneezes and looks aside, and that he accepts as an inevitable part of what the conveyor belt is bringing. But he resolves not to take his pleasures, like most people, from those moments, or, like most people, to attempt to expand those moments into a lifetime, to grab them when they occur, and attempt to keep them still and enduring, to hold onto them for dear, dear life.

Because, Walter has learned, the people who have managed to render their worlds as static as possible simply do not see what is happening before their very eyes. Sometimes he looks at Penny sitting on one corner of the blue couch in the living room and feels quite certain that no matter what he did, she would not take notice of it: that he could, say, lead Dora Sibley across the room and up the stairs, unbuttoning her blouse as he went, disappear with her into the bedroom for an hour, and later return and settle down in the armchair across from the couch all without Penny so much as glancing up at him or asking what's going on.

The way he has actually put this prospect to her has been to suggest that he could stroll through the living room with a lion on a leash and she wouldn't take notice, but all she has ever done has been to look up from her book and respond with that classic little twist of her mouth, and Walter has never known whether that wry smile indicates that she agrees with him or thinks him a perfect ass or has, in fact, not even been paying attention to what he's been saying.

Most people, Walter has found, do not pay any attention to what you are saying to them, no matter how significant the message you bring. And Walter knows that in his work he often brings people the most significant message they will ever hear: the news of their imminent deaths. Even then they do not seem to attend to him: which makes Walter's work considerably easier, of course.

"I am here to kill you."

"I beg your pardon, what did you say?"

"You asked me what I wanted, and I said, 'I am here to kill you.'"

And still they bow their heads and go on signing letters the secretary stacked on their desk before she shut down her computer and left for the day. Or they say "Just a moment" and go back to dusting the Hummel figurines on the mantel. They hardly acknowledge Walter's presence, and yet it is he, as they turn once more to their tools or their telephones, holding one finger up into the air, as if to suspend this moment in time, who is about to bring them what they most seem to desire. It is Walter, stepping up close beside them as they bend to open a drawer or note pad, who is about to render their world static forevermore.

55. Motion

Walter's own world is never static, though, not even in the silent, small, motionless pool of light in which he sits in his study. When it's static, it won't be his world anymore. But meanwhile, time passes: oh, how it passes! Walter knows: it's the very stuff he's working with here. In but also *with*: even now, tonight, he sits alone, in his study, hard at work with it: aware of, among other things, how it does not hold still for him.

It is late and everyone else in the house is sleeping, long after party time: a time which strikes Walter as being a most peculiar sort of time, because it will recur next year, at, as his colleagues assured him when he and Penny took their leave this evening, "the exact same time"—which is probably, thinks Walter, the most improbable expression he can imagine—and will not be substantially different from this time: or rather, he has to correct himself, "that time." It will be like the midnight striking of a clock, with only a few different sets of ears around to remark on the fact that it's today's midnight and not yesterday's. And midnight, which it almost is, is a confusing enough time anyway, bordering as it does upon tomorrow.

And tomorrow, which is no time as yet, will be for Walter still another kind of time, in which he has agreed to meet Dora Sibley for a drink following their afternoon classes. That makes it, too, a peculiar sort of time: one which has never occurred before, hence quite the opposite of party time. And likewise, thinks Walter, will probably never occur again, being only a brief, aberrant moment in the way time moves for him. No, perhaps it will never occur at all, perhaps it's only a supposition in time, a hypothesis about how time can move, whereas something else will come up in time to keep it from occurring at all.

And now? In this time? Now, like many other late evenings, is the time which Walter spends with time: with the time of *Time Lapse*, which he has now on, in, his hands. For some months already he has had the lengthy introduction which he's promised to write for the new critical edition mostly completed. But even now, reading through its forty some pages, letting them sift through his hands from one pile to another, he's not satisfied. It sounds good, but something is missing and he cannot quite seem to get his hands on what it is that's missing.

I can handle the time, he thinks—naively, perhaps, but it's only a book he's talking about, isn't it?—but I cannot cope with the lapse: this book is driving me crazy.

In it time jumps continually forward, some improbable beast whose leaps, though never enormous, he cannot quite follow, though they still carry him, inescapably, along, from event to event. The important thing here, he can't help thinking—and he's said it in his introduction, though that hasn't seemed to explain or settle anything—seems not to be the events but the leaps—the lapses, the gaps—which tie the events together. Or cause them to come unstrung. And it's them, he whines a little to himself, that he cannot center on in his essay: them I cannot follow. What's, he wants to know, the point?

Or are they, he wonders, in fact the point, those gaps and lapses, the inexpressible absences that glue together the inescapable presences, the mysterious gluons of understanding, the unknowns that bond the polarized knowns of this book's world?

So alongside the book itself, yet one more time again, he neatly stacks the pages of his own manuscript and clips them together. Maybe, he thinks, maybe I really can't fit this together, make the necessary connections, all by myself. But to whom can he turn? Well, he thinks, maybe what he ought to do is to seek out the author of this book, wherever it is the years have carried that strange man off to. Yes, he could do it as a summer project, maybe even get another small travel grant from the University research fund; it's probably too late to apply this year, and, besides, there are other commitments he's already made. Pleased, all the same, and knowing that exploring grant possibilities is one thing he will do for sure with his time tomorrow, he stands, slips his manuscript into a manila folder, the folder into a drawer of his metal filing cabinet: time will pass and a summer will come, the next if not this one, and who knows, perhaps it will bring some answers along with it.

He puts himself in the hands of time and goes to bed, trying not to think, as he slips in beside his sleeping wife, about the possibility that some of the answers time may be bringing might be answers to questions that others are pursuing.

CHAPTER VII

56. Gardening

Dora's basement apartment in the rear of the building is dark and stuffy. "They call this the garden level. Those must be my flowers," she says, pointing out the window, one of three set high in the living room wall, to the row of garbage cans lined up beside the garages.

"But it is a garden in here," Walter protests, turning about in the center of the room, his gaze sweeping over the multitudes: plants lining the windowsills and bookcases, covering the tops of several small tables, hanging from lamps and curtain rods, edging out, the larger ones, in great pots set on the floor: everything green but nothing flowering. Walter recognizes some of them: the philodendron and shiffleria, the jade plant and rubber tree and several ivies and ferns. More he doesn't recognize: except as green plants and not flowering types.

The only thing flowering in the room, much to Walter's surprise, is Dora herself: dressed for a change not in the pants and sweaters she wears to teach in or the grey suit she's worn on more formal occasions—a concert or a dean's reception—or the warm-up suit he has sometimes seen her in, but in a floorlength, almost gauzy print of lilac flowers on a pink background. One of the most delicate dresses he has ever seen, thinks Walter, watching the light outline her body in it as she passes between him and the window to lift one of her plants off the sill. But then he wonders: is it a dress or is it a robe or even, seeing how thin it is and how it reveals her shoulders, a nightgown?

"What is it?" he finally asks, as she sets the plant on the floor beneath a lamp and begins to examine its leaves carefully.

"This?" she says. "An African violet, my first attempt at a flowering plant. Only it won't flower."

"Too big a pot," Walter announces, surprised himself at the authority with which he speaks, then suddenly pleased to remember that that statement, recognizably not his own and therefore for a moment rather troubling, was his mother's regular proclamation about African violets everywhere.

Dora looks up at him, but Walter, looking down at her, can't focus on either her eyes or the plant she cups between her palms because her dress, robe, gown, whatever it is—a whole flowering world—curves softly open at the top, bent forward as she is over the violet, and down it Walter can see two small but beautifully rounded breasts, nipples pale inside the shadow of the fabric: the most beautiful breasts, he is sure, that he has ever seen, and he aches to touch them as he kneels down in front of her, lifts his eyes at last to look in hers, only to find that she's still looking at the small pot that holds her African violet.

"This is too big?"

"This is just perfect."

Walter leans forward to touch her breasts through the delicate fabric: first one and then the other, moving his hand gently over each small, firm breast, touching his fingers down like a pianist's on each hard nipple. And when he feels her lean forward against him, he reaches one arm around her back, puts his mouth down against her hair, the lobe of her ear, into the hollow of her neck, still keeping his right hand securely in contact with one of those perfect breasts: wishing he never had to let it go and, at the same time, wanting to let it go at once so he can get underneath the fabric to skin itself.

Touch, touch, touch, touch, touch, says Walter's hand.

Down along her slender back his left hand glides, along the bony ridges of her spine toward her waist, her hips. She's curved one arm loosely over his shoulders, but seeking out her lips he finds her still staring at the pot she holds in her other hand.

"You really mean this size pot is too big? How do you know that? Who told you that?"

"My mother," he says, releasing her breast, letting his right hand slide down along her belly and hip, down her thigh and leg to the hem of her skirt, beneath which it begins the slow trip up again, flesh against flesh.

Carefully setting the plant down on the floor, Dora puts her other arm around his neck, too, then leans back, arching her neck, closing her eyes as she pulls Walter down upon her: "Hmmm."

57. Talking

Why he said that, Walter doesn't know: who hardly remembers having ever spoken with his mother when he was a kid. Not that she wasn't around: she was a full-time mother then just as she became a full-time businesswoman after his father's death. And for his part, he remembers being a full-time kid: basically solitary in spite of a handful of neighborhood playmates, generally preferring the indoors to the out. She was around and he was around, but still he can't recall them having much to do with each other. Up to about age five or six, in fact, he remembers nothing: which allows him to assume that they must have had a lot of contact back then; or none; or to wonder if perhaps one of them did something in that unremembered lapse of years that became a bar to further contact. Who knows, perhaps she was just too busy meeting the demands of her other children.

He remembers that he played by himself a lot, read, looked out of windows, listened to the radio, and eventually found a place for viewing the television set when it belatedly took its place in the household. In the midst of a full-time mother and four full-time siblings, to say nothing of a part-time father reasonably visible evenings and weekends, it was not easy to be solitary, but somehow Walter accomplished it: sitting in the farthest corner from the television set, using his top bunk for a playground and reading room, alert to the value of the spaces behind couches and chairs. He learned early to avoid crossroads: doorways, staircase landings, hallways, the spot right in front of the television that lay in the multiple pathway connecting the front door, kitchen, dining room, and living room couch. Dangerous places, crossroads. That, he can at least say, was never my problem: there is some solace in solitude.

And still he felt exposed. Someone was always finding him: reading a book under the dining room table, sitting on the dark basement steps nibbling one of the onions his mother stored in string bags there.

"Here's Walter!" his discoverer usually cried out: to someone out of sight somewhere, in another room, not to Walter.

"Such a nice, quiet boy," said the neighbors and relatives:

to his mother, his father, each other.

Who talked to Walter?

Not his mother, apparently, though he remembers growing up beside her, a small woman steadily diminished by the years that made him taller and taller. Yet he knows her as a talkative person: on the phone or in person, with his siblings, his father, her friends and relatives and business associates and anyone who happened to be around. When he thinks of her, he thinks of her talking. No matter how he tries, he cannot call up a silent image of his mother. He sees her short, gold-tinted hair bobbing, her red nails flashing, bracelets jangling, her mouth moving, always.

But he does not know what she says.

He does not think that she says it to him.

58. Everything

"Talk to me," says Dora.

Finished with their sudden love-making on the living room floor, they have gotten up, still mostly dressed, and Dora has led him down the hall to her bedroom, both of them shedding clothes as they go: Dora just her light shift, but Walter a bit of everything, hopping along behind her as he tugs off a sock, lets his pants drop to the floor. Now, on her unmade bed, lying on their sides facing each other, playing gently with each other's bodies before they begin again, Dora touches his lips with the tips of her fingers and whispers, "Talk to me, Walter."

"About African violets?" he teases quietly.

"No."

"Flowering plants," he says, leaning forward to take the pink bud of her nipple between his lips.

"Sensitive plants," She squeezes his sticky penis in her hand.

"Pollinating plants."

"Don't even think about it."

"So to speak. But not for a few minutes yet." He moves his lips to her other breast.

"Talk to me, then." She wipes her sticky palm along his ass, then keeps it there.

"About what?" he says resting his mouth between her breasts: "I'm all out of plants."

"About you."

He looks up, a little startled, from between her breasts, and says, pretty truthfully, "I don't know anything about me."

Dora knows a few things, and tells him: about his teaching and scholarship, his presence on campus, his reputation with students and colleagues, his family, now that she's met them, and how he is with them, now that she's seen a little of that. She has even read his dissertation, on microfilm, which puts her one up on everyone else in the department. But what she knows about Walter, nice as it is, she knows only from a few facts and rumors and some decade-old scholarship; what she wants to know about Walter she wants to know about the Walter who lies beside her on her bed now, circling her left breast with his tongue. She has come to the source, but even the source wonders what the source knows: the Nile itself begins in a murky, ignorant swamp from which little can be learned about its great delta.

"Background?" says Walter. "Parents? Siblings? Childhood friends? Mumps and measles? Education? Summer camps? What is there to know about me? I'm just like everybody else." Or so he has recently been informed.

"No you're not." She slides her hand down around his ass, between his legs, to caress the inside of his thighs. "For one thing, you're a better lover than anyone else."

"Not hardly," he says, remembering how quickly everything happened on the living room floor. Walter doesn't know whether to be flattered or embarrassed; consequently, he's a little of both. Nor does he know whether she's teasing him, genuinely praising him, leading him on, or some of all. Therefore all he can think of to say is, "You seem to know more about me than I do."

She laughs and pulls his penis against herself: into herself as he responds by rolling over on top of her: "Tell me everything."

"Or what?" he asks, lifting himself on his elbows to look down into her face, flushed and a little sweaty now, darkly veined lids closed over her eyes as, elsewhere, she opens to him.

"Or," eyes still closed, "I'll have to make up things about you, I'll have to invent you, I'll have to hold you here till I'm done."

"Well then," says Walter, his own eyes closing as he settles down upon her, thrusting into her, "everything."

"Everything," he thrusts, "everything, everything, everything . . . ."

59. Everything Else

There are times when he thinks this is everything, others when he thinks: if only this were everything. Mostly the latter. The world intrudes, more often than not, announcing itself as everything: or almost everything. Well, thinks Walter, it may be everything, but it is not enough. And this? Does this come close to being enough even though it is, demonstrably, not everything?

"Enough, enough," moans Dora, although her motions tell Walter quickly enough, when he begins to relax beneath her, that it is by no means enough yet. Two or three times they have rolled over, trying out the top, the bottom, various intermediate stages, and somewhere in those gyrations, at some moment suddenly past when he held one of her breasts almost wholly in his mouth, Walter has already come: enough but, as he finds when he begins to move beneath and within her once more, not enough, either. She pulls him over on top of her and, legs wrapped tightly around him, moves and moves and moves until Walter, still a long way from coming this time, begins to wonder if maybe this isn't everything after all. If it isn't, what is? And when he gets to the end of everything—which he suddenly realizes, as Dora, head back and eyes clenched shut, rides back and forth beneath him, squeezing and squeezing on him, is going to be sooner than he anticipated—what then?

At the end of everything lies everything else: mostly himself. Like everyone else, he supposes, Walter resides at the center of a sphere defined as everything: the everything within which he lives, the everything which revolves around him, the everything into which he continually thrusts himself: and thrusts and thrusts . . . until suddenly at last everything explodes around him and he within it, a fiery rush of time in which there are no suppositions or realizations, no definitions, no questions. And then, once more, that time, no time, has passed, the ashes of everything are drifting down upon him, and he is alone, again in the center, with everything else: himself.

Everything else is a question, and Walter does not know the answer. He knows it's where he lives, and perhaps that's why he's so interested in thrusting out of it and into . . . everything. But he wasn't kidding when he said to Dora, some minutes back, "I don't know anything about me." Fact.

Oh, he knows the name, the statistics, well enough. He knows he likes filet of sole and broccoli with hollandaise sauce and a handful of contemporary authors and willow trees and certain people and . . . and this, of course: this woman surging beneath and around him, drawing him deeper and deeper into her "oh"s and her "enough"s that are clearly not enough. And he knows what he's doing, too, and what other things he does when he's not doing this, and when and where and how well and with whom he does them all. Mostly he knows what he does. And he knows that all he knows still fails to meet that classical instruction to know thyself.

What he doesn't know is what is missing.

Which is, right now, nothing, except perhaps his mind, since everything else is in touch with . . . everything, more and more in touch, and faster and faster. Everything moves rapidly beneath him, setting a rhythm, not his, into which he enters as surely as if it were, as deep and firm and quick, until he feels he is touching, at every thrust, the farthest limits of everything, and everything explodes around him, and he explodes with it, with it.

Oh he has been with everything, and now Dora falls back, exhausted, sweaty, arms outflung beneath him, gasping: "God, I haven't had anything like that in ages"

And now he falls back too, beside her: back into everything else: he doesn't know what.

60. The Same Thing

Not that this question of identity is of any concern to Professor Job in his modern literature classes. He lectures not on who the characters of contemporary fiction are, or even who they think they are, but on what they do, what happens to them. His thesis: the same things happen to us all. What, therefore, does it matter who we are, who we or others think we are?

So when a tall, blond woman approaches him after the concluding session of this semester's Monday night seminar, after an hour's summing-up lecture and another hour's discussion of the kinds of things that happen over and over again, to the characters in *Time Lapse* as well as in the other novels they've been examining, to complain that she really cannot distinguish the protagonist in this book from a great many other characters, he struggles briefly to restrain himself from replying condescendingly that that is precisely the point he has been laboring to make for the past one hundred and twenty minutes. Only a foggy sense of appropriate classroom behavior, all that remains to him after a long day's teaching and much else besides, plus a clear recognition of the fact that she is not wearing a bra, collaborate to keep him from driving her away at once. Not that her breasts, bulging freely through her thin cotton sweater, nipples erect in the cool evening breeze that sweeps through the room now that the door is open, bear any comparison to the firm little delights he has just discovered in Dora's, but they have a depth, a resonance, that he can't ignore, either.

And because he also cannot ignore the fact that she has already written a brilliant mid-term exam and one of the most thoughtful term papers he has ever seen from this particular course, something else resonates, too: his failure to get across to her the main, uh, thrust of tonight's class. Of the course, maybe. Or perhaps even of contemporary literature: the same things happen to us all: it doesn't matter who we are.

Can it be? he wonders, gathering his books off the desk and watching her walk out the door, leaving both of them unsatisfied. From her slender back and smallish ass, he would never have guessed she had such large breasts. Can it truly be, he wonders, that it does matter who we are? That the reason I was not convincing tonight is that I'm no longer so sure of what I'm saying?

A lot of time has passed since Walter first began, in his dissertation, to formulate and develop this thesis he has just been presenting to his class. He is well past the point of taking it very personally. But if all the activities of his own life haven't led him into wondering about who he is, and whether he is or is not just like everyone else, Dora's questioning, only this afternoon, along with Penny's recent statements about the same issue, have. Can an understanding of the twentieth century begin to be undermined so quickly, and by such a simple question?

Well, time passes, he knows, and things change.

Does that happen to us all?

61. Flowers and Things

Walter comes down from his shower wearing a flowered print caftan Penny made him out of a sizeable piece of material for which she could find no other use. The flowers are enormous, dark blue and orange on a lilac background, and quite improbable: he has never been able to find anything like them in her books on botany and gardening. In this caftan, in fact, he feels rather large and improbable himself: like a floor-length drapery with no window to hang in front of. Well-covered, he feels totally exposed in it, and therefore won't even wear it when the girls are still up: what defense is there against the laughter of children?

 He is hesitant even about wearing it in front of Penny; she may have chosen the material, but whenever she sees him coming toward her like a surreal vision of a tropical garden, the look in her eyes conveys a strong sense of suppressed hysterics. He wears it, though. The plaid, flannel robe his mother gave him several Christmases ago is hot and dirty, and he feels just as uncomfortable in it. He has never felt comfortable in a robe: there's something loose, unfitted, about them that doesn't suit him. The caftan he wears, though: Penny made it, the plaid robe's dirty, he doesn't feel like getting dressed again at this late hour. So down the staircase he comes, feeling like an obscene floating garden and ready to defend himself against the derisive look Penny will throw him from the couch. Only he doesn't get it.

 She is sitting with her back to him, engrossed in Weissman's *Sex Against Death*, and doesn't even glance up until he settles down in a chair opposite her, cocks his head to check out the title on the book jacket, and says to her, "Who's winning?"

 And even then all he gets from her is a little smile. At the absurdity of his question? The absurdity of his costume?

 Neither, as it turns out. He frowns and she points: at the fact that he hasn't yet learned how to sit while wearing skirts.

 "*Contre le morte*," he says, quickly covering himself up by tucking the skirts of the caftan between his legs. He should have known what that cool draft shriveling his testicles meant.

 "What?"

 Obviously he knows she wasn't listening, since her French

is so much better than his: since, in fact, she can speak the language while he can only paste together a few trite phrases. Come to think of it, she wasn't talking, either: only pointing, above her book, and then disappearing beneath its horizon again.

"I was speaking against death myself," says Walter: "death by freezing drafts, death by icy looks, death by being frozen out, death by frigidity . . . ."

"Walter," says Penny, very carefully: a sign that she's aware just how thin this conversational ice is that she's just been pushed out on: "Walter, I would be happy to make love with you more if only you were around here a little more these days."

She has come up a little from bit her book to say this, or rather lowered the book somewhat so Walter can see she's giving him her full attention for the moment, but she's already raised its thick barrier between his eyes and hers again when he speaks.

"Are you having an affair?"

Now the book drops all the way back down into her lap, her right hand sandwiched between its pages to hold her place and her left spread across the cover, so that only one large word from the title shows, in bold red type: SEX. Not even what Walter had meant to query her about. Honest: the thought hadn't even crossed his mind till he uttered the question. Even now he doesn't know why he said it: he doesn't think, or have any particular reason to think, that she's having an affair, and even if he thought she was he's not sure he would ask her about it. Granted they don't make love as much as they once did, he's certainly not feeling sexually deprived, hasn't come downstairs in his caftan to entice her back upstairs to bed with him, feels his penis still aching, in fact, from this afternoon's activities, though at the same time inexplicably hardening between his cold thighs, reminding him who's really having the affair.

Penny stares across at him from the couch: "Walter, you're not serious about that, are you?"

62. Nothing

Walter, naturally, doesn't know whether he's serious about his question or not. Not having thought about it before asking it, he can't know what he intended. All he can do is think about what he wants from it now. And now, having pushed her into a corner, he feels like he's the one who's trapped.

What's responsible for this feeling is that book she's reading, hiding behind, raising between them, its clear duality like a flag of war: *Sex Against Death*. But he knows which side he's on, doesn't he? The thing between his legs tells him so, a firm reality. He's not under suspicion, is he? No one in here, in this safe place, is trying to get him to admit he's ever collaborated with the other side. He knows where he lives and thinks he's always made his loyalties clear: where there's sex, he chooses sex. Haven't his actions always made that clear? Unless, of course, to choose death at any time is to choose against sex, which he's always chosen whenever he's had the chance.

Sex Against Death: the book seems to insist on his acknowledging which side he's on. Still and thick in Penny's lap it lies. Her hand slides absently across the cover—she's paying no attention to the book, only watching him with large eyes—covering the red SEX, uncovering DEATH in its huge black letters.

Doesn't he know what this book says, anyway, even without reading it? The cover tells him enough: to elect sex is to deny death. He's sure he's always known this: screwing proves he's alive, while dying—though he doesn't know this part quite as well, at first hand, yet—only proves you're dying: and kills off everything else, too: sex, others, the world . . . . everything.

The conflict reminds him of that old kids' game: scissors, paper, stone, each with its power over something else, each under the power of something else: paper covers stone, is cut by scissors, which are crushed by stone. Sex obliterates death; death obliterates sex. The problem is that there's no middle term here: each is at once in power over and powerless beneath the other. So where's the game here: how do you choose, how do you know whether to reach out with a fist or an open hand? Only, he wonders, isn't death the more powerful, finally, because its power, once obtained, is everlasting, whereas the power of sex, no matter how often achieved, is only temporary? A fuck for life needs to be followed by another fuck for life, and another and another and another . . . . But a death . . . a death is a death: followed by nothing.

Does this mean he's taking sides at last? Which side, then? Who's to say that permanent is better than temporary? All he knows is that permanent is more permanent than temporary. Time passes, no matter what: sex, death; death, sex. Time passes, leaving him still transfixed, silenced, by this duality. He has not yet answered Penny's question, which came in answer to his question: Is he serious about this? Does he have a choice about being serious in such a matter, when faced with a book so thick and boldly titled as this, which, though he has not read it, he can surely tell by its cover? Time passes, and he gets the feeling that the whole struggle is written all over his face in giant black and red lettering for Penny to read. Surely he, too, can be told by his cover, which Penny, an inveterate reader, watches closely, tensed and silent, waiting for the words from within. Walter sees her hand slip nervously out from between the pages: losing her place. She tangles the fingers of both hands together over the cover of the book, so that he can no longer read the title. Time passes.

"No, forget it," says Walter at last: "Never mind. Nothing. I didn't mean it. I don't even know why I said it. I'm sorry. Just forget it."

For the moment, neither sex nor death.

63. Something

Because he has realized that Penny could be having an affair — though he doesn't really believe she is and therefore doesn't choose to pursue the matter—Walter also realizes she could die. Penny could die, Judy could die, Janey could die, his mother and sisters and brothers . . . who else does he really care about? Dora could die: that's not quite the same, but still, Walter has always known, in some unspoken way, that to love was to tangle yourself up in someone else's mortality. Sooner or later the someone you loved was going to be taken away from you: by death—if not theirs, yours—or—here he finds part of the connection he has been looking for—infidelity—theirs or yours: all love's old refrains of permanence—"Forever?" "Yes, forever"—only sad, sweet attempts to cover up its inescapably transitory nature.

But maybe it's only a transfer of terror, from your mortality to theirs. No one really loves who's not aware of dying, who isn't already dying maybe—some sort of death: boredom, poverty, suffocation, lack of all that love supplies. Love comes riding passionately to the rescue, dragging you out of that quagmire of mortality and carrying you off with a promise of excitement that could easily be mistaken for life, a new life, when it is, in fact, only another death: from which you can flee, of course, to another and another, thinking each flight an escape from mortality until some day it dawns on you that each escape is only a further entanglement with it, that you are now so entangled with mortality that there is no possibility of escape: which of course brings Walter right back to what he has always known, since he first looked up from himself into love's sad, spectral eyes.

This is what Walter is thinking about, with an odd confusion of person—"one," "who," "you," "he"—while Penny, having refound her place, reads on in *Sex Against Death*, and the TV, which Walter has turned on but not up, unreels the silent panorama of late news before his eyes: which are turned elsewhere. Having quickly examined the list of who can die—everyone, but mostly those who matter to him—he wants to rush upstairs and check on his sleeping daughters. At the same time he wants not to give in to such a sucker's sentimentality. There's nothing wrong with the girls, they're only sleeping, they haven't got a thing to do with death.

Oh yeah? thinks Walter, remembering a bedtime conversation with Janey only a week ago. He came in from Judy's room, having left his younger daughter wrapped up in her blanket and nearly asleep already, to give Janey, in turn, her ritual kiss and hug goodnight, only to find her sitting straight up in the middle of the bed, on top of her blanket and obviously nowhere near sleep.

"Do you love me, Daddy?"

"Yes I love you, honey, I love you with all my heart," he answered. And he sat down on the bed beside her and squeezed her to him, feeling her heart beating through her thin cotton pajamas. But, either unfinished or unconvinced, she stiffened her arms into the tiny space between them and pushed back from him.

"Will you always love me?"

She looked up into his face with a real question in her eyes, though Walter couldn't imagine where it had come from or why it had arrived at this particular time. He believed in children being calm and restful at bedtime, but this didn't seem to be a calm and restful line of thought she was pursuing.

"Of course I'll always love you, honey": because he meant it, because he believed it, because he didn't want to see her kept awake with restless anxiety or insecurity: "For ever and ever and ever."

"No you won't, Daddy. Some day I'll grow up and get married and move away and then you won't love me anymore."

"But I'll still love you, Janey, grown up and all."

"No you won't. Maybe I'll work on a spaceship."

"Honey, I'll love you wherever you are."

"No you won't."

"Yes I will."

"No you won't."

Yes, Walter realizes, that's what they've got to do with death: the same thing they've got to do with love, with him: everything. Because he loves his children so passionately, they can die. So can everyone else, of course, but it's not the same. Their deaths aren't connected to love, like this. Every night before he goes to bed he slips for a moment into each of the girl's rooms to lean over their beds, rearrange the covers, give them a last, gentle kiss on the cheek or forehead or hair, but just so easily, he realizes, could death also slip into their rooms, the moment he leaves, no, even while he's there. For that matter, the small seeds of death can drift through a closed door as easily as an open one—typhoid, influenza, meningitis—or may be there ripening all along—leukemia, Hodgkin's disease, brain tumor—and nothing he can do about it.

 About this maudlin line of thought, though, he does intend to do something. The worst literary trick he knows is for an author to drag the death of a child onstage to work the audience for all the cheap emotions it's possible to arouse. Most of all he hates it when it's done in the movies, where he knows he's being taken in by one of the sleaziest emotional clichés the films have ever hit upon but feels the tears beginning to come all the same. Maddening. But there are no children dying here. The children are upstairs, sleeping. Between the two of them they have never had anything worse than scraped knees, chicken pox, and the common cold. The children here are healthy and asleep and Walter successfully resists the urge to go upstairs and check on them. Death is nowhere around. Walter will check on them before he goes to sleep, as usual. Meanwhile he watches Penny, silently immersed in *Sex Against Death*, and the equally silent television set, where a film clip on the late news shows a squad of policemen huddling behind a protective metal barrier as they set off a small pipe bomb in a gravel quarry. The bomb goes off with a tiny puff of white smoke, like a firecracker. It doesn't make a sound.

CHAPTER VIII

64. An Easy thing To Manage

Halfway, more or less, through the actuarial promise of his life's span, Walter presumes to have learned a few things, among them this: that death is an easy thing to manage.

Having managed it a good many times, in various places and sundry ways, he should be in a position to know: having managed it in Dubuque and Waltham and Albany and Santa Barbara, Macon and Wheeling and Albuquerque and Walla Walla; having managed it with knives, guns, blunt objects, poisons, and even, on occasion, his bare hands; having managed it with doctors and ballplayers, waitresses and executives, housekeepers and barbers, teachers and an occasional minor politician, with men and women of every color and religious persuasion—oh the prayers he has heard uttered at the last moment!—with the wealthy and the unemployed, the active and the infirm, with wise men and fools, with sinners and, for all he knows, a saint or two: he should certainly know.

Tomorrow he will manage it in Lexington, Kentucky, with the owner of a small contracting firm: with a piece of piano wire and no more fuss or mess than usual: a demonstration, if yet another one is needed, of how easy a thing death is to manage. He will phone his victim—already he thinks of the man as his victim, though he is still a full, safe twenty-four hours away from actually being one—less than an hour before the mid-afternoon appointment he has set up by telephone, on the pretext of an urgent business matter, confirmed by the use of certain names in the construction business with which he has been supplied. He will explain that his flight has been delayed in Indianapolis because of mechanical difficulties, that he will not be able to make it till six or after, that it is important they talk today since he must take a connecting flight out in the evening, and will thus arrange for the businessman to admit him to his office after the rest of his staff has gone home for the day. Walter will, of course, already be in Lexington, making his call from a coffee shop or a corner phone booth, having arrived by rented car from Cincinnati early enough in the morning to have counted the firm's dozen employees coming in to work, just as he will count them out again in the evening, until he's sure his victim is alone. He will wish he could spend the rest of the afternoon at a movie, but movies are hard on his eyes; they do funny things to his perception and he doesn't trust them.

So he will wait, as he has often done—in a coffee shop, in a park or museum, impatient with towns like this that have wretched little parks and no museums at all—until it is time. Then he will meet his victim on schedule and sit with him in his office and stand to open his briefcase full of diagrams and reports and watch him bend over to study these photocopies Walter has made at the University library from an economics text selected at random, and finally he will take the piece of thin wire from his jacket pocket and twist it, quickly and firmly, around his victim's neck. And when he has let the dead man slump back into the swivel chair, he will roll the wire up and put it back in his pocket and, touching nothing else, gather up his papers and briefcase and depart. He will drive the easy hour and a half on the freeway back to Cincinnati, where the Society for the Study of Modernist Aesthetics will have completed the first day of its annual July meetings, and he will be aware, once again, how, just like that, a death will have been managed, so very easily.

He likes the sense of quiet with which such things can be done as much as the ease. The preferred tools of his trade are ones such as he will employ tomorrow: the thin wire, the razor-sharp knife, the chloroformed cloth, the blunt object. When the rare situation calls for a gun, he uses a silencer. He has not heard the full report of a gunshot since he left the army; noise like that makes its own mess: intrusive, disruptive. Walter surrounds his activities with silence, and he likes it that way.

And he has no reason to think, when he thinks about it, that his own death will be any noisier or more difficult to manage than this one: easier, if anything, since he will probably not be called upon to play such an active part in it.

So all in all he considers himself, on the basis of both knowledge and experience, an expert on death. From which he concludes that death is an easy thing to manage.

Life is another matter.

65. Lead On

Life is what people go home from funerals to lead. When Walter thinks of the funerals he has been roped into attending, the grieving homes where he has had to pay more than just a token visit, he sees signs of life in them all. The main thing he remembers about his high school sweetheart is the almost violent passion for life she exhibited after her father's death. He does not even remember her breasts anymore—though he remembers months of being absolutely astounded by their beauty and thinking he would never forget them, ever, for they were the first he had ever fondled—but he remembers coming home with her after the funeral to her family's cramped apartment: its tiny living room stuffed with old upholstered furniture and relatives who seemed even more ancient. They had not been back half an hour, hardly long enough to set out tea and coffee, cold cuts and cakes and sweet kosher wine, before she was insisting that he get her out of there for a while: "Take me for a drive."

    He was a little bewildered by her demand. His own family, he was sure, would have been horrified at his callousness if he ever expressed a desire to leave a scene of family mourning. But she not only asked but got her mother's ready permission—a wise woman, Walter now sees her to have been, though at the time he only thought her a dumpy little housewife from whom such liberality could never have been expected—and the pats and blessings of her relatives as they threaded their way through the crowd standing about in the living room on their way out: "Good, good. She ought to get out for a bit. Take her for some fresh air."

    No sooner were they in the car than she was climbing all over him, before he could even pull away from the curb, plunging her tongue deeper into his mouth than he had ever known a tongue could reach, pulling his hands to her breasts, to the buttons on her blouse, and then, when he proved too slow, undoing the buttons herself and pulling his hands inside.

    Finally he had managed to extricate himself and drive off, panicked that some arriving or departing relative might find them indulging in more than fresh air. But before he had the engine turned off in the wooded lane where they often parked, she was all over him again, with her blouse off and her bra unhooked.

"Hey," he said, when he finally managed to unplug her tongue from his mouth for a moment, "are you sure you want to do this now?"

That he can now perceive as one of the most naive statements of his early career in naivete: of course she wanted to do that. She knew exactly what she wanted to do: she wanted to live and she had no hesitation about showing it. Her father was dead and she was alive and even her mother and relatives had certified her right to express that fact. If there was anyone there who didn't know what to do—what it was all right to do—Walter knows who that was. But he hadn't known, back then, that death was so easy to manage. That was not a secret his family had ever let him in on. Nor did he know that, in managing it, one could be permitted to reveal how easy it was. Simply by taking one's clothes off. By now, however, he has had a couple of good and willing teachers—one of them death itself—so any slowness in catching on that persisted he could only take the blame for himself.

Slowly then, as funereal occasions arose, which they did with an undeniable regularity, he began to put together a few observations on the business of death: for example, that the whole point of following the corpse to the cemetery lay in being able to return home, after the burial, alive—and preferably to celebrate that life, that return from death, at the sort of party which someone in his own family usually staged after funerals, where crowds of relatives greeted each other with only barely repressed gaiety around tables laden with food and drink.

At times, young Walter was appalled by all this funereal gusto, though not sufficiently so to let up on stuffing himself with roast beef sandwiches and chocolate cake while the great aunts he saw only on these occasions pinched his arms and told him how much he looked like his father. Later on, still working slowly away at catching on to how the world of death operated, he began to take a more sober view of all this levity: understanding it as only a temporary respite before all these greeters and eaters had to return to the more difficult and burdensome business of life. Only then did he manage to relax at funeral feasts: to actually enjoy the paté and shrimp and the little flirtations with cousins from distant cities.

66. In the Gap

In this way he finally began to understand that all the funerals he ever attended were alike: in much the same way that all the murders he has committed are alike, though they occur in different places, with different persons, and by different means. Walter appreciates the fact that their similarity arises on purely formal grounds, as cause and effect combine to provide them with the same general shape or outline, though it is up to the individual participants or the individual occasion to fill in the details. This grants them—individual and occasion both—a sense of uniqueness, but Walter knows better by now: that the same things happen to all of us, whatever those things are. That they happen to different people in slightly different ways fools a lot of people, but not Walter, who doesn't consider himself to be like lots of people. When he finally gets down to considering this issue that the two women in his life have recently raised, he has to admit that he considers himself sort of, yes, unique.

Likewise his children, about whom he is even more determined than himself: the same things will not happen to them, whatever those things are. Walter knows, by now, what those things are and that, of course, is why they can't happen to his children.

Also he knows they will: just as they happen to everyone.

What he doesn't know is how to resolve the difference between will not and will. Thanks to that woman—he remembers her as a girl, but somewhere, he knows, she's a woman now—who first began his instruction, thanks to his own more formal and objective education on funereal occasions and his later and more intensive training on the graduate and post-graduate level, he has learned an enormous amount about the ease of managing death.

Not everything, however: there are certain deaths he knows he would not be able to manage with anything remotely resembling ease, deaths that would make life look like a breeze by comparison. There are, in fact, only two such deaths he can think of, two so difficult that he doesn't even dare approach them by name, and he doesn't believe he will ever have to confront them: children, he has already argued with the insurance salesmen who have badgered him from time to time about taking out policies on his daughters, have no right to predecease their parents—but he also knows . . . .

What else does he know?

He knows that anything can happen, and he knows that, given enough time, anything that can happen, eventually will.

He knows that there is not so big a gap as he would like between will not and will.

He knows that that gap is where he lives, which is what makes life so much more difficult to manage than death.

He knows he will just have to keep on working with death, then, until he gets it right.

He does not know how much work he has to do on life, at the same time. Or: instead of.

67. Connecting

Maybe a little bit of death in one place, he thinks a bit woozily, leads to a bit of life in another. A couple of drinks in the hotel bar with a trio of colleagues from other institutions, who ignore his apology for having missed this particular paper because he was at that other session, is all it takes to remind him, once again, that life goes on. On and on, he thinks, tuning out, mostly, their interminable discussion of a presentation he can only feel he was lucky to have missed, and meanwhile hungrily devouring the bowl of mixed nuts on the table because he's only just driven back from Lexington, has had no dinner.

As soon as he comfortably can, having accomplished the end of making his presence at the conference known, he excuses himself and retreats to his room, where he is instantly, without so much as removing his jacket and tie, on the phone ordering up dinner from room service. The bottle of white wine he surprises himself by requesting is something he can't explain, even to himself, but when the little table is wheeled in with its white cloth and single candle and covered dinner plate, when the silent server lights the candle, uncorks the wine, pours a first taste, and returns the bottle, its shoulders wrapped in a white cloth, to the ice bucket, Walter is delighted with himself for having done so. He is even more delighted that this whole ritual has been enacted as a pantomime, not a word having passed between him and the server since the first knock at his door, and only a nod, almost a bow in fact, when he hands over the signed chit with an extravagant cash tip and the young man backs out of the room.

Now, with candlelight flickering on the little table, and a blurred view of the Ohio River and the Kentucky hills beyond through the one enormous, floor-to-ceiling window in his room, Walter relaxes. He has shed coat, tie, and shoes. He sips the wine, finds it, to his satisfaction, so chilled as to be almost tasteless, and pours himself a full glass. When he returns the bottle to the ice bucket, the little cloth the waiter has wrapped it with slips to the floor, and he doesn't bother to pick it up. He is a little drunk—those two quick bourbons on an empty stomach have hit him harder than he expected—and he's tired, too, having left the hotel at five this morning. Extra efforts are beyond him at the moment, and so, surprisingly, is his appetite, which seems to have quietly slipped out of the room along with the silent server.

This sudden weariness sits him heavily down on the armless chair the server has pulled up to the table. There was some connection he was trying to make a little while ago, he remembers, between today's little bit of death and the little bits of life—food, drink, conversation—with which he's tried to follow it, but he can't seem to piece together the fabric of that reasoning just now. He lifts the cover off his dinner plate and sets it aside, an action that seems to take all his energy. Is this what he ordered, this veal . . . veal something? There is saffron rice on one side of the plate; slender spears of asparagus stretch across the other. Walter picks one up with his fingers, leans over his plate, and bites off its tip. It's cold, and it takes him a minute to realize that that's the way it was meant to be. And, he has to admit, it's quite tasty: fresh, crisp, lively. His appetite stirred somewhat, he tries the veal but finds both the meat and its heavy white sauce too rich, cloying, so he lays his fork down across his plate, returns to his wine, drinks, refills his glass, tries once again to stitch together those earlier thoughts: a little death, a little life . . . then what?

Not for a moment, even in this condition, does he believe in some sophomoric doctrine of compensation. Emerson be damned, he says to himself, raising his wine glass to the darkened window that mostly returns his own reflection to toast his far more sophisticated perception of reality, but all he can get from his glass by now is a last drop or two. To his surprise, the bottle itself is also empty: and do not think, he tells himself, that that means that somewhere else the bottle is full. The world is full of empty bottles and full ones: it doesn't mean a thing. If there's a connection, I can't connect it. Here I am, a full bottle, having just consumed a bottleful, while that contractor in Lexington is an empty one, but I do not understand the connection between except that they happened one right after the other, just like that; time, good old time, leapt straight on from one to the other, and because I did not have enough time to separate them, they actually seem to happen together, they actually seem to fit together, a bit of death and a bit of life, one in each hand, not even tugging against each other but just there.

Here. Fortunately I know which is which.

One in each hand makes it seem to Walter, at any rate, like a kind of balance, wobbly as it might be, some dizzying sort of dance. A little bit of death, a little bit of life. Turn to the left, turn to the right: balance, if not compensation. Maybe it's just the wine, he thinks, getting unsteadily up from his chair and heading for the bed that spreads its queen-size invitation in the middle of the room, but nothing feels quite in balance here. After all, he concludes, despite his attempts to balance these events, to lay the question of compensation on a scale that evens everything nicely out, there is really no such thing as a little bit of death.

68. Disconnecting

Waking up, early, in the room in which he forgot to close the curtains last night, a room unambiguously brilliant with the light of a summer morning, Walter, without even fitting his glasses to his face and sitting up in bed, has a sudden clarity of vision: Why, he thinks, I could stay here forever. Not here, exactly: this room, this hotel, not necessarily this city. But, yes, here, out here, somewhere: disappear into that sort of here and never be seen again. He lies on his side, facing the wide-open window, and says, almost aloud, "And why not?"

Others have done it, surely. From what he knows by reading the weekly news magazines, the country simply hums with the activity of runaways: men, women, and children. They drop from sight every day, fleeing jobs and creditors and spouses and parents and problems, and no one really knows where they disappear to, many of them, not the police, not the families left behind, not the investigators often hired to take up the search when others have failed. Mostly, they are simply never seen again. It's a big country to get lost in, thinks Walter, and no one knows where they go, though I doubt they can go anywhere with quite the financial resources that I have stashed away.

It's cold in this thoroughly air-conditioned room, where Walter still lies in bed with the blanket clutched to his chin. Looking out the uncurtained window he faces, he can see, even without his glasses on, what the sun says: another scorcher, just like the one he arrived in the day before yesterday, bright and cloudless and, given the humidity of this classic Ohio valley season, pretty unbearable out there. In here it's cold, however, and for once Walter's happy to be in a building where the air conditioning runs all the time, though he still has a hard time accepting, in principle, windows that won't open. A common enough practice, he is aware: no handles to pull them up or down, no cranks to wind them in or out, not even any locks, just tightly sealed double panes, and in between a defiant, unbridgeable chasm of dead air. Sealed off forever, he thinks: I doubt you could even throw yourself through one of these. From either direction, he presumes: they would never find me in here.

Not that he thinks this huge window was put in for his convenience: but, he wonders, whose? To whose advantage is it to be kept so isolated from the outside world, to be cooled all summer and warmed all winter without variation in temperature, to have no wind sweep papers off the desk, no dust collect upon the window sills? When he puts on his glasses and gets out of bed and wanders around the room he will notice how the windows are set directly into the wall, with only a rubberized seal around them on all four sides. In tornados they have been known to pop right out, sucking the room and its inhabitants along after them.

Not ready to get up yet, however, thinking instead of the possibility, remote as it might be, of not ever getting up and out again, but of settling in here—some sort of here—forever, inside some sealed and airless and sill-less window where neither the heat of the sun nor much else can reach him, not ready to see or be seen just now, at any rate, he does not reach over to the nightstand and pick up his glasses preparatory to rising, but squirms, instead, slowly around in the big bed, turning away from the window, twisting up the sheets and blankets around his naked body as he goes, until he has got himself deeply buried in the bed clothes again. He couldn't do that with his glasses on: can't see a thing now, down in the dark here, can barely breathe, for that matter, with nose and mouth firmly lodged here: a dark and airless haven where the world doesn't intrude.

Sooner than he thinks he will have to come up for air, though perhaps he'll descend yet again: and have to come up again. Again. And still he will have to come up again. And, one of these times, get up. And stay up.

69. Banking on It

For most of his fellow citizens, as still-sleepy Walter well knows, it's a terrific financial crisis to drop out of sight— how, on what, will they live?—but not for him. Thanks to a decade's work, he has a safe deposit box stuffed with cash in almost every major city in the nation and a number of minor ones as well: a triumph of security, of possibility, of—since he wants to see it like this—human ingenuity and survival. Even now he can imagine himself standing in bright sunlight on the wide, white sidewalk in front of, say, in this particular city, the Central Trust Bank, feeling the warmth of the day soaking through his skin as he digs around in his pocket for the key, sorts the right one out from an envelope full of others. It's a unique key. He likes the little talk he's gotten each time he's rented a safe deposit box, informing him that his is a unique key, that no one else has one like it, that if he loses it, it cannot be duplicated, that no one can get into the safe deposit box without it. He likes the feel of it in his hand as he walks into the bank clutching it: it's his and it's hard and it makes him aware of the sweaty hand he holds it in.

Inside the bank, leaving the sunlight abruptly behind, he finds everything unexpectedly dark and has to pause for a moment, adjusting to the light, nosing around on the threshold to familiarize himself with where he is before he's ready to proceed. Then he sees, and remembers, the stairs leading down to the vault, and moves quickly across the thick carpeting of the lobby to descend them. Just outside the vault his progress is temporarily halted. He signs the entry card, careful to use the same false name he used when he rented the box. The attendant confirms his identity. Yes, he's the same person he was before, and so is she: he even remembers her red hair and freckled face as she leads him quickly now into the vault itself, through its wide, thick door and across to the opposite wall where his box is located. She has a bank key that she turns, first, in the door to the box. Then he shows her his key and she points, silently, to the slot where it goes, but he has trouble inserting it so she takes it in her own hand and slides it in and turns it easily and the door pops open at her touch and she slides the tray out and hands it to him, still closed, but there it is now.

He's obviously enjoying this, smiling broadly now that the

box is in his hands, and she seems to be enjoying it too, standing beside him smiling. She asks if he wants to take it into a booth, so he does, and closing the door behind him, he lays the tray on the little table there and immediately pops the catch on the lid, forgetting as he does so how tightly packed the tray is, so that as soon as the catch snaps free the lid springs open and the bills, jammed in there far more tightly than he remembers, come leaping out, spilling all over the inside of the booth, over the table and chair and down onto the floor, spilling everywhere inside the booth, all green and fresh and plentiful.

70. Obviously

He wakes again, abruptly—was that a knock at the door? housekeeping already?—thinking, Where have I been?

Away, away, he realizes: far away into the netherworld of societal drop-outs where no one will know his name, no one will know what he's done or what he's failed to do, no one will know who he's left behind or where he's going next, no one will know what he's after or, especially, what's after him. No one will know where he is. No one. No one will know. Or care.

Actually, where he's been is only still here: the bed where he shucks off the blankets, sits up, affixes his glasses to his face, stands, heads for the bathroom. Stepping under the shower he thinks: Of course I know where I've been, why was I asking that? Nowhere. Where else would I have gone, have I ever gone? But why, he wonders, am I standing here under this lovely stream of hot water explaining to myself where I have or haven't gone when it's perfectly obvious to anyone, which means me, where I've been, which is nowhere: asleep, dreaming. Why, he wonders, is he then berating himself with the obvious?

It does occur to him, shortly after, while toweling off, that if knowledge of where he's been is so obvious, then it could possibly be something else he was asking of himself. But what?

And yet, he thinks, propping one foot up on the edge of the sink to examine his toenails, perhaps the obvious needs to be stated. Not to be confirmed but to be verbalized. Perhaps it's not enough that the obvious is obvious; perhaps it has to be made obvious that the obvious is obvious: which only words can do. His toenails definitely need clipping, but he puts his left foot down and lifts his right one up to check it out, too. Yep. His toenail clippers are in his travel kit, sitting right there on the bathroom counter. But he just stands there, right foot still propped on the sink, wondering about the obvious: why isn't it enough for things to just be, for the obvious to be obvious? It isn't like teaching, where one seeks to make the obscure obvious, or like that other work of his where one labors to make the obvious obscure. Or, for that matter, like a lot of scholarly writing he has seen, which only makes the obscure more obscure. This is something different: both more humble and, he suspects, more important. The saying of what could just as easily not be said, to one's self even, with no real gain or loss of information. For the sake of the words, then. But what do the words do?

In the still slightly steamy bathroom he tries out a few: "These toenails definitely need clipping." Embarrassed, he looks quickly around, not sure whether he has spoken these words aloud or just shaped them in his head. Satisfied that he doesn't seem to have made a complete fool of himself by saying what he's said to no one, in an empty room, out loud, he opens his travel kit, takes out the clippers and begins trimming his nails. First the right foot, then the left. There, that wasn't hard. He said what he said and did what he did and was where he was: obviously.

71. Presence and Absence

Still, if he decided to take off, just like that, to drop out, vanish, skedaddle, the way people do when they suddenly drop out of sight, into wherever it is they go, would he want to make it obvious by uttering words to that effect?

Getting dressed—a shirt and jacket, no tie, will do for today's stuffy conference sessions—he thinks not: with words, you are in danger of giving too much of yourself away. He stands, threading his belt through its loops, in the midst of the bright patch of sunlight that flows through the window, creating an illusion of warmth. If you're really going to go, the thing is, just to go. Words won't get you going, not very far, anyway, no further, probably, than the bathroom or the office or the conference in some Cincinnati or other. Words are much better for staying around, a way, if anything, of staying around even if you're doing a little going. Tokens of the self. Tokens of the self that others want from you: when you're not there, surely, but also when you are: because they say you're really there.

Words for presence, then, and silence for absence. You can go away into silence even if you don't go away in fact, but the only way you can go away in fact, really away, is in silence. No wonder, thinks Walter, sitting on the edge of the bed with a shoe in his hand, it's words that are wanted of us when what's really wanted isn't words but us. Words as us. Any words. Well, almost any words, so long as they're ours and not the words of others: clichés. So long as they are uttered in the spirit of presence, not as if we were not there: absently. Words to be there with, words to be here with: when we speak them we speak ourselves. For the sake of others we bespeak our presence. For our own sake also: without presence, where are we?

Nowhere, once again, he realizes. And then: just like that federal agent, shrouded in silence's cloak of invisibility, whose unspoken absence concerns Walter far more than an articulate presence would, that bespoke a who and a where.

And where would Walter, silent Walter, conferee and killer, rather be? Not here, he knows, abruptly shedding his blazer, rolling up his clean white cuffs. He'll breakfast in the coffee shop—it's early yet—schmooze and be seen, sit in for half a session, and be gone, to, why not, that other zoo, the real one.

And does, by mid-morning, in high summer heat, wandering sweatily through the almost empty grounds, passing quickly by that comic philosopher the walrus, which Penny likes to think of as an escapee from grand opera. He seeks out the big cats, but they're sound asleep, each and every lion, tiger, puma, ocelot, and leopard. He's also partial to the African antelopes: wildebeest, zebu, springbok, harte's gazelle: the silent and quick and graceful ones. In the background, a seal barks, a donkey brays in the children's zoo, monkeys chatter on their moat-surrounded island, bird cries rise from the nearby aviary, an elephant trumpets, loud and long, somewhere out of sight.

72. AT HIS BACK

When Walter arrives at the hotel's entrance late the next morning, suitcase in hand, he finds there's not a taxi available in the sudden summer downpour. He regrets not having made arrangements ahead of time, though he's never found that necessary before. The doorman shrugs: what can you do in weather like this? Walter steps outside for a moment, is wet by the time he sees there's not a cab in sight, quickly turns back through the revolving door. Just inside the lobby, he stares out at the heaviest rainfall he thinks he's ever seen. He doesn't wear a hat, never has, but thinks that perhaps he'd better start, if he can only figure out what kind of hat would suit him best. Now, however, is not the best time for considering that. Besides, he wonders, what good would a hat be? This kind of rain is like being under water: another world. Perhaps at the other nearby hotel, just a block or two west, he'd have better luck.

Halfway there and soaked through, he spots the open doorway of a large building, where he figures he can take shelter and watch the street for a passing cab, finding, as he ducks inside, still another reason for rejecting the notion of a hat: nothing that might accidentally be left behind.

Inside the tall gothic arch of the doorway, he sets his suitcase down, pleased to recognize that even in the midst of drowning he has been thinking like a professional. He removes his glasses to wipe them dry with his handkerchief, but the handkerchief turns out to be soaked through, so that when he puts his glasses back on he finds them smeared worse than before. He is not yet worried about missing his plane: as always, he has left himself plenty of time, and sooner or later a taxi will show up or he will get to another hotel or he will ask to use the phone here to call one. He does not subscribe to anxiety, though he briefly wonders, turning about toward the dark depths of the arched opening, whether, if he wants to preserve that posture, he hadn't better stop subscribing to those newspapers whose silences on the one subject he searches them for are the primary contributors to such anxiety as he has. He also wonders what to do with the dripping handkerchief in his hand: stuffs it into his jacket pocket and steps forward into a murky darkness like what he'd expect to encounter many fathoms beneath the surface of the sea.

There is something going on here. While his eyes adjust through their smeared lenses and a small puddle forms at his feet, Walter begins to make out that he is in some sort of church. There is an altar at the far end across which several figures move like slow, ungainly swimmers, and there are other figures submerged in the front rows of pews. But what kind of church he is in, leaning wetly against a stone pillar at its rear, he cannot imagine. Nothing around the altar defines it: no cross, no icons, no tablets of the law, no crescent, no idols or candles or incense, not even a hymn board. Nor can he understand what's being said up front, though he suddenly realizes that sounds have been drifting back to him all along: not English, he's convinced at first, but then he begins to wonder. Perhaps it is English after all, and he is only deluded by the harsh accents and unusual rhythms of the ceremony or the building's own echoes. He listen attentively: to gurgling, garbled noises, more like those of a violent argument. From time to time the congregation surges forward onto its feet like a heavy wave and growls angrily back at those on the altar, then settles down again, bowing its head, while harsh, guttural sounds pound down upon it.

Would they even understand me, Walter wonders, if I were to ask to use the telephone? And what sort of place have I taken refuge in here: what church, synagogue, mosque, temple . . . are there other names for houses of worship? Walter only knows enough about the world's major religions to think he would recognize any of them he might wander into the midst of, but here he recognizes nothing except the sounds of violence. He feels the pressure of its unexpected depths and begins to wonder what might happen when he's discovered lurking behind his pillar in the darkness at the rear. Human sacrifice? He wouldn't be surprised. He realizes he's waiting for flashes of lightning and great peals of thunder from outside to join the ferocious tones of the service within, but all he hears is the steady, liquid flow of rain: that and someone breathing huskily just behind him.

He waits before he turns around, waits for his anxiety level to drop down to where he can deal with whoever is there and knows even as he waits that there was no one out there when he entered, no one saw or followed him, he's done nothing here to call any attention at all to himself, nothing more is known about him than ever has been, and the newspapers remain full of the same old silent nothings: not, he knows, recalling those old parental silences, that there is nothing behind nothing. Not to be panicked into releasing his grip on either of the twin streams of time he clings so steadily to—slowing it all down as he hangs on with both hands, letting it move at his speed—not to be panicked into some sudden, jerky chronology in which his world would speed up and rush away, beyond his control, he turns slowly and easily about, an act of casual curiosity.

And is nonetheless surprised by the figure standing there, outlined by the dull haze of rainy sky through the open doorway: wearing a shiny badge and a cap with a glossy beak.

73. Other Worlds

The badge bears the taxi driver's permit number: the first three digits by classic coincidence identical with the first three digits Walter dials to contact his contact and the last three digits simply and repetitively classic: and Walter, as they cross the ancient suspension bridge into Covington and head up toward the river bluffs on top of which the airport sits, wonders, What sort of beast is this? The beast of time, perhaps, since it appears he's going to miss his plane after all: it's due to depart in fifteen minutes, and fifteen minutes is what it takes to drive from the bridge to the airport, a coincidence of time, impossible time, for which Walter credits the beast in the front seat, in whose presence Walter has watched the afternoon thunderstorm wash away the solid half hour chunks with which he had sandbagged himself against just such contingencies as this.

"The airport," said Walter, as soon as he had penetrated the murky light of that . . . church and identified the meaning of the cap and badge. And he picked up his suitcase at once, ready to step right out into the downpour.

But the driver hesitated: took off his cap, shook the water from it in a fine spray, ran one hand back through his thick yellow hair, and finally said, "In this?"

"It's just rain," Walter objected, shifting his suitcase, damp and heavy, to the other hand. The driver, he realized, watching him rub the back of his hand against a nearly hairless chin, was just a kid.

The kid, peering out the open doorway, took a cigarette out, tapped it against the pillar next to Walter, stuck it in the corner of his mouth, and lit it with a sudden flash of fire from his other hand. Walter, aghast, who had never known of anyone smoking in a house of worship, watched in silence as he exhaled a thick cloud of smoke and announced, "No, I don't think so."

The roar of the congregation splashed up again behind them. Walter, turning, saw them rising and flowing up the aisle, toward the altar. It looked to him like the final stage of the ceremony, except that where a gentle benediction might have been expected, the central figure on the altar, a shadowy presence in the distant darkness, was screaming wildly at those processing slowly toward him, raising his voice in what echoed back to Walter as a high-pitched squeal and tugging at his robes and pounding the podium. Still, thought Walter, it might be the end all the same, and soon the congregation, worked up to some high pitch of rage itself, might splash up against the altar and be thrown back, surging down the aisle toward the open doorway: where Walter did not particularly want to be found clutching his suitcase in the company of a kid taxi driver smoking a cigarette.

Just what he anticipated might really happen in this place Walter didn't know. What he did know was that though he came to Cincinnati often—it seemed to be a regular crossroads on his travels—and felt he knew the city well by now, there was always some sense, rarely so overt as this, that it was another world here. Not his. The rest of the world—the world where students paraded through his office with incredible excuses for turning in work late and children climbed on his lap to ask for help with their buttons and grown strangers dropped to the floor at his feet, no longer breathing, after some intricate maneuver of his hands— that world was his, surely enough. But this one, even though he knew well enough that the same things happened here— that people ate and screwed and killed and spoke to each other in scores of different ways—this one kept revealing itself, in little ways most of the time, never so dramatic as this, as different. And every time that revelation came, Walter wanted to be someplace else. Back in some other world: his: where, of course, precisely the same things happened.

But he couldn't remember any other world he had been in where it had rained like this, in great, heavy, solid-looking sheets of water, and where a kid taxi driver in patched jeans and a shirt with frayed cuffs, who could obviously use the money, had refused first a ten dollar tip, then a double fare, and finally a flat fifty dollar offer before finally confessing, as he rubbed out his cigarette against the stone pillar both of them were leaning up against by then, "It won't start."

74. Time's Winged Chariot — I

It wouldn't start. At Walter's persistent urging and with the help of a ten dollar advance tip whether it started or not, which the kid took with a shrug that reminded Walter of his own, they fled out into the rain just ahead of the congregation recessing down the aisle like a flash flood. In the aging Plymouth that wouldn't start, which the young driver informed him died even in light showers, Walter wondered about their intentions: he hadn't been able to make out their expressions as they crested down the aisle toward him, had not paused in the rain to look back, and once in the car, its windows had steamed up so quickly there had been no chance to see what happened to them: whether they had drained away or were still splashing around out there.

They are still out there somewhere, Walter thought: after all, this is their city. But he did not know what they might be doing out there: going back to work, stopping for coffee, lying in wait for him, shopping at the supermarket, devouring their children. Anything can happen here: it is a different world, just like his own. Walter has read enough science fiction in his perambulations through the various sub genres of twentieth century literature to know that that is exactly what men expect to find out there in space, on other inhabited planets: different worlds, just like their own. Worlds where you suddenly find that things you would never have taken to be human beings—not any more than you would take a string of symbols on a printed page for human beings until they, too, suddenly came to life as characters—are busy doing the same sorts of things that human beings have always done. Just like in Cincinnati. But in this depressing downpour, which was about to make him late for his plane, Walter was in no mood for cataloguing those things that human beings have always done. Suffice it to say that anything was possible.

"Anything is possible," Walter mused aloud.

The driver, apparently taking this as a hint intended for him and attempting to justify his advance tip, tried the ignition. The car started at once, and the defroster quickly cleared the windows, so that Walter could see that there was no one out there, nothing but the ominous congregation of thunderclouds unleashing itself loudly, messily, upon them. Nothing but a last half hour before plane time, into which Walter persuaded the kid to drive, taking various unfamiliar byways to avoid the risk of stalling out again on the freeway, meeting the predictable stop lights and traffic, until at last Walter climbs out of the taxi at the very minute his watch tells him his plane is to depart, leaving the kid in the front seat shrugging his shoulders and folding several tens into his wallet.

In the waiting room to which he dashes, suitcase banging harshly against his leg, Walter finds another youngish man waiting with a similar shrug, leaning back against the metal railing as he watches Walter run down the long concourse toward the departure gate. Walter pauses, panting, in front of this neatly attired stranger, whose thumb gestures back over his shoulder toward the observation window, through which Walter can see the Northwest jet slowly swinging its nose away from the boarding platform and out toward the runway, can hear the whine of its engines: "Too late, we missed it."

There is, Walter realizes, no accent at all to this voice he hears: nothing of Cincinnati, nothing that is not Cincinnati. Nor is there an out-of-place hair on this man's head to indicate that he, too, has been running to make the plane, or a wrinkled jacket to show that he's been out in the rain. I have a suit just like that, thinks Walter, setting his suitcase down to brush his hair back from his face and wipe his rain-smeared glasses again with his soggy handkerchief, wondering just why this fellow is really standing here, calmly, almost as if he's been waiting for him: only a shade darker, and I would never choose a tie like that. And he is not so young as I thought: there is a kind of unrivaled absence of emotion in his face, he is probably within a year or two of my own age. And Walter, thinking of his age, remembers that he does, in fact, have a tie just like that, which his mother sent him on his last birthday. He has never worn it.

Smoothing its maroon and grey stripes against his white shirt front, the stranger suggests a Delta flight that will enable them to make connections at O'Hare, not so fast as the non-stop, but Walter, who has been considering precisely that alternative himself, shrugs, picks up his suitcase, and falls into step beside him.

75. Time's Winged Chariot — 2

It is raining heavily when his plane takes off from Cincinnati, heavily and steadily. Dark clouds beneath them over Indianapolis indicate the same weather there, and at Chicago, where he has to change planes and where the stranger who has sat silently beside him winks at Walter as they disembark and then quickly disappears in the crowd, the rain is so heavy that lights are on everywhere, even in mid-afternoon. Departures are already hours behind schedule, his own included. By the time he's finally off the ground again, violent thunderstorms are battering Milwaukee and the captain reports that tornado sightings have closed Minneapolis. Tornado activity keeps them away from Des Moines and Omaha; St. Louis and Kansas City are shut down by dense fog.

Walter finds himself aloft in a world of visibility zero, ignorant of where he is, wondering how long they can stay up, how far they'll have to go before they can come down again. He doesn't want to spend the night in Salt Lake City or Philadelphia, but from what the pilot says, the area in between, which is a lot of the country, doesn't appear very promising.

Up here, however, it doesn't look so bad: sunset and voluminous clouds billowing up under them, only their dramatic heights and shifting colors betraying the mess below. And even down below, as it turns out, there are some accessible spots, though they are not spots that Walter has ever had it in mind to visit. Since it's not Walter's choice, however, they do descend from time to time: to Green Bay, Duluth, Sioux Falls, all of them fading into the darkness that falls through already dark clouds. From the vantage point of their airports, from the inside of an airplane in which most of the other passengers seem to be comfortably asleep, Walter doesn't think he can tell one of these cities from the other. He can't, and when they take off from Duluth with a promise of improved conditions only to land at Sioux Falls in the face of a newly dismal forecast, he might as well be back where he started from. He is, in fact, in the same place all along, as the same smile on the face of the same flight attendant filling his same coffee cup all the long evening assures him. But the same place is not the place he wants to be.

I have been, it makes him think—as the loud speaker in the coach compartment offers a vaguely worded promise that they are heading, at last, toward home—in the same place too long. And if you are too long in the same place, sooner or later, someone is going to find you there. Someone you will not recognize at first, but someone who has been devoting a lot of time and effort to looking for you, is eventually going to sit down beside you and say, "Ah, here you are."

This is what he knows: if you know both that you have been in the same place too long and that if you continue to stay in that same place you are going to be found out there, and if you still remain in that place, knowing what you know, then it must be because you want to be found out there. Presence is the key to the self: here I am, therefore here I can be found.

Found by whom? Everyone, anyone: myself, among others. Even Walter doesn't know which discoverer he worries most about: himself or others. He does suspect who's looking harder.

And so what he knows, as the plane comes down at last on a runway he has been assured is the runway he has been wanting to come down on for a great many hours now—though as far as he can tell it looks like every other runway he has seen tonight—what he knows is, that it is time to think about being someplace else.

All the same, he is thankful to find, as he disembarks into the familiar airport, that he is not someplace else, that he is home, or almost home: where it's only raining lightly and visibility, he finds—as he peers out the exit doors into the night before stepping into the phone booth to call Penny to come and pick him up—is considerably improved.

CHAPTER IX

76. NOT JUST YET

Back home, as the months go by and the fall semester returns Walter to his old activities, he can't get Dora's interest in what he knows about himself out of his mind. Not that she's a nag: it's the idea that nags at him, more than he cares for, though just now his attention is elsewhere. He lies very still with his cock inside her, not moving. If he moves at this point it will be all over, and Walter is not ready for it to be all over, not only because he has been enjoying it so much but because he knows, they both know, that they may never do this again. Oh, they can do it again this afternoon, as many times as they can manage it over the next couple of hours—as a result of which a part of Walter is more than ready to get it all over with right now so they can rest a bit and then begin again—but after this afternoon it seems likely they will not do this again.

Therefore Walter does not want to think about what will happen, or not happen, after this afternoon, because when he thinks about that he thinks about the reasons why they will probably not do this after this afternoon, and those are the same reasons why they should not be doing this this afternoon and should never have done this for the first time, and when he thinks about all that he feels tense and on edge and ready to explode and have it all over with, so that all this will be past and they will not be doing it anymore and he will not have to be thinking about it, and the reasons for not doing it, anymore.

Actually, he prefers to be thinking about what they are doing right now, about the way her mouth clamps to his neck and her body presses with a kind of absolute tightness against his, about her hard little ass which he clutches with his right hand and her small breasts, which he can't even feel in the absent space between their bodies, though he can feel the pressure of her hard nipples against his chest. But this sort of thinking begins to edge his body into motion, toward a finish he most surely desires but . . . not yet, he tells himself, not just yet.

No, actually he would rather not be thinking at all but simply moving. Simply and purely moving. Purely and briefly. All too briefly. Not yet. Thinking, on the other hand, postpones this motion that will be all too brief because they have already postponed it all too long, touching and mouthing, opening and entering, tongueing, rolling, moving and stopping, moving and stopping. Stop: the pressure of her hand on his back stops him. It's amazing how fast he's learned these little signals, for it's not the pressure of her hand on his back that stops him but his knowledge of what that pressure signifies: not yet, not yet. Thought suspends action. Then her long fingers slide down the small of his back and over his ass and pull him closer, deeper: saying now, now. Thought begins action. He begins to move, feeling her begin with him

    Now he cannot say whether he is thinking or not thinking.

77. Now and Again

After the second time, they lie side by side on their backs, breathing heavily, a few inches of wrinkled purple sheet between them, the cool spill of air from the room air conditioner mounted high on the opposite wall washing over them. At first its steady hum is the only thing active in Walter's consciousness, but after a short while it's joined by other sensations—the sweat trickling down his belly to join the other liquids with which they've anointed each other, the sight of her still erect nipples, big as the first joint of his little finger—and at last by thought.

I want to do it again, he thinks, I don't want to do it again.

Rolling over on her side and seeing him looking at her, Dora says, "Pretty flat-chested, huh?" She has said that, or some slight variant, as she does every time they come together like this, a couple of times already since the moment when they closed her apartment door and immediately began touching each other.

"Pretty beautiful," murmurs Walter in response, placing a hand over one of those breasts he adores—the left one—and feeling its nipple tickle like a finger against his palm. This is as much conversation as they have engaged in since entering the apartment because for most of the past hour they have had their tongues in each other's mouths and what they could think of to say, they have said before they got here, in Walter's office, in Walter's car: we should not do what we both clearly want to do, we should do it but only this once more, better not get started again, better get it out of our systems, someone will find out, no one will ever know, I want you, I want you. At some point they found themselves beyond talk. Now they seem to be returning to words again. Dora, at least.

"Your wife has bigger breasts."

"I wasn't doing a comparative study, I was making love with you."

"But she does," Dora pushes on: "You like breasts, and she has much better breasts than I do, doesn't she?"

Walter objects, sluggishly, abstractly: "Bigger is not necessarily better."

It is all true: Penny does have bigger breasts than Dora,

Walter has not been doing a comparative study, he likes breasts, and no, as everyone knows, of course bigger is not necessarily better. And Walter has begun thinking, vaguely, of his wife: this is the first and only time in this or any city where they have lived together that he has gone to bed with someone else. And as he knew before, as he has been thinking with some irritation during, and as he is fully aware now, afterwards, it is not a good idea. Was not. Has not been. He does not like the idea that Penny might find out, though he knows that is highly unlikely—he is on enough committees this year to have meetings as alibis for almost any afternoon, since it is at meetings that he mostly spends his afternoons anyway—and probably no real threat to their marriage anyway. He does not like the idea that others in the department might find out, though that also seems unlikely since Dora is no gossip, has no close friends there with whom she might be apt to exchange confidences.

There are other things he does not like, too, such as the pressure Dora might put on him when the question of her future in the department arises, though they both know that future isn't up to him and he's sure she isn't the kind of person to take advantage of their relationship. Neither does he like the idea that all these possibilities exist whether they ever do this again, on another afternoon, or not. Suddenly he wants very badly to be at home, which up till now has been, for many years, in this city, that center of his existence from which he has not let himself be distracted. But at the same moment he becomes acutely aware of the tickling sensation in the center of his right palm coming from the nipple against which his hand is still firmly pressed.

"Do you really like it?" says Dora, laying her hand on top of his.

For answer, because he really does like that thick, sensuous nipple against which she is now rubbing his hand, because he really does like breasts and is delighted to discover that size is of no importance, because in spite of all his mental reservations he really has enjoyed what they have been doing this afternoon—enjoyed the strength and hardness of her body and her way of squeezing him tightly from within, where he wants to be again every bit as much as he wants to be somewhere else—he slides his head over toward her and takes the other nipple firmly between his lips. Then she does something no one has ever done to him before. She puts her hand in his crotch and begins to run her fingers around through all the heavy, stickily-drying juices there, back and forth through the tangled wetness of hair, and around his scrotum and moistly down the inside of his thighs. Walter is not wholly sure that he likes this—partly because he knows that sooner or later her wet, sticky hand is going to plant itself sloppily somewhere else—but he is sure he likes the feel of her dripping fingers sliding up and down the length of his cock now, up and down, up and down its slippery thickness as she pulls him toward her one more time.

The last, he thinks as he descends, for the third time, into that unthinking darkness. Probably the last, but what do I know?

And for the moment, indeed, he knows nothing: nothing of what is possible beyond what is, nothing of what might yet happen despite both their better knowledge, their mutual agreement: nothing of Dora, really, nothing. And of himself?

78. Self Knowledge

As to himself, what he can't seem to get out of his mind is Dora's argument that she knows more about him than he does himself. Or was that his argument? He suspects that there are probably several people around who know more about himself than he does: Penny, for that matter, who, in spite of what she says, has probably forgotten more about him than he's ever known.

He remembers Penny looking at him on their anniversary several years ago, leaning forward across the candle-lit table in the glass-enclosed restaurant at the top of the hotel, staring at him across her *sole bon femme* and saying, not for the last time, "Walter, sometimes I think I don't really know you at all."

He can't recall how he replied. What can you say to something like that? A woman you've lived with intimately for years, who has seen you day and night, sick and well, bad moods as well as good, habits and hopes, friends and family, who's heard you both serious and silly, who's taken you over and over again deeply into herself, suddenly tells you she doesn't know you at all.

Perhaps no reply was called for. Or perhaps, Walter sees now, if he knew himself better, then he would be able to help others to know him. But then, perhaps, they wouldn't want to.

Ah, now he remembers. What he answered was: "But I'm no mystery." And he meant it, though a considerable portion of what he's done has become the stuff of mystery to others. And that, given what he hears, or rather reads, or in fact doesn't read, these days, is itself mysterious: a mystery to him. What's going on? The *Times*, in a back page article on Columbus Day, reports that there is nothing to report on an ongoing investigation into a nationwide series of presumably connected murders; its sources remain anonymous. *Newsweek*, the week after Thanksgiving, does a feature on "Great Unsolved Murder Cases of the Century," listing the same investigation in its "Top 10" sidebar, including a photo of the still-unnamed federal agent assigned to his case, with the face so effectively blurred that Walter can't tell if it's a man or a woman, but saying nothing about the case in the text. And why a picture, Walter wonders, that doesn't picture anything? What about this great talent, as it was once reported to be:

is it a talent mostly for concealing itself, turning itself into a mystery while it goes mysteriously about its business, creeping like some night thing—dare he think it?—ever closer? But it doesn't obsess him; he treats it like one of those unscratchable itches in the middle of one's back, learning, mostly, to ignore it, though how he manages to do that is a mystery to him.

Yet he isn't really interested in being a mystery himself: not to himself, not to others, at least not to the others with whom he's so closely linked. Perhaps, he thinks, it's only a matter of achieving further self-knowledge. But so much work. And for what? There is much to be learned about the self, he's sure, that is not worth learning.

79. A Brief Visit

Ditto for other folks: though Walter, with a chance to stop over in his old home town on the way to a conference in Atlanta late in the winter, almost spring, decides he will take the opportunity to look in on the matter of his grandfather, an act of curiosity more than duty. Walter has two grandfathers, both of whom he will visit on this trip: one in a cemetery and one in an old folks home. He visits the first first: out of affection and familiarity, because that grandfather, his father's father, was the grandfather he knew as a grandfather while he was growing up: the grandfather who took him fishing, taught him how to whittle, let him practice driving on his old Ford when Walter's father grew sharp and impatient about what Walter was doing to his new Buick. That was a grandfather, as Walter's respectful nod at graveside indicates. And here is his father, too, taciturn as ever, in the very next plot. But what am I doing here? he wonders. Flowerless, wordless, he has no idea how to address the dead. He doesn't mind carrying his meaningful dead with him, but these token visitations to the spot where they have supposedly been put to rest are another matter altogether.

Nothing, however, is more another matter than visiting his mother's father: that "other" grandfather whom Walter hasn't seen, he's sure, a handful of times in his life, has never even heard called "Grampa" but only referred to as "your mother's father" by his father or "my, uh, father" by his mother.

Whatever the old man's done to warrant such semi-ostracism Walter still doesn't know: only that in earlier years, whenever he asked, after one of those rare and brief visits, why he didn't see more of that grandfather, his father always said. "Because he's not a nice man," while whenever he brought the subject up in more recent times, his mother always closed it off with, "Don't speak to me about that man": for which reason Walter has chosen not to let her know he's in town, to make this visit entirely without her knowledge. Whatever it was the old bastard did, Walter can't see that it makes much difference now that he's ninety six years old, in poor health, and tucked harmlessly out of the way in a home for the aged.

Even at the home Walter finds the old man tucked away: six floors up in a ward for the chronically ill. Like the family skeleton, thinks Walter, riding up in an elevator that moves as slowly as the residents he saw making their cautious treks across the lobby: the crazy ancestor secreted away in the attic. But why have they conspired to keep him at such a distance, Walter wonders, not only out of sight but even out of conversation? The elevator creaks slowly upward, the ancient groans of its passage revealing it to Walter, despite its modernity, as a prop from a Gothic novel. This is ridiculous, he thinks, as it grinds slowly to a halt several inches out of line with the door at the top, what danger can he possibly be to anyone, now?

The elevator doors start to open, then stick after only a few inches. He pushes the "Door Open" button on the panel, starting them again, but they stick just as quickly. Finally he leans into the opening and shoves them, until at last one of the doors gives and slides smoothly open all the rest of the way. The other remains stuck. And exactly what is it, wonders Walter, stepping out, puffing slightly, that I want from him now?

I know, I know, he answers himself, looking up and down the hallway: I want to know what he's doing up here, I want to know who he is, I want to know what's been going on. Or maybe, he thinks, I just want to know what I want to know.

What makes him think this old man can help him, he isn't sure, but all the same he gets directions from the nurse's aide stationed at a desk near the elevator and heads down the long hallway toward the ward. More a ramp than a hallway, he feels it sloping sharply away beneath his feet as he follows it. Your traditional crazy attic, he can't help thinking, though he can readily see that it only slopes like this because it connects two buildings whose floors aren't level with each other. A nice touch all the same, he acknowledges.

As is the fact that the ten old men in the ward all seem to him to look alike—frail bodies nearly invisible beneath the sheets and shiny skulls gleaming through sparse strands of fine white hair—so that it takes another nurse's aide to point out his grandfather: whom Walter's sure he wouldn't have known even if they'd all looked different. But he's the only one not in bed. He sits in a wheelchair instead, next to a pair of wide French doors that are opened, on this almost springlike day, onto a small sunporch. It's the most pleasant vista Walter's seen in the home, but no one's on the porch, and when Walter crosses over and introduces himself to his grandfather and suggests they move out there where they can talk in private and in the sunshine, the old man refuses with a terse shake of his head.

"That way," he says, pointing out the ward doorway where Walter entered, and then when Walter steps around behind the wheelchair to push it, the old man reaches around and slaps him sharply on the arm: "Think I'm not strong enough?"

He quickly proves he is. Bony arms sticking out of his over-sized cotton robe, he wheels himself straight across the ward, ahead of Walter, and then, more slowly, up the sloping hallway. Walter walks beside and a little behind him, ready to grab the chair if the old man weakens and it starts to slip back. He doesn't say anything, wanting to let the old man concentrate his strength on the chair, thinking: he'll talk when he's ready.

Almost at the top of the slope, not far from the desk and the elevator, he does indeed talk. He turns the chair sideways across the hall and looks up at Walter and says, "Go pee."

Walter's a little dumbfounded and looks it, but the old man looks at the door just beside them labeled MEN, points at it, and repeats himself: "Go pee, boy."

"But I don't have to," Walter, suddenly the rebellious child he never was, starts to plead, not altogether aware of just how much he gets out before he thinks better of it, decides he's going to have to humor the old man to get whatever it is he wants from him, pushes open the door, and enters.

Inside he fumbles for the light switch as the door swings shut behind him, flicks it on after a moment's darkness, and is just in the midst of deciding he might as well try to pee anyway, as long as he's here, when he hears a scream from outside. He pulls open the door and rushes out, hand still on his fly, to see the nurse's aide standing by her desk covering her scream with one hand and pointing with the other back down the long, sloping hallway where, turning, he sees the wheelchair with the old man in it speeding away from him. Down the sloping hall it sails with hardly a sound, already beyond any chance of his sprinting after it and catching up with it: down the hall and into the ward already, and swiftly across the ward headed straight toward the open French doors on the opposite side, and through the doors in a flash and out onto the sun-porch before the aide in the ward can react. From the top of the hallway Walter sees the wheelchair crash into the low railing of the porch, tip forward, fling the old man in his white bathrobe over the edge, and then balance itself for a moment, wheels spinning in the air, on the edge of the railing, before following after him.

80. Another Glimpse

So who needs a grandfather anyway, Walter tells himself: it'll be a cold day in hell when I visit that selfish old bastard's grave.

This is ridiculous, he also tells himself: I've just killed the old man and now I'm blaming him for it.

It is ridiculous: partly because he's still sitting in the coffee shop in the lobby of the home because when he came downstairs and started out the door a few minutes ago, after what little there was to say to the people upstairs, he saw that they were still doing some clean-up work out in the street. He stirs his coffee, wondering just what he did that could have had such an impact. He arrived on the scene, hoping for a chance to clear up the mystery that surrounded this old man, and immediately the mystery erased itself: which, of course, doesn't make it any the less a mystery. Is there something to be learned from this?

If anything, he realizes, it adds yet another mystery: the mystery of how this effect was achieved. He can tell himself with a reasonably clear conscience that, however much he expected, he didn't do anything. He tries it: I didn't do anything. Good enough, nobody thinks he did. Everybody knows he was in the john, though some are possibly wondering what he was doing in there at just that moment. Nothing, he knows. But if it isn't what he did, then he's only left to conclude that it's who he is.

Who is he?

Among other things, he is a man who had a grandfather less than half an hour ago and now no longer has one, a man who is sweating heavily without knowing it and letting his coffee cool without drinking it, a man who ought to be phoning his mother to tell her that her father is dead, but who knows that all she will say is: "Then we don't need to speak of him anymore." And he is a man who was looking for something here but doesn't want to get up and go out in the street now and look at what's there.

Also, he is a man who knows, from long experience, that he can do this sort of thing. But he hasn't known he *was* this sort of thing.

No matter how much cream and sugar he keeps adding, the coffee, when he finally sips at it, tastes not only cold but bitter.

When the waitress passes by his end of the counter, Walter asks for a fresh cup and she quickly obliges, obviously a nice person who doesn't think any the worse of him for the cup he's already wasted, though he sees no more of her than a yellow apron, couldn't say whether it's starched or stained. The yellow that passes, blurred, out of focus, in front of him, as he begins to stir cream and sugar into this fresh cup of coffee, quickly fades, and mostly what he sees is the billowing white of his grandfather's robe, all too clearly focused, as the old man goes sailing out into space over the edge of the sunporch. All he can see is the white robe ballooning out as air fills it from beneath. He cannot see the old man in it. Again and again he goes over the image, looking for someone inside it, but for all he can see it might as well be an old sheet flapping in the wind: except for how quickly, after a moment's hesitation, it plummets out of sight below the edge of the porch. Only a solid weight inside it could pull it down like that, and who could believe one of those papery frail old men, who looked as if a breeze could float them right out of their beds, weighed enough for that?

There was no one there, Walter tries to tell himself: the nurse's aide in the ward never did scream; the other old men just continued to lie silently in their beds; after a while someone came in and closed the French doors without a word. In Walter's mind the doors blow open again, rattling against their frame, and he sees a tattered old white sheet sailing away in the wind over the iron railing of the porch. Filled with nothing but air, it just drifts there, flapping lightly in the sunlight, as if to say, See, nothing in here, nothing to worry about, light as air, you never had a grandfather, you are not who you think you are.

"Who then?" breathes Walter, his face damp from the steaming cup of coffee he's been leaning heavily over.

Then suddenly the white robe plummets from view, and Walter stands up from his stool at the counter, hands hot and tingling as if he's been pushing with all his might against something, though in fact he's only been squeezing his coffee cup tightly between them.

81. A Mother's Glance

Is it reasonable, Walter wonders, to be this upset when in fact he hasn't done a thing? What bothers him is that even though he didn't do anything, the effect was exactly the same as it's been on many occasions when he did do something: and there's a dead body around here somewhere to prove it.

Walter doesn't want to know exactly where and isn't too comfortable with the fact that he's still around here himself, having abandoned the coffee shop to wait in the lobby for his mother. The director of the home has phoned her and Walter has promised to wait, though he'd rather not. She'll begrudge the time away from work and be further annoyed that Walter didn't let her know he was in town. All in all, a combination as unproductive as death, wherever they've hidden it away just now.

Though he doesn't want to know precisely where it is, Walter doesn't wholly like not knowing, either: death he's used to seeing in a specific place from which, once it's occurred, he can move rapidly away without attracting attention. Just like he slipped away from the ward upstairs, feeling that there was a lot of it around there, all of it looking almost exactly as his grandfather had looked right before he plummeted from sight.

In the lobby, where he's the youngest person by twenty years or more, Walter feels too much the center of attention. The walls are papered with flocked maroon fleurs-de-lis, matching the color of the dresses worn by many of the old women who shuffle through and the slippers favored by the old men, while Walter himself sits all in brown, from hair to shoes, on the edge of a couch covered with some sort of velvety fabric, also maroon.

He's pleased to see his mother come pushing through the front doors dressed in dark blue shoes and skirt and jacket, very businesslike, in no danger of going soft and maroon on him, looking trim, a good ten pounds lighter than when Walter last saw her, and not at all pleased herself. She looks a little taller, her plump face a little less doughy, when she's intent and busy like this, and Walter can almost mouth her first words as she hurries across the lobby to him.

"You could have at least let me know you were coming."

Since indeed he could have, there's little to say to this.

Standing in front of the couch, he nods, reaches out to hug her, accepts her quick peck on his cheek, her hand under his elbow.

"Let's make this quick," she says, steering him around the receptionist's desk and toward the director's office.

And Walter scurries along with her, happy to make it quick, not too happy with how much he feels like a child being dragged around on one of his mother's shopping trips. He'd thought he wanted to find out something about what kind of person he was in the presence of a mysterious grandfather; he is finding out that in the presence of one's parents, one is always a child. So he sits silent and attentive, a good boy, posture erect, an appropriately serious look on his face, while his mother discusses with the director what's necessary for two such adults to discuss: to which he pays an appropriate lack of attention.

He's thinking, instead, of where he's arrived at on this journey: one visit to the long dead and one visitation of death to him: as sudden and easy as he'd always known it was, and, like everyone else, he wasn't paying attention.

As his mother chatters away at the director, he knows that when this interview's over she won't have nearly so much to say to him, particularly about his grandfather, dead or alive. She will stand in the lobby trying to define the details of his stay.

"I'm on my way to a conference," he tells her. She already has one hand against the heavy glass door, but pauses to give him a funny little look, forehead furrowed.

"You don't want to see your brothers and sisters?"

"I didn't make this trip for family or I'd have brought Penny and the girls. I made it for me."

She shrugs, looking like she's beginning to sag a little: practical and efficient so far but beginning to wear down. But then she straightens and leans into the door, pushing it half open: "I've got to get back to the office."

"It's all right, mother, I have to be at the airport soon."

"I'm sorry, Walter, I haven't got time to drop you."

It's all right: Walter doesn't want to be dropped. He has other things to do: he has to go on to Atlanta to spend the night in the hotel room he won't check out of when he leaves for New York tomorrow morning.

82. A Busy Season

For Walter it has been what his brothers and sisters would call, if they were dealing with a similar rush of activity in the family business, "a very busy season." What's just happened emphasizes it, but Walter is at a loss to explain it. He knows what makes for a busy season in the soft drink business, he's been there: party time or hot weather, it's as simple as that. But what accounts for a run on murder?

    He's been there, seen the statistics on that, too, in the daily papers and weekly newsmagazines, where he sees most everything: lunar charts, weather graphs, economic indices. He knows how the turning world twists up human biorhythms, thermostats, and pocketbooks onto its spindle, flinging helpless men and women into the streets to commit unspeakable acts of violence. But he neither sees himself as helpless nor believes he commits true acts of violence. What he does he does through knowledge, forethought, and choice: professionally, not at the whim of earth's odd forces. And this year he possesses, when he acts, the same dispassion as last year and the year before, when he acted far less often. No feelings of anger or passion disturb his concentration or alter the steadiness of his hands when he acts: not before, not during, not after. Not ten years ago, which is the last time he can recall such a flurry of activity, and not today.

    Today he only wants to kill and be quick.

    Tomorrow is Janey's birthday, and he's promised her he'll be home for her party in the afternoon. Promised to show the films he's already borrowed from the public library on the projector he's already borrowed from the University's Media Services department. Promised Penny and promised himself, too. And he's sure he'll be there: Walter is a man who keeps his promises.

    What he isn't sure of, given the speed he'll have to act with now, the tight plane connections he'll have to make, all the squeezes of time he's usually so careful to avoid, not liking to feel rushed, not wanting time to nudge the hand or mind he concentrates on keeping steady, is why he didn't just turn down this job and stay home. It wouldn't have been the first job he's turned down, nor would the refusal have created any problems. The level at which he's worked over the past decade has pretty well established the level at which he's willing to work, the number of jobs he'll take or turn down, but suddenly, now, without even realizing it at first, he's working more than he has since his first years in the profession. And as if his willingness were making itself known, the calls for his services have been coming more and more frequently, a new one sometimes awaiting him when he phones in to report on the completion of the last one.

There are various possible explanations he can think of: his employers are advertising their services more widely, for example, or the number of professionals like himself has dwindled, so that everyone left is now busier than before, or he is in demand simply because he's better than anyone else.

Or, he considers, it is not the world that is having a busy season, not the usual manipulations of supply and demand, but only he himself, Walter Job, who is having a busy season.

Almost, he thinks, as if the more active he suspects his pursuit is becoming, the more active he himself becomes. Could it be charted? Maybe so: for years—he can count them—with no sign of pursuit, the level of his activities held more or less steady. Then, abruptly, pursuit appeared, or so the media reports—he's certainly seen no signs of it himself—and subsequently so has an increased level of activity on his part. Is there a causal factor operating here? No, he admits, nothing relates to the reality of pursuit, only to signs of pursuit: perhaps they—he, she, it—are no closer than before.

But I am, he thinks: I am close to setting a record this year, when there's not even any reason for keeping count. I am going to come close to missing my daughter's birthday party tomorrow. Right now, even, I am cutting things very close indeed. He looks down at his watch as he steps up onto the sidewalk out of the subway station, looks up then at the lights beginning to flick out on the fourth floor of the building across the street, and hurriedly steps into the intersection at the very tail end of the traffic light, listening to the taxis lined up there angrily revving their motors for the charge.

He is, as he says, getting very close indeed: though he doesn't know to what.

83. Coming Close

It's close to six o'clock when Walter pushes the twelfth floor button on the elevator's panel and then quickly steps out of it into the small, marbled, first floor foyer of the office building. Behind him the elevator doors close swiftly and smoothly, and the old-fashioned arrow above them shows it rising slowly towards the top floor: not to be summoned back to reveal its contents, Walter presumes, until morning, which is time enough. He will wake early back in his hotel room in Atlanta, where he has already spent the previous night, and get up as if there had been no day trip to New York at all, and shave and pack and take the limousine to the airport; he will breakfast aboard the plane that will get him home in time for Janey's birthday party at noon. Perhaps he'll arrive while Penny is serving hot dogs and potato chips to half a dozen little girls from around the neighborhood. Hopefully he'll get there before she's begun to light the candles on the cake. It'll be close, but not too close.

He exits through the swinging glass doors of the office building not even close to worrying about being recognized: his medium height, thinning brown hair, metal-framed glasses over brown eyes, his smooth and ordinary features in combination with his neat and ordinary clothes, brown suit and shoes, tan shirt, undistinguished tie, all so close to looking like anyone at all that he's not likely to come close to resembling anyone in particular. Passing the doughnut shop next door, he looks in the window and sees the waitress behind the counter filling a thermos of coffee for the elderly night watchman who stands by the cash register, ready to go on duty precisely at six. It's that close.

And close is what counts, thinks Walter, flowing back down into the subway with the evening crowd: and not, as they say, only in horseshoes. How about cutting things close, playing it close to the vest, being close to someone, or, worse yet, closing in on something: a notion that itches him briefly in an unreachable spot in the back of his mind before he just as quickly reaches around there with his well-practiced habit of ignoring it. How about not even being close?

He takes the first train that comes along, not bothering to

look up at the lighted destination signs. The last one to enter the car, he feels the sudden rush of air as the doors close behind him and thinks: close may say it all: close shows good timing, a willingness to accept the risks, full participation, thoughtfulness, action, care, precision. Close is well done.

He rides, standing, just three stops, leaves the crowded car as soon as the doors hiss open and climbs at once to street level where, not bothering to look about to check his location, he flags down the first taxi that comes by and quickly climbs in. The taxi plunges away into traffic even before Walter has slammed the door and finished asking to be taken to LaGuardia: almost, he's left feeling, while he's still got one foot on the sidewalk. And that's close.

Not to be close, on the other hand, signifies a certain failure of judgment: too much time allowed, time to get sloppy in; or not enough time allowed, not enough to get the job properly done. Not to be close is to be too open, too loose, easy, unstructured, wide of the mark, distant, distracted, abstracted, off target, messy, out of things, careless.

Walter watches with admiration the way the taxi driver moves in and out of traffic, changing lanes with speed and precision, darting unhesitatingly into the gap between two cars and then quickly out of it again and into the next advantageous opening. He wants to tell the driver that there's no real hurry, that he has the ride well-timed for making his plane, but he knows there's no sense saying anything of the sort: this taxi driver not only knows how to play it close, but, like every other taxi driver whose cab Walter has ever been in here, and unlike the kid in Cincinnati who hadn't quite fit himself to the job yet, she drives as if there were no other way.

So Walter relaxes in the back seat as they hurtle across the Tri-Borough Bridge into the tangled bi-ways of Queens, respecting the professional bond between them: a closeness arising from how they do what they do. Walter studies the face that stares back at him from the identification photo on her permit: long dark curls springing wildly out from under her cap, coarse features, a wide nose and heavy jaw: a face he'll never see again once he's paid his fare. Yet in some ways, he thinks, I am closer to this woman than to my own wife.

That being the case, he wonders, what does it really mean to be close?

To whom or to what, he wonders, am I really close?

He also wonders whether this sort of wondering is likely to lead him closer to . . . anything: anything he wants to be led closer to. And then, at the airport, he tips the driver so extravagantly that she actually climbs out of the taxi to thank him, stands there on the street side staring across the car roof at him, before he turns away toward the building, as if to memorize this face that has suddenly so far exceeded her expectations. He shakes his head a little foggily, haranguing himself for his extravagance, as he heads toward his gate: too close, too close: too wide of the mark and too close at the same time.

84. Taking Notice

If one of Walter's goals is to see how close he can come, another is not to be seen too closely himself. Observing every detail, he'd rather pass through life unobserved himself. If he takes notice of every birthday and anniversary, every class hour and committee meeting, all the memos and appointments cast in his direction, every charitable request and uncharitable complaint, every demand for assistance and every plea to be left alone, every need expressed or unspoken, every change in appearance or weather, every mood, every meal, every item of news, gossip, memory, imagination . . . if, in short, he takes notice of everything, then perhaps no one will take notice of him.

    He doesn't, of course: who can? But he tries to come as close as possible, given his awareness of his own shortcomings: that he does not remember people's eye color, hair style, or family history; that while he's enjoying the meal he cannot, for the life of him, recollect, as his hostess seems able to do with such relish, the wines and delicacies she served the last time he and Penny were over, a year or more ago; and that his accuracy in judging other people's emotional states, especially the people he's closest to, is as often as not a little off the mark.

    It's hard work. But he never wanted to be noticed as the one who's paid so little attention to the drift of the conversation that he's still smiling while all the others at the table have assumed looks of concern; who's standing alone in the middle of the intersection when traffic begins to move because he didn't notice when the "Don't Walk" light came on; whose socks don't match, who applauds between movements of the string quartet, who enters the lecture hall late, causing others to shift around in their seats to make room for him. Walter has taken great pains not to be caught in the center of everyone's attention: noticing the things that have to be noticed so that he can take his place, unnoticed, among them.

    "Walter," he wants people to say to him after a party at which he and Penny thoroughly enjoyed themselves, "were you at the party the other night? I don't recall seeing you there."

    It doesn't happen that way, of course: others take more

notice of things—some things, anyway—than Walter does. But he tries. He sits quietly in the departure lounge reading *The New York Times* until his plane is called. He's checked to make sure his fly is zipped. He moves expressionlessly along the line, boarding pass in hand for the gate attendant, letting the businessman in front flash her the big smile, the one behind call her "Honey" in a soft, Georgian drawl. Having used the toilet at the airport to avoid being seen lurking up and down the aisle during the flight, he takes his window seat near the middle of the coach compartment, crosses his legs, folds his newspaper open to the editorial page, latches his seat belt. Only then, feeling safely anonymous as he reaches awkwardly upward to flick on the overhead reading light, does he notice who's sitting next to him.

85. Prophecies

Fear of pursuit is an interesting phenomenon. Walter remembers an optometrist who, while examining him for new glasses at age seventeen, announced that he'd be wearing bifocals at forty five. Although he dismissed this prophecy at the time with the cavalier disregard of youth for the future, Walter has thought of it every couple of years lately when he's had his eyes refracted, every couple of months, even, when he's stopped in at the optician's to have his frames adjusted. Less of it, in fact, than of him: the optometrist with such assurance about his powers of prediction. Walter can no longer visualize the man, can't recall whether he's tall or short, whether he wears glasses— perhaps, by now, wears bifocals himself—doesn't know whether he's still practicing, still alive. But he does have a strong vision of that optometrist waiting for him out there in the future, and not just vaguely in the future either, but at a specific point which Walter, if he keeps on moving into the future, will have to pass whether he likes it or not. A ghost from the past—an invisible ghost, since Walter can no longer picture him—who has leapfrogged Walter's present to lie in wait for him in the future, there is no avoiding him: he knows more about Walter Job's future than Walter Job does.

Is that something to be afraid of? Walter doesn't generally fear pursuit. Other prophets have pursued him as well. His grandmother, long dead: "You'll be an important person when you grow up, Walter." His mother: "Don't do that, Walter, you'll be sorry." Even his father, otherwise usually silent: "Walter, if you can just remember to change the oil regularly, it should last forever." Like the fading images of his relatives, their predictions lurk around many of Walter's daily activities: too vague and inaccurate to constitute a menace, as Walter, who has always changed the oil on schedule, knows. Their pursuit is blundering, hopeless, a mixture of dim threats and promises of no more substance in his present or future than his teacher's comment on his third grade report card: "He shows no respect for books." In fact, he loved books, even then; that's why he scribbled in them.

The optometrist's precise prediction, however, pursues him with the solidity of fact: so confident that it can simply take up a comfortable position and wait knowingly for the event to happen, a pursuit so precise and inescapable that it reverses the normal order of things, settling down to watch Walter catch up with it, whether he chooses to or not. And how could such pursuit as that not inspire a certain fear, a certain awe?

"Well, Walter," says the man in the next seat, who is not Walter's old optometrist—not the presence Walter doesn't need anyway to remind him of pursuit—but only an old college acquaintance, whom he hasn't seen since they roomed together as sophomores. Even before the name comes back to him, Walter remembers the farewell remark this one-time friend tossed out to him as they parted on the railroad platform at the end of spring semester: "Walter, you'll never grow up."

"It's you, Carl," says Walter a little disbelieving, as well he might: the undergraduate athlete who swam in the winter, ran the half mile in the spring, and exercised diligently morning and evening at all seasons, now sits beside him in the shape of an aging, overweight banker. Greying hair, eyes with heavy lids above and dark pouches below, thin, unsmiling mouth and smooth, sagging jowls startle Walter with the image of a man who has, indeed, grown up. Is this what he meant by growing up, Walter wonders: aware that whereas Carl probably no longer even remembers making that remark, he himself senses yet another prophecy coming alive: he feels as if, in the company of this weighty adulthood, he has been made a little child once again.

Can it be, thinks Walter as they exchange brief summaries of the past fifteen years while the plane roars off down the runway and climbs its many miles into the night sky, can it be that this man and I are of the same generation? Is this what I'm going to look like if and when I grow up? Walter wishes that, like a woman, he had a purse from which he could extract a mirror to check on whether this is happening to him yet. I am grown up, he insists: what's this fat man that I should be so upset by him?

This fat man, né Carl—Carl what, Walter still can't remember: maybe when he grows up he'll have a better memory for names, but as it is he can't even recall what prompted Carl to make that long ago crack about him. Carl is not, it turns out, a banker, grey suit and face notwithstanding, but a union organizer. All the same to Walter: a heavy, solemn citizen, wheezing out for Walter's benefit the dull narrative of his steady progress toward the grave. Walter's ecstatic to discover, as they wait in the taxi line in Atlanta, that they're staying in different hotels.

"All the same," says Carl, backing clumsily into his cab, "I'm sure we'll get together again."

They won't, of course, so why do these words sound so ominous to Walter? Because, he tells himself as he climbs into a taxi of his own, because why didn't Dora say that? Why didn't my mother say that? Why is it only the Carls who say that? The fat Carls who don't even know me.

Well, he rationalizes, maybe that is because the people who know me know they will get together with me again and so don't have to say that. And maybe, the thought itches at him, that's why he's heard no further assurances about getting together from the one person who has presumed, publicly, to know him well enough to have promised that they will soon be getting together. "Soon" is the word he scratches most vigorously at.

CHAPTER X

86. CHARACTER

So Walter is being pursued by a word, by presumption and promise, by the intangible unscratchability of language, by an itchy someone with neither a name nor physical attributes: what Walter's familiar with from his browsings in the literature of the supernatural as a wraith, but a wraith, he understands, with some tangible accomplishments to its credit. A quiet, competent wraith, the scariest kind to Walter's way of thinking. What Walter knows he only knows from the daily newspapers, the weekly newsmagazines and the evening news on television, and so far the former two have had little substance to provide this wraith with and the latter even less, which leaves him feeling like a man who's been given one side from which to determine the nature of the triangle: out of such meager information it's difficult to determine what angle of acuity or obtuseness the world is bringing to bear on you.

Walter would like to have some idea—however fictitious—of the name and face of his pursuer so that he can better imagine the confrontation they might finally have. But no one offers him the data he needs for his sense of realism. He wants to be able to see this person, to speak a name, not in order to devise a climactic scene of violence between them—his mind doesn't turn in that direction when he thinks about their coming together—but only to imagine the conversation they might finally have.

He cannot, however, imagine himself in conversation with a wraith: he is too firmly grounded in reality for that. It only yields an image of the ridiculous: himself talking to a blank wall, to an emptiness in the room, a shadow, a puff of smoke. If there's one thing he doesn't want this final confrontation to be—assuming that it has to be at all—it's ridiculous. He cannot even imagine, in order to avoid the question of name and face, carrying on a telephone conversation with his pursuer; he needs a voice to develop such a scene convincingly: deep or high-pitched, masculine or feminine, solemn or sharp. He needs, for the sake of reality, the participation of at least one of his senses.

But what little news he has so far doesn't appeal to his senses, as perhaps it's not the nature of news to do, which only abstracts what's deemed significant from the daily flux of events, which bestows no life though it certainly goes hand in hand with a lot of death. Even that is of the abstract sort: reporting the death of so-and-so, of such-and-such and age, from this place or that: never a hint of the limp or the smell of his after-shave lotion or the passion she felt for her life, though Walter doesn't stop to think that in his own associations with death he, too, has generally tried to abstract himself as far as possible from these telling little details of life.

The only detail he's ever been given is that someone—an "agent": man or woman?—with a considerable record of previous accomplishment has been assigned to work on a number of unsolved murders, believed, for reasons unstated, to be related: among them, according to the sampling in that newspaper article that so disrupted breakfast almost exactly two years ago, some that Walter recognizes as his own handiwork. For all he knows, the whole proposition may be merely a fiction, designed to frighten him away from further such activities or into some sudden, revealing action. He doesn't actually think so and can't, of course, operate on such an assumption. But unless this agent is fleshed out somewhat more—he doesn't want anything special, just the usual attributes: sex, age, size, hair, teeth, eyes, posture, dress, a few background details—he has no way of knowing how the world is coming after him: with what realities as well as what fictions.

It surprises him to realize that what he wants from this . . . yes, character, whose reality for him is limited to a construction of words in a newspaper, he would not want from a character in *Time Lapse*, that other interminable occupation of his, whose reality is also limited to a sequence of verbal constructions. And of a more substantial nature than a newspaper, he tells himself on an April night in a houseful of sleepers, when he picks the book up off his bookshelf and hefts its weight in his hand.

Walter is an intelligent, mature adult of the late twentieth century, far too much a man of his age to demand of the literature of his age that it provide him with the accoutrements appropriate to the literature of a previous age. In all the arts, he explains to his students, not just in literature, the age of realism is long past: it is the boon or bane, take your choice, of the contemporary artist to know that the constructions which art provides are just that: constructions: in a novel, constructions of words. And to think of characters as if they had some life outside the pages of the book, to speak, as used to be done, of characters so real they seem able to walk right off the pages, is to seriously confuse not only the times but the nature of art.

But it appears that what he wants for his art and what he wants for his life are two different things: right now he'd give the whole of modern fiction since Joyce and Woolf for this one character realistically presented.

Not getting what he wants, naturally, he can only conclude that life has, indeed, begun to imitate art. Either that or art has attached the nature of its constructions far more firmly to life than he'd ever realized, or thought possible. A dismal conclusion either way when he comes to examine, in the pale fire of art's reflected light, the nature of his own reality.

87. Dialogue

What kind of dialogue does he want to construct between these two characters, should he ever manage to establish a sense of their reality?

Without that reality it's hard to say. He needs to have them doing things—pacing about the room (he needs to have a room), lifting a book down off a shelf (the same book he still has in his hands?)—in order to know how they'll be saying things. The idea of voices in a vacuum only gives him a sense of the vacuum, and he wonders how you can get anything from a conversation while you're suffocating for lack of air, the air of reality.

He knows he could sit down and write this dialogue if he wanted: sit down at his desk, lay aside the book, pick up a pen. Like everyone else, he's read enough fictional conversation to have some idea of how it's done: "'Like everyone else,'" he says, "'I've read enough fictional conversation to have some idea of how it's done.'"

But no one replies. No one says, "Of course you can, you're a very skillful craftsman." No one even says "Prove it" or "Ha!"

If there's to be an answer, Walter sees that he'll have to construct the character who does the answering himself; no one's taking on that task for him. But that doesn't seem quite right. After all, this is a character who's reputed to be in pursuit of him, and if the pursuit is successful, he, Walter, is the one who will have to pay the consequences. The more real and active the character, then, the more real and active the pursuit will be. If anything, he ought to devote himself to de-realizing this character, though he isn't exactly sure how such a deconstruction would be accomplished. He suspects that it couldn't be done in any way that wouldn't involve his own deconstruction as well: destruction. This isn't just a character in a book, it's a character who exists on exactly the same plane of reality as himself. Whatever that is, he wonders, and meanwhile what did I do with that book I was walking about with only a minute ago, or did I set it down somewhere? It's so easy to lose sight of things.

After all, he only wanted to try and imagine what kind of dialogue he might have with his pursuer if and when the two of them finally meet. That shouldn't be so hard, should it? He's not sure how he's managed to get himself all tangled up like this, and misplaced his book besides, in the process of trying to figure out how to go about constructing a hypothetical dialogue on, say, the nature of the final coming together of the pursuer and the pursued. But it is hard: enough so that he considers simply abandoning the enterprise. The best reason for doing it now is to be prepared for it when it happens later. On the other hand, he's no longer too keen about doing something now that could only add greater substance to what only might happen later.

Still it's interesting: only hard, damned hard, to know what to do and what to say, how to do and how to say. And if it's hard to know what to do and say oneself, it's even harder to imagine the doings and sayings of another: especially another such as this one, behind whose long silence Walter truly has no idea what's going on. Oh, Walter knows silences well enough—as his mother used to say, he was always a quick study—and he also knows what lurks behind them. His whole ancestral line—his father and, now, both his grandfathers—could speak to that, if there were any way to penetrate their lifelong and now permanent silences. Maybe that's why he wants this dialogue with his pursuer: to let the pressure off the violence he knows that silences bottle up. And that's what he feels in the silence of his own unknowing: stifled, bottled up, breathless, in need of hearing things aired, in need of good, fresh, open, unthreatening air.

88. A Scenic Overlook

On a pleasant spring afternoon, when he has neither class nor committee—nor, any longer, Dora—Walter sits on a park bench on a small promontory overlooking his life and wonders about many things he has done. This and that, he thinks, this and that: I don't want to name them all, they're too obvious, and whatever they are, they've been repeated over and over: even to repeat them in the mind, in words, is a redundancy at this point.

Picking through a little brown bag of leftovers scavenged from the refrigerator before he drove off alone to this little spot he likes along the river, what he thinks he wants to know is: what does it all mean?

A sweet pickle, a dried-out slice of ham, a hunk of yellow cheese going white with mold, two black olives: whatever was there and about to become a loss for lack of attention, he took. What he really wants to know is: how does it all hang together?

The pickle is soggy with age, the wooden bench warm with May sunshine against his back, the river between the steep green banks in front of him smooth and glossy as oiled hardwood: looking solid enough to walk out on. A little ways upstream, to Walter's right, two young boys, playing on a sandbar on the opposite shore, do indeed seem to be stepping out onto the surface of the river, the water so shallow there, so close in color to the sand, that it's impossible to tell just when they enter it.

Walter isn't interested in miracles, however; he's only interested in the obvious—the bridge just upstream with the big red city buses crossing it—and the not so obvious—the bridge downstream, around the long curve in the river, just out of sight, where he cannot tell what is crossing now. The buses, he knows, never use that bridge: a slight difference, he realizes but still a difference. A trivial difference, he'll admit: but it's only by such bridges, with their insignificant differences, that we manage to make both sides of the river hold together.

Pulling the white fat off the edges of the slice of ham, he tallies the bridges, upstream and down, including the railroad bridges: a dozen, as far as his knowledge will carry him, which is not too far upstream: what a lot of work we go to, to make things hold together. He tosses the string of fat out toward the river, but it falls into the bushes not far below him, where its arrival is greeted by a sudden scurrying in the underbrush. Nothing visible, but he might well have known something was there, busy as the unseen bridge downstream, and flowing with life.

But not meaning, he decides, nibbling at the ham, taking experimental little nips around the edges to make sure it doesn't taste spoiled: I am not one of those people who's going to be reduced to looking for meaning in his life. No thank you. Finally he just stuffs the whole slice in his mouth and pops an olive in after it, for a little flavor.

What he's done he knows. Not everything, of course: he knows the last time he killed but not the last time he ate ripe olives. What he knows about what he knows is that it's he who's done these things: which, he's the first to admit, doesn't endow them with any special meaning, only a sense of continuity. I could easily have done altogether other things, he argues as he sets about scraping the white mold off the cheese with his thumbnail: things just as meaningful or meaningless; but if everything one does is equally meaningful, then nothing one does is truly meaningful: which is to say, full of any distinctive sense of meaning or unmeaning from which its values can derive: meaningfully or meaninglessly. Take your choice, there's nothing there.

Stripped of its mold, the pale yellow hunk of cheese tastes absolutely bland. He sniffs curiously at the thumbnail he used for a scraper: ah, that's where the flavor disappeared to.

And the only thing that holds all these things together is, he concludes, the fact that I did them: I am like a series of bridges tying together my own life, which is otherwise divided by a river of ignorance, and every time I make a new appearance a little further downstream, a fresh crossing, it makes a little more sense of my life, of what I do. Not meaning, mind you, just coherence: if it doesn't say anything else, it says it's me.

But in between, he wonders, gulping down the last of the cheese and wishing he'd brought something along to drink, to make it easier to swallow, in between these bridgings, these structured appearances in which he knows what he does: what makes it hang together in between?

89. Walter Goes to the Movies

It's like a film, he decides: each frame presents the same image as the preceding frame, with only minute variations, and a sequence of such frames, no matter how nearly identical each is, produces, set one after the other, the illusion of motion: life. From time to time there is a cut to a new and different sequence of nearly identical frames, a cut informing us that something has happened—time has passed, to save us from boredom there has been a lapse in continuity—but the same thing is still happening, as the new sequence demonstrates at twenty four frames per second.

In this sense he finds life quite like a movie: quotidian events pasted together to produce the effect of movement. From one to the next it's hard to tell that anything's happening. No matter how carefully you inspect each one, it looks just the same as the one before. But string them one after the other and keep the sequence moving steadily along in front of you, and presto: the illusion of life! Leap ahead to another sequence and discover the same semblance of progression. No one knows what went on during the gaps over which the cut has jumped: the same things as in the sequences shown, doubtless: life: the illusion of life: life without attention drawn to it: things just as significant as the ones seen, perhaps even more so for not being shown.

Suddenly, in a brief spasm of *deja vu*, it occurs to Walter that this film needs a name. He'll call it *Time Lapse*: because he remembers the rumor that once circulated—had one of his colleagues actually read it in *Variety*?—that the film rights to *Time Lapse* had been bought by Hollywood: well, not Hollywood exactly, but an independent studio in which some big Hollywood names were collaborating. For weeks there was talk at lunch with his colleagues as to what kind of movie it would make, where it would be set, who would star in it, but then interest in the subject waned and so far as Walter, who did not see a great many movies, knew, no film had ever been made of it. He understood how that sort of thing happened to a good many literary properties, which were bought and then dropped, but he also knew that even when films were made of them they often emerged in unrecognizable form and under titles which gave no clue to their original source.

Perhaps *Time Lapse* had been filmed after all. Possibly it was never released, or had only a short run, or, for all Walter knew, won a whole shelf of Academy Awards. No one might know where it came from: it could happen like that. Perhaps one night it would appear on television, the late night movie, and only after hours of watching it unfold, piecemeal, before his eyes, between commercials, would he realize what he was watching. Though he knows that the kind of movie he could see in it bore very little resemblance to the kind of movie Hollywood would see in it, still he wonders what kind of film it might make.

A film full of multitudes of characters wandering in and out, most of them playing their roles reasonably well. If one of them, particularly a minor character, plays a role badly, it's only because, in Walter's version of the film, the nature of that role is to be played badly. In that character's own film, the one in which he or she is a central character, the role is played just as badly. If it were, Walter thinks, his own film, it would be a relief when someone as adept as he considers himself to be appeared on the screen, however briefly, to play a part well.

What happens in that less capable character's film, most of it anyway, is, Walter realizes, the very stuff of the lapses in his own film, which cuts and jumps as it does because it cannot follow everyone, every moment, every thing that happens, every strand of development, the working out of every passing life, however well or badly portrayed: because, in short, it cannot really show life at all. Life lingers in the multitude of lapses, unattended to. Perhaps the lapses possess a sequence of their own, if only it could be seen, a sequence implied by all the sequences that are shown. Perhaps not. Perhaps, Walter thinks, what is seen is indeed only an illusion of life, a substructure, no, actually a superstructure—elegant or entertaining or suspenseful: whatever the director chooses to make it, within talent's inescapable limits—behind or within which the real life, which can never be seen, goes invisibly on. Like the cinematographer who fills the screen with the image of an office building, implying thereby the inexhaustible quantity of human activity that goes on behind its walls: even though those walls may only be a façade. Like the composers who argue that silences are where the music really is.

Or the subatomic physicists who explain how the photograph of the particle only proves how the real life of the particle has slipped out from our grasp and sped away.

Well, no wonder, thinks Walter: no wonder they couldn't make a film of *Time Lapse*. It would have had to consist of precisely the material that gets left out of all other films: the gaps that exist for only a fraction of a second between the separate sequences of the montage. Then, quickly, the splice is made, the two sequences sealed tightly together, as if that's the way they always were, and ever shall be; the gap disappears, and the film goes on as if it had never existed. Yet those lapses across which the cuts in the film stride, presuming to make sense by the act of omission, defining the world with an editing machine, philosophizing with scissors and paste: those lapses . . . .

Don't be fooled, he wants to say, by the scenes of sex and death played out here before your very eyes. They only seem to be what they seem to be because of everything that gets left out.

Everything, he begins to realize, has been an obsession for far too long: perhaps it's time to turn toward everything else.

Even this, he thinks: just because these thoughts, these words, occur one after the other, discrete frames of mental activity strung together on a celluloid grammar, does not mean that they make sense. An illusion of sense, perhaps. Perhaps the real sense resides in the things unsaid, ungrammatized, unthought, too ordinary to seem worthy of having any attention drawn to them: in everything else.

90. The Speed of Light

When Walter does go to the movies, it's not like anyone else goes to the movies. When he finally gets up off the bench and stuffs the paper bag, with one black olive still left in it, into his back pocket, and walks away from the river and up the street, past where he's parked the station wagon, to the nearest bus stop, and catches a bus that delivers him downtown where he buys his ticket and walks into the first theater he finds, not even aware that it's the only downtown theater left, he doesn't even know what movie he's sitting down in the dark of.

It's the middle of the afternoon and the theater is practically deserted, but Walter wouldn't know it. The same movie's been playing here all spring, and probably every moviegoer in the country has seen it at least once by now, but Walter wouldn't know that, either. Walter isn't looking at the few odd characters who lurk in his vicinity in the darkness and he isn't looking at the even odder characters exhibiting themselves flagrantly on the screen. He's looking at the passage of light as it rushes soundlessly over his head, not stirring the least breeze, and splashes without a ripple on the giant screen in front of him.

From time to time Walter turns to look over his shoulder at the pinpoint spot of white light high on the rear wall of the theater: the small, bright circle from which the light emerges, stretching itself, thinning out, expanding as it surges down the length of the theater to reassemble all its waves and particles on the screen in front in, miraculously, the shape of a rectangle. From somewhere behind Walter, cigarette smoke rises, in unpunished violation of the law, allowing the beam of light to display itself even more lucidly in mid-passage, depriving it of none of its final impact. The light hovers in the shifting cloud of smoke, not seeming to move, and Walter, who as a man of his times has some idea of the speed of light, though he could not give an exact figure just now, wonders: how does it do that?

Then he turns his full attention to the screen, concentrating as hard as he can on what the light is doing there: not on the characters, the scenery, the furniture, the colors, bright and clearly defined as all these things are, but on the way light establishes itself on the screen: trying to see through the continuum of its passage to the breaks between the frames, to isolate with his own vision the tiny segments from which this illusion of life to which he's paying no attention is constructed.

Of course he can't do it.

Eventually, eyes aching, he abandons his seat and backs up the aisle, still thinking that they have to be there, dark little lines through which even the miracle of light can't pass, brief dreamless nights separating the bright daytimes of the frames: exactly the way the world is constructed. Not to see them is not to know how it's put together: not to be granted a rest from its relentless brightness, which is giving him the beginning of a headache just now.

Movies aren't at all like life, he thinks.

Behind him, on the screen to which he turns his back as he reaches the end of the aisle and stretches out his arm toward the door, a group of armed and uniformed men batter down a doorway and burst into a large, brightly lit room packed with frightened, unarmed civilians, men, women, and children of all ages, backing hurriedly away from the force that shatters the door, but with nowhere to go. With only a moment's hesitation, the uniformed men begin to fire indiscriminately into the terrified crowd trying to shrink away from them, and abruptly all motion slows: writhing bodies barely turning, arms stretching and stretching outward against the oncoming bullets, faces contorting and slowly bursting open, waves of blood spraying against the walls and floor, against other bodies drifting downward through their red tide, all in the relentless choreography of slow motion so as to be seen and seen and seen . . . .

Walter, pushing through the exit door, steps quickly across the small lobby and out into the street where the afternoon sun slashes a bright new pain into his eyes.

91. Humpty Dumpty

Walking the bright streets well away from downtown now and watching leaves fall as sudden bursts of wind shake the treetops, Walter knows it isn't autumn. But trees are dying: dutch elm disease and oak wilt have taken root deeper than any of the local shade trees, and nothing seems able to shake them loose. Crews move slowly through the city, taking down infected elms to slow the spread of the disease: impressive monsters seventy or eighty feet high, causing the boulevards to be closed off for a day to accommodate the careful process of removal. Often, to Walter, they look as healthy as others left standing, except for their crowns, browning or already barren, and the condemning marks of red paint city inspectors have splashed on their trunks.

Soon, Walter can see, the streets too will be brown and barren, as open and unshaded as they were a century ago, as he has seen in photographs from that era, when the city was still mostly treeless prairie. Soon there'll be no protection from the hot sun the crew blocking the street in front of him is sweating away in or from the winter winds roaring in from the west: the trees won't shake any longer, but the windows will rattle. Walter sits on the low brick wall that fronts one of the boulevard's luxurious homes and watches four men, bare-chested and dripping but wearing hard hats and heavy gloves, slowly dismantling the giant elm across the street. A chain saw roars above the rumble of idling trucks. The tree comes down chunk by chunk, with ropes and pulleys as well as chain saws, as if it were an important historical monument being dismantled brick by numbered brick for reassembly at some distant location. But Walter knows they are only trying to avoid power lines, cracked pavement, damage to neighboring property, only reducing the tree to manageable pieces, and that the trucks hauling away those huge rounds of tree trunk are not delivering them for reconstruction but only dumping them at a riverside burning site. Some things you take apart you cannot put back together again, he concludes: not nowhere: this is Humpty Dumpty speaking, and I should know.

The chain saw screams, a car horn honks: orange sawhorses barricade both ends of the block, but somehow this woman in her station wagon full of kids has gotten through and now, right under the condemned elm, her car up close against the dump truck angled across the street, leans on her horn to demand passage. In the back of the truck, two workmen, waiting to handle a heavy limb being lowered toward them, stand with their hands on their hips, looking down at the station wagon, obviously swearing, though Walter can't hear a word they say.

One of the workmen climbs down from the truck, walks over to the car, and pokes his head in the open window on the driver's side. He is talking, though Walter cannot hear him, leaning one arm on the door of the car and, with the other, pointing upwards. Abruptly the honking stops; at the same instant, the roar of the chain saw also stops. No one is talking any more. The man steps back from the car, removing his yellow hard hat and wiping the sweat off his forehead with the back of a glove. The car door opens and the driver steps out, letting the door swing shut behind her. The solid clunk of its closing is the only sound in the street. As she tilts her head up where the worker is pointing again, Walter recognizes her: Sally what's-her-name from down the street, Penny knows her, whose twins go to Montessori School with Judy. She stands beside the wagon, leaning against it with one straight arm, head tilted back, throat stretched, as she looks up: an ex-model, Walter recalls, who seems to know she's taken a striking pose. The workman beside her, gloved hands on hips once more, staring at her, open-mouthed, adds a touch of realism.

So does the heavy limb swinging overhead. One end of its arc brings it over the back of the truck, the other end out over the station wagon. The creaking of ropes and pulleys silences everything else in the street. Nothing else seems to be moving. Walter looks around for some sign or sound of life, some movement that will end this pantomime, and sees that the sidewalks and lawns are lined with people, all standing in silence, watching the swing of the huge limb as it arcs back out over the station wagon once again, reaches the end of its swing, creaks back toward the dump truck. Even the children in the back of the car are silent: silent, Walter realizes, as only Montessori children can be.

My god, thinks Walter, sliding down from the brick wall, Judy's in there: today's their day at the Arts and Science Center. What's that stupid woman doing? I could kill her.

92. The Tie That Binds

Walter doesn't ordinarily take killing personally. It is, he has long since realized, simply an act, like any other: more common, perhaps, than a lot of others, and like many others probably done best if one is not too personally involved in it. But they are human acts: involving him whether he will or not.

Before he can involve himself in this one, however, he hears the car door slam, tires squeal, as Sally backs away from the truck, jerks to a stop, then starts forward again, swinging the car in a screeching U-turn in the middle of the wide boulevard, on the curb of which Walter now stands, mouth open, in the midst of coming after her—to do what, he doesn't know—as she completes her turn and accelerates toward the sawhorses blocking the same end of the street where she somehow managed to enter. Just as she reaches the far end of the block, a workman appears and drags one of the sawhorses aside. The station wagon plunges through the gap in the barricade without the slightest flicker of its brake lights. Only as it disappears down the long boulevard, speeding away under the shadow of the remaining elms, does Walter realize he's been left behind with the image of a child staring at him from the rear window: hands pressed against the glass, eyes wide, face pale, mouth open: his own daughter!

My god, he thinks, I'll kill that stupid woman yet. Looking around, he sees that the crowd that had collected on the walks and lawns has begun to drift away: drawn by the sudden silence of the chain saws that have been roaring in their neighborhood for weeks, they retreat when the noise starts up again, as it now does. The hovering limb settles with a loud thunk into the back of the truck, and high up, out of sight, the saw splutters into action, motor roaring, teeth grinding into the flesh of the tree.

No, thinks Walter, I won't kill her. She looks like a pretty unkillable type, though he knows there's no such thing. The spectators have all disappeared, though Walter never saw where they went off to: down the street, back into their houses, away into the shops on the next block over. No one's interested in what isn't happening. At the rate the station wagon was going when he last saw it, the children are probably wandering happily around the

Arts and Science Center by now, poking their heads between the rib bones of the stegosaurus, Sally herding them along, puffing away at a cigarette in spite of the "No Smoking" signs posted all around her.

Still, thinks Walter, something should be done. But between murder at one extreme and pranks at the other, like slashing her tires or making anonymous phone calls, he can't think what, except maybe talking to her. And he doesn't want to talk to her.

I don't like her well enough to want to talk to her, he mutters, hoisting himself back up on the brick wall. Even thinking about her fires up his rage again, and he begins to see a little scenario in which their voices rise and he reaches out— up: she's taller than him—to grab her thin arms and shake her, but she looks down at him, eyes expressionless, face haughty, simply waiting for him to be done, her cool, unruffled look juxtaposed in his mind to the wild look on the face of his daughter peering wide-eyed at him out of the rear window of the station wagon. By god, he isn't finished with her yet. Gripping her arms tighter, he forces her down, down, till he can feel himself leaning forward, over her, out over the edge of the brick wall, from which he slowly begins to tip forward, and reaching out his hands to balance himself, pull his body back, he's suddenly aware he has the beginning of an erection.

Damn, he thinks, I don't even like her well enough to want to fuck her: what is this thing?

He knows very well what this thing is: no, what these things are: lust and violence, love for his children and hatred of stupidity, all the death out there and all the sex, all the directions passion can take. The thing he doesn't know is: why does he have anger in his heart and an erection in his pants? What binds him so personally to all this, ties these things together?

Maybe it is me, he thinks, hopping down off the wall. He stands for a moment in the middle of the sidewalk, brushing off the seat of his pants.

Maybe, he thinks, this thing I do not know what is only me. Across the street the chain saw roars suddenly loud and clear, and an enormous branch cracks loudly and swings out over the street, dancing at the end of its ropes and pulleys.

And maybe too, he adds, it is anyone.

93. A Last Lecture

Listen, Walter, afoot now, asks himself, what is the truth of this matter?

First he answers himself simply: There is no truth.

Or: you cannot know the truth.

On this subject he then lectures himself as follows: what friends, is truth? "Absence makes the heart grow fonder," for example, is not truth. It sounds like truth but what it is, is bullshit, because for every such sound resembling truth there is another sound that contradicts it: "Out of sight, out of mind." Therefore there is no truth. Or you cannot know the truth. Or there are many truths, some of them contradictory: which is the same as either of the above.

I know that there are some among you, he continues to himself, who will argue that mathematics alone can give us truth. As in two plus two equals four. But what we have to remember to ask is: four what? two oranges plus two oranges equal four oranges. All right so far. But two oranges plus two apples equal four what? Fruit? OK, maybe. And two fruit plus two people equal four what? Objects? Hmmm, maybe. Keep going. Two objects plus two ideas equal four what? I'm not sure. But I know that the only way two plus two can keep equalling four is to keep the categories locked up tight. But the categories are always changing. One professional killer plus one family man equals what? Well then, finally eliminating the categories altogether. Two plus two equals four. But two what plus two what? Equals four what? There can only be truth so long as the symbols are abstract and no longer refer to anything in particular. The only way mathematics can provide truth is by giving us a truth that is not the truth about anything. Except, perhaps, itself. And I do not believe that is what we want from truth.

No, reasons the lecturer, that isn't truth. That's tautology. Like: I am what I am.

And I don't know what that is, the lecturer tells himself in an aside, so I cannot possibly judge it as true. Or not true.

The lecturer now draws toward a conclusion: If truth is what we want, and what we want is the truth about something, and if mathematics alone can provide us with truth, but a truth which is not the truth about anything, then we are in real trouble.

On the other hand, what's so hot about the truth?

The truth, as one of you will doubtless counter, will set us free.

But free from what? From the untruth? From all the other truths? Or is that only a moralistic claim, no more objectively demonstrable, no more, as it were, truthful, than saying, "The untruth will set you free"? From the truth, of course, if only you knew it. From mathematics, perhaps.

Well then, he continues, if we cannot have the truth, what are we left with? Not the untruth, which is indistinguishable from the truth. Not even mathematics, which is true not to us but only to itself.

My friends, I conclude we are only left with what is.

Whatever we conclude, he concludes, that is.

Like again, for example, he resumes, after a short pause: I am what I am.

That tautology again, which isn't a truth but only a statement of what is. And I do not pretend to know what that what is. The truth of it, so to speak. Or only the whatness of it. What it is is a snake of a statement biting its own tail. Besides, he adds, I do not even know that, having said it, I am it anymore. Perhaps what I have to say is: I am what I am but I am not what I was. That is, not what I was when I said, "I am what I am." Etcetera. That doesn't get us any closer to the truth, but hopefully we have abandoned that matter by now and no longer even feel the loss. Perhaps it doesn't even get us closer to what is.

Nonetheless, I like the sound of that better than the sound of truth. It isn't any clearer, but at least it announces that we are, at last, in pursuit of what is, whatever that is.

Lecture finished.
Close notebooks.
Go home.
Find out.
What is.

94. THE PROFESSIONALS

On the way home, having walked all the way back to pick up the station wagon at the riverside overlook, Walter spots a flatbed truck parked in the weeds on an empty corner lot, a sign advertising fresh sweet corn stuck into the ground beside it, and stops to pick up half a dozen ears. A middle-aged man in grimy work clothes sits on the back of the truck, so engrossed in *Farm Management* that he doesn't even look up at Walter as he fumbles—deliberately, Walter assumes—seven ears into the paper sack and absently pockets Walter's dollar bill.

Walter, who admires professionalism in any activity, is delighted to discover that there is a journal like this for real farmers and that real farmers actually read it. He has always known there were periodicals for the so-called gentleman farmer: back issues of them on the Fosbergs' coffee table have continuously advertised the fact that they are not truly city dwellers, that their hearts reside on the abandoned forty acres they own in Wisconsin. But this is different, and the farmer, still lost in the pages of his journal as Walter drops the sack of corn onto the front seat, is an intellectual. At times like this Walter wishes there were a trade magazine for his own profession: and he doesn't mean *College English* or *Modern Language Notes*.

Where, for example, did the farmer learn that little trick about the extra ear of corn? Seven for six and probably thirteen to a dozen: it doesn't cost him much, especially on a slow afternoon with most of his load unsold. And where, for that matter, did he manage to get fresh corn at this time of year, getting the jump on everyone else by a good two months? Hmmm, says Walter to himself: but nonetheless he'll probably drive this route more often and keep an eye out for the flatbed truck on the corner. An intellectual, by Walter's definition, is only someone with an idea, and this farmer is clearly a man with an idea, which he is likely to have gotten from the same kind of place where Walter got his ideas for unravelling the themes of *Heart of Darkness* or Walter's plumber got his idea on how to bend that little rod that connects the toilet's water inlet valve to the float at just the right angle. Walter, never able to fix these things so the water shuts off properly, has only yesterday had his respect for professionalism enhanced by seeing the bill for the five minutes of labor his plumber performed two weeks ago: and knows that, as with his doctor, he is paying not for the act but for the education that made it possible.

Not that Walter sees money as the mark of professionalism: plenty of unprofessional hacks make a fortune, mostly, he supposes, because a gullible public lets them get away with it, fails to insist upon high standards for whatever it is they are doing: teaching, social work, psychiatry, tree pruning and bricklaying and food packing and baseball. No, not baseball: sports fans are the least likely, it seems to Walter, who remembers plenty of boos from his irregular visits to the ball park, to let anyone get away with a performance of less than professional caliber. It is not the salaries of the superstars that make them professionals, but the way they perform, and for Walter this means combining a spirit of amateurism with a—what shall he call it, *modus laborandi?*—of professionalism: matching delight in the job with a thorough knowledge of how to go about it.

Sitting at the last traffic light before turning down the winding street to his own house, Walter, drumming his fingers on the steering wheel, reflects on how many of his own colleagues do not meet this notion of professionalism, either because their knowledge is soured by a distaste for the job or because their delight in teaching lacks the knowledge to back it up. Or both: a case or two of that on the faculty also occur to him. Or because the knowledge is combined with the wrong job: Fosberg, teaching ineptly instead of doing the research he is qualified for and interested in. That Fosberg's teaching and chairmanship bring him in more money than a research grant only confirms for Walter the lack of any genuine connection between money and professionalism. It's Dora, after all, bursting with both knowledge and enthusiasm, who is by far the poorest paid in the department, but like any professional she does her job well simply because she is a professional and that is the way professionals do their jobs: the public's judgments—cash and applause—though a pleasant reinforcement, are always secondary to a pro's own.

Swinging wide around the last bend, Walter sees his house

blossom into view, gleaming white and brown in the late afternoon sunlight against the dark green background of trees in his yard and the neighbors'. Last fall painters did a thoroughly professional job, and Walter is glad that he didn't give in to Penny's desire to save money and do it themselves. He is glad he called in the expensive tree service to remove the dying box elder that used to shade the kitchen window and glad he has at last found a reliable mechanic to work on their cars: a young man at the independent service station near the University who not only does what has been asked of him but also explains, when Walter comes to pick up his car, what else ought to be done, and why.

Janey and Judy are sitting on the front lawn when he pulls into the drive. They wear matching blue sundresses and sit with their legs spread, rolling a big red plastic ball back and forth between them like a pair of professionals in a scene from the perfect childhood. And Walter, lifting an ear of corn out of the paper sack and waving it out the window at the girls as he brings the car to a stop, feeling the fat, firm, even rows of kernels lined up professionally beneath the husk—though he still wonders where it came from—California? Texas? Mexico?—is glad to know at a time like this, that he, too, is a professional.

Where did he come from?

95 . The Amateurs

"You may be a professional," Penny tells him, as they sit side by side drinking coffee with a scoop of chocolate ice cream in it at their kitchen table later in the evening, after the girls have gone to bed and Walter has spent some time explaining his theory of professionalism, complete with examples: "You may be a professional as a teacher and you may be a professional as a scholar. But as a father you're strictly an amateur."

Funny, but it's never occurred to Walter to think of this as an area where standards of professionalism might be applied. He likes being father to two young daughters, but he's never thought of it as a job; he does not exactly know what he is doing as a father, but neither, he presumes, does anyone else: hence the blank look he bestows upon Penny in response to her unexpected complication of his theory of the nature of professionalism.

One thing Walter can always be sure of with Penny: her ability to complicate things.

"Hmmm," he says, a verbal shrug through his sip of coffee, recalling their marriage as a move, among much else, to simplify things. Things, he thinks: you can simplify things; it is people who are always the complication. Aloud: "I didn't know being a parent was such a complicated thing."

"Then," says Penny, a note of hostility creeping into her voice as she sets her coffee cup very, very carefully down, "how come you couldn't make up your mind to support me when I was trying to be firm with Janey after dinner?"

"I didn't know it was such an important thing." He doesn't mean "thing": he means whatever it is people mean when they say "thing" to refer to what happens between people, knowing that it has nothing to do with things, that there are no things between people, there are only the people: which is plenty.

"Important enough for you to stand there with your mouth open looking like a helpless dummy."

"I didn't know you needed help."

"I was looking at you for help, for god's sake! I thought one of the marks of your precious professionalism was knowing where to find the god damned resources?" She rolls her cup around on the table between her hands, and Walter, for lack of knowing what to say, does the same: until he accidentally sloshes some of his coffee over onto the table top.

"Hey," he says quietly, as he rises to get a paper towel to wipe up the mess, lowers his voice to change the tone: "did something I said about professionalism upset you?"

"It didn't upset me, damn it, it made sense." Penny has not lowered her voice to match Walter's. "It made me realize what a tough job I'm trying to do with a fucking amateur for a partner."

Walter, his single paper towel inadequate, has only managed to spread the spilled coffee over the table top: there is more of him here than he thought: "I'm sorry."

"Don't be sorry, just try to be . . . ," Penny hesitates, "more useful, more helpful, I don't know, more god damned professional!"

Tired of being berated in his own terms, Walter drops the towel in a puddle in the center of the table. "I suppose," he says, making a weak pass at sarcasm, "I am supposed to read the bloody journals." "Bloody": a word he picked up from her in their first years together. Now she doesn't use it any more. He says "bloody" and she says "fucking"—and "professional."

"Yes," she says, "read the fucking journals and try to be a little more professional."

She gets up and stalks out of the kitchen, returns in a minute with a pile of magazines in her arms. Standing in the middle of the kitchen she pokes through the stack she holds and pulls out the relevant copies. Splat they go as she slams them down, one by one, on the wet table in front of Walter: *Modern Parenting, Psychology Today, Ms., Woman's Day*: each, Walter sees, headlining an article on how to be a successful parent, a supportive parent, a good parent, a non-destructive parent, a . . . parent: a professional parent.

"Aw, look," says Walter, slumping down defensively in front of this journalistic display, "you have to find your way through recipes and decorating ideas and . . . ."

"And where in hell," demands Penny, "do you think a parent operates? In a vacuum? In a zoo? In a laboratory?"

"Enough," begs Walter, his way of conceding that she's made her point: that the scientist needs to know how the lab works before setting up the experiment, that the tiger who is not a professional about the jungle will never find its prey. But he never realized before that people had to be professionals about being people: had to both love that occupation and know how to do it well. A difficult, a tiring, thought. He lifts the magazines, one at a time, and moves them to the far, dry side of the table, turning them upside down so that their coffee-soaked back covers can dry. Wearily he pushes the soggy little ball of paper toweling around in the remains of the spilled coffee: "I'm really tired. I think I want to go to bed now."

96. CRY OF THE WILD

Alone in bed, Walter stalks a jungle of self, trying to hunt down the beast of amateur parental behavior, but what he sees in the brightly lit clearings there doesn't look so bad: a harmless looking creature that likes to play with children. Sometimes it prefers to lean back by itself against the knobby roots of giant trees, sometimes it slips away into thickets where he can't follow, but all in all, how much harm does it seem capable of? Now and again he finds it in some dim grove grabbing one child by the shoulders or chasing another away with a growl and a snap, but even this is not like other things he sees: beasts who seize their young in their mouths and drag them down narrow forest paths, letting their heads bang against the encroaching trees; beasts who shove their young out of those trees, growling to keep them from climbing back up again, until at last they slink away. High in their perches, these beasts glare silently down at Walter staring up at them: until at last Walter realizes that the reason they do not growl at him is because they recognize him as one of them and are waiting for him to climb up and join them, half-hidden among the leafy treetops. There is nothing to do but dig his nails into the trunk and begin the long climb, though he doesn't want to be a part of that crowd, hadn't been aware that there were so many, perched on almost every limb of almost every tree in sight, no doubt hidden from view till he has approached this close by the heavy shade of the overhanging forest and the dense foliage and their own striped or spotted protective coloration.

"But I don't belong there," says Walter, inching, all the same, steadily upwards. He almost chokes getting those words out, feels like each of them is a gag stuffed down his throat as he struggles, gasping, to repeat them: "I don't belong here."

Feeling the leaves brush against his hair, he seems to hear another voice echoing from somewhere above him, "Belong where?"

Are they taunting him? Eyes stare out of dark foliage, their nighttime glow informing Walter it's taken all day to make this climb; deep into the night now he is gagging on words he can no longer get out: "No, I don't . . . ." But he no longer wants to just speak them out, one at a time, he wants it all to come out at once, everything, to gasp it all out in one gigantic sobbing breath, choking it out, gasping and weeping, "I don't . . . ."

And suddenly he is sitting up in bed sobbing wildly into the darkness. He clutches his pillow in his lap with both hands, his fingers buried deep in it, tears stream like a rain forest downpour over his face and neck and bare chest, and Penny, one arm around his shoulders, sits up beside him, stroking his head with her other hand gently as a leaf moving in the forest wind as she asks, soothingly, "Don't what, darling, don't what?"

"I don't know," he wails, gasping for breath between sobs that control his body independently of anything he wills, leaving him too weak to will otherwise, only to cry and cry into the dark.

"I don't know," he cries, "I don't know, I don't know."

97. A Lesson in Resilience

He's not lying: he really doesn't know. Sobbing into Penny's arms, he doesn't even know where she's come from, doesn't remember her coming to bed, doesn't know what's happened, doesn't know why he's leaning limply against her spilling all these tears he never even knew he had. And he doesn't know why Penny's mothering him like this, her lips against his cheek and her hand brushing his damp hair out of his face, or why he's letting her mother him like this; he only knows that when he makes a brief attempt to choke back his sobs and pull himself straight up, away from her, he hasn't the strength for either. So all in all, he doesn't know much, and what he does find out is mostly discouraging.

Therefore he cries even harder: cries and cries into the middle of the night, his tears flooding out Penny's soothing words and her occasional quiet, worried question and the sound of cars in the street and the ticking of the alarm clock on the nightstand: by whose dimly glowing hands he sees, when he has at last cried himself out, cried himself into an exhaustion so total he can't get a single coherent word out to Penny, that it is three in the morning as exhaustion drops him at last, like some beast hunted through the night until his strength is gone, heavily from Penny's arms into sleep.

Nor does he know much more when he wakes automatically, with no assistance from the unset alarm, at six thirty. Standing in the bathroom, brushing his teeth, he knows the face in the mirror is his, but he's unfamiliar with the eyes. This redness he has rarely seen before, only at the end of the summer on days when the pollen count is at its highest, and as to the dark circles beneath them: he never has circles under his eyes. What happened?

The night is a mystery to him.

The morning, less mysterious, still has its puzzles. Penny hasn't yet woken by the time he's shaved and dressed in jeans and a sweatshirt and left the bedroom, but the girls are up, lying on the living room floor in their pajamas watching cartoons on television. It's spring and the house is a little chilly this morning, so Walter chases them off to put on robes and slippers, then stands there in their absence watching the cartoon world flashing and exploding in front of his tired eyes: animals smashed wafer thin by enormous weights dropping on them rise, slowly at first, then suddenly pop back into their rounded shapes once again; other characters zoom off roads into the empty air above deep canyons, pause there, puzzled, and only when they look down and see that there's nothing beneath them do they begin the long, whistling plunge to earth; still others are hurtled into the world with such force that their limbs stick deep into solid rock, or are struck by objects thrown so hard that their bodies are stretched out, like elastic, almost to the breaking point, before they snap back into place again. Not only a violent world, thinks Walter, but also a very puzzling one, physiologically speaking: nonetheless, quite a lesson in resilience.

By the time Janey and Judy shuffle back in in red robes and fluffy slippers, he has flicked off the television set and gone off to the kitchen to boil the water to make the coffee to put some bounce back into his own life this morning. And before they arrive in the kitchen whining their complaints against his turning off their programs, he has managed to get the juice pitcher onto the kitchen table, the butter into the frying pan, and the eggs cracked into the mixing bowl, and is busy measuring out coffee into the filter cone.

"Janey, pour the juice and set the table. Judy, go get the paper."

Their whining stops, as mysteriously to him as it began, as they turn to the chores he's assigned. Perhaps they're only hungry. The mystery of their appetites eludes him: one day it seems impossible to fill them up, the next impossible to get them to the table. This seems to be one day rather than the next, as Janey lays out butter and jam, starts the toast, fumbles around in the dishwasher for clean silverware, then pauses beside him on the way back to the table.

"Don't make my eggs runny."

He shrugs, never too sure of his control over how the eggs turn out. While they cook, the teakettle whistles; he pours the boiling water over the coffee, waits as it filters through, then pours again, finds that the eggs are by now indeed no longer runny, and serves them up as Judy returns with the morning paper. They all sit down together and Walter, reaching for his juice with one hand, flips through the sections of the newspaper with the other: there is no sports section.

"What did you do with the sports section?" he starts to say, correcting himself after the first word—Judy, who can't read, can't tell one section from the other—to say: "Where's the rest of the paper?"

"That's all, Daddy," she says, smearing too much jam on her toast.

"Are you sure that's all?"

She nods her head, too much jam already in her mouth to talk. But Walter decides to look for himself and gets up and walks to the front door, which Judy has left open and from which he can see, down the walk to the driveway, that there's not a scrap of paper around. He pushes the screen open and goes out to check further under the bushes, but finds, naturally, nothing. Where is the sports section?

From the kitchen, with the door open, he can hear, now, Penny's voice: "Where's your father?"

98. Bouncing Back

That terrific question Walter, standing on the front lawn at seven thirty a.m. without the sports section of his morning paper, is not particularly prepared to deal with. Therefore he calls out, as if it explains anything, "Here I am!"

Where he is it's a lovely May morning, warmer outside than in, the sun shining, only a few fluffy little clouds showing on the horizon in the south, birds singing which Walter, of course, cannot identify, and not a soul to be seen out on the streets. No one rushing out, slamming doors, late to work or school; no cars starting up or automatic garage doors grinding down; no one hollering out after anyone else about forgotten lunch bags, dentist appointments, dinner parties. It is Saturday morning, and Walter has never seen the neighborhood so quiet, so pleasant and devoid of people. The lawns glisten with dew, and he does not want to go back into the house.

But when he looks up at it and sees Penny standing just inside the front doorway, her face blurred by the screen, he begins to move slowly up the front walk toward the house. He stops outside the door, in no hurry to give up the morning sun that soaks into his back, and stares at Penny, still inside, staring out at him. The screen breaks her face into countless tiny dots just like a character on television or in the comic strips, thinks Walter. But Penny breaks out of the cartoon by the simple act of pushing open the screen door and, still wearing only thin cotton pajamas through whose top Walter can clearly see the dark shape of her nipples, steps out to put her arms around him, lean her head, this time, against his chest. The screen door slams behind her, jarring Walter into appropriate response: he raises his own arms slowly, puts them around her, gently hugs her to him, understanding none of this: just last night, wasn't she launching an all-out attack against him? Just last night wasn't there a chasm between them as empty as the neighborhood is this morning? Just last night wasn't he whisked alone and weeping and far away? Just last night: what happened last night?

What's happening now is that Walter, hugging Penny, one hand on her shoulder and the other in the small of her back, feels the softness of her skin, still warm from bed, through her thin pajamas. He lets his lower hand drift downward onto the upper curve of her ass and feels, in response, her body tighten against him and her mouth slide open along his neck. His own face buried for a moment in her fine, dark hair, his mouth moving down around her ear, he does not understand this, either, though he knows well enough what is happening: his penis bulges between them and in a moment their mouths are together, tongues twisting around each other as they cling together in the warm spring sunshine on their front walk in this quiet, unpeopled neighborhood.

At least Walter hopes the neighborhood is still empty: less from any sense of propriety than from something—something he'd like to know more about—in the kind of effect its emptiness was beginning to have on him. Before Penny's arrival that is, and this, this other kind of effect, which he'd also like to know more about: not just in the sense that he and Penny share, as they both let their mouths part so that they can turn and move, still holding each other, only a little more loosely, back into the house; but in another sense that he fears is his alone, a sense that asks, is this all, after last night, after everything, is this what it all comes down to?

This he likes, to say the least, but still he wonders: and wonders besides, as they close the front door behind them—awkwardly, their bodies still close—just what kind of excuse he is now going to present to Janey and Judy so that he and Penny can assure themselves of a brief stretch of privacy without their absence drawing too much attention to itself.

"Listen, girls," he is about to say, not knowing what's going to come next, as they pass through the living room, hip against hip. But he sees the pair of them once again far too engrossed in their television cartoon to pay the least bit of attention anyway. So Penny precedes him up the stairs to their bedroom, and Walter, in hot pursuit, follows as close as he can stay behind her, both hands on her ass.

CHAPTER XI

99. Alarms and Diversions

Everything that happens at this point in Walter Job's life he takes personally. Not just what that happen to him, either, but what happens to the world at large, so long as he becomes aware of it: as he does in his usual way, via daily papers, weekly newsmagazines, evening TV. Anything he becomes aware of, in whatever way, he turns toward himself.

I'm not an egotist, he tells himself, but everything counts.

So when he reads that hundreds have been slaughtered in the latest outburst of warfare in the Middle East, dozens in a new flare-up of IRA activity in Northern Ireland, another handful in a fresh round of militarist repression in Chile, he can't help reflecting on the insignificance of his own few actions: paltry numbers and minor effects. When he sees the thousands slaughtered in automobile accidents, outbreaks of food poisoning, epidemics, earthquakes, landslides, he can't help admiring the deliberateness of his own activities: the virtues of intention and choice. But when he reads the obituaries of the old and rich and famous, he can't help concluding that the ubiquity of death, which takes everyone sooner or later, eventually deprives his own activities of the significance he has just managed to restore to them.

Death, the world reports to him, is, like nothing else, absolute: total, one hundred per cent, perfect. And inasmuch as he takes everything that happens personally, he reads the balance of the message as an announcement that in the machinery of such perfection, you, Walter Job, are only the tiniest cog, no more significant in the total contribution of your life's activities than a cross-country bus driver's fraction of a second of negligence, an arsonist with the striking of a single match, a potato salad in repose on a picnic table on a hot summer afternoon.

Walter doesn't know whether to be relieved or insulted by such comparisons: doesn't the fact that he brings deliberateness —choice, intentionality—to what he does make a difference?

In the long run, says the world, which is far more adept than Walter at seeing things in the long run, no.

Everything that happens tells Walter that. The late news reports the death from leukemia of an All Star third baseman on whom Walter, out of sheer admiration, once refused a contract. In a weekly newsmagazine he reads that a British poet whose work he has always thought highly over-rated has been slashed to death for unknown reasons by an unknown assailant. The morning paper headlines a double suicide pact by a young local couple of whom he has never heard.

What Walter understands from this is that he could have done any or all of these deaths: could have taken the contract, played the anonymous literary critic, proffered release to the anguished lovers. The fact that he didn't doesn't seem to have made any difference. Someone, something, did. Look, he can tell himself, thinking of the desperate lovers, where I'm not involved some of them even take on the job themselves. And sometimes, he knows, when he hears the ambulance go screaming past in the street, when he sees the film clips of the body plucked still breathing from the river beneath the bridge, sometimes they botch it: wouldn't his own skills have been preferable to that?

Well? A little muddled—because there's so much that happens out there and it's so difficult to know how to take it all in relation to himself—he can at least try to assure himself that none of these deaths that have been happening, or not happening, concerns him. If whoever is pursuing him is reading the same newspapers, watching the same network news, why, if there's a whole team assembled by now to deal with his case—a possibility Walter knows is all too likely—there's nothing there to connect Walter with what death really does. Why should he be concerned?

But of course everything concerns him. He takes it all personally. He can see quite clearly that somehow or other everything that happens relates to his own predicament.

100. His Own Predicament

What, exactly, is "his own predicament"?

When he gets up in the middle of the next night, a Sunday well on its way toward Monday morning, and leaves his sleeping wife in bed and wanders about the house, looking in on his sleeping children, rearranging their covers, checking the locks on the outside doors, rinsing the glasses and dishes dirtied by their bedtime snack and stacking them on the kitchen counter, folding yesterday's newspaper away in the corner of the kitchen closet, he thinks: probably this is all there is to my predicament: to get up at night and look in on the children and check the doors, clean up the kitchen and put away yesterday's news. All in all, just like anyone else: so why is this a predicament?

It's a predicament, he thinks, turning out the light and sitting down at the kitchen table in his pajamas, because it doesn't fit. Because it's like these pajamas that get all twisted up when I roll around in the bed. They're for sleeping still and straight in, just like this house, but I'm a turner and tosser.

As his eyes adjust to the dim glow from the corner streetlight that edges through the kitchen window, Walter discovers a banana on the table in front of him, last of the bunch. He picks it up, peels it halfway, and nibbles at it, thinking that if people were aware of the other actions of the man who lives in this house just like they live in their houses, they would feel that it was those other actions that did not fit, whereas it is part of his predicament to feel that, as a man well aware of his other actions, perhaps it is living in this house that doesn't fit. By the time he has reached the end of this thought, he's also finished the banana. He gets up, wanders about the kitchen for a minute with the banana skin dangling from his hand, starts to drop it in the sink but thinks of the noise the disposal would make and instead opens the cabinet under the sink and dumps it in the wastebasket. Feeds himself, cleans up after, doesn't wake a soul: he's good at living here.

He's also good at doing the other thing he does.

He sits down again at the kitchen table in the almost dark, wondering if this is all there is to his predicament: to do two things well which do not fit together: to be like pieces of a jigsaw puzzle which don't come together to make a unified picture: pieces which he begins to suspect of not being capable of making a picture, maybe pieces to two different puzzles. He hears the low hum of the electric clock mounted on the wall above the sink: a blue clock, but he can't see its blueness in this light or read its hands or know anything from its tickless murmur that speaks of time passing. I have wandered around here in the dark, he thinks, like some nocturnal beast, until I have managed to get each foot caught in a separate trap, and still I sit here, while time hums invisibly by, thinking I am free to get up and do whatever I want. Soon it will be dawn, and the hunters will be coming around to check their traps.

He gets up and wanders off into the living room, finding the blue couch easily in the dark and settling down into it. I'm not bad at this dark, he thinks: maybe my real predicament is only a tendency toward the pretentious image, a tendency fatal for the poet but what difference does it make to me? I'm not trying to create a poem, only a life. In a poem, besides, everything has to fit. In a life . . . .

Suddenly tired, he stretches out on the couch, which just fits his extended length. He takes off his glasses, feels out a place for them on the glass cocktail table, and closes his eyes. The three big cushions on which he lies are soft, too soft if anything, and he rolls around on them trying to make himself comfortable, edging over onto his side, then his stomach, then turning over onto his back again: managing in the process to get his pajama bottoms twisted up around his legs, the top twisted around his torso. He sits up to straighten out his pajamas, then slowly, drowsily, not to tangle things up, lets himself down on his back again, realizing as he does so that he can now see the couch taking shape about him, that even without his glasses he can make out the table in front of the couch and the two chairs beyond that and the bookcase on the opposite wall.

And this too he takes as part of his own predicament: that just as he's about to get comfortable and drop off to sleep, the room about him begins to fill up with light.

101. Everything Fits

Walter lies half asleep on the couch, no closer than before to knowing what fits and what doesn't, to being able to define with any precision "his own predicament," while around him the room grows slowly brighter: fuzzily brighter to him, without his glasses, when he lets his eyes flicker open. But less and less does he open his eyes now, or make the necessary progress toward a daylit recognition that everything fits. Having decided that he's good at the dark, he lets himself subside slowly into what's left of it, eyes tightly closed. In an hour or so, waking early as usual, his daughters will slip downstairs to amuse themselves with the early morning cartoons on television and find themselves even more entertained by the spectacle of their father asleep on the living room couch, pajamas all twisted up around his chest and legs, defenseless in the face of their giggly high spirits.

Meanwhile, everything fits: this home where, after considerable restlessness, he has at last fallen asleep in the wrong place; the more traditionally placed sleepers above him or, for that matter, all around him now, and those who do not sleep as well, those who may even have him in mind as they do not sleep; those who may have him in mind first thing upon waking, like the wife who will arise startled to find his usual place in the bed beside her vacant and descend to find the children perched on his chest and thighs, and those who will never think of him at all; those who will be dead by the time he wakes, dead by the hands of persons or diseases unarrested, dead by cataclysms of nature or their own hands, and those who will be busy transcribing those deaths into the early morning news reports, and those who will attend or not attend to those deaths, those reports, as they rise and move on out into the day. Everything fits, being part of that world into which time, humming undetected on the wall above the kitchen sink, brightening the living room minute by minute even through the drawn drapes—so that one by one each object carefully fitted in there over the years, each chair and pillow and shelf and book and vase and painting, stands forth bright and distinct in its own entity—moves all the sleepers unawares.

Everything fits: fits like an infinitely-fingered glove around Walter Job: that predicament.

102. Boxed In

Thus fitted, in daylight and everything, Walter dreams of boxes within boxes. "The first one is yours," he's told: "stop there." But he doesn't know whether "the first one" signifies the outermost box or the innermost one. The outer one contains only other boxes, all of them tied with brightly colored ribbons, so he sets about opening them one after the other, in pursuit of the inner. Perhaps he's already transgressed the rules: "Stop there." Rapidly, not to be stopped now, he unties ribbon after ribbon, tears open box after box, discovering only that there is no stopping. Open boxes, tossed aside, pile up all about him and still he goes on. He is making a terrible mess and still he goes on. He stands inside the enormous box he opened first, tossing other, smaller ones out as he opens them, but many fall back in and the ribbons that tied them float in the air, tangling in his clothes and hair and glasses. The boxes he is now opening are the size of his fist. Inside each he finds still another, smaller box and inside that another, yet a little smaller, and inside that still a smaller one, smaller and flatter now, flat like little books, those remarkable little books the size of a fingernail, made with unbelievably thin paper and microscopic print, which yet manage to contain volumes, all there is to know, if only you could read them, if only your eyes were good enough and your fingers not too clumsy to turn the pages, if only you had sufficient patience and time. If only you had a whole lifetime.

103. Ringing the Changes

No one, thinks Walter, getting up in the middle of the couch in his tangled pajamas, a child snuggled in on either side of him, has forever. A bell will go off, like the duplicitous alarm he can hear ringing faintly even now in the distance of the bedroom upstairs, and nothing afterwards will ever be the same.

Walter's life is full of bells: his day today, only barely detached from yesterday by, among other things, this sound he has just detected: a veritable ringing of changes. These are the sounds of alarm that mark the turns of Walter's day:

The solid, pretentious, televised "bong" that announces "Faces in the Evening News."

The lucid tinkle of silver on crystal: well, stainless steel on glass.

The silver ring of coins, unpocketed, unspent.

The clang, clang of an ambulance's departure, hard upon the harsh siren of its arrival.

The three-pronged chime of a doorbell—g, a, c#—upon which a life could be impaled.

The ring of the telephone, the ring of the telephone, the ring . . . .

The coarse buzzer of the so-called bell that signals the end of a class hour.

The buzzer of the kitchen clock timer, which buzzes even now, signalling to Walter that it is time: time to disengage his arms from around his two cuddly daughters and get up and take the two soft boiled eggs he presumes Penny has put on for him off the range and eat his breakfast and go to work, where classroom bells and telephones will ring his day along.

"Aw, do you have to go, Daddy?"

"Yes, can't you hear the buzzer, honey?"

104. SYNECDOCHE

Except for the harshness of the sound, it doesn't bother Walter when the bell buzzes to bring the class to an end while they are still in the midst of discussing "Mario and the Magician." The young man in the back row whose name Walter has not managed to learn all semester, who had his hand raised ready to ask a question in response to Professor Job's summary of Mann's position on the issue of free will, comes, head lowered, down the central aisle now towards the desk at the front of the room. Walter will listen to him with care, will make a note on his question or comment and then look up at the young man, smiling.

"We'll take this up at our next meeting for the benefit of the whole class, Mr. . . . . ?"

And the student will fill in the blank in Walter's question with his name or—flustered because here at the very end of the semester it is the first time he has raised his hand in class and now he has another class he must rush off to—will not fill it in, and then he will leave the room and Walter will gather up his notes and books and leave right behind him, pushing out against the tide of students flowing into the room for the next class, Hapsburg's seminar on *Paradise Lost*—endless poem!—and will not be bothered in the least that they have not completed the work set for today, that it will dip over into the next hour, in which they are scheduled to begin Kafka, "Metamorphosis" and a couple of other stories and then *The Trial*, that Kafka's unfinished, disordered work, will then slop over into the time reserved for—it doesn't even bother Walter than he can't remember who's next on the reading list after Kafka: ah, no one, that's who: the end of the semester, the summing up.

None of this sloppiness, this failure to fit the contents into the container, bothers Walter, despite his passion for neatness, because of his knowledge of, his faith in, both the contents and the container. It is the nature of the contents not to be contained; it is the nature of the container to do the containing which cannot be done. For Walter, this constitutes a perfect match, in which his role is basically that of referee: overseeing the containment into a sequence of structured segments of time of the body of that which cannot be contained. If some small piece of the corpus has to be lopped off and fitted into the next time box, Walter can be perfectly satisfied: Mann will have been dealt with, the needs of the story completed, student inquiries satisfied, or at least addressed; and the container itself, his course, held firmly in place by identical containers set on either side of it—it is the Gothic Novel that meets here in the previous hour—will have survived, not only unchanged but also invisible: ideal containership, into which, it pleases Walter to reflect, the University has ruled that anything can be fitted, from a discussion of a gigantic insect to a microscopic examination of the smallest microbe, from the natural functions of the mind to the functions of a mindless nature: the fifty minute miracle.

Not that there is anything sacred about the fifty minute hour, Walter realizes: it could as easily be thirty seven minutes or a hundred and twenty two. The mere fact of its being there takes precedence over its size. Sitting back in his office after class, fitting the fictions of Mann and Kafka between the bookends on his desk, he considers a new philosophy in which simply being there precedes even dimensionality and things of any size can be reduced or shaped to be fitted into whatever is there: nothing so large or so small, so orderly or so chaotic, so simple or so complex, that it cannot be encompassed within one or more ordered segments of time, once you have them in place.

What Walter is thinking as the telephone on his desk starts to ring: I can contain anything.

105. Short Circuit

The telephone contains the familiar voice of Walter's contact: not the female socket into which he plugs himself from time to time but the male plug which she inserts into him, if it is ready when he calls. Today's direct connection constitutes a short circuit, and the telephone crackles with alarm.

"I am speaking of your trip to San Jose a few months back," says the voice that Walter has, after all these years, gotten accustomed to thinking of as "Buddy": though not for a minute does he believe that's its real name. Today, however, Walter, listening closely, would like to have a firmer handle to grip it by. He has never heard this voice, usually easy and jovial, sound anything like this, so close to losing control, so much on the edge of anger, so un-Buddy-like: barely able to contain itself.

"Everything was fine in San Jose," says Walter, a simple repetition of the statement he remembers having made by phone shortly after his return, months ago: what could be wrong there now. Nothing, surely: all was fine, as he reported. No surprise to anyone: for Walter everything has always been fine: in San Jose, in Houston, in Providence, in Jacksonville and Cleveland and New York, frequently and recently in New York. Here, today, however, everything is not fine.

"Everything is not fine," the voice, an uncaged tiger, growls: a little louder and one of Walter's colleagues from a neighboring office will come running to ask if he is being attacked by an angry student. Carrying the telephone with him, Walter walks around his desk and kicks his office door shut. The long cord lets him pace his office while he waits for Buddy's anger to settle down into information, but what he cannot do is settle himself down again behind his desk while it continues: this anger has unseated him. Though nothing has been said yet, he still does not know what to do with it, where to go. For a moment he perches on the edge of his desk, then he is up and pacing again, receiver in one hand and cradle in the other.

As he paces, he recites into the telephone, speaking against what he feels is a wall of anger though in fact nothing but silence meets his words, the details of his visit to San Jose. These events he narrates in a carefully constructed code, so that no one eavesdropping on his conversation could imagine that he had done more than keep a scheduled appointment, on behalf of a mutual friend, with a business acquaintance while he was in the city for other purposes altogether. When he is finished, Walter stops, leaning against his desk, waiting for what he knows all too well lurks behind such silences.

And at last it comes, so brutally loud that Walter pulls the telephone away from his ear, holds it—as if to keep it away—high up, at arm's length, behind his head. And hears it quite clearly all the same: "You visited the wrong customer!"

Suddenly Walter knows where he has encountered that voice before, knows its name even, and letting himself slide down into his padded desk chair he sets the telephone cradle back down on his desk and reaches across to pull the text out from between the polished, matching geodes he uses as bookends, opens it—no, lets it fall open itself, it's been used often enough—to one of the stories he had been preparing for the next class meeting and reads, aloud, in a husky whisper, not even aware he is speaking into the telephone: "the noise at his rear sounded no longer like the voice of one single father; this was really no joke . . . ."

106. No Joke

"This is no joke, Walter," was what his father had said when Walter finally got home and, having forgotten his key, hesitantly rang the front doorbell, which chimed him unhesitatingly—bong, bong, bong—into his father's presence: "Your mother's really upset about this."

What Walter immediately noticed was that his mother was not anywhere to be seen. Neither were his brothers and sisters. Except for his father in the living room and his friends hanging in the front doorway behind him, the house was deserted: a haunted house, with his father the ghost and his hovering friends daring him to enter and spend the night there. In the morning they would return to find him mindless, deranged, his hair turned white; already his knees felt like they were buckling underneath him. Ready to brave it out all the same—after all, he had his four best friends supporting him from close behind—Walter flew the flag of good humor on his face: a small, forced smile and a quip he had been preparing all the late way home. But his father got there first, however redundantly.

"I told you, Walter, this is no joke."

The voice echoed through the house, affirming its emptiness. His father, having backed off after opening the door, now sat erect in the big living room chair, silent, his hands clutching the arms as if to thrust himself upward and out towards Walter at any moment. He wore a short-sleeved shirt, and Walter could see the muscles of a man who'd built a business loading and delivering cases of soft drinks himself tightening in his forearms. Without turning around, Walter could tell that his buddies had edged back: had withdrawn the foot each had loyally planted inside the door, on the living room carpeting, right behind him. He knew that in a moment he would hear the screen door slam shut, that he would hear feet scuffling on the wooden porch and voices mumbling goodnights, and that if he turned around he would be just in time to see them disappearing into the fading summer twilight. The last thing he heard was Donny Hochstetter's awed whisper: "Jeez, it's just like my old man."

Walter, who had seen from time to time on Donny's face a

red, ugly welt, which was no joke at all, sincerely hoped not: knew, in fact, that those bulging muscles in his father's forearms were not pushing him out of the chair but holding him in it and that the hands fiercely clutching the arms of the chair were not about to release it. And knew that this was no joke either.

107. Favors

"This . is no . . . joke," says the voice on the telephone, setting each word carefully down on the threshold of Walter's hearing with a quiet, restrained anger Walter has long since learned to appreciate.

Walter, who out of habit has let the receiver drift back from arm's length to its normal place against his head, now removes it again, looks at it curiously, in front of him, as if it were a thing from another world, before bringing it back to speak into it, slowly: "I don't find it very funny myself."

"You made a mess," says the voice in the telephone, "and now you got to clean it up."

"Yes. Certainly."

Walter can understand cleaning up; it is the mess he does not understand. San Jose was no problem. He has had problems—never serious ones, but situations that took a little more time and effort: to guarantee privacy, to determine identity, even to find that he could not do, on a particular occasion, that which he was supposed to do—and knows that this was not one. He had plenty of time, plenty of privacy; as usual he even took the precaution of double-checking the identity of the victim with the victim himself. Who else would be at work in the offices of a small electronics firm on the last Sunday of the month if not the owner himself? Middle-aged, balding, a ring of greying hair set like a drooping crown down around his ears, wire-rimmed glasses, and the remnants of a German accent: "Ya, of course I am Friedrich Eberstadt, but who are you und how did you come in here?"

"I am here to kill you, Friedrich Eberstadt."

Only for a moment did the man look startled, his glasses suddenly going opaque—though Walter knew it was just a trick of the lighting—as he lifted his head up from the ledgers strewn across the desk in front of him. He closed one and set it neatly in a corner of the desk, picked up another to lay on top of it but then dropped it back down in the spot he had lifted it from and leaned back in his desk chair.

"So," he said, pushing the chair back from the desk, letting his arms hang limp. "So do me a favor, young man. Do me a favor and kill me."

And Walter, without further ado, had done Friedrich Eberstadt a favor. He had done him a favor and killed him, from across the wide desk, with one quick shot, and had waited only a moment after the silencer had whispered its farewell to see that the job had indeed been properly done, and then he had left. But what kind of favor Friedrich Eberstadt had done him by pushing back from the desk and dropping his arms and holding still for a perfect target, Walter is now having a hard time figuring out. The telephone, still open, lies in his lap: no help. Walter does not rely on the telephone for help, only for contracts. For help he trusts, mostly— only?—himself.

So, he wonders, who would have been sitting at Friedrich Eberstadt's desk, at a time when only Friedrich Eberstadt should have been there, working on Friedrich Eberstadt's books and calling himself Friedrich Eberstadt and asking to be killed, as a favor? Walter can imagine the man denying that he is Friedrich Eberstadt. That sort of thing he has heard before: "Believe me, I'm not really Friedrich Eberstadt. Ha, I was just joking. You don't want me, it would be a big mistake." But someone who is not the victim claiming to be the victim: that is something else. That sort of thing Walter has not heard before: clearly, you can't even trust people regarding their own identity.

But who would consider it a favor to be killed? A little voice deep inside signals a ready answer to that one: someone who is in big trouble. Someone who sees it as the easiest way out. Someone who is in way over his head, doing things he shouldn't be doing and perhaps even wishing he were not doing them but not knowing how not to be doing them. Someone who was in Friedrich Eberstadt's office doing things he should not have been doing with Friedrich Eberstadt's books.

Walter lifts the telephone from his lap and, too impatient for code at this moment, says clearly: "The bookkeeper."

"Very good, mastermind," says the voice at the other end, more patient-sounding now: "You have, in fact, eliminated one of our clients."

108. Compensation

"One?" says Walter.

"Previously there were two. Now, thank you, there is only one."

"I don't usually ask for explanations," says Walter, a bit hesitantly.

"And I don't usually have them, but . . . ."

"But," insists Walter.

"But to some people it now seems best that we understand the mess on our hands. Your hands. Granted it has taken some time to appear. Your visit produced a certain fear and trembling. And silence. Now, however, it comes to light. The gentleman was indeed the bookkeeper. His colleague is unhappy with recent events and has decided to complain, despite his fears, since he does not feel he got full value. He has a company of his own, this businessman, not unlike the one the bookkeeper worked for. It seemed to these two gentlemen that this company, and naturally they themselves, would prosper far better if they also had control of the other company. Things were progressing rather nicely toward that end, requiring only the elimination of one last stumbling block. Now there has been a setback. Our client despairs."

"The stumbling block can still be eliminated," protests Walter, knowing this is neither the right answer nor one he could safely engage in.

"The stumbling block has been forewarned, we must now presume. The stumbling block has read the financial news on the bloody pages of his ledgers. What he does not know is who did him the favor of publishing this deadly little item, and why."

Well, thinks Walter, another favor: a favor for the bookkeeper, who was probably terrified at what he found himself doing, and at the same time a favor for Mr. Eberstadt, who was no doubt likewise terrified to find out what was being done to him. For the remaining client, however, he has made a mess. It's the last time, he tells himself, that I will take the victim's word for his own identity. For himself this has made a mess, too. Two favors, two messes: there is at least a kind of doctrine of compensation at work here: and that's twice, too. Someday he will have to go back and read his Emerson again, very carefully, but meanwhile what he needs is a shift in the balance. In Emerson's world there may be compensation, but in Walter's world everybody wants the same thing: a favor. What kind of favor can Walter do that will also do a favor for himself, by cleaning up this mess.

That is the biggest favor Walter can imagine, and naturally he does not want anyone to do it for him. Naturally no one will. Such is the way of Walter's world, and he has no objections to it. Seen from the inside, it is very simple: chaos surrounds you, as far as you can see—if you are nearsighted, like Walter, then you had best assume that it continues well beyond the limits of your vision—and you may either lose yourself in this chaos, as some choose to do, or, like others—Walter among them—you may choose to oppose this chaos, establishing yourself as a tiny monument to order in the midst of chaos, bit by bit extending the principle of order as far around yourself as you can reach.

Given his vision of the order—disorder—of the world, given that Walter offers no objections to this vision, he is, then, a very accepting person, one who can understand the kind of tricks a chaotic world plays on him, giving him a Friedrich Eberstadt to kill who is not really a Friedrich Eberstadt. That sort of thing is the very nature of chaos.

What he cannot understand, however, is the paradox of an act of his intended to raise the level of order in this world increasing instead the depth of chaos. That sort of thing is not, he must believe, the nature of order: or of his own intentions. What happened to Friedrich Eberstadt—or what did not happen to Friedrich Eberstadt but happened to someone else instead—was only a small slip-up; in truth no one could blame him for it, since he had been told it was Friedrich Eberstadt's custom to work alone in his office on Sunday afternoons and since he found a man there who matched Friedrich Eberstadt's description, spoke with his German accent, claimed his very name.

But this is one of the few times in his career, since its very earliest days, when Walter has been made directly aware of any adverse effects of his attempts to provide order. Once upon a time, when he knew his clients on a more personal level, the effects seemed always highly beneficial: clear problems resolved and order clearly restored. Now, perhaps, the problems are no longer so clear, the achievement of order so simple. What is it he does when he does what he does? He has long thought he knew the answer to that: the ordering of the world about him, whereby he is himself established in the midst of chaos.

Now he wonders: for example, in comparison to those who allow themselves to be lost in chaos: has he lost himself in this quest for order?

109. Keep Talking

"Have you lost your mind?"

"Huh?"

"This call is costing me, and you aren't saying anything."

"Oh, sorry. I didn't know it was long distance."

"The long distance has been since you said anything. Say something."

Walter is not altogether happy with this emphasis on talk. Usually, from him, action has sufficed and words have been kept to a minimum, by everyone's preference, to everyone's satisfaction. This, however, is a different case: so he must say something. Words, as usual, will not do the job, but all the same something must be said: a quandary, Walter realizes, not unlike the teaching of literature, among other things.

Therefore he says, "Let's look at this from both sides."

"There are two sides?"

"There's the subject's side and there's the object's side."

That's a beginning; at least he's said something, though it's never in the past been Walter's way to acknowledge that there were sides, to say nothing of taking a side. He has merely, if that is the word, served, so to speak, as the finalizer of the relationship, and he has finalized, by now, a good many relationships while having no idea of the relative value of the two sides. Without having an idea at all, in fact: only an act to perform, which, freed from the burden of ideas, he has performed exceedingly well. Until now. Now he needs a new beginning, an idea how to proceed afresh.

His idea is: "Suppose we were to reverse the roles?"

"Keep talking."

"Reverse the roles: let the object become the subject and the subject the object." There are all kinds of appeals in this: aesthetic as well as moral. The main appeal to Walter, however, is the practical one: a way to clean up the existing mess.

"Keep talking."

"As things now stand, the object is aware that he is the object, aware that someone has been trying to objectify him. Let's give him the opportunity to objectify his objectifier. He should even be willing to pay for the pleasure." That should strike the right note, thinks Walter: it's not only fun but it's good for you: i.e., profitable. Good for us: for me, for my Buddy here, for Mr. E.

"Keep talking."

"As to the subject, there's no way we can satisfy him at this point. He's lost his partner, certain activities have come to light, anything more he does now will only serve to connect him to what's already happened, and even if you give him double his money back it's not going to satisfy him or make up for lost opportunities. He's an object already of the unpredictable. Nothing we can do for him will satisfy him any longer, but something we can do with him will satisfy someone else."

And of course, adds Walter to himself, bring his dissatisfactions to an end once and for all, though he wonders, seeing how this tidy new plan has come to be, if this doesn't somehow reveal chaos to be managing things after all. Can chaos work through order? Walter, only wanting to clean up a bit of a mess, is willing to use any tool available, though like any other craftsman he needs to have control of the tool, not let the tool control him. Perhaps that's what this little flip-flop represents: he's beginning to get a handle on chaos itself now, learning to roll with its tricky little punches and turn them to his own uses. There's something to be learned from this, he's sure, not all of it practical, though in the short term now the practical surmounts everything else: learning to cope. Not just learning but making a virtue of it: even a profit.

"Besides," adds Walter, " . . . ."

"Stop talking."

"What, then?"

"Do something."

110. THE FIRST NATIONAL WAY

What Walter does shortly afterwards is to go to the bank—not his neighborhood bank but a bank across town where he keeps his only local secret safe deposit box—to get the cash he needs for the doings he will have to do. This done, he walks out of the bank side by side with a heavy-set, middle-aged man who, the moment they step out into the sunlight, suddenly crumples up and drops to the sidewalk. Coins ring noisily as they spill from his pocket and roll across the walk, into the gutter. By the time his head touches, last, silently, upon the First National's expensive pebbled conglomerate, Walter is back in the shadows of the doorway, his eyes roaming up and down the street for some telltale sign: some car in sudden speed-up, man on the run, flash of light on metal or simply a hand inside a jacket pocket.

Walter sees none of that, though by the time he's finished his quick survey there are a number of people on the run, all centering on the stricken man. Walter himself retreats into the bank, reaches for the phone on the first desk inside the door, but it rings just as he's about to pick it up. He lifts it all the same, presses the button to disconnect the call, dials 911, reports the incident and its location. When he hangs up, he steps not to the door but around behind the desk to a wide, tinted window that looks out over the sidewalk in front of the bank. The receptionist who has been sitting behind the desk staring at his abrupt commandeering of her telephone rises to stand beside him, and together they hear, already, even through the heavy, double-paned window, the sounds of the approaching siren.

Outside, Walter can see, the man has been propped up against one of the square concrete pillars that support the bank's overhanging roof. His jacket has been pulled back off his shoulders, his tie undone, his shirt loosened, but his legs sprawl in a helpless V in front of him and his head lolls to the side. His tongue protrudes slightly and his eyes seem partly open, though Walter can't tell whether that's just an illusion of the dark lids that droop over them: whether, in fact, the man is still breathing or those motions he sees come from the jiggling of the man and woman who kneel on either side, trying to keep his limp body propped upright against the pillar. The sagging face looks flushed, and it takes Walter a moment to realize that the color he sees is the effect of the tinted glass he's looking through.

But, he thinks, there is no blood: it's just a heart attack or a stroke, a diabetic collapse, a fainting spell: just. But the attack has come from within. No one out there has done this thing. In particular, to Walter's relief, no one out there has done some violent thing to this man by accident, while in fact attempting to do some violent thing to him, Walter.

"He's a goner, isn't he?" says the receptionist.

"Probably," says Walter softly, who has seen that look, or something very much like it—the sagging flesh, lolling head, tongue and eyelids out of control—on the features of any number of older men when they have finally heard him, on the third or fourth time he answered their queries by stating his business, and realized he was in earnest. They were all goners.

"You didn't look so good yourself when you ran in," says the receptionist, "but you sure acted fast."

Walter does not remember that he ran in, but maybe I did, he thinks, maybe I did: a cooling layer of sweat coats his chest and belly. Not from the run, he knows: it was only a dozen steps, if that, to the phone. But never before, not even for a moment, has he thought that he might be the object of a murderous attack. Now what, he thinks, now what? Is something happening here?

Outside, two blue-uniformed paramedics, faces dripping with sweat, have double-parked their ambulance in front of the bank and are lugging oxygen equipment toward the fallen man. Inside, beside Walter, not a bead of sweat mars the smooth forehead of the young receptionist beneath the even line of her bleached blond hair. She wears a tight, lime-green sweater. Of course, realizes Walter, she has to dress for the air conditioning. He shivers slightly in his own thin coating of sweat. Even her face looks carefully dressed.

"Did you know him?" asks Walter, aware as he speaks that he has already shuffled him off into the past tense, just as the attendants will soon be swinging him away too, on a stretcher with the oxygen mask strapped to his face, into the past tense of Walter's experience: "He was just in here."

"No," she says, turning away from the window. "He looks like my father."

Walter, looking down to check his watch, only hears, repeats, her last words: "Your father?"

"I mean the way he looked when he had his heart attacks. He had ten of them, every one while I was home with him." Tugging at the bottom of her sweater to pull it tight, smoothing the front of her skirt, she sits down and wheels her chair up to the desk. Walter can see her performing the identical gestures—pulling her sweater down over her hard, pointy breasts, patting down an imagined wrinkle in her skirt—as her father crumples to the living room floor beside her.

"I only missed the last one," she says, smiling up at him as he moves out from behind her desk where they were standing, "and I waited a long time for that one." Then the phone rings and she lifts it to her ear, pushing back her hair with her other hand.

"First National," she chimes in a light, clear voice: "Be happy today the First National way."

III. Life Eternal

The dead man on the sidewalk—on the other side of the street now from where Walter has crossed to get his car from the parking lot—is no news to Walter Job, who has seen plenty of dead people. Death isn't news to anyone, he thinks, noting that all the same, even in the early heat wave of this May afternoon, a crowd has gathered, hiding the body from his sight: what is it they're in such a hurry to see that they work up a sweat running down the street on a day like this? Death they've already seen, haven't they? Is there anyone who hasn't seen death: fresh and red in World War Two or Korea or Vietnam, in the streets between mangled cars, had home delivery of it in dying color, straight from the latest drug shoot-out, train crash, plane wreck, flood or fire anywhere on earth? What could be more common—less worthy of attention, devalued by overproduction—than death?

What would be far more interesting, thinks Walter, and not impersonally now, beside his car in the bank's parking lot, would be staying alive: not dying.

Because of the ambulance blocking half the street, traffic on the other side creeping along as slowly as possible to see what's going on, and pedestrians wandering across in the middle of the block, Walter has to wait to get out of the parking lot. He sits in his car with the motor running, drumming his fingers on the steering wheel, sweat forming along his hairline: feeling an impatience he would not feel if he were going to live forever. Quite suddenly he realizes that he would like to live forever.

A desire like that contradicts his entire education: which tells him that to live forever is to be a Struldbrug, to creep into eternity with mind and body in perpetual decay, shit and stupidity draining from his crevices; which tells him that he would only live to bury his friends and loved ones, that he would try everything to the point of boredom or satiation, that he would become a diseased outcast among those healthy enough to die and eventually, as millennia pass, an ape among the evolved; which warns him that a dying world, seeing him remain forever alive, would come to hate him and that he, longing for the world's natural benediction of death, would come to hate himself as well; which warns him that he'd lose track of all he does and sees, that suffering more than joy would be the portion of his endless life, that the sun would turn cold and the earth decay, that he would have to sit in a lot more traffic tie-ups like this one, that his wife in her aging flesh would despise him, thinking he despises her; that would threaten him, finally, with losing his humanity: for to be human is to die.

He has presented a lot of people with their humanity, then, and he does not know that many of them have been grateful for it.

He does not think that the dead man across the street—who, as best he can judge from the sudden shifting in the crowd over there, is now being lifted into the back of the ambulance on a sheet-covered stretcher—is any more human for being dead.

And the way the crowd edges back as the body is carried through its midst, so that some are forced off the curb and into the street and others turn away and depart and one old woman backing up on high heels stumbles and sits down hard on the concrete and has to be lifted to her feet by those around her, does not suggest that the people there, curious as they've obviously been, are totally enthralled with this evidence of humanity.

He knows that the desire to live forever is only an adolescent dream, that only those too young to note how the world is aging and dying around them can assume their own immortality, and that not for long: for to stay alive is to watch others die and maybe, he thinks, vice versa. The deaths of others that are supposed to remind us of our own mortality mostly serve to remind us that we're still alive. Therefore, reasons Walter, the more death we see the more alive we are, and thanks to modern technology we have been able to sit right at home in our living rooms and really live. It's nothing new, he's sure: mankind has always killed to survive: on the battlefield, in experimental medicine, in the exploration and conquest of new lands, in the construction of tunnels and dams and bridges, sanctioned by laws of inheritance: yes, life has always depended on the deaths of others.

Dependent Walter, watching the ambulance glide slowly past the parking lot exit, watching pedestrians return to the sidewalks and traffic begin to move along and thin out, noses out into the street at last, looks left after the flashing lights of the ambulance, and drives carefully off in the other direction.

112. The Fight for Life

"Walter, you're wrong."

Maybe he is: having tried to present a fresh outlook on immortality at the dinner table, he finds he's making little headway.

Janey's round little eyes dart back and forth from one parent to the other: "What are you arguing about?"

"Life and death," says Walter.

"We're not arguing," says Penny simultaneously, "we're having a discussion."

Both of them demonstrate their points: Walter by tearing himself off another hunk of Penny's freshly-baked French bread, Penny by restating, in a calm and rational voice, her thesis that life is only life because death is death, that life is a terminal condition by definition, that the beginning and the middle are defined by the end, that it is in fact death that creates for life its value, its piquancy, its, yes, meaning.

"Meaning?" inquires Walter, wondering at the same time if what he's hearing isn't an extension of his own thoughts about the tidiness of endings, the virtue of containers.

"Yes, meaning," he's told: "nothing has meaning without boundaries, otherwise it's just a shapeless, meaningless mess, but it's the boundaries, like birth and death, that give shape to things, and everything has boundaries."

"'Nothing has meaning,'" quotes Walter, providing an earlier boundary than her text has intended, "and I don't know where it's decreed that 'everything has boundaries.' But if my life has to have a meaning, I think I'd rather give it that meaning myself than have death provide it."

"And what kind of meaning would you give it?" asks Penny.

What kind of meaning would death give it? Walter's tempted to reply instantly: all death means is that it's over. Death means you're dead.

"Life means you're alive."

"Huh?" says Penny, caught in the midst of stuffing another wound-up forkful of spaghetti into her mouth.

"I mean," says Walter, a little uncertainly, poking his own

fork around among the last few strands of spaghetti sinking from sight in the great puddle of tomato sauce left in his plate, "life is its own meaning. Just being alive is enough, a value in itself. The more life, the more meaning. If I'm ever reduced to looking for meaning in my life, I won't look for it in my death."

"Suicides do," counters Penny.

Walter doesn't think so. He just thinks suicides don't like what their lives mean, though maybe they're the most devoted of all subscribers to the theory that death gives life meaning: they can't wait. Such a hurry! And, he thinks, such disappointment, if it's meaning they're looking for.

"If I'm going to give meaning to something," he says at last, "it's my life, not my death."

"But you still haven't told me what kind of meaning you'd give it."

Waiting for a reply, Penny pulls off a piece of French bread and wipes it around in her plate to mop up the sauce. Walter, waiting for a reply himself, does the same, only with all the sauce left in his plate it's hopeless. The soggy bread begins to fall apart as he lifts it from the plate, but he manages, leaning over, to get it into his mouth without too much mess. No one says anything. He tears off another piece, dips it into the sauce more cautiously, nibbles at its red edges, dips again.

Janey eyes their busy silence: "Are you done fighting now?"

113 . Freedom of the Press

Walter, concerned with the news the telephone has brought him today, no longer fights the surprises the media can bring him: though there are surprises all the same. Since he first encountered what surprises the newspaper can bring, Walter, unfolding it every morning, never looks for news that might concern him on the front pages, which report on wars in the Middle East, volcanic eruptions on the Pacific rim, assassinations in Latin America, legislative blunders from Washington, tank truck explosions on the interstates, tank ship break-ups in the international waterways, and outbreaks of weather everywhere.

These are the things that are happening: therefore the things the world is taught to be interested in. Walter, since that first eruption of the morning news in his own world, has generally been pleased to find that with him nothing is happening: nothing more than an inch or so of filler from time to distant time at the back of the local section. But he can't decide if he prefers this sort of couple-of-times-a-year nothing to absolute nothing: if he'd be happier never to find anything, not even in the back pages. Unsolved crimes, he knows, are not particularly newsworthy items, but little reminders that someone is working on them are sufficient to bring them, now and then, into the peripheral vision of the news agencies, and Walter would prefer that not even that much of an eye was being kept on him. He's seen other items from these same back pages—reports of a minor street incident in Lebanon, sales of weapons to an African nation, analysis of seismic activity in the Aleutian Islands—suddenly flare up into the front page as civil war, congressional scandal, earthquakes, and he does not want to be part of any such conflagration himself.

Walter wants the freedom of the press, much argued for in his country these days. He also wants the freedom to read the newspaper and watch the evening news without worrying about coming face to face with himself there: a freedom from fear that he does not have these days. It still amazes him how he just had to pick up that one single morning paper to be shoved into a world of such disquiet: a world where, as he has done daily for slightly over two years now, he finds he has to check quickly through the paper page by page before he can settle down at last to reading the sports section with any comfort. He does not know what he would do now if he found something there. He knows that anything he does find, no matter how infrequent or insignificant or well-hidden, keeps him from getting on to the sports page.

So far, of course, he's really found nothing worse than the old news that some old murder cases have been re-opened and that there's no new news on the old news, and though he knows perfectly well that most of those old cases were nothing he was ever involved with, even the current silence about the investigation isn't enough to alleviate his worries and open the sports pages to him with much relief if only because he knows that behind a silence there is always something: or someone. Nor does it give him any ease to not know in even the vaguest sense who that someone is whose name is never mentioned in the rare little back page news item reporting that that someone has nothing to report.

But now, this very evening, thanks to yet another branch of the media, which removes him from dining to living room with the solid gong that announces one of the few television programs that Penny tolerates watching, "Faces in the Evening News," Walter, for the first time, actually gets to see that someone, though he does not come away from the experience feeling that this viewing will be much of an aid to future recognition.

Walter and Penny arrive on the blue couch, in front of the television set, coffee cups in hand, dirty dishes abandoned on the kitchen table, just as the interviewer, a tough woman newscaster whose nasty demeanor in interviews Walter has always found refreshing if not especially likeable, introduces the evening's first guest by announcing that she cannot introduce her guest by name. She herself, she explains, does not know her guest's name.

Walter looks up from his coffee cup.

Across the table from the interviewer sits a man—Walter thinks it's a man—in a paper bag into which only a pair of eye holes have been cut. The bag comes down over both head and neck onto the narrow shoulders and across the top of the jacket and sweater of the person sitting motionless there.

"What do you think of this?" says the interviewer as the camera zooms in and the paper bag fills the whole screen.

114. Bagged

Walter, carefully setting his coffee cup down on the glass coffee table in front of him while the camera cuts away for a quick sequence of commercials, doesn't think much of it. Penny laughs the little snorting laugh that Walter knows means she doesn't think much of it either: in a different way, of course. The interviewer returns to the screen with an attitude indicating that she probably doesn't think much of it herself, as her questions gather only a minimum of information from the face that is hidden from the evening news. The voice from inside the paper bag—Walter thinks it's a deep enough voice to be a man's, though it has an electronically altered tone to it—acknowledges that he—Walter decides he might as well assume it's a man—is an investigator for a government agency which cannot be named, that he's working on a number of unsolved but not unconnected murders that cannot be further specified in a number of different cities that cannot be designated, and that his own identity, obviously, cannot be revealed.

Walter watches, silent. Penny snorts her sense of the ridiculous as the interviewer burrows along with her usual relentless technique, only managing to elicit negatives: what the paper bag cannot say, cannot reveal, cannot provide any details of, cannot discuss, cannot....

"And just what can you do?" she finally demands with considerable sharpness.

"I can solve these murders," rasps the odd, muffled voice from inside the paper bag.

Walter is glad he's still not holding his coffee cup in his hands: he's feeling what he thinks he'd be feeling if he were to discover that he was currently on television himself. Penny is jiggling with unrest: it's apparent to Walter that for her this interview is going nowhere, even though it's gone almost all the way to him. The paper bag is motionless, placid with the assurance of its last statement. The interviewer is dubious, edging her chair forward as if it were just remotely possible that she was either going to be let in on the secret solution at last or about to rip the paper bag off her guest's head.

But the bag remains untouched, and when the secret isn't

forthcoming, she fills the silence by asking for it herself: "And just what makes you think you can do that?"

"I cannot say," says the paper bag.

Walter, sitting as far forward on the edge of the couch as the interviewer on her chair, finds this reply just as disconcerting as she seems to. She turns away from the paper bag and stares into the camera's eye, into Walter's eye, the way it comes out, with a mixed look of frustration and disgust.

Right, thinks Walter, what the hell does that paper bag think it's doing on this program anyway? And what kind of answers can you expect from a paper bag? Walter's not at all sure he even wants to know what's in the bag. How, he thinks, a little fearfully, can you be afraid of an ordinary brown paper bag? And the interviewer begins to look like she no longer believes a paper bag is worth interviewing.

"I don't suppose," she says, without even bothering to look over at it any longer, "you can tell us what means you'll use to solve these crimes?"

"I'm afraid I cannot say."

"Or even what kind of bag you're hiding in?"

"Kraft Number Five."

"I'm afraid our time is up."

Walter actually thinks, at this conclusion, that he hears the paper bag crinkle in a smile, though obviously neither he nor the interviewer feels like smiling at this.

115. Cutting It

Not altogether pleased to go about haunted by a vision of a paper bag, Walter suspects, all the same, that it could be worse. He could have a specific vision of a man with bright red hair, a man with a goatee, of a woman with a large mole on the side of her nose, or a limp, or a wide straw hat . . . . And then he would find himself startled by, having to cope with, every odd walk or birthmark that appeared in his vicinity, every flash of red or white in the corner of his eye. But someone in a paper bag could be anyone, and everyone could be anyone, and no one can be startled by or try to cope with the presence of everyone.

So, as Walter knows, things could be worse. In fact, the image of the paper bag does not stick with him long. Although at first, after the television interview ends and Penny switches the set off, he considers the possibility that every trip to the grocery or hardware or discount store will bring back, as he carries home the brown bags, an instant recall of the interview, he knows, more rationally, both that sacks of food and hardware pose no particular threat to him and that if there is, in fact, someone out there closing in on him, watching and following him, that someone won't be walking the streets wearing a brown paper bag over his or her head.

So he is at ease again with paper bags: carries out the garbage in one, watches Penny pack his lunch for tomorrow in another, decides it's possible to continue using them for storing dust rags, old newspapers, other paper bags. Even now, barely an hour later, he is sitting at the kitchen table making masks out of two medium sized paper bags, probably the same kind of bag the person in the television interview wore. Janey and Judy sit on either side of him, each waiting with a fistful of crayons while he snips out two eye holes and a mouth hole in each bag, tries them over the girls' heads, then removes them to enlarge the eye holes, bringing the eyes closer together. Then he rises and leaves the bags and the table to his daughters, who begin at once with great intensity to crayon in the faces they have imagined for themselves. Master of the brown paper bag, Walter departs from this kitchen scene of domestic tranquility quite fearlessly.

Back in the upstairs study from which his daughters have called him forth, Walter finds, however, that he is still clutching the scissors ferociously in his right hand. An old pair of scissors, long and pointed and darkly rusted along the blades, Walter is surprised to discover himself hanging on to them like this, almost angrily. They're only ordinary scissors that have been around the house forever; he doesn't remember when or where they acquired them, but knows he's used them to open packages, cut wrapping paper, trim bangs, that he's seen Penny cutting dead leaves off house plants with them and snipping coupons from the newspaper. An old pair of general, all-around, useful, household scissors, he thinks: what is this grip I've got on them?

Scissors still in hand, he sits down at his desk, thinking he will drop them in a drawer and get on with some of the niggling paper work he's been asked to do here at the end of the semester, like writing up his course descriptions for next fall. Instead he rips a piece of lined yellow paper off the legal pad lying on his desk and begins to snip away at it. He doesn't remember which drawer he got the scissors out of anyway; probably he didn't even find them in his desk. Every time he looks for them they seem to be in a different place: kitchen drawer, bathroom cabinet, tool chest, Penny's sewing box: they appear to move around with a freedom of their own, just as they seem to be doing now on the piece of paper Walter holds up in his left hand. He thought at first about making some pattern out of this, but the scissors, instead, seem merely to be making a sequence of random slashes across the paper, first vertical, then horizontal. The center of the paper remains intact, but all four sides are in shreds, and now each additional slash sends a shower of confetti-sized bits of yellow paper sprinkling down over the top of his otherwise uncluttered desk. The scissors make sharp, decisive snips, quickly reducing the paper to a small, oddly-shaped fragment held between Walter's left thumb and forefinger, and then in amazement he watches that, too, disappear in a flurry of yellow scraps drifting down over his desk.

My god, he thinks, leaning back in his chair, I've never seen my desk in such a condition as this.

The scissors, still firmly hooked to his right thumb and

forefinger, stand erect in front of him, ignoring the havoc they've wrought. With some effort he wrenches them loose and throws them, clattering, into a drawer of his metal filing cabinet, which he quickly closes upon them. Then he picks up the wicker waste basket from beside his desk and begins to scoop the scraps of paper carefully off the desk top into the basket. Some of the scraps fly up as he slides his hand among them, however, and drift down to the carpet around his desk as he works, and the sharp, metallic clang of the scissors he tossed into the filing cabinet still rings in his ears like a final echo of all the little changes that have been rung upon him today.

CHAPTER XII

116. No

Awkwardness sends Walter and Dora scurrying back and forth to each other's offices in a way that will soon have everyone in the department guessing what's going on between them if they don't stop it. The source of all this activity is a three-day summer seminar in San Francisco, scheduled to begin not long after the semester ends. The title of the seminar is "The Death of an Idea," but Walter is not so much interested in knowing that the idea whose death will be examined is Modernism as in taking advantage of the opportunity to clear up the mess death has left him with in nearby San Jose. And he doesn't know why Dora's interested in the seminar, but she's willing to tell him.

"Three whole days together!"

"But you're a medievalist."

"Walter, I am also interested in the history of ideas."

"But," he says, who has been thinking, not without relief, that their affair has been over since the end of fall term, who has heard it rumored that she has been dating an Assistant Dean in the School of Engineering, but who is suddenly quite conscious of his swelling penis even as he stands there talking with her, "I thought we weren't going to, uh, see each other anymore?"

"But your wife won't be there, Walter. That was your problem, wasn't it, that she was here? It'll just be us this time, for three days, anyway."

She's seated behind her desk, tapping on it with the eraser end of a pencil. He is acutely aware that he's standing in her open doorway: "I can't believe we're having this conversation here." He retreats to the safety of his own office and its closed door, but soon there's a sharp knock and the door opens.

"I'm expecting a student," he lies.

"Walter, what are you so worried about?" She closes the door behind her.

He's worried because he thinks that somehow he should have known something like this was going to happen. She's wearing her grey suit, which he's observed she only wears on important occasions. It's both business-like and attractive. He says, "It will be perfectly obvious to everybody what's going on."

"Because colleagues go to a conference together? What right do they have to draw assumptions from that?"

"They don't have any right, but they'd certainly be right."

There's another knock at the door: the propitious and unexpected student, whom Walter quickly motions to a chair. Behind the young man's back, Dora leans seductively in the doorway, hand on hip, to give her exit line in her flattest, most businesslike voice, "I'll check on flights."

An hour later, they are checking on each other again, seated on opposite sides of Dora's desk, her pencil in hand again—Walter realizes that he's never seen her at her desk without a pencil in her hand—but the door closed this time. Walter explains, truthfully, that he's also planning, as part of his ongoing editorial project and with the help of a summer research grant from the University, to use this trip to initiate a quest for the author of *Time Lapse*, who he has reason to believe is living on the west coast. She taps her pencil on the desk and shakes her head at Walter, who then adds, less than truthfully, that his wife is considering accompanying him on this trip.

"Walter, everybody knows your wife doesn't go to conferences with you."

"If you go, she'll certainly be suspicious. Someone's bound to say something, sooner or later. I think she's already uncomfortable about you." Is she? Walter wonders. Or was it just indifference that turned Penny's head away the last time he mentioned something about Dora to her?

"The question isn't whether I go, Walter, it's whether you go. I'm interested in the seminar, the U has travel money, I need a break, and I've never been to the Bay Area. Besides, I can stop and visit my folks on the way out." She taps her pencil once for each item in her catalogue, lays it down on the desk when she's done, then picks it up again and adds: "If you come along, you'll just have to figure out a way to deal with it. At the moment, I'm not even sure I want to spend my time there with you."

Wait a minute, Walter wants to say, this was my idea, I was the one who was going to go to the seminar first. But before he can complain he's stricken, in quick succession, by a recognition of how childish that sounds as well as by a feeling of frustration at this sudden loss of control and, quite unexpectedly, a solid thump of jealousy: who would she spend her time there with? Is that handsome young Assistant Dean just waiting for the chance to go flying off to San Francisco with her? And why should that bother him, anyway? Isn't he the one who couldn't handle continuing their affair, the one who couldn't cope with the deception?

She seems to think otherwise, answering his thoughts with a quick smile: "Besides, Walter, you seem pretty adept at matters of deception."

"No," he responds instantly, not sure whether he's saying no to his talent for deception, the seminar, Dora's trip, the possibility of resuming their affair. Just no: confusion brings him to a full stop.

"No what?" she asks, but he just sits there.

"Walter, there's something more to it, isn't there?"

"No," he says, almost jumping with the sudden awareness of how tightly she's clutching her pencil in her fist.

"No," he repeats: "What?"

"I don't know, Walter, but something. Something."

Walter just sits there.

"All right, then," she says, loosening her grip and casually tossing the pencil down on her desk, "have it your way."

His way, thinks Walter: is this his way? He doesn't even know what way this is that he's told he can finally have it. Is this, whatever it is, the way he wants it? His way?

No: "No."

117. WHY?

Walter sits in his office after all his colleagues have gone home, drumming his own pencil on his own desk and wondering how this is going to end. Walter doesn't drum his pencil on his desk and he doesn't hang around late in the day. Unless there's a committee meeting he has to stay for, he leaves early. In recent years he has met the University's service requirement by accepting appointments to numerous committees; it's never a problem—and usually the truth—to tell Penny he'll be late because of an afternoon meeting, since most meet from four to six. Not today. Nothing keeps him on campus late today, sitting in his office drumming his pencil on his desk and wondering. Wondering isn't something he prefers either: not any more than staying late and drumming on his desk with his pencil. Walter doesn't believe in wondering what he does, just in doing what he does.

Except lately, he thinks: lately he's been doing considerable wondering. Like today: wondering how this will end.

When he stops thumping on the desk like an infant banging its head against the end of its crib, he also wonders how it began. He waits and wonders, lays his pencil down on his desk and sits back in his chair, but no explanation presents itself. The clock over the door, already indicating he's going to be late for dinner, suggests that maybe there is no explanation other than time. Time passes and things happen. It was just time. One day, he thinks: one day he was kneeling on the floor in Dora's living room leaning over to touch her breast. One day. After that came another day. And another day. And so on. Then there came a lapse of days, weeks, months now: nothing. And now, today, something again. Maybe he shouldn't worry about it: sooner or later, just as it was eventually today, it will eventually be tomorrow. And something will happen: maybe something else.

Against the grain of not wondering, against the realization that he's hungry and wishes he were home already, he wonders: Is that all there is to it? Time passes and the things that happen happen? But such things! And this thing rather than that thing: today this happens, another day that; to me one thing happens, to another person something else: why?

Abruptly he stands up, grabs his pencil off the desk, snaps it in half, throws it in the waste basket and grunts, "Ugh!" for "Why?" "Ugh!" for the world of "Why?" he's wondered into: not a world where he wants to be. Many people have asked him "Why?": their final question. And he has always answered with a quick non sequitur. And still the world is full of people wandering about asking "why?": for whom the reply, whether he provides it or not, will be the same, eventually: time's reply. And Walter's? If he doesn't ask the question, maybe he won't get the answer.

So off he goes: out of his office, closing the door snugly behind him, out of the building and across the almost empty parking lot and into the station wagon and on his way. No more asking questions, no more pointless wonderings, when he could be home instead. No more whys when he could be happily at home eating dinner with his family. No whys when he can be home eating dinner and playing with his children and making love with his wife.

But at home, he will soon discover, at home they also ask "Why?": especially when you're late for dinner.

118. Because

"Because," explains Walter, "it's a non-valid, useless, counterproductive, self-defeating, and lethal question. That's why." Or: that's "why?"

"That's an awful lot to put on a little three letter word."

Now that the children have gone to bed, Penny and Walter are free to resume the bickering that was suspended for the sake of a digestible meal and a reasonably peaceful evening. The meatloaf survived his tardiness—nearly intact, given the general lack of appetite at dinner—but Walter's beginning to wonder if he will. Penny doesn't begrudge his lateness: she only wants to know why: is it such a terrible question?

"'Little things mean a lot,'" sings Walter: "a little word, a bullet a couple of centimeters long, a tiny cyanide capsule, the single surviving spermatozoon, the first mad cancer cell."

"My, my," interrupts Penny, "aren't we being snide and knowledgeable tonight."

Chair pulled up tight against the dining room table, to which they've returned—who could say why?—to complete the argument that began there, Penny slides the sugar bowl back and forth from one hand to the other as if it were the only piece left on a giant game board spread between them. Only there's no checkered table cloth: no squares, no rules, only the wide expanse of oak, coarse-grained, with sudden edges all around.

And Walter at the far end: defending, he thinks, his life: "Would it really make such a difference to know why?"

"Yes, Walter, it would."

"Even if it was only that I was sitting in my office thinking?" Now he sits with his hands clasped behind his head and his chair tipped back on its two rear legs.

Penny, squeezing the sugar bowl between both hands now, sits forward and thinks: "Is that really the reason, Walter?"

"See!" cries Walter, leaning suddenly forward so that his chair bangs down hard on its front legs: "See: that's where 'why?' gets you: more questions. You give one answer and right away someone wants to know if that's the real answer. Are you sure there isn't some other answer? If that's the answer, why is that the answer: why did you do that? Why didn't you watch the clock? Why didn't you call? Why did you have to sit there and what were you thinking about? And why didn't you come home to do your thinking? Why don't you think in your study here?"

Walter doesn't actually make a speech like that: not his style. What Walter says is, "'Why' kills."

Penny releases the sugar bowl, arches her back, stretches, arms out: "Bad as that, huh?"

"Every bit," answers Walter, leaning forward to put his head down on his arms as he talks, slowly: "You answer one Why? and you open up a dozen more. And a dozen more for each of that dozen. You die before you can answer all the Why?'s. You have to stop living to even begin to answer them. There's no end to them. Once you're in their grip, you're lost. They take you nowhere. They don't let you live."

Penny stands: "You look tired, Walter."

"No." He raises his head, sits up. "Not really. Only a little. Do you suppose that if you never asked 'Why?'—if you never had to answer 'Why?'—you could live forever?"

Penny comes around to his side of the table, puts her arm over his shoulders and pulls him toward her: "Still thinking about living forever, Walter?"

He puts his arm around her hips and squeezes. His other arm, too, burying his face in her belly.

"Sometimes," comes his muffled reply.

"Come to bed," she says softly.

Tilting his head back, both arms still circling her hips, he looks up at her and wonders aloud, "Suppose I asked why?'"

"Oh, I have lots of reasons," she says, smiling down on him, "and all good ones. Two of your favorites are right in front of your face."

119. ALL WOUND UP

Walter wakes to the loud ticking of the bedroom clock, reaches for it over sleeping Penny, face down on her pillow, lifts it off the night table on her side of the bed and turns off the alarm before it rings. Only as he sets it back down, very quietly, still leaning over Penny, does it dawn on him that this clock, which they have had beside their bed for many years, is an electric clock. Why, then, does it tick like that?

Very carefully he lifts the clock and its trailing white cord over Penny, over the wooden headboard, over to his own side of the bed, where he sits up, puts on his glasses, which have been lying as usual on the night stand on his own side, and begins to examine it. The clock is shaped like an old-fashioned windup alarm, with a black metal case, a big silvery bell on top, and several over-sized keys and knobs for setting and winding it on the back. And a white cord trailing out of the bottom. It was a gift but he cannot remember from whom: his mother? her father? What he does know, even without trying it, is that the big wind-up key in the center of the back won't work. Why should it?

He tries it anyway; it spins loosely at his touch.

When he lifts it to his ear, he can hear, beneath its loud, regular ticking, the steady whine of its electric mechanism. Somebody, he thinks, has gone to an awful lot of trouble to make an electric clock that resembles a wind-up clock right down to the tick: somewhere in here—perhaps for the benefit of people who like wind-up clocks, who like them ticking beside their beds but cannot remember to wind them—they have put, in addition to the electric clock works, an electric ticking mechanism. For the forgetful, for the nostalgic, the clock is always wound up.

Walter sits up in bed studying the back of the alarm clock: how has he managed to let all these years slip by without discovering its secret? Tempted to open it up and see what makes it tick, only the doubt that he could put it back together again restrains him. Instead, he fiddles nervously with the keys and knobs until at last, more or less by accident, he sets off the alarm, and the silver bell, activated like the rest of the clock by some unseen electric mechanism, rings loudly, almost in Penny's ear. Unlike the real wind-up clock which it resembles, the alarm bell on this one does not run down. It rings on and on.

At last Penny props herself up on her elbows and looks over at Walter sitting there beside her holding the clock, which is still ringing, electric and relentless.

"For god's sake, Walter, what're you doing with the clock?" She reaches over and shuts off the alarm herself.

"Somebody," says Walter, "somebody, even in this quiet electric age of ours, sure wants us to know that time is ticking by."

120. In and Out of Synch

Standing in the center of his stuffy office on the last day of spring semester, Walter practices a kind of mental syncopation, setting up the beat of the alarm clock in his head and then popping his mind's fingers not on the obvious electric ticks but on the brief moments of silence between them. Only he can't keep this attempt to get himself in synch with time's regular little leaps going for more than a few beats before other patterns intrude: his regular breathing, the irregular crawl of sweat drops down his forehead, the unmusical rhythms of thought scratching for a larger share of attention, and the monotone hum of the big electric clock above his door, which is about to buzz its disruptive buzzer even though classes are no longer in session.

It's not just the last day of classes or the last day of exams, but the very last day Walter has to be at the University until freshman orientation in the fall. He's only here to turn in his grades, to deposit his gradebook in his desk drawer, to stack term papers and blue books on the table outside his door for his students to pick up at their leisure, though he knows that most of them have departed for home already and that most of these essays and exams will still be lying there in September: only a long pause away between the two loud ticks of the semesters.

But still he stands there, sweaty, leaning forward, hands gripping the back of his desk chair. The door is shut, windows closed and latched, desk top perfectly bare, all his notebooks stacked away in his locked closet, all the books he has been using throughout the semester returned, last week while his students were writing their finals, to their proper places on his bookshelves. He doesn't hear a sound in the building: not the whoosh of the air conditioning, which won't get turned on till summer school opens, not the voices of his colleagues, whose intrusions he doesn't worry about: they are still at home grading exams, and many of them, he knows, won't meet Friday's deadline for turning in grades: they never do. But these meager attempts to stay out of synch with official time, Walter thinks a little snidely, are only rationalizations for fully synchronized incompetence. The clock on the wall, equally incompetent, emits fifteen seconds of raw noise, summoning no one to class.

It is, Walter sees, letting go his grip on the chair and standing up straighter than his customary slouch admits to look up into its face, in synch only with itself and others of its kind. He spins the swivel chair around and lets himself down onto its padded seat, wondering, on the other hand, who he's in synch with: who he could turn to who would be—would dare to be—attuned to his own pulses and rhythms: not just the loud, obvious ticks of family, job, family, job, either, but the regular, deadly silences in between, which are, as he's discovered this afternoon, the hardest to get even his own self in synch with.

121. Getting Going

All right, then, who? Who is there he can talk to not just about a part of his life but the whole: if, he thinks, spinning the chair back to face the desk, it makes a whole. And even if it doesn't, who? Who besides the bathroom mirror that others always seem to be waiting to have their own consultations with, or the photograph in his closet that only dizzies him? Who? To almost anyone he can talk about his family, his teaching, but to whom can he speak about the silent, unspeakable in-betweens? To whom can he speak about Dora but Dora herself? And she's already gone: not necessarily more efficient but simply determined to get her work done and take off for Denver, as he knows she did last night, to visit her parents before going on to San Francisco. To whom for that matter, can he speak about murder but the victims? They'll talk, of course, but those brief, edgy conversations, however emotional, never seem to get around to his own feelings.

Well, he could talk to his pursuer, but that conversation, he can see, might come too late to meet his needs. Or, thinks Walter, besides himself, to whom he doesn't really want to talk about the subject—aside from himself, who is his own and only best friend but a little too intimately involved to be able to offer much in the way of perspective—there is only, that he can think of, who isn't likely to be upset or revolted or offended or angry, his contact, his—admit it—Buddy. Why not?

Because, he realizes as he finishes dialling the second number, the one to bring him in contact with his contact, and hears it begin to ring at the other end: because he is not supposed to be talking, he's supposed to be doing, so even here he can expect rejection: and gets it in the immediate tone of voice that responds to his own quick offering of identification.

"Listen," Walter explains, "I just need someone to talk to."

"What talk? Don't you have things to do?"

Yes, Walter thinks, I do. But "What talk?" Because I need a friend, and look what I've come to for a friend? Because I need someone to whom I can say, "I am not who you think I am?"

Says his Buddy, "I know exactly who you are."

Did I say that aloud? Walter wonders: or is someone reading my mind? Maybe, he considers: hasn't this unseen contact, this disembodied voice at the far end of the line, served him like a fairy godmother all these years, granting him his every wish—well, at least his one wish over and over again—most every time he's called, and generally without his even having to voice it?

"Well?" A voice reminding him that someone's still there.

Well? If he's only used up one wish, shouldn't he have two left? The first of which, he thinks, might be to do something about this hot, suffocating, sweatbox of an office he's shut himself up into. Agh. The last wish he knows you have to save to clean up the mess resulting from the first two, but meanwhile, apropos of this, this stifling little hotbox in which he feels he can hardly breathe—96 degrees, registers the thermostat on the wall beside the door—this airless cube he's so efficiently sealed himself up in—doors, windows, closets and drawers all shut up tight, no one there, here—this paper bag he's pulled over his head without cutting any air holes in it, this book he calls his life with its tightly-closed covers into the V of whose once-open pages he feels he's slipped and been squashed, breathless, this . . . all this: isn't it time to get going from this?

"I think," Walter gasps into the telephone, "I think I'll just get going now."

And sure enough, the voice at the other end grants his wish: "Get going, Walter."

122. Some of the Ugliest Places in the World

To get going means not to spend the summer spading up the flower garden for Penny, trying to repair the punctured screens and awnings and ending by having both professionally done, chauffeuring the girls to recreation department swimming lessons and accompanying them now and then to the beaches himself, re-reading *Time Lapse* yet one more time while desultorily polishing his own insufficient sentences about it, taking advantage of the girls' absences while they play at the homes of friends to make sweaty love with Penny on hot afternoons, and reading, of course, the newspaper, from first page to last, at breakfast, sweating through every little item found or imagined there, waiting for the silence-shattering headline that reads AGENT SAYS END NEAR.

To get going means to let these usuals lapse, means to lurch forward, less knowingly, into something, certainly, else: but, wonders Walter, does it have to be into this? This?

Because this, he has made a point of saying since their arrival, is one of the ugliest places in the world. Oh, he was willing to come here, as Penny's quick to remind him every time he starts to sound off, but he was agreeable to going anywhere the girls wanted for a little trip before his own summer travels got underway. But the choice of a tour of the elegant horse farms of Lexington, Kentucky, whose white-fenced bluegrass pastures spread their rolling acres out before him now, was Janey and Judy's. This, ugly? They have all been suitably shocked. Well, he's entitled to his opinion, isn't he?

"But Daddy!"

But Daddy's been here before, if not exactly for the scenery. And perhaps he's exaggerating. It's been suggested: in the car, in restaurants, at the motel. Maybe he is stretching it a bit by saying "in the world," that exaggeration signifying not the world's extremity but his. He hasn't, after all, seen the industrial midlands of England, the slums around Mexico City, or the unsalvageable wreck of Calcutta, to name a few that he's at least heard about. Penny has made it clear that his opinion is not adding much to the beauty of the trip, and Walter himself isn't sure why he's so insistent on this issue. In his defense, he argues, mostly to himself, it's the ugliness that's insistent.

But for his daughters, even Walter has to acknowledge, Lexington, Kentucky, is not a place with a dingy little downtown, an unattractive university campus, an unplanned sprawl of suburban shopping centers, and an all-too-well-planned, it seems to him, concentration of black slums, but merely a name for a vacuous center—though it's just such emptiness that Walter's own dark gaze seems unavoidably drawn to—ringed about by one of the seven wonders of the modern child's world.

And the other six, thinks Walter, turning his back on the pastures and leaning over the half door of the stable to look in upon one of Calumet Farm's immaculate horse boxes, are probably all Disney Worlds.

123. Travel Is Broadening

Maybe this is Disney World, too: there are horses but no horseshit. The Calumet stables are just about the cleanest living quarters—animal or human—that Walter has ever seen, just like all the other stables they've seen on their tour of the bluegrass breeding farms. The straw, they have been told at every stop, is changed twice a day; the floors and walls are scrubbed down with a frequency and thoroughness that would shame the most meticulous homemaker. Everything glistens with fresh white paint in the June sunshine. The oats are first quality, as are the daily groomings and the plentiful acreage of the white-fenced Kentucky bluegrass pastures, each with its picturesque thoroughbred stallion.

Just such a perfect scene does Walter see again as he turns away from the stable, shading his eyes in the afternoon sun: a gleaming white fence, not unlike the one whose peeling paint marks the boundary of his own backyard; a rolling bluegrass pasture; and, in the distance, a solid, chestnut horse grazing in the shade of a large oak. The girls prance about him, begging him to take a picture of this beautiful horse and finally agreeing to pose for him—Janey leaning against the fence and Judy perched on the top rail—when he explains that the horse is too far off to show up well in the pictures and hopes that its enormous penis, which astounds him even at this distance though they have been looking at remarkable studs all day, won't show up at all.

At his daughters' urging, he has already taken fifteen or twenty pictures of horses, all of which, he's sure, live better than many of the people in this ugly little city. The horses eat the best oats where some people lack oatmeal; they have clean, private living quarters and acres of sunny backyard to play in; and people who already have more money than they know what to do with actually manage to increase their income by losing money breeding and raising and racing these beasts.

"It's disgusting," he mumbles, peering through the viewfinder at his two pretty little brown-haired daughters who, isolated from the rest of the world in their flowered blouses and sky-blue shorts against a white fence and a background of rich green pasture graced with the statuary presence of one perfect them stretching their arms out impatiently against the white fence as he hesitates, blinks, sees them stretching upward into young women against this perfectly framed isolation, and mutters again, as he clicks the shutter and waves them down off the fence before the tour guide can come to chastise them, "Disgusting."

Only when he hears Penny, behind him, giggling, does it occur to him that, given part of what he's been aiming the camera at, she must have been more than a little amused by his remark, thinking he was focusing on, commenting on, a piece of equine anatomy no different than what they have both noted on dozens of other oversized stallions throughout the day. Whereas what he himself was surprised by was this sudden appearance of a rudimentary social conscience. Well, he thinks, turning about to glare at her, she might show a little of that herself: though he realizes it is Penny, of course, who has been active in all the liberal causes of the last decade.

But just how fiercely he's glaring he can't imagine, until he finds himself asking why she's backing away from him. Camera in one hand, he reaches out toward her with the other, and still she continues to back away step by step as he advances, until she's almost pinned up against the wall of the stable. And the more she backs away, the more something else, something a long way removed from social righteousness, creeps up on him, until he realizes, stepping toward her, letting the camera drop from his hand to snap and swing from the strap around his neck, watching how the dark pupils of her eyes focus unblinkingly on the face he can't see, that what he'd really like to do is to slap her, hard, right across the face, open-handed but hard: one hard, clean, sharp, open-handed, violent, slap.

124. THE DISCOVERY OF THE INTERNAL COMBUSTION ENGINE

"Walter!"

Why? he thinks, watching her start to raise her hands to ward him off: why?

And then: Oh no, I'm not going to let myself in for that.

"I've never seen you look like that before."

All the same, he thinks, why?

"I'm sorry," he says, pushing his hands up under his glasses to rub his eyes: "Maybe it's time to go back to the motel," where, perhaps, he will find some way to understand how outraged social consciousness lighting terror in the eyes of a presumably sympathetic observer should in turn ignite in him the flames of a purely personal violence. Something in his eyes he hasn't let shine through before: one small, unexpected crack in the dispassionate armor of professionalism through which he's always approached the world and suddenly, it seems, everything flashes through. He's been seen.

Oh, seen: yes, he's quite sure of that. He can feel it; he feels suddenly naked and observed, seen as he was just moments ago ready to do something he's never even thought of doing before. Why? No: he knows it's not "why?" but "who?" He, of course, knows who. And so, apparently, do others, now. They've seen, they know: he's sure of it, as he quietly herds the girls into the station wagon for the drive back to the Holiday Inn: where the linen is changed fresh daily but the family of Job is herded, at the bargain family rate, four into a room.

And this, thinks Walter, looking about the crowded room, suitcases lying open on the floor, the girls bouncing on one double bed to the extravagant rhythms of the television set, and Penny stretched on her back on the other, book in hand but eyes on him, where he stands in the midst of it all, right between the two beds, this is a mess.

So he shakes his head, signifying helplessness, and departs for the little oak-paneled bar off the lobby, where, all by himself at a little oak table, leaning forward over his untouched bourbon and ice, he thinks: this, too, is a mess. Or: wherever I go these days is a mess. Or: only with great diligence have I, all these years, kept the mess, which is everywhere, from surfacing. The more he broods about it, the more "or"s there are, and the further they carry him: toward himself:

Or: there is no mess here, or anywhere; there is only me.

Or: yes, there is too a mess: everywhere I am.

Or: there is only me, and I am a mess.

And: so finally I am in synch with myself, but is this the self I want to be in synch with?

Also: do I have a choice?

He pauses to think about that one, and then, as if to demonstrate that he does indeed have a choice, gets up and walks out of the dark little bar, leaving his drink untouched behind him, and across the lobby and out through the glass front doors and onto the asphalt of the parking lot, where he stands blinking in the hot, late sunlight, amid the multicolored glare of cars. There are choices, he thinks, all these makes and models and colors, but when it comes to the self, really, what choice is there? If I get tired of this model, or if it's been too badly used to be serviceable any longer, can I trade it in? And if I could trade it in, is it likely that the model I got in trade would be any different? Or isn't every single one run, deep inside, by the same internal combustion mess? Naturally, with effort and practice, we keep the hood closed and the chrome polished, most of us, most of the time, except when some legalized emergency lets us run stripped-down, souped-up versions wherever we want, even over the crowds of bystanders on the sidewalks. But the mess is there, all the same, all the time, and we know what the name of the mess is, oh, we know it, we know what's purring along deep inside us, man woman and child we know it, and know it in others, know it when we see it even if we don't always know it when we feel its relentless little electric hum pushing us along, know it in you and you and you and, of course, in me, know it for what it is, which is: violence.

What we don't know, he concludes, threading his way through the cars, across the parking lot, is what to do with it.

Because, he continues to conclude, spotting the blue station wagon in the next row, we have to do something with it.

Just because, he offers as a final conclusion, digging his key out of his pocket and unlocking the door, it's there.

Here: he sits down behind the wheel of the stiflingly hot station wagon, bouncing the keys in his hand, letting the door hang open: here. Here: end of lecture. No more lectures, ever. Nothing more to say beyond "here."

Except that here, where he is by choice—some sort of choice—does not really seem the best place to be. Here, in this ugly little city where it does not surprise him to recall that he has killed as often as in any other city, even New York, since in no other city but here and New York has he ever killed more than once; here in this city where he has, in fact, killed recently; here, he thinks, sitting behind the wheel of his station wagon with the door open and the light from the low angle of the sinking sun filling the inside with brightness and heat, right here: here is not a good place to be.

125. Not a Good Place To Be

If Lexington, Kentucky, is not, now, a good place to be for Walter, where, exactly, is a good place to be?

On the little commuter hop to Cincinnati, where he will catch his connecting flight to the conference in San Francisco, Walter cannot think of one. He has chosen to fly, rather than drive with his family, because the girls, for whom the whole world now seems to consist of good and beautiful places to be, have thought of one more where they'd like to be: Mammoth Cave. And they have persuaded Penny, who also thinks there are good places to be, to take them there before they start homeward.

"I don't understand what this place has done to you, Walter," she has said at the airport, even as Walter stooped to hug his goodbyes, one arm around each of his daughters: "Really, I've never seen you like that before."

And Walter, seen, has winced, has only managed to say, one more time, "I'm sorry."

And feels even more sorry now, sorry that because of the sorrowful mess he's made, because of these sorry rhythms of the self that thump so silently and heavily between—against—the rhythms of love, he cannot even feel, with any certainty, that home will be a good place to be when he finally gets back there: which, given a three-day-long conference and an old mess to clean up and the plans for seeking out the author of *Time Lapse* to which he's also committed himself, he and Penny both know could stretch out to a couple of weeks. He wishes they'd splurged on separate rooms at the motel and been able to make love last night, this morning. A family room wasn't the best place to be.

About such stupid financial limitations with so much money around, the mess of having to deal with only what's allowed to be seen, he's also sorry. Confusion of love and money: and he's sorry, missing the love. He knows where the money is, which is almost everywhere now, just as he knows where it's come from: so once again death and sex tangle themselves up in his presence, and he's sorry: now that he senses the nature of the opposition, he doesn't like the growing realization of which side he's placed his money on. That, too, doesn't seem like a good place to be.

So: standing in front of a bank of telephones in the Cincinnati airport, from which he's been intending to call back to the motel, to try to catch Penny and the girls again, before they depart for the rest of their travels, to say one last goodbye, Walter still can't decide what place would be, for him, a good place to be. He stands with a coin in his right hand and his left on the telephone that can take his voice quickly, if briefly, back into the one place that has felt like a good place for him to be all these years.

But despite that pull, which he can feel urging the receiver from its cradle to his ear, the coin doesn't drop. Like the quarter he holds between thumb and forefinger, Walter himself just hangs here, a creature that's fouled its own nest and knows not where to turn. It's a long moment and one he thinks could go on endlessly, leaving him in Cincinnati—well, northern Kentucky, to be exact—forever. But Cincinnati doesn't seem like a good place to be either. He knows, squeezing the cold coin in his fist, what's brought him here: death, or at least the route to it. And suddenly, pausing before this long row of pay phones, waiting in this airport for a change of planes, he sees this city as a crossroads on his deadly journeys.

Ah, he chides himself, it's only Cincinnati: the Queen City of the West, old Porkopolis: but fragments of the Roman general's sword, only half-heartedly beaten into a plowshare, stick in his mind: this is the crossroads of his travels, a spot through which—always for good, practical reasons—the airlines have taken him time and again. Only now it occurs to Walter, withdrawing his hand from the receiver and pocketing the coin, that a crossroads is not a good place to hang around. Too much traffic passes through a crossroads: sooner or later, almost everyone. Walter doesn't relish making his presence available to everyone.

But on the long evening flight to San Francisco, on the big jet that spans two thirds of the country's breadth in the twilight beneath him, Walter can't come up with a good place to be. Every place he can think of that's a place he thinks he might like to be—every decent, cultured, liveable urban center in the United States—is a place where he's already been, a place where he's already done, as he prefers to say, what he does. Except at home, in the city where he lives: Walter's never wanted to live with what he's done. So he considers the possibility of living elsewhere, outside his native country, before quickly deciding that he does not want to live where they do not speak—precisely, not even in Canadian or British ways—his language: which he's only beginning to learn how to speak to himself.

So where is a good place to be, Walter?

Maybe, he thinks, standing in the crowded lobby of the St. Francis Hotel, looking around, nodding at a few faces he's seen before at meetings in New York and Chicago and Philadelphia, at places he's gone to partly because, like this one, they've given him the opportunity to go still other places, do other things: maybe there is no good place.

Maybe, he thinks, tilting his head down over the front desk to fill out the registration card, maybe, considering where I've been and what I've done and who I am, maybe there is no place that's a good place for me to be.

126. MAKE A WISH

Well, if no place is a good place for him, then maybe no place is where he should go. Here, someplace in this huge edifice, Dora waits for him: or doesn't wait, but is here, somewhere. That was their simple, mutual, last agreement: that they'd both be there, that they'd see. But Walter's seen and been seen. Something's been seen, and here, which is not no place but someplace, among other things the place where Dora is, he doesn't think he wants anything seen again, especially himself.

San Jose is someplace, too: someplace where it's thought he ought to be—where he knows he has an obligation to be, and soon—but he knows what's to be seen there. What's been seen already. Walter sees it: he doesn't think he likes the look of it, either.

So where then? What place is no place? A muffled cough, reminding him that he's still some place, alerts Walter to the patient desk clerk, stiffly waiting for him to complete the task of registration. Walter looks up at the man: no, at the uniform: the neat blue suit and the red and blue striped tie he's seen, it seems, almost everywhere. Walter doesn't look on up at the face, but just hands over the pen and straightens up, picking up the uncompleted registration card and turning away. Without even looking down at the card in his hand, he tears it in half, neatly dividing the name he's just finished printing on it. Walter. Job.

That exit doesn't much take him anywhere, of course, not even nowhere. It only leaves him standing on the streets of downtown San Francisco, long after dark, with his suitcase on the sidewalk leaning against his leg. A soft rain has begun to fall and Walter, with no place in mind, picks up his suitcase by its wet and slippery handle, wanders along, hatless as ever, while his glasses blur almost to opaque with rain, and eventually finds himself in the vicinity of the bus station, thinking, Well, maybe a bus is the way to go, because if you're going no place you had better at least keep in contact with the earth and not be in too much of a hurry, for fear of missing it.

But where is it? What is it?

Well, there were three parts to Walter's western trip, not counting Dora's unplanned intrusion, just like the three wishes he remembers thinking about earlier: the conference in San Francisco, the mess in San Jose, and the quest for the author of *Time Lapse*, anywhere. Having given up on the first two—shredded the registration card, mentally canceled the clean-up job—there's still the third: the one he's been saving, for when he needed it.

The only problem is that this is the sum total of what his efforts during the last semester to locate—even to localize—the author of *Time Lapse* have netted him: nothing. This is the grand total result of his calls to the editor at the house that published it, to the agent whose name the editor gave him, to the ex-wife whose name the agent gave him and the old friend whose name the ex-wife gave him, and the CPA whose name the old friend gave him: nothing. The CPA has a letter from the Internal Revenue Service, the old friend has a power of attorney, the ex-wife has the three children, and the agent has a postcard three years old with a picture of Mt. Rainier on one side and a brief message on the other announcing the title of a work in progress: *The Past Recaptured*. Extinct, thinks Walter, who's seen that snow-covered volcanic cone, that title, himself. And all Walter has to connect himself with all this is a polished and re-polished draft of his own fat introduction, a career in contemporary literature, and a decade of concern. That's it: who has anything more?

Is it possible, Walter wonders, not for the first time, for someone to simply disappear like that?

He knows it is: Walter has disappeared some people himself. But yourself?

127. Gate Two

Walter stands, a little dazed, in the midst of the lights and smells and motion of the bus station, gaudy posters advertising See America Travel Passes on the walls above the rental lockers, candy wrappers in puddles of rain water tracked across the concrete floor, sailors banging in and out of the men's room: a lonely figure, like most he sees here, hauling his dripping suitcase across the filthy floor toward the ticket windows, where he sets it down in yet another puddle and, his hand wet and cold and a little cramped from the tight grip with which he's been hanging on to things, lays out the requisite number of twenties for the purchase of sixty days of unlimited travel: See America.

See Walter.

Walter stands, wet and chilled, shivering a little though it's quite warm in here, by the door marked Gate Two, waiting for the next bus out, Seattle bound, for starters. On the other side of the doorway, opposite him, stands a smallish person in a thick, white, cable-knit sweater and grey pants and a flat woolen cap, whom Walter has mistaken for a young boy.

But then he hears the bus outside, and the sudden rumble of its engine through the closed doors makes him want, more than anything else, to call home. Not that he knows what he wants to say. Probably nothing: "Hello." But he knows desperately that he wants to hear the voices there: Penny's, Judy's, Janey's: the only voices—he cannot conceive of ever picking up a telephone to call anyone else again—who attach him to any place, the only voices capable of calling him back from wherever he's headed: no place. But then he realizes that they're not home either. They too are traveling: somewhere between Lexington and home, via Mammoth Cave, somewhere out of the direct way home, settled down for the night in some motel by now, nowhere, really, in particular, ready to move on again tomorrow, sleeping, silent: he cannot call their voices to him.

There are a lot of other things he cannot call up, call back, either. But can he let them be? Is it possible to do something and then leave it behind? To detach yourself from all—or even part— of what you've been and done, and just go on from there? And if you can, if you do, who or what are you then, in that going on? Anything, Walter wants to cry out, or anyone: let someone else do what I've been doing. But then, he thinks, isn't that exactly what I'm trying to become: someone else? Do I buy a ticket out of the town of who I am just to arrive where I've been all along?

Walter, shivering slightly again beside the bus station door where he senses the presence of other people beginning to gather behind him now, waiting, feels a kind of shuddering moral revulsion at this: much as he might think, if he were given to anthropomorphizing, a snake might feel shedding its old skin only to reveal an identical new one. Fortunately for the future of this thought, he isn't given to anthropomorphism: an approach he's only barely learning to call upon when he thinks of himself. And this thing, this thing that's trying to shuck off its very being — well, its very been—is it him still? Can the new skin differ from the old or will he just be, still, snake?

Maybe if he ever came face to face with the object of his quest, the author of *Time Lapse*, he could try out, for openers, an assertion on this subject they're both obviously concerned about. "I am giving up my old I am what I am," he could say, hopefully: "Now I am not what I was." Old athletes might mutter such an expression in despair, but not Walter Job.

But the question is: If not that, what? What else is Walter to be? Not that identity's his main concern: those little flashes of the self emergent, expanding until it takes on the dimensions of reality, until the conviction arises that there is something there, don't concern him much now. Not what I am, he thinks, reduced to these old fragments of perception, but what I do.

But what he wants to know is: is he to be a something else that will do something like deny, with no more hesitation than a snake, a long and deadly past that is, undeniably, his? Or is that just one more inhuman thing for this him-thing he's so busy unwrapping to do? Walter has to remind himself of his intolerance of applying the word "inhuman" to things humans do. No matter how they abuse and torture and kill one another, he always insists that these acts be called human, not inhuman: because humans do them.

Why should he deny himself equal status before this law of language: which, he feels, struggling to define his own humanity with it, is probably the only law there is for him here, now.

So who has a word for this man? Not necessarily a good word—he's in no position to ask for much: who is?—just a word: a word to tie him down to what he is, a word to set him free from what he is: to do both, if there is such a word. But maybe there isn't. Maybe no amount of words is capable of doing so much. Maybe, for the likes of Walter Job, language isn't sufficient.

The only sound he hears now is the deep rumble of the bus idling at the loading platform outside. Not to the voices that inhabit this station at a level he cannot make sense of, or the rattle of papers, or the shuffling of feet and luggage, does he attend. For a moment, looking up and out of himself, he awakens to the number of people who have gathered about him at this doorway. Abruptly he's aware that it's not a young boy standing opposite staring blue-eyed from under that grey cap toward the loading platform after all, but a woman, her hair pulled up under the cap. The fine network of lines around her eyes, suggesting that soon they might begin radiating outward over her whole face, tells him she must be his own age, at least, and that, like him, she waits now, intent and silent, like him. And only the deep rumble of the bus, which will carry him no place he's particular about, because he's just going, but will—for he hears its heavy door hiss slowly open at last—soon carry him and a lot of other people out into the western darkness, fills this silence.